I0589447

Beyond the Sapphire Gate

BOOK ONE OF

THE FLOW OF POWER

R.V. Johnson

Publisher's Cataloging-in-Publication data

Names: Johnson, R.V., author.
Title: Beyond the Sapphire Gate, Book One of the Flow of Power / R.V. Johnson.
Series: The Flow of Power
Description: South Jordan, UT: Lost In New World Publishing, 2015.
Identifiers: ISBN 978-0-9861655-0-4
Subjects: LCSH Magic--Fiction. | Fantasy fiction. | Swordplay--Fiction. | Science fiction. | BISAC FICTION / Action & Adventure |FICTION / Fantasy / Epic | FICTION / Fantasy / General.
Classification: LCC PS3610.O37265 B49 2015 | DDC 813.6--dc23

This book is a work of fiction. Names, characters, businesses, organizations, places, events and incidents either are the product of the author's imagination or are used fictitiously. Any resemblance to actual persons, living or dead, events, or locales is entirely coincidental.

For information contact; http://www.authorrvjohnson.com

Cover design by DHMDesign

ISBN: 978-0-9861655-1-1
EBook ISBN: 0986165506
First Edition: March 2015

For all those who enjoy losing themselves in a new world, if only for a few bells. I am of like mind.

ACKNOWLEDGMENTS

I wish to thank my editors, Kelly Hartigan (Xterra Web),
editing.xterraweb.com and Bryce Anderson for all their hard
work. Much thanks to proofreaders, Crystal Harris and Gary
Fannin, to name but two. The writing group's astute critiques
helped keep me in check as did the beta readers.

FREE DOWNLOAD

Sign up for the author's new release list and receive Beyond
Terra, the stunning new novella in The Flow of Power series
http://www.authrrvjohnson.com

INDENTURE

A fine dust haloed from the glossy leather-bound *Tiered Tome of Symbols* as Crystalyn Creek closed the cover. The beautiful symbols of white on the front and back had drawn her attention the instant she'd spied the book on the podium. Now they worried her. More accurately, the *behavior* of the symbols caused her unease when she focused on them.

She picked a symbol at random, again testing the unnerving conduct by tracing its beautiful circled pattern with her vision. The symbol churned, slowly at first and then spinning into a maelstrom, its myriad looped circles spiraling down into the dark hole of rotating turbulence at the center. As she glanced quickly away and then back, the symbol rotated to a stop.

Such disturbing motion made her believe she was slipping, her brain misfiring again. At a mere twenty-two seasons, she was spiraling into madness. Who would take care of little sister Jade? Dad was too weak.

Yet, she'd been unable to leave the book alone; gathering knowledge of the symbols inside the old tome overrode the aberrations. The pattern she'd just tested was under the heading titled defensive symbols in chapter two of the book. How a symbol could help with defense was beyond her. Symbols conveyed a meaning or many denotations, entwined into one. Perhaps whoever chronicled it had meant for it to signify a defensive implication for the object inscribed?

Unfortunately, Crystalyn only knew one person who may have the answer: her Indenture Service Provider, Ruena Day, but she couldn't ask her. Ruena would believe she'd slipped for sure.

Sitting straighter, Crystalyn stretched, working the kinks from the small of her back. She'd sat at the plasicrete podium perusing the book much too long. The mid-morning transport shipment still sat on the dock along with many other end-of-shift duties she should've completed. Now she'd have to scramble to finish. At least today, there hadn't been any new artifacts to scan, to *dot map*, as she called the process of converting a relic's exact dimensions to a digital image.

A throaty voice spoke from behind. "There's work to be done, and there you are lounging."

Crystalyn jumped to her feet. The ragged, low-tech stool she'd been sitting on rolled across the floor and banged against a thrust motor crate. "Oh! I didn't know you were here."

Ruena regarded her. Surprisingly, no frown marred her features, though her full dark-shaded lips had compressed to their usual thin line. Pulled back, and braided on the sides, her generous black hair displayed the two thin locks that arced outward above her eyes and downward to end on each side of her fine cheekbones. The dragon scythes—as Ruena called them—accented her rounded nose and sharp face but failed to pull attention away from the woman's vibrant almond eyes. "Don't belabor the obvious, Crystalyn. Did you get the new arrival finished?"

"Yes, the artifact from Low Realm is complete. The collection was measured, dot mapped, and converted to a holo image early last night."

"Good. Have you sent them to me?"

"No, the collection is too large. I had to write them to a protein gel drive. It's secured with your genetic imprint and on your desk."

Ruena smiled. "I'm going to be working with it soon."

Again, Crystalyn was surprised. Her service provider *was* in a rare mood. Did she dare ask? "Will you let me take the book home tonight? I'll dot map it and copy every symbol in it on my free time."

Ruena's smile vanished. "What do you mean?"

Crystalyn moved to the side.

Seizing the *Tiered Tome of Symbols* from the podium, Ruena gave it a quick glance. "How did you get this? I locked it in my desk a long time ago."

"I found it here. Honestly, I thought you left it for me to dot map and holo replicate."

For the longest moment, Ruena's eyes bored into hers. Finally, her dark gaze flicked to the dusty tome in her hand and she frowned.

Crystalyn quelled her rising anxiety with difficulty though it shouldn't have been so hard. She'd used the new way of activating her med cylinder at lunch, implanting it in her eye as Physician Ralston had directed, but how could she really know it was working?

Tucking the book under an arm, Ruena folded her arms at her chest. "Besides security, you're the only one who knows the current code to my office," she said, raising a fine black eyebrow.

The book of symbols hung tantalizingly close. Crystalyn avoided a direct look at it though it tugged at her. Instead, she focused on her ISP. "True, but how would I get in your desk? I don't have a key."

Ruena regarded her, her eyes dark coals. Crystalyn stared back, refusing to look away, though her anxiety rose.

Abruptly, Ruena spun and marched to the neural scan door that led deeper within the warehouse. As she stabbed her black mane into the red beam, it switched to green, the door whisked open, and Ruena marched through. "Come with me" hung in the air behind her.

Crystalyn scrambled to stay close. Beyond the threshold, the flooring changed from plasicrete to the spongy air-infused sealant of older times, which deadened the sharp sound of Ruena's spiked heels and the thud of Crystalyn's boots. They tramped between the hover crates Crystalyn had personally programmed for optimal space planning and ease of retrieval. Her eyes automatically noted the remaining empty spaces' shapes and sizes for future arrivals; few remained bare even though the most valuable pieces were stored in a monstrous titanium vault, taking up the entire north wall, she'd dubbed the mausoleum. Even Ruena called it the mausoleum now.

Built for observation of the mausoleum and most of the storage area in the warehouse, Ruena's one-way-glassed office resided in the eastern interior. Circular in design, it brooded like a giant horror wheel of darkened glass triggered by motion to light up and reveal different terrors trapped within to frighten the unwary.

Ruena's lengthy strides soon brought them to a standstill in front of the office's sole entrance. Touching an unobtrusive spot beside the door, Ruena slid her fingers to one side. A small keypad activated in the shadowed glass. Her slender digits danced, entering the code for the week. The lock clicked its release, and the heavy glass door swung inward with a whoosh. Glancing sharply over her shoulder, Ruena paused at the threshold, her eyes glinting in the sterile, overhead light.

Returning the woman's penetrating gaze, Crystalyn kept her face smooth; she hadn't done anything wrong. Well, perhaps, she shouldn't have spent the day reading, but Ruena could dock the day's six credits if she must. It would hurt, but losing her indenture would hurt far worse.

"Wait here," Ruena finally said. As the door closed with a soft hiss, her purposeful steps carried her beyond the glass-topped desk facing the office interior.

Crystalyn stared at her distorted image reflected back from the dark glass. She'd disliked the horror wheel office from the first day of winning her indenture four and a half seasons ago. Surprisingly, Ruena had picked her then from a pool of more than ten million strong. The moment she'd first seen it back then, she'd thought the same as she did now: the office was too big and so *ugly*. It certainly fit Ruena though. The bigger and gaudier something was, the greater her ISP liked it. Sometimes, it seemed, Ruena considered her station in life to be higher than the king of High Realm. Though, in a way, perhaps she was above the king. Much of the royal treasures had ended up in Ruena's office or sat displayed in the mausoleum.

Even so, it didn't fully explain how the book had come to be where she'd found it. If the Mistress of Ancient Artifacts hadn't left it on the dock, then who had? Ruena was right about access. Only Ruena, security, or Crystalyn could get into the Big Ugly. Yet no one had a key to the great desk except Ruena. Why would anyone remove something so valuable from inside the desk and then leave it lying around the most insecure area of the whole complex? It made no sense.

The office door's barely audible hiss forewarned of Ruena's

arrival. "You're still here? Isn't it past time for you to leave?" she asked, arching a fine black eyebrow.

To Crystalyn's disappointment, Ruena had left the book behind. Though she'd expected it, bitterness still left an acrid taste in her mouth. "You told me to wait."

"Yes, so I did. Come, I'll walk you out."

Ruena set a brisk pace back the way they'd come. Crystalyn fell in beside her, disappointment fueling a growing anger which made little sense also, but the afflicted part of her brain didn't need much—if anything—to set her off. The book was a possession of her ISP; Ruena would do as she chose.

Ruena broke the stillness. "What did you want with the tome? Speak quickly and truthfully."

Surprised she'd bothered to ask, Crystalyn hurried to reply before the woman changed her mind. "Symbols fascinate me, they always have. Did you know most could be redrawn and combined into one giving them a meaning much higher in complexity? Even those elaborate ones in the book. Let me work with it for a while, and I'll map them to holoscreen, combine, and redraw them. You'd have your measured images of the original symbols and my combined ones, all replicated in holo formula in half a service day. Overnight, if you allow me to take it home."

Silence pervaded the warehouse beyond their footsteps. Had she pushed too much? Crystalyn sensed the irritation radiating from the older woman, but she couldn't ignore the matter of the symbols swirling on the book. Was it really a clear indication of her slipping, though she combated her affliction with medication, or something else? "Can I ask you something?"

Ruena glanced sidelong at her. "I suppose you must."

"Why would someone create so many symbols in the first place? It must've taken an exorbitant amount of time, as well as an artistic aptitude, to draw them all with…ink. Is the book that old?"

Ruena's lips thinned. Their pace quickened.

Once again, the neural door loomed close. Pausing only long enough for the scan, Ruena strode to the dock stairs where she halted, both hands going to rest on her firm hips. "I have decided. The book's age makes it quite valuable; extreme care is essential. I will map it for replication personally. Clear it from your thoughts. This time, I shall set the security system and inform the guard of the early armament. Please, be certain your exit is secured behind you as I buzz you out."

So there it was. She would never see the book again. Ruena hadn't yet budged from a decision once made.

Crystalyn grabbed her daypack from the spot on the floor she'd taken to storing it upon her arrival to work and slung it over a shoulder. Seven steps—she'd counted them so many times—brought her down to the exterior door, but it failed to budge when she put her shoulder to it.

"There is a final item to mention before you depart."

Crystalyn suppressed a sigh. What could the woman want now? Hadn't she done enough? "Yes?"

"Be prompt at first light; I'm expecting a shipment. Replicate and record it in my holo database, then store it in the mausoleum."

"But that's my one free day!"

Ruena's fine black eyebrows rose. "Is there a conflict? Perhaps I haven't selected the right assistant, as I believed. Another could easily be located. Training someone new to measure, replicate, and list the acquisitions will be annoying, yet it should not take—"

"No, no conflict. I'll be here."

"See to it."

The irritating buzz of the ancient door unlatching grated on Crystalyn's ears as Ruena fingered the button hidden on the underside of the plasicrete pod. Again, she wondered why the infuriating woman insisted on its use. High Realm had higher technology to offer, such as the neural scan door. Ruena could easily afford it. In all probability, she was the richest person anywhere on the three realms, besides the king.

Shouldering the door before it relocked, she stalked toward the manned security booth a full block south, another of Ruena's egocentric security holdovers. With the overhead dome's protection, the woman didn't need the added cost of a live guard. Entrances and exits could be set up with a remote holofeed, coupled with a transparent trip beam.

Crystalyn should thank the One, the Great Father, that Ruena *had* chosen her above the rest for indenture. With her mother vanishing from home seasons ago and her dad losing his servitude as head of the king's security a season after, the three of them who made up her little family had relied heavily on her earned credits.

Still, she fumed as she walked, trying to make sense of Ruena using the excuse of the book's value. Crystalyn had personally handled enough valuable items over the last season alone to buy a palace or two on High Realm. If anyone were willing to sell—which she doubted— as scarce as real estate had become.

To keep her indenture, she had to give up her one free day with her family and receive yet another shipment. The one bright spot was she'd receive triple pay for the day, which in itself was unusual. Ruena had never paid the triple credits for such a service before. What was so special about the new arrival?

It all made little sense, which *was* normal for Ruena. The woman never offered a single reason for her demands. It was all so...so infuriating.

Pausing, Crystalyn shifted her pack to her front and rummaged inside. Where had she put her bloody med cylinder?

SPIRAL CURTAIN

The soft whir of hydraulics engaging sounded when Crystalyn removed her finger from the print scanner. With a soft whoosh, the stainless steel door retracted into the mausoleum's shell. Using the laser cutter she'd carried from the dock as a pointer, Crystalyn motioned her younger sister Jade to maneuver the hovercart inside, eyeing the wooden crate on it with fresh amazement as it passed. Though rough-cut, the crate looked assembled from real wood, a cost so extravagant her curiosity about its contents grew.

Settling the cart at the floor's center, Jade turned in a slow circle, gaping at the mausoleum's glittering contents. "Wow! You actually get to indenture here?" Not waiting for a response, she dashed to a nearby glass shelf where a gold sundial inlaid with diamonds and rubies glinted on a silver stand. With barely a pause, she raced to several gem-studded statues grouped beside glass displays of jewelry, her lengthy auburn hair trailing behind. "Oh—" Jade breathed, awe thick in her voice.

Crystalyn smiled. The first time she'd worked in the vault, her reaction to the gold scales, jeweled bowls, gilded armor, and formal headdress—all artifacts Ruena had acquired somewhere—had been similar to her sister's. Even now, she found the mausoleum captivating. Much to her delight, on occasion, she would happen across artifacts she'd never seen before—Ruena had an eye for the exquisite.

Today, Crystalyn found it hard to enjoy the room's objects after the swirling symbols of yesterday. She'd fretted over them the night through. Returning to her service work made the occurrence so much more real.

Now, she had to mention it and find out if the one person she was closest to—one of the two she cared most about—thought she'd slipped beyond fixing this time. "I'm glad you like the mausoleum, Jade." Crystalyn spoke softly at first; gradually she gathered momentum, keeping her voice steady. "Nevertheless, I brought you along for one other reason besides your physical help. I've struggled with telling you something that happened yesterday. Before I do, you have to promise me you won't tell Dad, not right away. I'm not sure his heart could stand another issue about me, not this one." Crystalyn paused to draw a long breath. "I don't know where to begin, so I'll blurt it out. Believe it or not, I found a book, a *real* book, of symbols that swirled when—"

"Oh, I'll believe anything now," Jade interrupted. Folding her arms across her stomach, she leaned against the door, her green eyes round. "Something happened to me too, *is* happening right now. Please, hear me out, Crys. I'll try to explain."

"All right, hurry though. You're the only one I can talk about anything with."

"Well, I know where to start, no problem there. I was chatting with Dad, about the time you would've finished your indenture yesterday, when…when I noticed *something* rotating around him."

Crystalyn felt a twinge of anxiety. "What rotated?"

Jade hesitated, sucking her lip in her mouth.

Crystalyn opened her mouth to tell her to stop abusing her lip, but a look of resolve dulled Jade's eyes and slackened her face.

Her face pale and stony, Jade spit out her lip and continued. "A gray fog, a mist, something like that, circled around him. Vague shapes spun slowly inside, they were so odd…I concentrated on seeing through the vapor. The harder I looked, the slower the rotation revolved until I could see they were…images. Dad had three; I could see that, but slowing the images for viewing tugged at my mind like a storm wind ravishing Low Realm. I couldn't hold it long. After I let it go, I had to lie down. I was so weak, I could barely breathe."

Crystalyn's stomach lurched, her anxiety rising faster than she could quash it, a certain sign of a panic attack. Though she didn't want to, she may have to inject another med. Though lately, she'd come to rely on them too much. "What kind of images? Can you describe them?" She was almost afraid to ask.

Jade's face drained again, giving her a ghostly white complexion. Her deep-green eyes widened as she stared at something beyond Crystalyn's shoulder. Crystalyn glanced where her sister looked, but nothing new stood out with the artifacts shelved there.

Her voice sounding frail, Jade continued. "What's worse, when I look at you, yours is chaotic...how should I put it? There's a shadowy mist rotating around you in constant flux. Images flash by as it rotates. Right now, there are three repeating. I can halt the rotation on whichever one it lands on...if I concentrate...it's so hard, willing it to slow, but I'll try. You're running toward something unclear. It reset. Now you're running, again. There's a gray shape looming out of the mist. It reset. You're running, the shape has broken free from the mist, it's...oh, no! I can't hold it! It reset. But I've...I've seen it."

"What? What did you see?"

Jade hesitated, her lower lip quivering, as if she wanted to pull it inside her mouth but thought better of it. "I don't know what it is, only that it's a creature. Somewhat like the dog at the Farm yet much different and far larger. You seemed worried, or frightened. Your...viewing frightens me. The rotation is dark, not gray, like Dad's..." Jade trailed off, her voice becoming small at the end.

"Why is mine dark?" Crystalyn couldn't help but ask.

Jade shrugged. "Dad has a shining sword, an empty glass vial stoppered with a black cowl, and a beating heart rotating around him."

Crystalyn's mind whirled as she struggled to grasp Jade's words. What did it all mean?

Jade's soft voice descended to a whisper. "Your viewing leaves me with foreboding. A strange creature stalks one side, a pool of blood spreads toward a darkness pacing you on the other, and an unknown planet spins around both. Something is happening. To you, to us, to our family, and I'm not at all certain it's a good thing."

Crystalyn gasped for breath as anxiety droned within. Perhaps, she wasn't the only one spiraling toward madness. It *could* run in the family. Reaching for her pack with the med cylinder, she hesitated. To dot map the shipment, she had to have the ability to think. Reaching out, she put her hand over her sister's and squeezed gently. "I'm not sure what's going on, but let's finish this project. We'll discuss it at home, okay?"

Relief flitted across her younger sister's face in an instant. Jade had over-emphasized her wide eyes again with too much makeup, something else they'd also have to discuss later. Her sister's fine brown eyebrows rose. "What did you want to tell me?"

"Never mind, we'll go over that on the way home."

Kneeling and using a focused beam to avoid starting a fire with the laser cutter, Crystalyn melted the heads from the old iron nails securing the rectangular wooden lid of the crate. Even so, the untreated wood still charred slightly around each one. She found the smell of the burnt wood pungent but pleasant.

Removing the crate's wooden lid released the sharp scent of tree bark, which filled the crate to the top edge. Again, she was in awe of the cost involved in the shipping. Someone had spared no expense. Scooping a pile of the bark onto the lid, Crystalyn exposed an unadorned, black-stained wooden chest. Lifting the chest from its fragrant bed, she flipped it open.

A small cry escaped her. Two artifacts beckoned for examination from a layer of blue velvet. She grabbed the first relic her eyes fell upon, bringing it close. Throughout her seasons handling Ruena's beautiful, immaculate collections, nothing had ever compared to what she held now.

An exquisite candle-shaped black crystal—light for its size—gleamed with polished ebony. Lovely white symbols etched around the base and shaft added stark color, drawing the eye from the candle's top where a black crystal ball resided, murky and opaque. Thorn-covered vines made from the same black crystal snaked around the top of the orb, a spiky garland.

A current of energy thrummed through her hand as if the candle drew power from inside.

"Ho! What have you got there?" Jade asked, reaching inside the chest. "Oh! I love it!"

Prying her gaze from the black candle, Crystalyn gawked at the second piece. Gripped in Jade's slender hand, a white crystal shaped as a candle blazed with a multicolored light. Like the black candle, the white candle had many symbols covering the base with less on the main upright. Unlike the black, every symbol set in the white candle was fashioned from multifaceted jewels, possibly diamonds. Two crystal wings protruded from a clear crystal ball mounted on the upright.

Something flickered inside the ball. Crystalyn leaned close and froze. A white mist raged throughout the wings and sphere, endlessly moving back and forth as if searching for an escape.

Jade lifted the candle close to her face. Her green eyes grew hugely magnified. "What's in there? Why is it moving?" she asked, her voice hushed.

"Who knows what Ruena purchases or why? Let's get going, I don't want to spend my one free day hanging around here," Crystalyn replied, standing and taking a final glance around. The allure of the room was strong. She'd spent many hours inside the mausoleum without a thought to the passage of time. Today was shaping up to be no different, over half of the day fled already. "I'll have to map them both separately before we can go. Let's use Ruena's office, something I rarely do, but I want to get it done."

Leaving the chest—she planned to use it to store the candles in the room upon her return—Crystalyn elbowed an unobtrusive panel in the vault wall. The door whisked open.

Setting a brisk pace, she led the way into what she thought of as the path of gloom. Created a long time ago, perhaps soon after the building was first constructed, the path led to a dreary storage area. Ruena had told her once it had its beginning as temporary storage until the mausoleum's completion.

Thankfully, the woman hadn't ever asked her to clean it up, for thrown against the walls and stacked ten high in places, dozens of discarded cryocrates loomed. Thermal containers turning green took up space beside filled and empty sarcophagi, and even big transport bins materialized in the way, creating a narrow walkway. As usual, Crystalyn's nose wrinkled, assaulted by mildew clinging to artifacts left in original packing.

She hurried to Ruena's office door and punched the code into the keypad. The smoky glass door sighed with release and fell inward.

Opulence sprang into view.

Poured into the plasicrete floor and providing an impractical traction, hundreds of steel masks from dozens of different cultures showed a part of Ruena's ostentatious way that Crystalyn disliked. She waved an arm at the expansive room cluttered with shelved artifacts and expensive furniture. "Welcome to the Big Ugly, sister." Striding atop the masks, Crystalyn went to a massive desk supporting two side extensions. Made from the same dark glassy material as the windows and door, the desk was big and bulky.

Dropping into Ruena's chair, Crystalyn touched the smoky glass surface on the desktop. Holo views flicked into life and displayed each of the three administration buildings' many rooms and common areas. At the same time, three-dimensional holograms sprang into view around the room on the walls of dark windows facing away from the mausoleum, some displaying other key warehouse areas, one entire wall devoted to the circumference of the mausoleum. One wall displayed archeological sites.

Current news events flickered to life on another without sound, showing the riots surrounding the palace grounds. Crystalyn felt sorry for the palace administration's security but supposed they had it coming after they'd booted her dad. A third, fourth, and fifth panel showed panoramic views of the vast mountain. Several panels showed the ever-present pollution cloud permeating the lower level, even though she could only make out dark shapes in it.

Jade shook her head with disbelief. "Oh, it hurts to look at it all.

Hasn't she ever heard of media overload?"

"You think so too? I always feel like I'm caged in some weird high-tech cave while the whole world outside riots. I should be out there helping them, like Dad used to do."

Jade smiled. "I don't think you'd make it as an admin security guard. You'd get too mad with all those people shouting in your face."

Crystalyn smiled too. Jade was so practical in a kind way. What would she have done without her these past few seasons of difficulty?

Jade's smile faded, her young face turning solemn. "What can I do to help? I'm ready to go home. I'm sorry, Crys, but this place gives me the creeps."

"Don't apologize. This place has a way of doing that. We should be going anyway before Ruena discovers I brought you with me. Let's start with the white candle. Hold it steady at the base. I need to get a laser scan of each symbol one at a time before I can map the candle's dimensions…hey!"

"What, Crys?"

"I've seen this symbol before. In the book of symbols, just before Ruena took it from me…wait, she didn't stop at her desk. She went past it."

"You've lost me," Jade said.

Crystalyn eyed some old-style shelves filled with small figurines. She pointed. "Hand me that dragon on the top shelf, please," she said, reaching out.

Jade placed it on her palm. Manufactured from a softer metal, the red dragon seemed solid enough. Flipping it over, her thumb brushed against a fine crack on the stomach. Grasping the dragon's head, she pulled downward. The dragon's upper torso folded back on its tail with an audible clink. A silver key gleamed inside.

Jade patted the desk. "Nice, I suppose that will unlock this monstrosity."

Crystalyn grinned. "It's low tech but definitely *her* style." As she fitted the key in the center drawer, a twist retracted a bar mechanism. A gentle pull revealed two books lying next to each other. Both had the same title: *The Tiered Tome of Symbols,* but there were notable differences. One had white lettering on a black background, while the other had black letters with a white background. The white-lettered one had Tier One gold embossed in small letters in the upper right, while the black letters had Tier Three imprinted the same way.

Jade inhaled sharply. "For love of the One, are they real?"

Crystalyn removed the white-lettered tome from the drawer. "I've already read this one." Placing it on the desk, she gazed at a symbol on the cover. As before, the symbol began to churn. "Tell me you see it, do you?" she asked, pointing with her free hand.

Jade's strangled gasp provided an answer. "Aren't you the least bit afraid of it moving like that?"

"As long as you can see it *is* moving, I'm not. For a while, I thought I was slipping again." Crystalyn opened the book and thumbed through the headings.

"But what if they're dangerous? How can you know they're not going to hurt you?"

Crystalyn looked up. Did Jade still see images in her aura? She wasn't certain she wanted to know; her sister's newfound ability was unnerving, worse than the spiraling symbols. "The symbols haven't hurt me so far, though according to the notations inside, some of them are used for aggression which is odd. I don't know how a symbol could be aggressive. It's something I have to figure out."

"Then don't touch them, put the book back," Jade said, her voice taking on a pleading tone. Flipping a stray clump of reddish-brown hair from her round eyes, she pulled her lower lip into her mouth, gaping at the tome as if expecting it to hurl a magic bolt from between its gold-edged pages.

Crystalyn felt an irrational spurt of irritation, which she quelled. The book couldn't possibly do that, could it? "Stop chewing your lip, Jade. Why don't you look around? There's a lot to see in the Big Ugly. I'm going to search for the candle's symbol inside here. If I know what it represents, I may add it into the white candle's inventory holo, the same with the black candle when I get to it. Knowing what the symbols on the artifacts represent changes everything. Ruena has to appreciate it, I hope."

"Okay, but be careful. There's something about those…" Jade said, moving away.

Crystalyn turned the book's pages with extreme care. Ruena would notice the slightest crinkle and rage throughout the warehouse like a radioactive squall ravishing Low Realm as she sought the person responsible. A turn of the page revealed the symbol she'd recalled in chapter four under the heading enhanced healing. Why healing?

"Speaking of symbols, what are these?" Jade asked, setting two blue objects in front of the desk.

Crafted from sapphire crystal, a pair of trim obelisks rose to door height, tapering smaller from base to top. Engraved a third of the way down, two intricate symbols with many curved lines, like links of a chain without end, stood out.

Crystalyn was delighted. "Whoever carved the symbols on them was very good, wouldn't you say, sister? They're intricate and identical. I don't remember them in the white-lettered book; I'll check inside the other one."

Setting the black-lettered volume next to the white one, she opened it slowly. Penned with dark ink, the matching lines of the links without end symbol stretched across half the first page under the heading travel. Underneath, black spidery handwriting went on for two paragraphs written in an unfamiliar language—unlike the white-lettered book.

Why travel? The symbol might represent a past agency; no one traveled anymore. There was nowhere safe left to go, except on top of the Mountain. But she had doubts about that; it was too complex, which meant it probably represented something else, for there was something going on with it…

A power resided within the symbol's pattern. Subtle, yet strong, chained to something vast. Reaching out to the symbol, she tugged the chain, not too hard, yet with the firmness of knowing it was right for her to do so. The chain gave way, creating an opening, inviting her to step through…a *gateway*. Her head reeled as the power she'd sensed thrummed through her. Or was it already within her?

Churning faster and faster, the symbol lifted from the page and slowed, growing in size. Suddenly, a beautiful sapphire color raced along the symbol's pattern, swallowing the black lines, glowing brighter.

"Crystalyn!"

The symbol floated across the desktop toward the obelisks. Both symbols on it spun in place. Black, translucent spidery extensions of their patterns raced up and down each one as the symbol from the black-lettered book soared between them. Locking in place, the symbol's translucence brightened. Jagged, azure bolts pulsed within the symbol's radiance in alternating directions, above and below. A dark blue mist drifted out of the symbol and scrolled to the floor, drawing a misty, clockwise swirl as it went. Deep within it, darkness stormed with a constant flux.

Stepping close, Jade stared at the spiraling, dark curtain. "What is it?"

Crystalyn gaped. "I'm not sure. It's almost like there's a storm brewing inside."

Jade inched closer. "You're right, it is a storm, and it's getting worse. There's blue lightning flashing above a dark, swelling sea behind the mist. Where is it? What is it?" Raising her hand, she reached for the alien landscape beyond the swirling symbol.

A sudden feeling of disquiet hammered Crystalyn. "Get away from there!"

Reality slowed.

Jade uncurled a fingertip to the dark curtain and vanished.

The symbol faded, and the mist dissipated.

From a great distance, Crystalyn heard a voice scream. "NO! Don't touch it! Don't touch the symbol!"

After a time, she clamped her mouth closed, putting an end to the screams. Motionless, the obelisks mocked her with their solemnity. Why had she brought Jade here?

Anger darkened her mind. Her vision blurred. Anxiety rose in the pit of her stomach. All were emotions involving her afflicted mind swings, she knew, but she cared not. Jade, her sister, her lifelong friend, the very person who'd helped her through the black times by putting up with her confrontational tongue and manipulative mind, the one who tolerated her illness for what it was, was *gone!*

Her eyes sought the symbol, lying chained and inert, in the book. A power still awaited there. She focused on it and got it floating between the obelisks.

The symbol spun translucent between the obelisks, the mist darkened behind it, and azure lightning flashed.

Her anxiety rose, stronger this time.

The dark curtain began to recede.

Gathering her will, she concentrated on the symbol's pattern, visualizing the intricate, interlocking lines and complex curves, the gateway hidden inside.

Once again, the doorway of spiraling darkness dropped to the floor.

Stowing the books in her pack, she picked up the black candle and climbed onto the desk. Taking a deep breath, she jumped into the swirl.

THE WHITE-LETTERED BOOK

Resting against rough stone in a narrow alley, Crystalyn found herself looking at two stout men facing a petite girl who gripped a dagger outstretched in one hand. One man leered at the girl, his stance relaxed. His cautious partner glanced toward the alley mouth and then back at the girl. Both men held short, hook-tipped swords.

Gazing the length of the alley, Crystalyn didn't find Jade though her sister must be close. They had both come through the same gateway. *Where was she?*

Her gaze returned to the swordsmen. Both sets of brown eyes stared at her, scowls fixed upon their faces.

Suddenly, the girl spun, moving with blurring speed.

A flash of metal brought white-hot pain lancing through her midsection. Her head banged the wall. A second lesser pain rang through her skull. Strength fled from her legs.

Time slowed. She slid slowly downward. Vague images of the girl and the alley floated in and out of her vision. Abruptly, she found herself sitting slumped over. Confused, she tried to stand, but her limbs wouldn't accept commands.

Darkness draped her mind.

Why was it dark?

Her eyes had closed. Forcing them open required a great effort. Distorted images flitted by. Blinking, she focused on her waist.

Her mind finally registered what her body understood. The hilt of a jeweled dagger protruded from her stomach.

Fatigue descended heavily upon her then, funneling her vision to a vortex. Closing one eye to focus, she fixed on the dagger, which seemed so far away, like gazing through the wrong end of a sight glass. The small hand of the girl encircled the dagger and pulled, releasing an appalling sucking sound. Her blood fountained.

Crystalyn plastered both hands over the spouting hole, despairing at the blood spraying from between her fingers. A cavernous cold leached into her bones then, adding to the weariness. Thoughts of sweet, dreamless, sleep slipped into her mind. She may heal with sleep…

A majestic white-and-silver image flitted into her mind. Lovely in its simplicity, the symbol was a perfect pentagram in shape, outlined in white, and the fine silver lines inside matched a spider's webbed design. Where had she seen it before? *Oh, yes, in the white-lettered book.*

Focusing on the symbol, Crystalyn projected it outward. The vortex of her vision expanded, snapping the world into acute clarity. The symbol hovered in the air near her head. Instinctively, she sent it toward her wound. Glowing silvery bright on contact, the symbol sank into her skin. Shockingly, her awareness still clung to it, caught in its wondrous webbed design.

Unraveling as it went, the white symbol followed the puncture, leaving behind a silver and white mesh as it pushed her vital life fluid before it. One-third smaller, it reached the main bloodstream.

Sealing her blood vessel with what she thought of as symbolic gauze, the symbol drifted across the artery, applying mesh on the opposite side.

Concentrating, she rotated the symbol a full turn, performing a quick reconnaissance. Her blood flowed normally, delivering platelets as usual. Slowly, she continued the rotation, only to halt at the gauze patch installed on the artery's far side. A dark green substance had eaten through part of the seal and was pouring into her bloodstream from deeper within her organs. Now what was she supposed to do? Scarcely half her symbol remained.

A symbol she'd read under the heading dilutions formed in her mind. Combining them, she redrew the symbol into a new one.

Intricate gold and silver lines, winding back and forth, filled the pentagram inside. Where webbing was before, there was now a hedge-like maze of lines with no beginning or end. Glowing faintly silver and gold, and triple the size, she rode it into the mossy stuff invading her organs and circulatory system.

On contact, the fluid vaporized into puffs of transparent mist, her bloodstream sweeping it away. The silver-gold symbol poured into the gap leading deeper inside her, filling it with an almost tangible fury. Finished, she sealed the opening with the remainder, releasing her awareness back into herself.

Comprehension of the outside world coalesced around her, bringing with it a splitting migraine. Consciousness began to slip away, draining from her like a mountain stream racing to a canyon's edge. She fought the sensation, willing her body and mind to coherence.

The alley sprang into clarity. Movement caught her eye.

The girl meticulously wiped the jewel-encrusted dagger on one of the swordsmen's pants leg. Once satisfied, she lifted her taupe dress to the thigh and stowed the dagger in a sheath. Then her small hands moved over the corpse with a practiced ease, patting the body. Several coins, a plain dagger, a small wood box, and several other items vanished into a leather bag hanging at her hip.

Crystalyn's stomach churned strong enough she felt she was going to vomit. Thankfully, the feeling passed. She needed time to replenish her strength, but she wasn't going to get it. The girl would soon realize she still lived.

As she used her legs and hands to push herself to a sitting position, dizziness assaulted her. Crystalyn rested her head on her chest, fighting the sensation. *Please don't let me blackout,* she pleaded in silence. *Please, Great Father!*

After a while, the lightheadedness lessened, and the pack at her feet sprang into clarity. Both leather-bound tomes lay half-exposed inside the main compartment. A warm feeling spread through her as she looked at the white-lettered book of symbols. It was a good thing she'd read it; the book had taught her the symbols to use. In a way, tier one of *The Tiered Tome of Symbols* had saved her life. What other wonders might she gain from the black-lettered book?

Soon, she would study every page. It might save her life or someone else's. Providing she lived long enough here—wherever *here* was.

Right now, her list-ordered mind demanded goals. First priority—search until she found Jade, no matter what it took or how long. Second, once she found her sister, both of them would look for a pair of obelisks. Third, once they found them, she would open the gateway using the *same* symbol. She was convinced the last part was important for a safe return trip home. It was a simple strategy. But it was *a* strategy.

Without straining her upset stomach as best she could, Crystalyn shoved the books in her pack, keeping the girl inside her peripheral vision. Busy with her macabre task, the girl ignored her as if she was no longer among the living. With any luck, she would continue to believe so long enough for her strength to ebb back.

Crystalyn stole a look around. Sunlight faded from the mouth of the alley, the shadows stretching long from it. Soon, darkness would claim it all, assisted by the stone buildings lining both sides. Grayish-black dust, ground fine from decades of shod feet, covered the ground, clinging stubbornly to sun-faded wooden crates that were intermixed with broken glass and rotting vegetables. Other unidentifiable refuse littered the ground in places. Nothing else caught her eye.

The "nothing else" brought anxiety gushing into her weary, pain-shrouded mind. The black crystal candle was nowhere in sight.

MAGICAL SUICIDE

Anxiety pulsed through Crystalyn. What could she do? This world was so different. Anger filled her with manic energy. It didn't matter. She would search until growing old if needed. She would find Jade. Blackness swallowed her anger, draining her newfound energy. Everything was her fault. She'd messed up again, ever since the bloody Hartwig kid incident. Why hadn't she seen it? Anxiety pulsed again. What would she do if she couldn't find Jade? What then? Poor Jade! Blackness pulsed. Dad and Jade deserved better. Why did they keep trying to help? Why keep trying? Anger pulsed, filling her with manic energy. *Stop it. Stop it, here.*

She couldn't afford to have her mind going in circles; it could easily become an endless loop. Besides, she needed the energy the anger provided. She felt ready to stand. Flipping her pack's strap over one shoulder, she gathered her legs under her and stood.

She swayed as nausea rose, but again she forced it down, only to have her head explode with a migraine, blurring her vision. Moments passed before she could focus on her surroundings.

The girl who stabbed her sat demurely on the chest of a dead swordsman. A cold smile thinned her lips. "I see you, outlander. You are most perplexing. Many before have fallen to my blade, none survived," she said matter-of-factly, her tone clinical. "Yet, there you are, moving around as if you just woke from a nap. You will explain how this is possible."

Crystalyn assessed her assailant, ignoring the mild command. Fine eyebrows, rounded nose, and jet-black hair shorn to shoulder length gave the girl an odd, aristocratic presence. Most notable was the girl's white skin, so pale it made her full lips appear as red as blood, while her brilliant green eyes shone with a belying innocence. *She's small*, Crystalyn thought, not much larger than her biggest stuffed bear. Of course, the girl was still growing. She couldn't be much beyond ten seasons of age. "Who are you?" she asked, her voice sounding as weak as she felt.

Tilting her head, the girl frowned. "You're asking a question to my question. Very well, I'll answer first. I am Atoi."

"That's a pretty name. I'm Crystalyn. My friends call me Crys."

The girl's impassive, ashen face never changed. "I don't care about your friends. Answer the question. How did you survive my blade?"

Crystalyn's head throbs rose with her ire. The girl was arrogant and dangerous, proving quite capable of handling herself.

"Did you not hear me? How have you survived this long?"

Crystalyn massaged her neck, as she scanned the immediate surroundings, looking for signs of the black candle.

The girl straightened. Crystalyn caught a glimpse of a dark silhouette on the body behind her.

Leaning from the wall, Crystalyn tested her balance. Nausea rose again, stronger this time, and her legs trembled. Perhaps she should have remained sitting for a while longer, but she dared not. Atoi might realize how weak she was and strike again.

Atoi's wide eyes narrowed a little. "You're not going to answer, are you? Well, you can at least tell me how you got behind me. I *know* this alley was empty when I led those fools in here. Only someone with the advantage of Using could've gotten behind me, methinks. Tell me, oh-so-oddly-garbed outlander, are you a User?"

Beginning to feel stronger, Crystalyn ignored the girl's strange question. One of Atoi's statements stuck in her mind. *Why would she lead those men in here?* "Where's the other one?"

"The coward ran off when I stuck Jewel in this one," she replied, patting the corpse's leg.

"You call your knife Jewel?"

Atoi closed her half-open mouth, her white face statuesque and regal. Suddenly she jumped upright. Gray dust mushroomed as high as her booted ankles before falling away. "Enough talk." Holding her right hand behind her, she patted her thigh with her visible hand. "Jewel will make you tell me everything, providing I don't scratch you too deep. You will die from her special lingering death. Methinks you're too weak to stop us a second time."

A gray-shaded symbol with a white outline set to a star pattern formed in Crystalyn's mind. Crystalyn combined it with another, redrawing it into a highly complex maze-like design, though it retained the same colors. How it would help, she was uncertain. Standing straighter, she almost cried out from the pain of her throbbing head. Grimacing, Crystalyn faced the little girl, praying her legs would hold for a while longer. The conversation had turned bad, possibly deadly.

An adage she'd penned in med school popped into her mind. *Wear the right emotional mask, and people will respond.* Perhaps she could turn the conversation around with her arrogant instructor mask, *if* she was strong enough to maintain it. She must hurry. *Please, Great Father, let this work.* Smoothing her face, Crystalyn tilted her head and looked down upon the little girl, straining to keep her voice steady. "Am I as weak as you think, little one? Is it worth the risk to find out?"

Atoi's expression didn't budge a hair. Her hard, green eyes shone with anticipation, matching the half-smile pasted on her pale face. The girl wasn't buying a single word, but she had another idea. "Perhaps I should melt your Jewel in her sheath. Would you want that?"

Atoi's fine eyebrows rose. "So, you *are* a User," she said. "I thought as much, outlander." Advancing slowly, Atoi glanced surreptitiously around. "You don't look strong enough to melt snow, though. You are pale like me and shaky…unlike me. You're much too weak to stand for long."

Atoi paused, cocking her head and nodding slightly. Her voice took on an odd, echoing quality. "I know how taxing using the Flow can be without an Interrupter. One of my hosts had the ability. I commend you for being able to stand at all. Using the Flow has drained you deeply, hasn't it, young User?" Atoi advanced a few steps closer, her smile thinned to a grim line. Strangely, her eyes looked aquamarine instead of the emerald she'd first thought.

Crystalyn was tempted to ask Atoi to elaborate, but she'd had enough. Time was passing too quickly. Jade could be anywhere now. Though her ruse probably wouldn't work, Crystalyn had to try convincing the little imp that stabbing her again would be a mistake. "Care to test your theory, little girl with the big mouth? Go ahead; give it your best shot. I've had my fill of attempts on my life. Well? Am I as weak as you think?"

Left hand hovering near her thigh, Atoi hesitated a step or two away.

Meeting her gaze for gaze, Crystalyn waited until Atoi's hand dropped to her hip and her stance relaxed. Then, curling her lip, she put on one of her best sneers. "I thought so. Now, show me what you're hiding behind your back."

Scowling, Atoi moved her arm to her side. Gripped in her small hand, the black candle gleamed darkly, caked with dried blood. *Probably my blood,* Crystalyn thought. *Wait!* Atoi had used her other hand to retrieve the knife. *Little Miss Dagger must be ambidextrous.* She'd have to keep an eye on both hands.

Atoi raised the black candle. "You have two books and don't really need this. Why not let me hawk it for you at the Under Market? We can make a great fortune. With a bit of work beforehand, I can raise interest for it and double the coin. Sixty percent will go to you, of course. Sixty-five, if you push." Atoi forced a wide smile upon her lips, though it remained far from her dark-green eyes.

Atoi wanted a quick sell. Even if Crystalyn agreed to her offer, she would receive little, if anything, from it. Worse, now that they'd spoken of negotiation, the moment Atoi left her sight with the candle, she'd slip away. Or the girl would lead her into an ambush. "The candle isn't for sale, little one. It's mine. Give it to me." Holding her hand outstretched, Crystalyn waited, redrawing the symbol back to its original gray pattern with a white outline. After all, she didn't want to damage Atoi too badly.

Atoi hesitated and slowly extended her right hand.

Crystalyn brought her symbol out to hover before her.

Atoi's aquamarine eyes widened.

Stepping forward, Crystalyn grabbed the candle as she released the symbol outward.

Atoi's free hand slipped into a slit in her dress, coming out as a metallic blur, stabbing upward.

Crystalyn's symbol spun and separated into stacked concentric circles of black and then rippled outward, dispersing a deep *faa-rooooom* sound.

Atoi's knife froze scarce inches from Crystalyn's hammering heart as the first of the circles slammed into the girl, ripping her from the ground. The second and third circles hit her in midair, flinging her faster backward end over end. Two-thirds of the way along the alley, Atoi landed with a dull *thud*. Sliding a dozen feet on her side, she crashed into a line of refuse barrels, the jeweled dagger still clenched in her hand. Gray dust exploded upward, hanging in stasis, before billowing down to coat everything with thick fallout.

Crystalyn gazed at the limp form. *Have I killed another person?*

As panic bloomed, Crystalyn squashed it. She couldn't go through that again. The blackness had nearly swallowed her last time. A single, monumental moment of uncontrollable panic could lock her inside her mute, screaming mind with no way out this time.

She paused to assess the situation with cold logic. What had gone wrong? For all her careful redrawing, the symbol had struck with much stronger force than she'd expected. The symbol *had* been under the aggression heading, yet it was only supposed to be a minor pushback, meant to knock an opponent away. Why so much power? Was she stronger than the book's author was? No, if anything, she felt weaker. Even the black candle seemed heavier in her hand though it gave off faint warmth...*wait!* The black candle...could it be augmenting her...her...*ability?* It was the only logical explanation. *Sweet Mother!* Now she had a weapon better than Atoi's bloody dagger.

Spying a pile of pallets stacked haphazardly at the back of the alley, Crystalyn brought out the symbol. Adding her touch of complexity, she combined it with another, changing the white outline to gold, the gray to silver. Sending the now golden-stacked circles soaring down the alley, they slammed into the pallets, generating a thunderous boom. The pallets burst into grainy particles. Behind them, chunks of stone and clay shingles rained from the wall and roof, clattering to the ground. Reverberating from the wall, a concussive wave swept toward her, blasting dust and debris higher than the alley walls on both sides.

Before she could think to run, raw energy knocked her to the ground, swiping oxygen from her lungs. Many heartbeats passed before the wave slackened enough to let her gasp for breath. She struggled to her feet. The throbbing in her head matched her racing heart, bringing on a nosebleed this time.

Well, that was dumb, I could've killed myself, she thought. She could see the holofeed now—"Crystalyn Creek commits magical suicide by being stupid." Wiping her bleeding nose with the back of her hand, she looked for something to stop the flow. Her eyes fell on the swordsman's corpse. A brown tunic clothed the man's torso, leaving his arms bare to the shoulder.

Crystalyn knelt and pulled on a seam with both hands. To her chagrin, the material proved to be stronger than leather, yet it felt as supple as silk. Grabbing the short sword lying nearby, she sawed a sizeable chunk free, trying not to nick the dead man too deep. Not that it mattered. It wasn't as if he could feel pain.

Applying pressure to her nose, she was grateful for the rag to stem the blood loss. Since the sword had proven handy, Crystalyn unbuckled the leather sheath from the unfortunate man's waist. Firmly grasping it, she stood, pulling the strap from under the corpse without having to roll the body. She nearly swooned with the effort.

Slipping the short sword into the sheath, she used the sheath's point on the ground to add stability to her weakened balance while making her way to the comatose girl. There, she knelt. Checking the little girl's pulse, she was relieved to find it steady. Atoi would be awakening soon. Crystalyn stood, studying the child who'd tried to kill her twice. How could someone so young be so prone to such violence? Was such violence common in this place? Her knowledge of this world was limited, to say the least. Not knowing what to expect could cost her life, or worse, her sister's life. Where was Jade?

"Well, that certainly cleared the refuse from the alley."

The dry, masculine voice came from the alley's mouth. A young man—not much older than she—stood there. Tawny hair, cropped at jaw level, fell alongside his clean-shaven, aristocratic face. He was clad in black leather pants and a velvety green vest that left his arms and shoulders bare. Crystalyn couldn't help noticing the way his well-toned muscles rippled when he drew breath. "Are you speaking to me?" she asked.

Grinning, the young man's dark blue eyes twinkled. "I do believe you're the only one in any condition to hold a conversation right now." As he looked at the comatose form at her feet, his smile faded. "Will she live?"

"She may. What do you want?"

"Ah, forgive me. I am Darwin Darkwind. You may call me Darkwind if you prefer. Most people do." He bent at the waist to execute a deep bow. "As I rode past this dreary alley, I was blown to the ground by an impressive display of Using. At least, to me it was, but I don't think my horse liked the giant push to the opposite side of Mud Street. I spent some time calming the poor thing down. Well, encountering such strong use of the Flow, I simply had to introduce myself to the User. You now know my name. I would consider it an honor to be entrusted with yours."

He was starting to sound like the girl, Atoi. "I suppose there's no harm in telling you. I am Crystalyn. I hope your horse is going to be fine."

"Oh yes, the mare blames me for some reason," he admitted, laughing easily. The big question is whether you're a Light User or a Dark User. Which one is it? I must know before I decide if a friendship is merited."

Crystalyn wasn't certain how to respond. "Uh, I haven't decided."

Darkwind beamed. "I was hoping you'd say that. As I said, your use of the Flow was impressive. We could certainly use one such as you within the Dark Citadel; all would hold you in the highest regard. Many soldiers and servants would obey your slightest whim. Please, consider this an offer to fight for the greater power. Dwell on it. When next we meet, I'll be awaiting your answer. I'm certain you won't disappoint."

Crystalyn stared.

A soft moan brought her attention back to the girl lying in the dirty alleyway. Fingers clawing at the ground, Atoi's legs straightened and went still. She was coming around, but Crystalyn had a few moments before she regained consciousness. Darkwind's weird offer had her interest; she wanted him to go on.

"What do you…?" Crystalyn froze. An empty alley spread out before her, and even the street beyond seemed deserted. Darkwind had vanished. Crystalyn felt a spark of annoyance. He could've at least spoken a farewell.

She put the matter from her mind and looked to Atoi. Prodding the prone girl with the tip of her boots brought Atoi's eyelids open.

Her eyes wild, Atoi sat up and then laid her small head in her hands, whimpering. Crystalyn kept silent, keeping a firm eye on her.

Atoi moaned through her fingers. "What did you do to me? I should've known you lied about your strength when you didn't die from the poison, except that should've killed you anyway. Jewel has taken down Users aplenty. I don't understand," she complained, releasing another moan.

"Did you say User?"

Atoi's head rose to regard her, a frown furrowing her pale brow. "Yes, a User of the Flow."

"It wasn't wise of you to attack me then, was it?"

"No. Are you toying with me? Why haven't you sent me to stand before Onan?"

What odd things for her to say, Crystalyn thought. Atoi certainly didn't sound as young as she looked. "Can you stand? I wouldn't recommend you try anything, though. My patience is wearing a little thin. I have questions. You'll provide answers."

Clamping her mouth closed, Atoi struggled to her feet. "My body hurts much like a falun tree fell on me," she said, her voice filled with wonder. "I have great interest in how this was accomplished."

Crystalyn didn't offer an explanation, or aid, when Atoi staggered and nearly fell. Miss Dagger with her strange way of speaking needed to know they were *not* friends and she wasn't here to help her in any way. Besides, falun trees were a mystery to her. She'd seen many images of trees in holographic images, but she didn't remember anything with that name.

"How did you do that? Anyone with some ability can tell when a User is manipulating the Flow; their eyes have flecks of color the same color as the power they have an affinity for if they have been Using for some time. You must have Used for a long time now with the power you are able to draw. The more you Use, the greater the saturation, the stronger you are. I looked deep into your eyes; there was no color. Only the black-and-white pattern hanging in front of you had it. Who are you? What are you?"

Crystalyn ignored the girl's questions. What was she going to do about her? Ah, yes…Atoi didn't know it yet, but Crystalyn's time spent at the Administration Farm and then lockdown inside Low Realm was going be bothersome to the girl. She decided it was time—no, past time—to put on her empress demeanor and read her little attacker the rules. *Wear the right emotional demeanor, and people will respond.* She really could use some loyalty right now.

Closing her eyes and lips to slits, partly due to her migraine and partly to make her point, she planted her hands on her hips. "I want to get something straight right now, Atoi, for the first and final time. I don't trust you. I may never trust you. Your trust is irrelevant. What is relevant is your utmost cooperation. I have questions. You will provide the answers no matter how trivial it sounds. Most important, you will be my guide until I release you. Do you understand?"

Atoi's emerald eyes widened, her little arms dropped to her side, and she stood immobile for a while. Finally, she stirred, inclining her small head.

"Good. Listen close. You don't have a function in life except to attend *me* in all things, whatever my mood. Am I clear?"

Atoi's jaw dropped. Nodding, she remained silent.

Crystalyn held back a smile with some difficulty. "Good enough. Now, I know you have credits. I'm famished, and if I'm not mistaken, it's about to get dark. Do you know a place we can go to eat, girl?"

"I…uh, yes, I do know a place. I have coin, if that's what you mean. I think I need to wash up anyway. So do you. That bloodstain stands out on your…uh…tunic? What kind of clothes are those?"

"I told you, *I* ask the questions. Don't make me repeat myself. Let's go. I'll stay right behind you."

Atoi spun and led the way through an iron-banded wooden door set in a wall of the alley.

Suppressing a sigh, Crystalyn followed. The large bloodstain discoloring her hoody was an issue she hadn't thought of.

RUMBLINGS

The dwindling light outside produced a greater radiance than the smoky room they entered. Round tables and low-backed chairs fashioned from dark wood crowded the interior. A dark-stained table was placed in front of a stone fireplace that extended along a wall. No one sat at the rectangular table, even though the high-backed wooden chairs beckoned to the weary. At least, they looked inviting to Crystalyn.

In contrast, the round tables sported patrons. A few of them glanced in Crystalyn's direction before quickly turning back to their private matters. Lit candles at each table accounted for the feeble light and some of the smoke. Oil lamps mounted near doors, lit, loose-leaf cigars, and tamped pipes contributed to the rest. Wooden booths lined the walls along three of the great room's peripheries. Most had occupants.

Raucous laughter and the dull clack of filled metal mugs banging together Crystalyn attributed to a group of longhaired, clean-shaven men, and boisterous women, some wearing armor. They mingled with swarthy townspeople wearing silken leather who sat alongside tradesmen wearing gaudy tunics and robes.

The low crescendo of many conversations droned throughout the room. Snatches of bodiless voices drifted to her ears. "I'm telling you," a female voice thick with frustration said. "Listen to me. I just left the front. We're losing ground every few bells!"

"What am I going to do now?" a nasal male voice asked. "The blasted Dark Citadel grows bolder, yet the Circle of Light does nothing." Crystalyn's ears perked. The boy, Darkwind, had mentioned a Dark Citadel in the alley, but the nasal voice said nothing else. "Somehow, the Dark Users have doubled their power in the past season alone," a swarthy man said quietly from a table nearby. "Never in my twenty seasons as captain have I lost so many good men in one skirmish. Yet, it's happened twice in this blasted war. The last one nearly took my life. Perhaps it would've been better if it had," he added, looking into his pewter mug and trailing off.

There it was. As plain as the man's mug. Rumblings about some war going on, and Crystalyn had dropped the two of them right in the middle of it, providing Jade had transported to this world at all. *Please, Great Father, help me find her here.* Her luck seemed to be running where it usually ran, in the wrong place.

Atoi slipped across the great room, headed for the sole empty booth tucked away in a corner.

Crystalyn rushed to follow. Two table lengths from catching her, a massive body slid from a darkened side booth. Crystalyn pulled up short. The humanoid barrier blocking the way had to be female. But was she human? Bare, well-toned thighs rose past Crystalyn's stomach. Clinging to the upper thighs, a leafy green dress snaked to mid-breast where golden hair cascaded past a generous bosom complementing muscular arms and toned hands. The woman towered beyond the meager lamp light and drifting smoke, hiding her neck and head in shadows too deep for Crystalyn to see through. A voice drifted down from the shadows of smoke filling the rafters, brusque and melodious at the same time. "You're with the Child of Dark, are you not?"

"If you mean Atoi, yes. Why do you call her that?"

"You'll come to know in time, possibly. She may not allow it. Right now, I would ask acceptance for my companions and myself to join you and her. Is this permissible?"

Crystalyn glanced at the booth the woman had vacated. Two large shapes sat at the back. "I suppose you may, if it's not too long."

"Excellent. Lead the way." The great body stepped to the side.

Slipping past before the big woman changed her mind, Crystalyn plopped into the booth opposite Atoi. "Make room, girl, we have company."

Atoi sat up straighter, looking to where Crystalyn indicated with a wave of her arm. "What are you doing here? Are you following me?"

The large woman wearing the green dress sat next to Atoi, facing her. Broad in face and nose, the woman was attractive, in a big sort of way. Delicate cheekbones complemented her fine eyebrows and eyes…there was something about her eyes.

"Our business isn't with you this time, Child of Dark," an elderly woman clad in a long white silk dress said as she sat down beside Crystalyn. Smaller than her companion, the old woman still forced Crystalyn to look higher. Wrinkles lined her weathered, motherly face, and her eyes…Crystalyn gaped. The old woman's eyes were a lustrous, glowing white with no visible pupils or irises.

Crystalyn looked at the big woman across the table. Her luminesce eyes shone from the darkness, facing her direction. Crystalyn had little time to gape; a third companion squeezed himself in next to the old woman. Shorter by several inches than his companions, the man's bulk still loomed over the booth. He held his broad jaw higher than most, and his deep, brown eyes regarded her, revealing little of what they wanted. At least he had normal eyes.

"Please, allow me to enlighten you who we are," the large woman across from Crystalyn said. "I'm known as Lore Rayna," she said, gesturing to herself. "The elder beside you is the Lore Mother or simply Mother. The choice is yours, but do address her properly as one or the other. Our protector sitting next to the Lore Mother is Cudgel," she added, flashing a quick smile toward the big, muscular man.

Crystalyn stole a closer look at Cudgel. The man's auburn beard made his broad face appear wider, yet his hair was a thick, fiery red. He sat rigid, and his pale brown eyes regarded her with open suspicion. Taken aback, Crystalyn looked away, toward the one speaking the introductions.

Lore Rayna had fallen silent, facing her expectantly. "Oh! My name is Crystalyn Creek. It's nice to meet all of you. I believe you already know Atoi?"

"We have known her for some time. For this moment, we're interested in you, dear," the old woman said, her vibrant tone belying her age.

Varicose veins branched prominently from her forehead to her deeply sunken cheeks. The old woman's mouth and lips had stretched so taut Crystalyn felt it must hurt to converse, though she'd shown no sign of pain. "Me? There isn't much about me to cause so much interest."

The Lore Mother laughed, a vibrant laugh, sounding strange coming from one with so many seasons. "Don't be coy, dear. I know when there's something special about someone. Particularly one with your…shall we say, strong Flow capabilities?"

"I knew it!" Atoi exclaimed.

Ignoring the outburst, the Lore Mother went on. "Besides, one does not usually sit speaking with an old woman like me while displaying such a large bloodstain spread across a waist as small as yours. In most cases, it would require seasons of advanced study to save someone with a wound that dire. Much longer than you've lived, I'd imagine."

Crystalyn kept silent, though she wondered how the woman knew she'd healed herself if that was what she meant.

"Let's talk about your apparel. I've never seen a tunic cut like yours, and I know a lot about clothes, believe me. It's a fancy of mine. Your clothes have an almost otherworldly feel about them, if I may be so bold to say." Before Crystalyn could answer, the Lore Mother turned her wizened face to Atoi. "I'm sure that's not all, is it, Child of Dark?"

"What are you talking about, insane old woman? Did I not tell you to stop calling me that?" Atoi said, her emotionless face contradicting her words. Sitting back, she dropped her left hand to her side.

For some reason, Miss Dagger's petulance irritated Crystalyn, and the little girl was too quick to reach for her weapon. "Watch your tongue, Atoi, and keep your hands on the table."

Atoi put her hand beside her other one on the table. "I do not know why the old woman keeps saying such things. What do they want with us? Make them go away."

Lips pressed together, the old Mother's pale, luminesce eyes bore down on Atoi's young frame. Presented with a side view of the woman's eye, Crystalyn saw only white. She wondered how the woman or Lore Rayna could see at all. Several heartbeats passed before the Lore Mother went on, her voice almost inaudible. "Tell me, little one. Did you create that ugly red stain on her attire?"

Atoi hesitated, looking at Crystalyn.

"Go on. Tell her the truth. I think she knows, anyway," Crystalyn said.

Atoi lifted her tiny head slightly. "Okay, fine. I did not do it with purpose."

The old woman went on, her raspy voice lowered. "Your dagger injects the magical properties equivalent to tree dragon's blood deep inside your prey, does it not?"

A sharp inhale from Lore Rayna and Cudgel brought to mind that they and the Lore Mother were part of a trio she knew nothing about.

Cudgel spoke for the first time, his deep voice a rumble. "Wise Mother, how can this be? A splash of tree dragon's blood will kill a warrior in a score of breaths!"

Lore Rayna interrupted. "Do you think she is the one, Mother?" Her large eyes remained fixed on the old woman. At least her head faced her, anyway. It was difficult to tell. Lore Rayna could've been staring at her, for all Crystalyn knew.

I—" the old woman began and then clamped her mouth closed.

A buxom barmaid, wearing a black skirt barely reaching her upper thighs and a matching vest that left her shoulders and most of her chest bare, appeared at the open end of the booth. "Can I get you all something to drink?" she asked, flashing a small, tired smile meant to include the entire table. Balancing a large wooden tray full of empty tankards and glasses, the barmaid glanced at Atoi, her blue eyes neutral.

"Yes, I want—" the little girl began.

"Go see to the Gray Dust envoy, Dawn. I'll see to this table," a gruff male voice commanded.

Shrugging her bare shoulders, the woman sauntered toward a boisterous round table.

A balding man of average height, sporting a black mustache, replaced the barmaid. A leather patch covered his right eye. Trailing out from under it, a jagged scar festered. "Well now, isn't this cozy," the man said, looking at the three big newcomers in turn. His one blue eye slid past Crystalyn without pausing, a stained rag draped over his right shoulder. "I don't need another trouble table, not this night. With all the trade envoys in town for the Snow Melt Festival, I have my hands full with everyone as it is, yet problems have plagued you three all week. Now here you are at the little one's booth. Why is that?"

Cudgel's red, bushy eyebrows pulled together, his gruff face darkening with each word the man spoke. In contrast, Lore Rayna's broad face smoothed as serene as a porcelain doll made to resemble a noble woman prepared to withstand the ages if handled with care. The Lore Mother's face resembled weathered stone.

"Don't answer that. I know you won't anyway, but I'll find out eventually. You know I will. All that happens in this forsaken town ultimately finds its way into the Muddy Wagon Inn, where I decide what to do about it," the scarred man said. Pausing, he fixed a penetrating stare at the end of the booth. Crystalyn tried not to gape. His good eye looked right at her this time. "Except, I don't think I know you, which I find quite curious. A new visitor never escapes the local townsfolk's gossip, particularly one as young and beautiful as you." His large muscles bulged as he lifted the rag from his shoulder and daubed along the scar's visible portion.

Crystalyn didn't know how to respond. Silence blanketed the booth.

"She's with me," Atoi said after a time.

"I know she's with you. She's in your booth, isn't she?"

"No, I mean, she's staying with me. I brought her into town and did not want to display her around, so we arrived…my way," Atoi said, her voice getting softer with each word.

Fixing his unblinking stare on Atoi for a long moment, Hastel's eye narrowed. "Very well, but if she's staying in your room, it'll cost you extra. You know that. See me in the morning. As for the rest of you," he added, glancing around the booth, "you'll also need to see me in the morning to go over your accumulating debt." Turning on his heel, he stalked off into the crowd.

"Blast him!" Cudgel hissed through his teeth, his deep voice echoing around the booth. Balling his beefy hand into a fist, he thumped it on the table, causing his chain mail shirt to clink softly. The table bucked. "One of these times, I'm going to relieve him of his good eye, then stand him near a cliff, and enjoy watching what happens next."

"Leave him…for now. We have larger concerns. The opportunity for your loving ministrations shall happen in good time," Lore Rayna said, a half-smile on her lips. "Right now, we have a different purpose."

"We do at that. You two stay away from Hastel. I shall handle him," the Lore Mother said. "I have something to show you, Crystalyn. I think you may find it quite…useful. Can I meet you tomorrow? Shall we say, at eight bells?"

Curious, Crystalyn nodded.

"Hey! Hastel never let us order our drinks. I'm hungry," Atoi said.

"I shall stop by the kitchen and have something sent to your room. We should all go to bed. The rest would do us good," the Lore Mother said, standing abruptly.

Cudgel slid hastily from the booth.

Pausing for a brief stare around the room, the Lore Mother stepped into the dimmer light of the smoky tavern center. "Not to mention, I want to have words with Hastel." The Lore Mother's raspy words hung in Crystalyn's ears long after the dim light closed in behind her.

Lore Rayna scrambled to her feet as Cudgel stared into the crowd, raking his curly hair back with a swish of his big hand. "I hate it when she does that! How am I supposed to protect her when she goes gallivanting off into a hostile area?" he complained, hastening into the crowd, breaking a new trail through fog of smoke.

"Will she be all right?" Crystalyn asked.

Lore Rayna smiled. "She's the Lore Mother. I think you'll find there's a much harsher side to her than poor Hastel realizes. Besides, she has the hairy, red-haired brute glaring over her shoulder at anyone who sneezes in her direction."

As Lore Rayna spoke, a flash of movement on the big woman's dress caught her eye. The green forest-fern leaves there formed an intertwined vine pattern. Each leaf fit with its counterpart so well they formed a body-hugging garb tight enough to repel moisture, Crystalyn believed. Such a thing wouldn't be impossible for some material, but that was not it; there was...*something*. Then, she saw it. The fern constricted and loosened with Lore Rayna's breathing, moving subtly back and forth. The dress was *alive*.

Lore Rayna pursed her lips. "You require food and a rest cycle to complete your healing. We will speak again in the morning."

Crystalyn watched her walk away until the smoke claimed her, her eyes on the green dress. With each stride, the foliage shifted, maintaining some invisible line for decency, albeit barely. She found the whole thing...disturbing.

Her head throbbed.

Standing, she looked at Atoi. "Come on. I want food, bath, and bed, in that order. Do they have bathtubs here?"

Atoi slipped into the narrow aisle. "My room does. I pay well for it."

"Good. I can scrub my clothes too. Lead the way."

Keeping an eye on the young girl's sinuous form as the little girl deftly made her way through a sea of faceless bodies, Crystalyn thought about how she'd never asked Atoi or any of the others about the rumblings. If there was a war, she wanted to know the details.

A war could be a significant deterrent to finding her sister.

BLUNT FORCE

Leaving his thrust cycle hovering at the parking locker, Garn confronted the gate wall. A holo image of a young male wearing a wide-brimmed security hat appeared high enough he had to lean back to view it.

"State your business" floated from the image, crisp and clear.

"Your boss wanted to see me."

"Are you Garnet Creek, Crystalyn's father?"

"I am."

"You have a great daughter, sir. We're lucky to have her indentured here." A loud whoosh from the wall preceded the gate retracting into it. Having overseen the security setup for the complex, Garn recalled he'd designed the gate wide for large cargo and had added a zoom holofeed for remote handling. "Please proceed to the warehouse, sir. She's expecting you." The image winked out.

Beyond the gate, a meter-thick, transparent plasicrete dome covered the complex from his suggestion, resting atop the wall. He strode along the spongecrete path with its hidden heat and weight sensors he'd had installed into the variation of plasicrete, this one softer for those on foot. Hovercraft transports never touched the surface until arriving at their destination, so a harder surface wasn't required. Blocky artwork, manufactured with varying colors and textures from the same spongy material, lined the path on both sides. The owner had purchased the artwork after he'd finished his consultation work. He didn't care for them.

The dome glinted with rainbow colors, reflected in the early evening sky like a clear, chemical bubble that refused to pop, silently deterring the uninvited from landing. Yet the open sky was still a much better view up here in High Realm as long as one didn't look down the mountain.

Now here he was, invited beneath the dome, smack into the Dragon Lady's great lair as he'd come to think of Ruena Day before his daughter's indenture. The king himself had asked him personally to consult with Ruena on security measures. There'd been a successful break-in at that time. He doubted there'd been a second one after he'd finished with his design. The strongest security was simple but effective, using a combination of old and new techniques. Surprisingly, Ruena Day had been one of the rare clients who'd accepted his method from the start.

For the hundredth time, he wondered what the emergency was here again. When he'd sent a feed to the warehouse to check on the girls' progress, the Dragon Lady herself had answered, asking for a personal meeting, which was odd; she'd always been a recluse.

When he pressed for specifics, she'd refused to discuss it over the feed, stating insecurities. Unless changes to his system design had occurred, the feed's encryption here, and elsewhere he'd installed it, had yet to be broken; a face-to-face meeting was not required, but it was fine with him. He had his own questions.

Staying this late was a first for Crystalyn. What was so important it had to be finished tonight? She could've hired half of Mid Realm to get the project done. As part of his former servitude as head of security for the king's administration he was privy to classified information. The woman had enough credits to purchase one of the realms should it be her desire. At least, she had when he'd been in the king's service before his wife's disappearance. Credits had a way of vanishing overnight. How well he knew.

Another first, Crystalyn had Jade with her, a much larger worry. They should've been home hours ago. Had something bad happened, perhaps involving a cargo container? He hated the thought of his daughter moving them around. Thrust motors failed every day. His chest fluttered as his unease heightened. Something bad better not have happened. He'd take the place apart with his bare hands, bad blood pump or not.

But he was creating his own anxieties, a bad habit he

admonished everyone else about whenever he noted it. Lack of information tended to do that to him. Perhaps the Dragon Lady was only extending a professional courtesy to him by telling him in person his daughter's indenture was terminated. No, the gate guard had mentioned how valued she was at her job, though he should've known it by now. As much as he hated to admit it, he hadn't been the best father, not lately. He should've been involved deeper in both his daughters' lives. Grieving over Sureen's disappearance had left little room in life to interact with his girls outside the daily routine of maintaining a household, but that was his own personal reaction and wrong. He should've talked to his girls at every opportunity.

The spongecrete path led past two large hovercrafts—the most advanced models available—to end at the rear dock's additionally widened, stainless steel door. The pulse curtain required the extra space on each end for its integrated neural technology to function. Garn did appreciate how the Dragon Lady had taken his advice by retaining some of the best features from the original building's design while integrating those with many of the latest advancements in security. Breaking in now would require someone who had knowledge in old technology along with new—a deterrent in itself—and had access to the tools required for both systems.

A much narrower sponge path pointed the way to an off-white exterior door. As Garn neared, the door buzzed loudly. Twisting the handle, he plowed inside before the lock could reengage.

The Dragon Lady waited inside.

Garn's pulse quickened.

Ruena Day had spent some time facing a mirror and it showed. Dark purple lipstick and eye shadow matched the orchids sewn on her black fishnet dress. The orchids strategically covered the feminine curves of her body the dress, which almost fell to mid-thigh, hugged. Black silk gloves snaked to her elbows, complementing the deep purple sharp-heeled boots that climbed to just below her knees. She still wore the two scythe-shaped bangs curling out from her forehead and down both cheeks that she called dragon locks. Each dragon lock sported mauve, orchid barrettes where it began at her head full of lush dark hair. The overall effect was startling. He was glad he'd selected his last expensive suit to wear or he'd have felt underdressed.

Eyes dark and shiny, Ruena gazed at him, a half-smile tugging at her generous lips. "Evening, Miss Day," he squeaked. Why was his voice so high? He never squeaked.

"Mister Creek, thank you for coming on such short notice," Ruena said, her voice a purr. She smiled, showing her white, even teeth. "I hope you can appreciate my attire, such as it is. I put some thought into it after we spoke."

Garn's face heated as he wondered what she meant, though he suspected he knew, but he found it hard to accept. Surely, she wasn't flirting with him. He was too old, though he'd heard some women preferred older men. Perhaps so, but he didn't feel like testing the validity of it. He would maintain a friendly relationship with her, for Crystalyn's sake. "Call me Garnet or just Garn, please. Everyone usually calls me Garn. Mister carries such an 'old man' image. At least, to me it does."

"Very well, just Garn. You may call me Ruena or just Rue. Do we have an agreement?"

"I believe so."

"Good. Now, if you will follow me, we can retire someplace comfortable." Spinning elegantly on one heel, she stepped onto the sealed plasicrete dock. Garn's body flushed when he noticed the orchids didn't stay in place as she moved. She did have an exceptional form. He shouldn't let her get the wrong idea, though. "Excuse me, Miss Day. I mean, Rue. Crystalyn mentioned you permitted her to bring Jade. Are the girls still here?" He scrambled to stay close enough to speak without raising his voice. Ruena's strides were long, even for him.

Ruena drew up short, twisting to look at him. A frown creased her forehead as her dark eyes penetrated his. Unable—or unwilling—to look away, he stared deep into them. The world froze. High intellect mixed with a fierce passion and...and something else drew him in, making him wonder. What could a much younger, beautiful, and supremely wealthy woman want with a dying older man?

How many moments passed, he couldn't say. Her face smoothed. She turned and led the way deeper within the warehouse, her weight balanced elegantly on her spiked heels.

Stopping at a door, Ruena raised an eyebrow, binding him with her stare. "Your daughter told you she asked permission to bring her sister along? I'm afraid Crystalyn told you…wrong. Her indenture is for her alone, and I never require her to work any Seventh Credit day."

"I asked her about that! I wonder why she insisted you had requested her service."

"I do not know. I dislike having anyone here, save for a small security crew, on the Seventh day. I do not agree with service on that day; everyone should have time away. After all, I may need some…time alone. Or I might wish to spend it with someone who intrigues me, as you do, Mr. Creek."

Garn swallowed hard. So there it was, tossed into the open.

"Ever since our previous interactions ended, I've searched for an excuse to spend some time becoming…acquainted," Ruena went on. "When you sent the message, I got the impression you wanted to meet in an intimate atmosphere. Was I wrong? Did you *not* want to see me in private, Garnet?"

Garn's lungs refused to draw breath as he gazed at her fine raised eyebrows and the question hanging there. Beautiful wasn't a strong enough word for her elegant, aristocratic features. Her sharp cheekbones curved down to a full, pouty mouth. Parting her lips slightly, Ruena leaned closer.

His body stirred.

Garn squashed the feeling, pulling back; he still hadn't found his daughters. When had he leaned close to her?

Lips curling playfully petulant, Ruena leaned on the door's exit bar, presenting a side profile.

He noted the dress she wore left no room for underneath apparel. His mouth dried.

"Come now, Mister Garnet, quit toying with me. Shall we go to my office? We can discuss anything you want there. I am certain you're parched by now."

He stood immobile, not trusting himself to move, unable to look away. She was a rare beauty, though he hadn't thought so in the past; she'd been too hard a taskmaster during the secure setup, demanding to know the precise details for each feature. He'd never met any woman matching his six-foot frame until back then. His wife, Sureen, barely reached his chin, yet it hadn't mattered. Sureen was the perfect size. They fit together like his best suit, manufactured from precise, robotic specifications. They'd been soul mates from the moment they'd met and every moment after. He could still picture her smile as if she stood beside him.

The sharp pain in his chest he'd lived with for six seasons hit him again. Everything within him ached to see her, to talk to her, to hold her. Sureen was the only woman he'd ever loved, or ever would.

The exotic beauty before him intruded into his thoughts, transposed for an instant with an image of his lovely wife. His chest constricted again. Head tilted back against the open doorjamb, her firm, full chest pushed forward, Ruena stared at him, expectation mirrored in her almond eyes, lips pursed. When had she opened the door?

As tempting as Ruena was, he knew he would decline her offer. He loved Sureen still, missing or not. As the One was his witness, he truly missed her. Not knowing if she was alive or dead was destroying him. He'd never given up on her, though it'd been many a long season since she'd vanished from their home without a trace. He *would* find out what happened to her. He was here for his children and nothing else mattered. He'd made a pact early on in his union with Sureen; their children would come first, always. They'd both wanted it that way. Again, his chest tightened. Ruena was still regarding him, her dark eyes shiny, expectant. "A drink is tempting, but I must go look for my girls."

Ruena's brow furrowed with rage and then smoothed so fast he wasn't certain he'd seen it. She smiled. "I believe I understand, now. You actually *are* looking for your daughters." Drawing and releasing a long breath, she straightened. "I won't apologize. I'm still glad you're here. I imagine you've already checked with Crystalyn's friend?"

A friend was something he hadn't considered. After the incident with the Hartwig kid, Crystalyn had been a loner. At least, he'd believed so. Again, he was reminded how much distance had grown between him and his daughters. He needed to make it up to Crystalyn—both of them—somehow. "No, I haven't yet."

"Crystalyn accepted a feed in my office yesterday from him. I'm sure we could locate the point of origin. Care to look?"

So the friend was male. He needed to find his daughters before trouble found Crystalyn. Worse, Jade was with her this time. "Yes, I would, thank you."

Ruena pushed the door open and placed herself beside it. "You have to promise to make it up to me, Garnet. I insist."

He half-expected her to use the limited space between her and the doorframe as an excuse to get closer, but she remained still—even inhaling slightly to allow him room as he slid past, her perfume making his head reel.

He hesitated at the threshold, noticing two blue obelisks positioned on each side of the door, as close to the inside wall as their bases allowed. A curtain of dark mist had dropped between them.

Oddly, the mist was moving with a spiral motion.

The whole setup sent a chill through his spine, yet he couldn't say why, perhaps from the sheer strangeness of it.

He lifted a foot to step back.

Blunt force slammed into his back, propelling him headlong into the mist.

FLICKER

Apprehensive, Jade cracked the tall door open. Made from heavy black iron, she was surprised how smoothly it moved. Beyond the doorway, a vast gray stone hallway lit with a purplish light sprawled for a great distance. Ornate amethyst pillars, carved with men and women in armor or robes, engaged in some activity, mostly battle from the look of it, lined the center. Two rows of the magnificent pillars led toward a wide half-circle set of beautiful cobalt granite stairs. A set of golden doors, as high as the hallway, reflected sunlight from a square hole bored through the ceiling.

Jade froze. Four guards stood at attention, two on each side of the golden doors. Two gripped tridents twice their height, and the other pair stood rigid with bulky crossbows peeking over their shoulders and double-headed axes dangling from their hips. Dark helms, breastplates, and gauntlets matched their chain mail armor.

Sucking in her lower lip, she ducked back inside, letting the door close with barely an audible click. Leaning against it, she nibbled on her lip, panic rising. Had they seen her? Perhaps she should check to see if they were coming. Her only chance at escape was to run. Midway to reaching the door handle, she froze again and then dropped her arm to her side. Peeking out again would add to the risk of them spotting her. The weapons they carried had one purpose: to slay with efficiency. That frightened her, worse than the ones designed to incapacitate and weaken as many opponents as possible in close quarters. At least with those—like some of the ones in the large room she'd found herself in an hour ago—she might have a slim chance of avoiding them by running.

Sitting, she put her back to the door, looking once again at the room. Racks of plate armor and vicious weapons stood malevolent and resolute. The weapons hung in orderly, open-faced rows designed for quick access, and the armaments—hung on iron pole trees—kept the pieces in one set. Each implement of death or dismemberment had minor nicks or gouges but no cracks or chipped areas. All were polished and looked sharp.

At first she believed she'd stumbled into another artifact storage place in the warehouse somehow, perhaps through some hidden passageway, but she'd only found the one exit. The one her back rested upon. Carved from some dark, amethyst stone—real stone and not some variation of plasicrete—the whole room had dim lighting from shafts, similar to the ones bored through the hallway's ceiling. There was no other exit. The immense hallway with massive golden doors, the armored guards who carried pointy weapons, and the tools of violence in this room made her situation too real. She wasn't anywhere near Crystalyn's work. But how?

Pain bloomed in her mouth. Jade spit her lip out, grimacing. If she kept chewing on it, there'd be nothing left but ground meat, though it was hard not to; she needed it for composure in times of stress. How she got here made little difference now; her main concern was discovering the way home. Thinking about it brought tears to her eyes, which she quelled. It was time to adjust the situation, as Dad would say, preferably in one's favor.

Standing, Jade adjusted her grip on the white candle, as she strode from aisle to aisle, making sure she'd missed nothing, perhaps a hidden trap door. She looked for anything wider or bulkier than it should be. As she gazed at weapon after weapon, a chill blazed an icy trail down her spine. How could she expect to survive in a place such as this? Panic arose again, but she stuffed it down, resisting the urge to bite her lip. Now wasn't the time to fall apart standing around grating her lip to shreds.

Completing a full, zigzagging circuit, Jade found herself facing the door, her disappointment sharp. Nothing new had presented itself.

Besides the war accoutrements, there was only the worn black leather bag hanging from an iron hook mounted on the doorframe.

Drawing a deep breath, she thumbed the latch a second time. Almost as an afterthought, she lifted the bag from the hook as she slipped through the door, letting it close—and lock—behind her. There was no going back. She hadn't found a key. Leaving it propped open was bound to draw unwanted attention.

Dropping the white candle in the bag, a soft *clink* bespoke it had other contents, yet its weight hadn't given her any indication. Exposed as she was, she resisted the urge to look inside. Slipping the bag over her head, she faced the hallway away from the golden doors. Walking with what she hoped was a normal pace, she strode along the rough-hewn stone floor on one side, avoiding the opulent rug lining the center between the rows of pillars. The last thing she wanted was to meet someone passing by there, as she tried to figure out which way to go.

She stole a glance behind her. The great hall appeared empty, save for the statuesque guards who stood in the same positions as near as she could tell. It appeared they hadn't spotted her, but she couldn't be certain.

Once out of sight, Jade picked up the pace, trying to project the confidence of someone going about important—but not urgent—business. The last thing she wanted was for someone to stop her and ask if there was an emergency.

Before long, she arrived at an intersection. Trailing her hand along the wall, she turned right, barely slowing down. Ahead, the corridor narrowed. Black- and red-robed people with hoods drawn surrounded a large oblong well.

She paused, feeling stupid. Her jeans and hooded jacket marked her as an outsider, and she'd wandered too close. Had she forgotten all of Dad's training?

The left side branched beyond the main hallway to reveal a similar picture. A large crowd gathered there too, yet there was a notable difference. The crowd surrounded a set of obelisks, like the pair in Ruena Day's office, except much higher and wider apart.

Excitement quickened her breathing. The obelisks were the last thing she recalled touching. The way home could be nearer than she'd thought. It meant crossing the huge hall and sauntering right through the people. As she watched, several large groups began the trek across the hall. Over half wore armor. The armor worried her. Anyone wearing it possessed a military heart. If nothing else, they would question her. What could she say? She arrived by accident, but would they believe her? It was doubtful since the whole place looked to be a fortress of some sort, but there was no choice. The tan-colored obelisks were her best chance to return home.

Changing course, she resumed the same pace, this time with a solid destination in sight. With luck, the mammoth obelisks would zap her to the warehouse before Crystalyn grew too frantic. The last thing she wanted was another angry tirade directed at her, though her sister's yell was preferable to this place of armor, robes, and stone. She'd never been far from Crystalyn or Dad her whole life. Or Mom, for that matter, when she'd been around.

The obelisks stretched higher the closer she went. Jade began to wonder if they functioned the same way as the sapphire obelisks. What would she do if they didn't? She couldn't wander around forever. At some point, she'd have to eat and drink. Perhaps, if she found someone wearing robes, away from the armored ones, she'd ask for some water along with help getting home. It'd require putting aside her shyness to ask, but she would.

Striding as fast as she dared, she rounded a massive pillar—the largest by far—shouldering the gray rock ceiling three stories above. Running lengthwise along the enormous hall, the granite pillars continued as far as she looked. Unlike the carved ones near the shining doors, all had been polished smooth, including the monstrosity. Reaching the far side, she halted.

A man wearing a dark red robe rested a shoulder against the pillar's smooth surface. Silver hair poked out in straggly strands from under a hood pulled back to a lined forehead. His steel-blue-gray eyes glinted, regarding her openly.

"Oh! I didn't see you," Jade said.

The man glared. "I did not intend for you to see me until now. You must be a new creation. I have never seen your kind in the Dark Citadel before." Pushing away from the pillar, he faced her. "What kind of abilities did the Great One bestow upon you? What is your use? You look human, yet your attire speaks a different tale. Are you a Dark User acolyte then? Speak now, before I lose interest and end this."

He spoke soft enough Jade wasn't certain she'd heard correctly. "What's a Great One? I'm afraid I don't understand."

Flicking his red robe to one side, he exposed a sword hilt. Resting a hand on the pommel, he stepped closer. "Do not think to play with me, little creature. I have tracked you from Lord Charn's personal armory," he said, his voice as hard as his eyes. "I shall ask one final time. What is your dark task?"

Fear swarmed inside Jade. What could she say? She didn't have the faintest idea what he wanted.

Unless…yes. He had an image like the one spinning around Crystalyn. Not black as Crystalyn's or all gray like Dad's. His was gray with a wide black streak in the center. Blurred miniature scenes flickered inside. Focusing her will, Jade halted the rotation and expanded the scene it happened to end upon, snapping it into sharp clarity.

Gazing intently over his shoulder, sword in hand, the red-robed man before her—garbed in silky brown leather this time—ran after a young woman wearing a leafy green dress. The girl carried a blue crystal candle in one hand and a wood staff in the other, an emerald orb atop it. As Jade watched, an unseen bowman fired an arrow; scarcely missing the man's head, it struck the girl under the left shoulder blade. Dark red blood ballooned across the girl's back as she fell. The man's face twisted with a soundless scream.

Pain exploded behind her eyes. Head throbbing, Jade released the image, allowing the rotation to continue on its slow, never-ending loop. Desperately wanting to rest her head in her hands, she clenched her jaw instead, staring at the red-robed man. "I'll answer your questions, providing I know the answers. But first, you have to answer mine."

The man frowned. As he did so, his eyes bled from a darker blue to a lighter gray, which she found odd. Wrapping his hand around the sword hilt, he straightened. "I warned you. Now you think to play games with me, dark creation. I have expended my allotted patience."

Fear crept up her spine. Once he drew his sword, it'd be too late. She'd have to be gentle if she wanted to survive. *No.* It wouldn't work with him. His pain was too sharp, too deep. Hitting him hard was the only way. "The girl arrowed in the back, who was she? What were you running from?"

The man's gray eyes darkened to blue, rounding with horror. After a time, he slumped, his sword hand falling limply to his side. Jade began to wonder if her questions caused his heart to fail. Suddenly he straightened, looking behind her.

Jade followed his gaze. A silken-robed crowd moved toward them at a marching pace, ragged-clad figures among them. Oddly, no one wearing armor was visible.

"Come. We have to leave," the silver-haired man said, turning around. He broke into a run, racing upon the ornate carpet between the pillar supports.

Jade dashed after him. Tucking the black bag under an arm, she ran as fast as she could, catching up. "Wait! Who are you?"

Slowing, he glanced over his shoulder, his blue eyes wild. "Now's not the time to speak. I delayed too long. Keep up or die horribly!" Bursting into a headlong run, he sped away.

Clamping her mouth closed, Jade pumped her legs, concentrating on the red robe in front of her. *Don't look back.*

Eerily silent except for the dull slap of their footfalls and her labored breathing, the red-robed man kept near the center supports running at a grueling, ground-eating pace. His hood blew back to reveal the full head of silver hair she'd seen in the image. Slowly, a pillar at a time, she was losing ground, straining for breath. Soon, he'd leave her behind.

Suddenly, he veered from the path, sprinting into a side passage. Jade followed, driving her legs as hard as she could. The passageway ended at an iron door where the man stood fumbling about in the pockets of his robes. Jade slid to a stop, narrowly avoiding a collision.

"Where's the blasted key?" he asked, digging in his pockets frantically. His flailing arms froze, reached into an inside pocket, and pulled out an archaic key. "Thank Onan," he muttered, fitting it into the lock.

Something dark slipped into the passageway. Malice, cold and reeking of evil, washed over her...bringing fear...*raw absolute fear*...she was going to die fearful. Flicker.

A profound serenity enveloped her. *Why had she ever thought it evil?* Relaxation soothed every fiber of her. Flicker.

Freezing terror gripped her at her core. Something powerful moved ever closer. A prevailing, unquenchable, thirst washed through the terror. *It must drink...must*...Flicker.

The sweet joy of profound happiness caressed her soul. How could she not want something so pure, so innocent, and so loving? Flicker.

Raw, gnashing hunger filled her mind. Raving, churning, all consuming...*must feed*...Flicker.

Pleasure spread through her in waves. It was delightful but *so strong and so...much.* Flicker.

Glee poured into her...a glee for the anticipated gain of a pure soul...*glee*...Hunger sated at last...*glee*...Flicker. Flicker.

INTENTION

A massive iron door swung closed in front of Jade. She blinked.

Sliced off in mid-glee, the terror beyond the door dissipated, leaving behind a faint wail of unbearable loss.

Unadorned, but expertly crafted, the black iron door fit the gray stone with no gaps.

Jade shuddered as the deathly cold thoughts dispelled from memory.

Two hands released a firm grip on her shoulders, surprising her. She'd not been aware they were there.

A man slipped past her, hanging his red robe on an iron coat rack. Underneath, he wore the brown leather outfit he'd worn in the image back in the hallway.

Bile rose in her throat when she thought how close she'd come to succumbing to the malevolence in the passageway. If not for the man who'd been about to kill her, she'd not be among the living. The same man who now stood relaxed without a hint of the urgency he'd displayed getting here. Of course, if she'd fallen behind, he would have left her to those…terrors. She shivered.

Her benefactor gestured toward a gray stone bench placed alongside a small rectangular stone-hewn table. "Please take a seat. I shall fetch something to drink to slake the thirst after our…little jaunt. Moving through a doorless entry, he vanished around a corner.

Only now realizing her heart beat wildly, Jade sat, resting both elbows on the polished tabletop. The light in the room was brighter than the hallway but not by much. Placed on gray translucent shelves mounted high, one to each wall, long gray crystal shards shed a dim light. Next to one shelf, a dark stain marred the otherwise polished wall.

Soon after her heartbeat slowed to normal, the older man returned carrying two silver mugs and a stitched leather flask. Setting the mugs on the table, he filled both. Shifting his long sword to the side, he sat down, blue eyes wary. "Well? Select which one you want. I am thirsty after such a run."

"Oh! I'm supposed to go first?" Grabbing the closest mug, Jade spilled a few drops on her hand as she brought it to her lips. Chilled, pleasantly sweet water coated her dry throat. Her next swallow drained the mug's contents.

Frowning, the silver-haired man replenished her drink. "So you are not a dark creation or the white ash leaves I ground into the water would have burned holes through you. Yet you do not know basic customs when sharing first sustenance. You are a bundle of mystery, young one."

Jade pushed the mug from her, spilling some of the contents. "Why are you trying to harm me? I've done nothing to you. I don't even know who you are."

He hesitated, staring down at her. "I suppose it is safe to tell you my name, now that I know which one to reveal. I am Camoe Shadoe away from this place. You may call me Cam, if you would like. I would know yours."

"Jade Creek, but everyone calls me Jade."

Camoe's blue eyes lightened to gray. "Very well, Jade. You're going to tell me in detail how you know about Maialene. Think carefully before lying. I will know, and lies raise my ire higher than you want to climb."

Stated matter-of-factly with such confidence, his last comment sent a chill through her. She'd only ever lied to placate Dad or Crystalyn's concerns with boys though they hadn't needed to worry. Boys were easy to control. Camoe, on the other hand, had the air of someone violent about him. "You mean the girl? I'm able to view images rotating around people. Well, with three people so far, you, my big sister, and my dad. With yours, I was able to halt an image and view it for a short while."

Camoe sat up straighter, the pupils in his blue eyes dark. "Are you saying you can read an aura? Then you *are* a User, as I suspected. However, I have never heard of a User with the ability to halt an aura. Certain specialized Users can see the aura rotating around us, what color it is, and *if* they are quite strong, they may get a glimpse of a vague shape rotating behind the fog, but that is all." He paused, his light blue eyes intent. "I do not detect a lie. Perhaps your skill is unique to you. I shall study it given time. Right now, I need to know something. Why is it that I cannot see your colors?"

Jade wondered why his eyes changed so much perhaps that is what he asked. "I don't understand. Am I supposed to have colors?"

Camoe scowled, his eyes staying light blue. "Every User has colors, and every User can see each other's color flecks that pulse in their eyes after they train and the Flow addiction saturates them. It gives some idea of a User's ability level for accessing the Flow and their current addiction. The more addicted, the less reasonable they are which makes them dangerous. Have you not been trained?"

Camoe was becoming impatient. Perhaps she shouldn't have told him so much about her images. "I suppose I haven't."

He nodded vigorously. "Yes, that would make sense. However, you are old to be a User without guidance. Most start with the first signs of potential. I may have to take it upon myself—"

His aura rotated, drawing her in and making her head throb. She looked away. "Would you please tell me what those…things are out there?" Jade asked, wondering what kind of place spawned such evil things. Her eyes fell upon the wall again. Nothing had changed with the crack, yet there was something about it. Perhaps it was the simple fact that everything about the room, even the ceiling and floor, was smooth. The crack stood out as the only blemish. Though, wasn't it only a stain when she'd looked before?

Clearing his throat before choosing to answer, Camoe regarded her as she regarded him. "They are wraiths the great lord releases after dusk. Some in the White Lands call them flickers, because they create an illusion of well-being in short increments to keep their intended victim from escaping. Their telepathic onslaught paralyzes their prey. A single flicker followed us into the passage. We were fortunate it went for you. I was able to ignore its weaker assault on my mind, so I am aware what you went through."

"Why would anyone want such horrors lurking around?" Jade asked.

"Simple, with those creatures roaming the halls, the great lord has no need for added watch, though some believe the flickers were here long before the Dark Users and their great lord. The wraiths patrol without rest only at night, searching for hapless souls caught beyond the protection of polished stone or iron. Once a season, Dark Users feed prisoners to them, swelling their ranks and keeping the flickers' voracious hunger sated for a while. Tonight was such an occurrence."

She wondered what he meant about polished stone or iron, but something else he'd said made her pause. "Why would their numbers increase?"

"You don't die—but I suspect you would wish you had—should they catch you wandering, or by design, in their area of telepathic onslaught. The Dark Users have developed what they call a soul lure to move them around for they cannot resist it. Once the flickers feed on your soul, you become like them, searching endlessly for a living, glowing soul, never satisfied."

Bitter cold seeped into her spine. These people feed people to wraiths. Why would anyone want to live here? The whole place sounded like a swarm of evil in one form or another. "Why are you here? Why take a chance with those horrid things?"

"If you have not figured it out yet, I am not going to tell you. At any rate, as long as we stay inside this room, we are safe. The flickers' corporeal substance cannot pass through iron or polished stone. There are no miniscule flaws as in regular stone or wood." Cocking his head to one side, his expression hardened, the lightening of his blue eyes blending toward gray added an emphasis to it she didn't like. "There is something I am at a loss to understand. You entered the great hall from Lord Charn's personal armory. How did you get inside? I have been trying for months, but there is no way to pick the lock without the dark throne room's sentinels noticing; they guard it in shifts. Even during a relief change, it is done two at a time, leaving two to watch the great hall and guard the golden doors."

"They watch the armory? Do you think they saw me?"

"Yes, they would not have missed your exit. Their function is to keep the uninvited from gaining access without a key, not question those who obviously do. You still have not answered how you came about your admittance."

"I, uh, arrived there by accident."

Camoe frowned, his eyes turning gray. "Accidental? How does one arrive inside a room by accident?"

Jade tried to keep the irritation from her voice. Why couldn't he accept what she told him? "I'm not sure. I'm beginning to suspect a smaller version of the big obelisks in the hall brought me here."

Camoe's frown deepened though his eyes began to darken. "Portable devices like the ascension gateways in the great hall?"

Jade found the name for the gateways odd. She hadn't climbed anywhere. "I guess so. They were a lot smaller than those, though."

"They must be portables. I've heard reports of powerful Users being able to activate portable gateways, but they are extremely rare. I have never seen one. The stationary ascension gateways here and elsewhere have only limited knowledge known about them, let alone the rarer portable. Most believe the Ancients put them where they are now. I do not believe the great lord himself or the combined efforts of the Circle of Light can move them. It is quite strange, I have no knowledge that the ability to create a portable gateway ever existed here or in the White Lands. You must be someone important to have used them," he said, slumping back, his eyes blue again. Then he froze. "Do you still have them?"

"I'm not important; my sister activated the…gateway but not on purpose."

"So you are not a User?"

"I don't think so."

"What about your sister? She activated the gateway, certainly she is one."

"I don't see how. Things like this don't happen on our world."

Leaning forward, Camoe's knuckles whitened as he gripped the flask. The blue in his eyes had vanished, replaced by a gray so light they were almost white. "Another world, you say? There is only one world: this one. Too bad, I was beginning to like you. I had thought we were going to be honest with each other. If I could be certain the flickers were not slinking outside the door, I would put you out in the passage."

"No! Please, I know I'm not on my world any longer. It's too different here, where am I? Tell me."

Camoe sat back, his face sullen, as his eyes slowly changed. "Are you toying with me, girl? If so, I cannot detect how you do it. Perhaps you believe a lie instilled in you all your life, which might do it. However, I am one of the few who knows other worlds are a myth mentioned in an obscure passage in the Surbon Codex. Most souls on Astura would not even consider it."

The codex sounded interesting, but she let it pass. "Please, tell me where I am. I need to know."

"I have already mentioned it, had you been listening. You are on Astura. I told you, I could tell when someone is lying. I no longer believe you are, but that means someone spent a lifetime, your lifetime, convincing you there is at least one other world somewhere. Or what I have always believed is the lie." Camoe fell silent. A frown added a line to his weathered forehead, but his blue eyes were thoughtful.

Jade was thoughtful herself after hearing his words. She was stuck on an alien world seething with danger, known as Astura. How could she survive long enough to get home? Convincing Camoe to help was vital, or she wouldn't make it far. But could she trust him?

She gazed at the crack below the polished ceiling. It seemed bigger now. No, denser, like a dark blemish that bled darkness; it seemed poised to consume the light of the entire room. She stared, mesmerized by the feeling. A black tendril flicked out into the room and then vanished inside.

Jade jumped to her feet pointing. "Something came out of that!"

Camoe spun on the bench. "Blast it!" he roared. Springing to his feet, he scooped up the flask. "Come! The bloody flickers have bored a way in; we have to head deeper within this infernal rock."

"They can bore?"

"Only if there was a flaw to begin with, but there is no time to explain. Follow me, and stay close." Standing the bench upright, he leaned the polished portion over the crack. Balancing it with care, he covered as much as he could. "It will not hold them long. Run!"

Jade dashed behind Camoe as he ran through the rear entry. Charging past a small kitchen table, he slid to a stop in front of a large iron stove built flush into the gray polished stone. Twisting an iron handle, he flung open the cook stove's door. A layer of ash packed the bottom. Beyond, a small opening gaped. "Our only chance is to follow the smoke ventilation chute. Go on, I will be right behind you." Without waiting to see if she complied, he grabbed a stringed leather bag from the table and moved to a cupboard. Sweeping some items into it, he dropped the flask in last.

Shifting her bag to hang on her back, Jade crawled into the stove belly on her hands and knees. Ash exploded with every movement; there was no help for it. Coughing, she paused at a dark, circular opening. Smooth gray stone led inward, sloping uphill gently before an ominous blackness swallowed it.

Camoe crawled behind her. "Keep going," he said, pulling the door closed.

Darkness enveloped her. "I can't see very far."

"Can you carry this?" he asked, thrusting a candle near her thigh. She grabbed it by the base, thankful for the meager light. Pushing her way into the opening, Jade awkwardly held the burning candle before her while pulling herself along with her free hand. Thankfully, the vent shaft was smooth, but even so, it was rough going uphill. Occasionally she could feel her bag drag along the vent roof. Sweat broke out on her brow. Pausing, she rubbed her eyes on her upper shoulder. Warm wax dripped on her hand. Soon the candle would be small enough it would burn her skin. Then what would she do?

"Do not stop! They may be able to get around the door," Camoe said softly, his voice urgent.

"I'm going to have to, at some point, or throw this candle away."

"Keep going. It may not go far."

Jade found that using her feet to push as she pulled her body up the tube with her free hand required far less exertion. Her pace quickened. Speaking was possible. "You've never been this way?"

Camoe's voice echoed past her as if he was right behind her, but she suspected he was still guarding the entrance for a little while. "Why would I? I have never been in any danger in my room. The flickers hunger for *you*, I can feel it."

She almost stopped. "What? Why would they want me?"

Finally, she could hear Camoe shuffling some distance behind her. His voice echoed past as if he was floating beside her. "I am not certain, but I suspect your aura ability and youth draw them. The Dark Users herd flickers around by taking advantage of their penchant for souls and innocence. You must be a bright beacon in their barren, colorless world. Desire to feed has thrown them into a frenzy."

Jade nearly stopped again. Feed, Sweet Mother, what kind of place had she brought herself to? "Wait...you said you sensed it? How can you? What are you?"

The sound of a mirthless chuckle drifted past. "I thought you would have guessed by now. Perhaps you are from another world. I almost killed you in the great hall; do you want to know why?"

She froze. Her instincts in the hall had been frighteningly correct. "Why would you do that?"

"I will tell you, but you have to keep moving. "Astura knows me as an essence druid; besides viewing a User's color, I pick up subtle hints of intent. Anyone or anything, living or not, has an intent exuding outward from them, and I can sense it. I have what they call the true sense. It has only happened a select few times throughout our history, usually when something catastrophic is about to occur. Without fail, my ability has always worked, until today. I get nothing from you as if you are a creation made by magic with no soul. Is it because you are from another world? I do not know, but I *intend* to find out."

Jade shuddered. Camoe's cold statement sounded like he intended to slay her if unsure of her motives. Her only intention was to leave his world as soon as possible. Surely, he couldn't fault her intent.

DARK THOUGHTS

Push-pull, push-pull. The chute seemed to go on forever. Jade kept going, snaking methodically onward and upward through the cooking vent. Mechanically, she focused on two words glowing in her mind. *Push-pull, push-pull.* Working her legs and then her arms, she undulated through the darkness like a robotic worm tunneling through space. Dark thoughts lurked in her mind, waiting for an opportunity to gain control, to leave her a gibbering mess. As soon as a random thought coalesced in her mind, it would turn dark, taking on a substance her fears found harder and harder to dispute.

Out of the nothingness before her, a thought seeped inside. She'd crawled into an impossibly elongated coffin ejector—built to propel the deceased sailing off the Mountain and into the gray ocean of the Wasted Sea. She was going to die in here. No one would ever find her in here. *Stop it,* she told herself.

Quelling the notion, she next wondered if she was going to run out of air. The vent tube was hot and stifling, her breathing labored. Was the air becoming thinner? No. The draft in the chute fanned ash past her head when she moved. It was a vent, after all, designed to draw smoke from the citadel fires. That brought to mind another fear. What could they do if someone lit a large fire below?

Nothing, they were as helpless and naive as a bug crawling inside a hover transport's combustion shaft. What were they thinking? Jade pushed on, worry hyperventilating the air in her lungs, each drop of her knee or hand made it harder to breathe through the cloud of unseen ash.

Push-pull, push-pull. Her thighs burned, her back hurt as if it carried the weight of the citadel above, and her lungs gasped like a fish trying to survive in one of the few freshwater lakes left in Low or Mid Realm. At this rate, she'd go as most of the fish had there, dorsal fin down and unmoving. She'd give much to know how much farther the bloody shaft was going to force her to crawl.

If only she could see something. The second time hot wax had splattered her thumb and palm, she'd cried out and dropped the candle. Darkness had swallowed her then. The dark thoughts had crept in not long after. Jade hated it. How had bats lived in pitch-blackness all the time? Would she ever see light again?

Push-pull, push-pull. Bleakly, Jade realized Camoe's shuffles behind had grown quiet. She stopped to listen. Had she finally moved beyond hearing him? Or had the flickers found a way inside? Fear knifed her gut as she thought about it. After a short, silent struggle, the flickers had consumed him. Now he was one of them, slithering toward her, his sightless eyes fixed on her vibrant, yummy soul. *Stop!*

Dark thoughts again. She couldn't allow *them* to fester or she'd end up petrified. All she had to do was just keep moving, one knee, one elbow, and one long and lonely shuffle at a time. She kept at it.

Another interminable struggle in the dark brought the realization she was no longer squirming uphill. In fact, she was going downhill at a sharp angle. She must have passed a vertical branch. Gaining momentum, she slid downward without effort, beginning to build an uncomfortable friction on the side dragging the vent tube bottom.

She rolled onto her other side, until it too got hot, but not for long. She was slowing, the incline lessening. Coming to a stop, the blackness seemed brighter somehow. As she gathered a second wind, her excitement helped pump her legs and arms faster.

The dark faded into a gray wall. *Push-pull, push-pull, keep your knees moving.* Now she made out patches of the purple-gray stone of the vent, giving her a burst of energy. Scrambling, she found golden light pouring through an open door comparable to Camoe's kitchen except larger. Firewood and fire starter was stacked in front.

Jade crawled through, sweeping chunks of wood and bricks of

starter out the door. A rough stone floor rose up to meet her, stinging her palms and bruising her knees. Blazing light lanced her eyes. Squeezing them closed, Jade rolled onto her back and extended her legs, working the cramps out one leg at a time, sighing with relief. After a short interval, she cracked her eyelids open, giving her vision time to adjust. Thankfully, the light wasn't as bright as it had first seemed, only glowing dimly from shards of amber mounted within a wire mesh from several places on the wall.

A shadowy figure moved near the stove.

Jade bolted upright and nearly swooned.

The figure turned.

Jade gaped. Mop-like hair, sunken yellow-orange eyes, and brown burlap-textured skin filtered through her disbelief. Unusual characteristics for certain, though normal compared to the thing's facial features that were drawn with thick, charcoal lines. Wide, scowling eyebrows, a round nose, and a grim mouth housing several jagged teeth kept her staring. There was no chin or neck; the face simply fused with the shoulders. But she had no doubts vitality flowed inside the figure. Its yellow-orange eyes shone bright with a candid self-awareness.

Looking closer, she realized there was something strange beyond the color of the eyes; something about the eyelids…they were nonexistent. Blinking wouldn't be possible. How dry the eyes must be to the creature. Except "creature" didn't seem right, and "figurine" fit better. The figurine looked contrived from whatever material someone had on hand. A white cooking apron covered the raggedy clothes it wore but exposed the oddly textured skin. The skin appeared as malleable as human's skin did as it stooped easily to retrieve a branch she'd strewn on the stone floor. The doll man dumped the wood in the iron fireplace to form a teepee.

She left the figurine to its task and looked around.

Lined in the center of the room, five black iron cauldrons hung suspended on twisted iron shepherds' crooks above metal bins banked with coals. Two cauldrons were bubbling briskly with a brown substance, and a whitish mash steeped in a third. The rest were clean and empty, tilted on their side.

Baking aromas smelling strongly of succulent meats and pastries from somewhere close made her stomach rumble—a painful reminder breakfast was the last meal eaten. Two large bread trays with many loaves inside, baked a golden brown, took up counter space along one wall, making her dry mouth water. On the far side, three smaller kettles filled with yellow vegetables warmed on a grill behind the big iron vessels. The figurine bent over near one of the pots and then pivoted toward the stove. Gripped in the jaws of iron tongs outstretched before the doll-like man, a coal ember glowed red.

Jade swept the wood out of the stove, scattering it on the floor.

The raggedy man-like figurine paused mid-step, one foot raised. Yellow-orange eyes considered her, unblinking. Then, spinning slowly, it marched back toward the banked coals heating the cauldrons.

Jade shrugged. It should buy Camoe time as she studied the movements of the strange, burlap-skinned…thing. Lifting and bending each leg with precise, jerky movements as if it was a wind-up child's toy, the raggedy man halted near a bubbling cauldron. Bending fluidly, the figure plunked the coal in a bin. Performing an about face, it began high-stepping back. It had no knees.

Ashes mushroomed from the fireplace, adding to the dust covering her.

Wiping her eyes with the back of her hands, she made out Camoe buckling his sword and sheath around his waist. Now she knew why she'd kept ahead of the druid. The limited space of the vent shaft had forced him to carry his sword in one hand.

Creating a second dust cloud, Camoe slapped his brown leather apparel as he regarded her. "Are you okay? You are grayer than if a death ambler had bitten you. I suppose I look it, too."

Before she could ask what a death ambler was, the raggedy man stepped between them, bending at the waist, to gather the firewood.

"Blast!" Camoe swore. Springing backward, he drew his sword.

Jade stepped in front of the raggedy man. "Wait! It hasn't

bothered me. I'm sure it's harmless."

Camoe's lip curled, his eyes a hard, light gray. "Stand aside. With luck, it has not yet reported to its master. Pray I am not too late." Raising his gleaming sword, he advanced.

Jade stayed put. Whatever the raggedy man was, he hadn't threatened her in any way. There was no indication it meant her harm. "You're not going to hurt him. It would've attacked me by now, had it wanted."

"You do not know these dark creations, Jade! Once created, there is a constant telepathic link to their master unless released by their creator. Most Dark Users have no reason to set them free and every foul reason to keep them under their corrupted control. Now, for the last time, stand aside!" Camoe's jaw tightened.

"Hold it," Jade said, raising her hands, thinking furiously. "What about the flickers? Shouldn't we be going?"

"What about them? I don't think they were able to get past the iron stove or they would have caught us easily. Now, stand aside."

"Wait! Won't it alert the master if you suddenly sever this link?"

"Yes, but we shall be gone from here by then. A dark creation's death can incapacitate the User for many bells. Particularly if it is a sudden and violent death, which I can make happen," Camoe said, his voice cold. The lack of color in his eyes showed he meant every word. He reached out to push her to the side.

Shrugging his hand away, Jade glared, holding her arms wide. "You'll have to kill me before I'll let you destroy it."

For a long moment, Camoe's light gray eyes shone with stark hatred. Jade stood with her arms out, determined to spare the raggedy man. Slowly, his eyes darkened to the familiar blue. Finally, he sheathed his sword. "Have it your way for now, my strange young companion. However, know this, should I detect the smallest hint your pet dark creation has contacted its master, I shall dispatch it without hesitation. For your sake and mine, I hope it is not too late by then." Stalking to a heavy iron doorway, he cracked it open.

Jade released the breath she was holding. Camoe could've easily thrown her to the side and sliced the raggedy man to pieces. She was glad the druid had elected not to; discovering what material made up the doll man's insides was something she didn't want to experience. Besides, her instincts screamed the doll man meant them no harm. Leaving him to light the stove, she slipped past the cauldrons.

Wrapping two steaming bread loaves in some brown broad leaf she found on the counter, she stuffed both in her black bag and then tied a nearby flask of water to her waist. As she finished, she remembered the white crystal candle had struck an object when she put it in the bag. Taking a moment, she fished inside while keeping an eye on Camoe. She didn't want him reneging on his word to leave the poor doll man alone. Her hand brushed something smooth under the candle, which reminded her of the arrow shaft protruding from the girl's back for some reason she couldn't fathom.

Suddenly, the rotation around Camoe froze. The scene continued where she'd left off. Halting long enough to scoop the girl into his arms, Camoe ran, tears streaming down his face. Arrows flew past. Stumbling into a copse of monstrous living trees, he set the girl on a tall horse tethered beside another. The girl held on weakly. Untying both horses, he vaulted onto horseback behind her and charged off, leading one of the horses. The scene faded as Jade caught another glimpse of the blue crystal candle gripped in the girl's delicate, blood-soaked hand.

Stunned by the image's clarity, Jade swallowed hard. It had seemed so fresh, so real, as if it'd happened just now. His look of frightened worry still shone clearly.

Removing her hand, she was surprised to find the object had come out of the bag with it. Wrapped around her fingers, a silver chain held a polished onyx arrowhead surrounded by a silver ring. Fastened by pins to the inside topmost portion, the arrowhead rotated freely, as did the silver ring it hung from. Halting its delicate spin, Jade ran her thumb along an outer edge near the tip, feeling the sharpness of it. Tiny symbols engraved around the silver ring and the arrowhead's center were too small for her to make out, but it didn't matter. Crystalyn would know what they meant. Slipping the chain over her head, she stowed it under her shirt for safekeeping.

As she strode to the room's sole exit, the flask hung heavy at her side, something she hadn't expected. Perhaps so much exertion had drained her or the image viewing had taken precious energy from her—perhaps a combination of both. It was surprising that Camoe's image had slowed without her concentrating on it, but she didn't want to dwell on it, for now.

Camoe would likely have some insight into the strange occurrence, but it was a delicate subject for her to broach with him. Performing an act of violence in some way was all he wanted, or so it seemed. Jade stopped at the door, gazing over Camoe's back as he squatted to peer into a dimly lit corridor. "Do you know where we are?" she asked keeping her voice low.

"I do believe so. We are near the soldiers' barracks, which gives me an idea. We may be able to escape this miserable place. Our only hope is to follow this hallway to the washroom. From there, we should have access to the citadel's drainage tunnels."

"You mean sewers?"

"Precisely, the tunnels must eventually empty into the black swamps. I cannot see them being too heavily guarded. Twisting to look at her and frowning, he allowed the door to swing closed. "Unfortunately, there is a major flaw in the plan. As I said, we have to walk past the soldiers' barracks and, worse, the food hall. I should have grabbed a pair of User robes when we left. Of course, they may not have held up. Soldiers and Users don't mix well. They prefer to stick with their own kind."

Jade gestured toward several cooking aprons hanging on wall pegs. "What about those?"

"There is not much material to work with there. Besides, I bet most, if not all, kitchen servants are like your pet dark creation. Made from the mind of evil to resemble a man but failing miserably," Camoe said, eyeing the raggedy man with narrow eyes.

Jade eyed a pile of burlap sacks. "Then, why don't we look like them? We could customize those sacks over there by the counter."

"Customize? What is that?"

"Never mind, find me something black I can use as a marker."

"You are speaking nonsense."

"Oh, right! I need something black to paint with or draw."

"Why not say so at the beginning? This should work," Camoe said, striding to a cold cauldron. Stooping, he retrieved a pointed chunk of coal from underneath. He handed it to her, a skeptical look on his face. "I'm not sure what you hope to accomplish with it."

"Just watch," Jade said. "Raggedy man, come here, please," she called, using her most innocent tone. She smiled to herself. The tone was her favorite. It had always worked well for getting Dad to bring her a drink or extra food. Crystalyn, however, usually flared with anger, making Jade bring something to her, instead. Her smile faded. She missed them both already.

Obediently, the doll man straightened from the stove and marched across the room to stand before her. She stared at his inexpressive face and textured skin. "This won't do. I can't keep calling you dark creation or thinking of you as doll man or 'raggedy man.' From now on, I'll call you Burlap or Burl for short. Do you understand?"

Face frozen impassively, the raggedy man bent his torso perceptibly.

"Mother Astura! Did it just try to bow?" Camoe said.

"It appeared so," Jade giggled. She was surprised but didn't want to let Camoe know. "Now, let me see if I can replicate our new friend." Squatting beside a pile of textured bags, she drew what she hoped was a good imitation of Burl's facial features. Finished, she held it up.

"With the aprons, it might work. Provided no one comes too near and the light remains shadowed throughout the hall," Camoe said doubtfully.

"Can you cut holes for our eyes while I draw the second one?"

Slipping a long knife from a sheath at his side, Camoe poked through the bag in silence.

Before long, Jade looked through holes in her burlap sack. A kitchen apron, tied at the back, finished the disguise. Camoe's blue-gray eyes regarded her from Burl's flimsy likeness, his apron smudged with ash to appear used. He was right, though. They couldn't get too close. Their eyes would betray them. They made a poor imitation of Burl—she was too slender, and they were both taller—which made them insane for believing they could fool anyone who happened to come close. What else could they do? Though she'd been gone less than a day, she had to get home. Dad would be frantic. Crystalyn would be frantic and manic. Something one should avoid bringing out in her sister no matter what. If one knew what was best for them.

CREEPING BURLAP

Another droplet of perspiration wormed into Jade's left eye this time. The sodium in it stung, blurring her vision, which caused her nose to well up. Wiping her eyes clear was out of the question, as they were nearing a wide, well-lit area.

Raising her knees to her hips, yet again, was enough to bring tears to wash the sting away; her body—or any human body for that matter—were not built to withstand such grueling repetition. Yet they'd been marching this way for hours. Her idea of mimicking Burl's choppy high steps when they'd left the kitchen behind now seemed questionable, but so far, the subterfuge had worked. Thankfully, the burlap disguises had held when dozens of black-armored soldiers trooped past them, going the opposite direction so many times she lost count. No one glanced at them long.

"Is it still coming?" Camoe asked.

Jade didn't have to look over her shoulder to answer. "Of course, *Burl's* still with us. Where would he go?"

Camoe halted, glancing behind. "Has he been carrying those kitchen rags the whole way?"

"Yes. You never noticed?"

"Not wearing these bloody disguises. I have not had the opportunity to turn around; you have seen all the activity we plodded past. Something is going on, but we cannot take the risk to find out. Why *is* it packing those rags?"

"They're dirty."

"I can see they're soiled. What does that have to do with it? Your befriended creation is going to draw unwanted attention, trailing behind us like a stray pet. Can you not see the situation not destroying it has put us in? It will not go away no matter what I say now."

Jade wanted to keep moving, but her legs ached to the point of screaming, and hot tears leaked down both cheeks.

Pivoting on a heel, she locked eyes with Burl. His orange, deadpan eyes peered over the bulky stack of well-used rags. No animosity, no carefully concealed cunning, and weirdly, no affection whatsoever slipped through Burl's ginger irises. She detected…nothing. It was as if his mind had no capability for emotion, however small. Yet he did have complex thought patterns. How else would he know how to do his job? Or even to follow them for that matter? Why did he follow them? Was he keeping an eye—or rather, two yellow-orange eyes—on them for his master?

No. She didn't believe that; there was no malice in them. Besides, it wasn't as if he had a say in his construction. No matter what the druid wanted, she didn't want to go on without Burl. His life seemed so menial, slaving away in the kitchens with no hope for any change; he was too intelligent for that. Was he alive? Perhaps he was just a mass of dark power created by some adept Dark User performing some forbidden arcane ritual, as Camoe implied. What did it matter? She got the sense he meant no harm from the moment she laid eyes on him. "Part of his job must be to ensure the kitchen linen is clean along with everything else kitchen related. Wait, didn't you say that we need to reach the washroom?"

"Yes, past the barracks there," the druid said, nodding his burlap head toward the well-lit widened area.

Great. Barracks meant military and the addition of men wearing armor. She was beginning to hate men in armor. How far could they push their luck? Lifting a generous stack of rags from Burl's outstretched arms, she deposited them in Camoe's hands. "Here, take some, we need to add to our creations." Slipping a hand under her burlap mask, she wiped sweat from her brow and tears from her cheek. The time for crying wasn't now, but it was sure to come. Adjusting the charcoaled sack for a better view, she took half the remaining linen from Burl. "These should give us an excuse to be in the washroom while helping to hide our too-human eyes."

Mask slightly askew, a cold blue—too-human—eye regarded her steadily over a pile of greasy black cloths that may have once been white. "There is so much more to you than I had originally believed, young one. Perhaps, we shall live to see another sunrise if we escape this forsaken cavern." Coaxing his burlap disguise into place with the soiled pile, Camoe turned and faced the corridor ahead. "Stay close, we have to continue without pause until we reach the drainages."

He resumed his awkward march, and Jade fell in behind. Right away, her legs protested every unnatural step. Not bending her legs at the knees was taking a heavy toll on her lower body. Fiery pain shot through her hip sockets with each high step. Again, perspiration broke out after a step or two. At the rate they were going, she would be a sodden, hobbling mess if they didn't reach their destination soon.

The well-lit area acquired its luminescence from beautiful white crystal shards wrapped in thin, black wire cages attached to the rock ceiling. The white shards provided the most luminous light yet, but also exposed her little group to several soldiers. The soldiers clustered loosely around two men centered in the widened stone corridor wearing heavy plate armor. Employing measured steps, the pair circled each other, swords raised, black helms pulled down. One stood tall and heavy, the other as tall but leaner.

Concentrating on maintaining the robotic march, Jade hugged the far wall. Glancing sidelong, she kept an eye on the scene enfolding in the miniature underground courtyard while looking beyond the circling soldiers. A line of black iron doors left hanging open illustrated rows of bunk beds cut into solid rock, accessed by ladders. The inside stone had been polished to a smooth sheen.

Movement drew her attention to the combatants. Lunging as if he held a spear instead of a sword, the heavier combatant disrupted the deadly shuffle. Nearly caught off guard, the leaner soldier whipped his sword to the side, deflecting his assailant's blow inches before it penetrated his chest. Reversing his parry, the leaner man sliced downward in retaliation. Fascinated by the exchange, Jade was slightly disappointed when they progressed past them. As much as she wanted to continue to observe the fight, it would require her to turn her head—something Burl, or a Creation like him, would never do, couldn't do. It was physically impossible with no neck; she'd have to stop and turn, or twist her upper body. Either way, she'd give herself away; no Dark Creation would care in the slightest how humankind killed each other. Each Creation performed certain tasks by design from their creator.

The harsh clangs reverberating around the stone cavern testified that the two men still fought in earnest. Not looking back required almost as much willpower as moving forward. After a time, the ceiling sloped lower than any other had so far, creating a feeling of immense weight pressing down. Lack of proper air circulation made the hall stifling. Continuing onward was fast becoming unbearable.

Rounding a sharp curve to the left brought a welcome relief. A pleasant breeze blew underneath the masks, bringing cool, moist air, which dried perspiration as it soothed dehydrated eyes. A few hard-won steps revealed the source of the breeze. Ahead, lay the washroom.

Sculpted from purplish-gray stone like every room so far, the washroom exhibited some significant differences. Most notable, calling the area a room was a gross misnomer. Wash *cavern* would be a better description.

Spreading many rock quarries in width, the cavern rose to a grand dome higher than the light inside could penetrate. Lit sporadically with glowing yellow stalactites growing to great lengths, the light provided a glimpse of a vast underground lake.

A series of shaped stone pools, varying in size and depth, lined the lakefront. Cordoned troughs distributed water from one pool to the next. Many white-liveried servants passed by as they moved back and forth along the hall, going in and out of the cavern, carrying out tasks for soldiers. No one wearing a robe was visible. Gaping about, Jade had to remind herself to keep marching lest she gave them away.

The pools on the left were clear, clean, and void of people except for those servants filling water containers. Most of the activity centered on the right side. There, half-clad and unclad men and women lounged on stone benches, sat in steaming pools, or stood knee-deep in bubbling pools as they wrung garments. Jade's face heated when she noted Camoe had chosen a path leading directly to one of the bathing pools before it wound past.

Though she wanted to look anywhere but ahead, she stared forward to remain in formation. Standing with both broad backs facing a bathing pool, two naked, muscular men stood glaring at the trio, as they trooped past in single file, their hatred apparent by their trembling bodies and balled fists. The images floating around both of them were dark and streaked with red, promising a picture of violence, or death, perhaps both. Jade shied away from prying too deep. "Go hide behind your slimy creator's robes, abominations, before I forget your masters are supposed allies."

The path led to one side, forcing her to look from the corner of her eye again. She wasn't sure which one had called out until she noticed the one sporting a goatee and square jaw was groping his side for something no longer hanging at his waist, probably a weapon. Her face grew hotter under the mask. She kept her eyes raised.

The angry man's clean-shaven companion spoke. "You're wasting your breath, Durg. There aren't many blasted Users strong enough to give voice to their no-breaths. Even those that can don't bother. It takes too much from them."

Durg, the goateed man sneered. "What do I care what it takes from them?"

"Just saying, those abominations likely don't even know you're talking to them. They only follow rudimentary instruction sets from their creator."

The path took them beyond earshot, much to her relief. Hatred for Burl's kind festered even here, though they were supposed to be on the same side. Jade resisted the urge to look behind and check on Burl. Instead, she focused on planting her feet on the path ahead. If Camoe didn't stop soon, her legs would anyway. No matter who watched, she'd fall over screaming. Biting her lip until she tasted blood, Jade kept going, putting one foot forward one step at a time. *Lift-step, lift-step.*

The simple act of moving worsened, becoming a pain-filled haze of agony, making her wonder if it was worth fighting so hard to escape. Yet Burl and Camoe deserved her strongest efforts; they struggled for all of them together when their odds were better for them to make it out alone. She fought through another hour, working up a litany to keep going. *Your friends struggle for you when they don't have to. Your friends struggle for you...*Focused on Camoe's back, she kept at it, each step sending another lance of pain deep into her lethargic brain.

When the path made a sharp right turn, Camoe abruptly stopped. Jade plowed into him. Flinging his arm out, he avoided ramming his face into a huge yellow and brown stalagmite, but only just. "Sorry, I can't go a step further."

Pushing away from the druid, she took stock of where they were. The far side of the cavern that had seemed so far away was very close. A small trough of gray water flowed languidly downhill toward a cave.

Standing without raising her legs felt so wonderful to her muscles, but the benefit was short-lived. They would cramp severely if allowed to contract after walking for so long with such an unnatural gait. Slowly, she bent them, one at a time, biting her ragged lip, tasting blood again, proud that she never cried out. When the pain began to subside, she fingered her mask. "Can I take this off? I'm tired of smelling like creeping burlap."

"Not yet," Camoe said, squatting and kneading his calves. "The entrance to the sewers is inside the cave ahead. The last time I explored through here, it was guarded."

Walking normally in place, Jade looked for Burl and found him standing slightly off the carved path, gazing at her stoically. He seemed to be aware of the need to stay hidden from prying eyes; the cluster of stalagmites he stood in blocked his outline from the pools. She smiled. Burl's gaze remained fixed on her, his unblinking eyes gazing out from his wide-lined, expressionless face.

Camoe stood and stretched. "You ready?"

"Yes, but I can't take this robotic walking."

Camoe frowned. "What do you mean by that?"

"Sorry, you wouldn't know. It's a term I coined for how we got here," Jade said. She mimicked the awkward process of moving without bending her knees. Even the three small steps she used sent a white-hot fire shooting from her legs to her hips. Her lip muted her cry.

"Oh," Camoe said, chuckling. "I have been calling it the golem march in my mind. It hurts, I know. Come, once we are in the waste tunnels, we can leave the heavy marching to the blasted dark creations."

Wincing, Jade resumed the march, clamping her mouth shut. Camoe's comment wasn't very different from those of the soldiers back at the pools. Burl hadn't been any trouble yet. In fact, he'd helped them get this far.

As they rounded several monstrous stalagmites tapering high enough to touch their stalactite counterparts, the jagged entrance to the sewers gaped before them. It was wider than she expected. Spanning a good portion of a large field, it resembled the extended, gaping mouth of a gigantic fish filtering food from water as several troughs converged into one.

Adjacent to their stream, a wide gravel path led them past spiky, black crystal shards lining both sides. Once past them, the cave narrowed. Pitted, rusty iron bars were pinned to the stone from floor to ceiling. The sickly bars allowed water to flow reluctantly past their purplish-orange spotted bottom submerged in the stream. An iron-hinged door, chained and locked, barred the way forward showing its own brand of rust.

Camoe's memory was terribly accurate. Four grizzled faces looked up from an improvised flat rock table cluttered with dice and tankards as they marched inside the cave.

Drawing his sword from under his apron, Camoe dashed forward and sliced through the throat of the nearest guard before he could rise. Reversing his swing, he lopped the adjoining guard's head from his shoulders as he attempted to stand. Gaining their feet, the two remaining guards shuffled backward, grunting in surprise.

Springing onto the table, Camoe leapt forward, thrusting his sword at a guard who fumbled for a great axe strapped to his back. A wet-sounding splotch testified the sword had found a mark. Bright red blood bubbled from the man's lips. Using his foot as leverage to pull his sword out, Camoe kicked the dying man in the stomach. His blade freed, he turned toward the final sentry, sword raised.

Towering over the druid, the bare-chested guard gripped an ugly jagged-toothed scimitar. Deep notches intruded along the blade's back and tip, cut at regular intervals. Camoe pulled off his mask, and the two men began to circle each other.

Jade pulled the mask from her head, fearing for her benefactor. He needed a distraction. Bending, she tugged at a rusty short sword from the headless corpse slumped over the table. The sheath resisted her pull but finally released its hold.

The guard suddenly lunged, executing a quick downward chop.

Camoe hoisted his blade at the last possible second, twisting away from the downward arc of the scimitar. The clang of steel against steel rang through the chamber.

Twisting his wrist, the big man slipped a notch over the long sword and pulled. Camoe's sword spun from his hand.

Bellowing with triumph, the guard swung a powerful blow at Camoe's head.

Camoe sprang backward. The sword tip nicked him above an eye. Landing near the end of the table, he slipped on a pool of blood, dropping to one knee. A red stain bloomed bright under his left eyebrow.

Grinning with malice, the big guard leapt across the cave, the scimitar point aimed for Camoe's head.

"No!" Jade shouted. She lunged at the man, the crude sword stretched outward.

Mid-step, the guard switched direction. Swatting her sword aside, he raised the scimitar, a glint of anticipation reflected in his eyes.

Jade vaguely heard the clatter of her sword dropping to the cavern floor. Her mind fixated on the flash of steel bearing down upon her. She could do nothing to save herself.

The sword slammed to a halt inches from her head, and the force of wind continuing past its sudden inert motion blew her hair back.

Burl's large, wood-grained hand gripped the big man's wrist, twisting it to the side with stunning speed. The sickening crack of breaking shoulder bone reverberated through the cave. The guard screamed. Seizing the sword from the man's unresisting hand, Burl silently flung it into the nearby stream.

In one motion, Camoe stood and thrust his dagger under the guard's chin, putting an abrupt end to the man's scream.

Jade struggled to comprehend. She was still *alive*.

Camoe followed the body to the ground. Once there, he pulled his dagger free. Dabbing the blood from the angry-looking cut above his left eye, he then wiped the dagger clean, sheathing it afterward. Rifling through the corpse's pockets, he collected some coin and a large black key, the head shaped in the likeness of the cave seen from a distance. He vaulted to his feet and hurried to the iron lock clasped with thick iron bands around the rusty door. Inserting it, he snapped the lock and swung the protesting door open, which gave off an ear-splitting screech.

"I'll lock this behind us. It may slow pursuit a little," Camoe declared, gazing over his shoulder, his eyes blue. "We should check their pockets quickly, though. It's too bad we can't stash the bodies, but there's no place close." His scowl caused the gash in his forehead to open wider. Blood flowed into his left eye, turning it pink. He blinked. "Are you all right?" he asked, absently wiping it with the back of his hand.

She stared. He had to be kidding, standing there with his pinkish, alien eye. A man just tried to bury a sword in her face. How could she be okay? The reality of the situation settled on her shoulders with the weight of the mountain. Stranded on a world where people killed each other, a world where humans created nonhumans which other humans labeled dark creations, a world where magic users penned humans with wraiths to satisfy their monstrous, inhuman hunger.

Almost every moment since her arrival had been spent running and fighting for her life. How could she be all right? She gaped at her companion with his demonic bloody eye before she realized the druid wouldn't understand. Violence was a part of him. "I'm starting to get feeling back in my arm, so I'll live," she said instead, biting back a sigh. "I do have a suggestion though. Why don't we pull the bodies through the door and let the stream move them for us?"

Camoe looked taken aback. "That had not occurred to me. It may get shallower after this, but it should work to get them out of sight. Let's hurry and check them for useful items first. We have a long journey ahead of us."

"I'll help drag, but don't expect me to go through a dead man's pockets."

Camoe chuckled wearily. "Come then. I'll do it before sending them to their final bath."

Gripping an ankle, she helped pull a corpse through the iron door to the stream. The current caught the dead man, carrying him mercifully downstream. As the body drifted downstream, it swept algae and fungus away that had grown undisturbed for who knew how long.

Jade gazed at a phosphorescent underwater plant left exposed from the moss. Was it native to the sewers? Sighing, she turned back to the grisly task of dumping bodies.

There was a lot to learn if she was going to survive on this world.

THE FLOW

Sunlight intruded upon Crystalyn's eyelids, brighter on her left. Outlined in orange, the radiated heat made thoughts of sleep vanish. Jade must've left the solar shield switched off again. How many times did she have to tell her? Rolling on her side, she faced the source, raising her lids a fraction. A giant shape moved, giving her a glimpse of green.

The events of the previous evening thundered into her mind.

"Good idea, Lore Rayna," a raspy feminine voice said. "The light has done it. I feared she may have exhausted herself beyond help, but she is awakening."

Crystalyn sat up, bumping her head on…a headboard, Atoi's headboard. A mother of a headache stirred to life, preparing her mood for the day. How she'd slept so soundly in Miss Dagger's bed was beyond comprehension. The girl had used her stomach to sheath her knife, and here she was lounging in the little vagabond's bed.

Sitting serenely on a wooden stool at the foot of the bed, the Lore Mother's glowing gaze seemed to be regarding her, concern apparent by the slight furrow of her brow. "Are your headaches getting worse, dear?"

"I suppose they are. How did you know about them?"

"You will address her as Mother or Lore Mother," Lore Rayna said.

Crystalyn squinted at the large woman who faced the window curtains. The same leafy-crawly dress covered her this morning, though barely. Drawing the curtains closed, Lore Rayna spun and faced her.

Lore Rayna's words irritated her. She wasn't Atoi's age. Her twenty-second season had passed months ago; she probably wasn't much younger than Lore Rayna herself. "Why should I call her Mother? She's not my mother. I don't need another one. I already have one." Missing for six seasons, alive or dead, she still had a mother.

Lore Rayna frowned. "It is a term of respect, small one, which you will use." Folding her arms, she leaned against the wall, beside the window. "Enough of your questions, Mother will ask them, and you shall provide truthful answers. I will know if you do not."

"Are you really that naive? You expect me to answer questions, yet you don't answer mine? Fair is fair, one for one, or you'll get nothing."

Lore Rayna's face darkened. "You are either a very brave or a very foolish person, much like the Child of Dark. Where is the little one lurking this morning?"

"She's free to come and go as she likes. I'm not her guardian."

Lore Rayna's eyelids hooded half the glow. "Perhaps you should be. She's quite dangerous, you know. You would be wise to keep a close watch."

"You want me to control her, like you do to the hairy brute. Where is he? Perhaps you should keep a close eye on him." It wasn't a fair accusation since Lore Rayna obviously cared for him, but she found it hard to care. The big woman had it coming.

"That is not your concern, *small* one! Do not—"

"Enough! Let her speak, Rayna," the old woman said, raising her voice. "Ask what you will of me, young one."

Glancing at the woman, Crystalyn opened her eyes wider and then squinted from the pain of her throbbing head. The bright, morning sun leaking around the curtains made it worse.

The Lore Mother had exchanged her white dress for a yellow gown. Sewn across the front, two rows of white three-fingered leaves made a simple pattern. The woman's glowing eyes burned with wisdom. There was a wealth of knowledge hidden there; perhaps help with finding Jade was closer than she thought. Her excitement grew, but so did her apprehension. Where to begin and how much would she have to reveal? Everyone wanted something here and seemed to have no problem killing to get it. Yet, to gain knowledge, one had to ask first. "You know I'm not from around here?"

A smile flitted across the Lore Mother's wizened face. "Many are now likely aware you hail from some unknown region after your bold stroll through the tavern. Most will not ascertain you are not from this world, however. It is not common knowledge that other worlds exist. I am one of a select few that believe there is the possibility of other worlds beyond our own."

Crystalyn sighed. "I don't know who I can trust. However, with you, I'm going to be candid. I have a goal. My sister is somewhere on your world. At least, the probability is high. I intend to find her no matter what I have to endure. I could use some help, but first, what do you know about my headaches?"

Lore Rayna and the Lore Mother exchanged a look. Shifting her toned bulk from foot to foot, Lore Rayna stilled. "So family is important to you?" she asked, raising a golden eyebrow. Her oversized orbs seemed to radiate brighter after the final word.

"Why wouldn't they be?" Crystalyn asked. For some reason, the question raised her ire. It made little sense. "Family and health should be high priorities in anyone's life. What kind of question is that?"

Lore Rayna gasped.

The wooden stool creaked in protest as the Lore Mother leaned farther forward. "Perhaps she is the One," she said, her tone deepening with the last word.

Crystalyn gaped at the two of them. "I don't have the slightest notion what you mean, but it's not important right now. Let's put a stop to the mysterious comments, okay? I don't know what you two want from me, nor do I have the time to wheedle it out of you. What I need to know is whether you can help me locate my sister. If you can't, you're wasting my time. You'll get nothing else from me." A little harsh perhaps, but she intended to be upfront from the start. Jade was all that mattered.

Lore Rayna grunted.

The Lore Mother nodded for a moment, her lips pursed. Abruptly, she sat up straighter, tilting her head slightly. "Your head trauma stems from your incorrect use of your…ability. You are likely pulling energy from deep within your system, possibly your bloodstream, robbing it of precious oxygen and bursting your red blood cells. At first, you'll feel the fatigue, then the headaches and nosebleeds. When you get to the final stages, you won't be able to feed yourself. That is if your heart is still pumping your lifeblood. Most hearts with this condition fail before anyone reaches the last stage. You now require advanced instruction, or you must abstain from using it altogether. Should you fail to do so, your blood will be too thin to carry the oxygen your body requires. You'll asphyxiate or bleed out from a simple cut or nosebleed."

Crystalyn's spine chilled at the woman's matter-of-fact words.

"As for your sister, I suppose I could attempt a contacting, but I shall need Rayna's aid and yours too."

"Me? What do you need me to do?"

The old woman rose to her feet with a grace belying her age. Smoothing her dress, she sat down next to Crystalyn on the bed. "Did you bring your stone and your orbs?" she asked Lore Rayna.

"Are you sure about this, Mother? What has she done to merit such a strenuous favor from us? This will require an interruption of great magnitude."

"Hush, child. We shall attempt the contacting. In so doing, we may learn additional knowledge of her."

"I'm right here," Crystalyn had to say and then quieted. They were helping her find Jade, after all.

Lore Rayna avoided looking at Crystalyn. "Shall I act as the focal point, Mother?" she asked.

Crystalyn gawked. As Lore Rayna put her hands behind her head, the dress moved, exposing a silver-twined strap. Releasing a clasp at her neck, Lore Rayna tugged it from her ample bodice. A glowing white stone resided inside a small slit—looking similar in size and shape to her eyes. Placing it on her forehead, she tied the end of the straps behind her head, centering the stone on her forehead. Reaching into a pocket Crystalyn hadn't noticed before—or the dress had grown around whatever contents the wearer placed there—Lore Rayna removed three hand-sized stones from her hip, seemingly. The smooth, pea-green stones, or orbs, as the Lore Mother called them, seemed precious. The big woman handled them with reverence. Raising a fine eyebrow, Lore Rayna hesitated, facing her mentor.

The Lore Mother drew a deep breath. "Yes, my daughter, you have focal point. You need the practice. I shall guide you while I interrupt the Flow. The conduit will be open for you to draw upon should you require it. Align the contact orbs; sit at the point."

Lore Rayna did so, sitting cross-legged and arranging the orbs in a triangle with the tip pointed at her.

The Lore Mother offered her hand. "Having never met your sister, you shall hold my hand and repeat her name. Concentrate on what you know and love best about her, what comes to mind first when you think of her. Can you do that, Crystalyn?"

Pulling her legs free from the wool blanket, Crystalyn slid next to the Lore Mother—discovering she'd slept in her undergarments. In the absence of sleepwear, she had no choice. "I don't have any idea what you're talking about, but thinking about my little sister isn't a problem. It's what I do lately." She held out her hand.

Clasping her hand with surprising firmness, the old Mother's age-spotted hand was softer than her own. "It should suffice, though I must warn you. Once we begin, do not attempt to interrupt the Flow. It could be catastrophic to us all." So saying, the Lore Mother's eyes burst into a brilliant luminosity—painful to look at—as she extended her free hand toward the floor.

Crystalyn froze. The floor melted to transparency. Below, a stormy river flowed. Stormy river *was* the best description for it. Clear and unpolluted, the river ran swift, frothing with a misty, gel-like substance. Individual curls of frothy white roared amidst intermittent flashes of jagged streaks of rainbow lightning.

Lore Rayna sat serene and immobile, supported above the river by nothing but air, or so it seemed. Leaning closer to the floor, Crystalyn could feel the power crackling with each flash of lightning as the river sped past on its endless path. She was awestruck. The river was very close, within her grasp. All she need do was extend her awareness.

The Lore Mother's voice broke through her reverie. "Give us your sister's name."

Crystalyn gaped. A sheer tube projected from the Lore Mother's downcast palm, penetrating the river. The stormy, hoary substance filled the tube.

"Jade. My sister's name is Jade," Crystalyn managed to blurt. The whole situation was a little frightening. How did these people survive with this kind of power available at anyone's fingertips? Panic crept into her mind. What unthinkable danger had she thrown Jade and herself into this time? No. She couldn't let it get to her. The panics would set in again. She *would* find her beautiful little sister. Crystalyn could see her now. Chewing on her lip, frightened and alone, her vivid, emerald eyes filled with worry.

"She has provided the link, Rayna," the Lore Mother suddenly said. The old woman's voice was strained yet loud enough to be commanding. "She is much stronger and closer to her sibling than I expected. Quickly, tie it to your orbs!"

Before Crystalyn could ask what link, the white stone embedded in the strap on Lore Rayna's forehead shot a bar of hoary light to the top orb in the triangle. Emitting a brilliant flash, a golden bar of light connected the two remaining orbs as it flowed back into itself. Countless colored dots stacked upward faster than the eye could follow—forming a three-dimensional image inside the triangle, ending at ceiling height.

Crystalyn gazed transfixed at the image. Blackness prevailed. *Plop, slurg, plop, slurg* echoed from out of the blackness. Something clumped together glowed with a phosphorescent green. It drifted along the bottom of the image where it vanished near the triangle tip.

Halfway up, a tiny, yellow-white light moved away in the distance.

Suddenly, the blackness inside the triangle darkened palpably. The light inside winked out. Darkness, absolute, consumed the image. Black, writhing tendrils sprang outward from the triangular image along the ceiling, as if a monstrous squid had risen from the depths of an underwater crevice.

Someone screamed.

BLACK CURTAIN

Tepid water ringed outward when Jade dislodged floating clumps of phosphorescent green that clung to larger growths of fungi. Soaked to the thighs, her legs weighed her down, requiring greater and greater effort to raise them. Each step she took disturbed the water's slow course—though calling the brackish liquid "water" did stretch her imagination.

Jade tried not to think about what they'd slogged through after disposing the guards' bodies. Thank the One, she'd worn her black lace boots to Crystalyn's work instead of the flats she usually wore. At least the boots provided a small measure of protection against whatever debris exited through the tunnels, though liquid still leaked inside. Whatever constituted the liquid, she didn't want to think about. Was there no end to these tunnels? "I can't go much further. We've been splashing through this mess for so long," Jade finally said, her voice echoing into the dark for a longer distance than she cared for.

Camoe swung the torch they'd taken from the gate guards' wall sconce in a half-circle, back and forth. Ahead, the tunnel widened into a small cavern, and two dark openings lurked at the edge of the torch's light, opposite the main drainage. "I am certain we have walked the night through, but we have yet to come across an area dry enough to rest. We are in dire need of such a place. We cannot slosh through this filth for much longer without risking an illness, but I am uncertain of the way forward." Lowering the torch, his shoulders slumped.

Slogging beside the druid, Jade pried the smoldering torch from his unresisting fingers. She took her last apron strip she had soaked in the oily substance back at the gate and wrapped it around the torch.

The torch flared with new life. Jade was reluctant to ask how many strips the druid had left. What would they do when they ran out? They couldn't wander around in the dark; it was too dangerous.

Underneath Burl's apron, when she'd removed it for strips, they'd found a soiled rope looped around the makeshift pants he wore, but Camoe had been reluctant to use it unless they had no other alternative, thinking it might come in handy, though they might not have any choice soon. As soiled as it was with kitchen grease, it should burn for some time. Raising the flame high, she sloshed forward to pause in the center of the small cavern. Both curved openings were similar in structure, revealing little but pitch-blackness, though the right one *seemed* better for some unknown reason.

"I say we follow the right side."

Camoe straightened. He looked at the left tunnel first and then to the right. "It appears both directions are heading up at a gentle slope. Probably ventilation shafts or access chutes for large debris removal, but why there are two when one is enough is beyond comprehension." Squaring his shoulders, he took the torch from her hand, turning his back on the left route. Dragging his feet through shallower water, he waded inside the tunnel mouth. His splashes ceased, and she heard him stamping his feet on dry-packed earth. "Come on. One's as good—" Though it was amplified threefold, Camoe's soft voice cut off with stark abruptness.

A curtain of blackness, darker than the tunnel, draped over her. Settling in like a collapsed tent, it encompassed her with an overpowering presence that weighed on her with the pungent, suffocating smell of mold long since forgotten. The torchlight's defiant existence vanished.

A presence intruded upon her mind. Something dark loomed, immense, intelligent, and powerful. Alien and aware, it crept forward, exuding a suffocating sense of indomitable willpower that packed the space around her. Arrogant with the knowledge of its supreme power, the alien intelligence compressed upon her mind, forcing its will upon her self-awareness of who she was, of what she knew of herself.

Instinctively, Jade recoiled to a corner. Gathering her will, she installed a protective barrier of resistance around herself, formulating it into a dome.

The compression gained intensity, pressing on her bubble of resistance with stunning power, exuding a great malevolence. The telepathic onslaught pounded against her barrier mercilessly, with the single-mindedness of supremacy comfortable with its complete mastery of all it had ever encountered, having no concept of any single being ever thwarting it in its long memory.

Yet thwart it she was. Her resistance remained firm. There wasn't a single spot weakening anywhere, even though the assault doubled in intensity, again. How long she'd be able to maintain resistance she did not know. For now, she felt confident she could keep it at bay.

The bombardment ended as fast as it began. Jade sensed the alien evil methodically spreading putrescent feelers around her bubble, searching for a hint of thinness, some infinitesimal flaw, however small. Discovering nothing, its frustration reverberated through her awareness as the feelers shifted to the base of her dome and grew still.

They were at a stalemate. But she was in a horrible predicament. Trapped in a tiny corner of her mind, eventually her body would need sustenance. Prevented by the foul thing inhabiting her from acquiring water, she would die. She had to do *something*.

A piercing white light stabbed through the center of the inhuman presence.

The malevolence stiffened.

A small, white screen opened inside the darkness. Swiftly, countless three-dimensional colored rectangles stacked around the screen, and a cloudy, three-dimensional image formed inside her mind. In the image, Crystalyn sat on a rustic bed next to a large, ancient woman wearing a yellow dress. A white three-leafed pattern stood prominent across the front. Both gazed at an enormous woman wearing a headband inset with glowing white stones. The large woman sat cross-legged on the floor facing Crystalyn at the head of a vague triangular image rising from floor to ceiling.

Joy raced through Jade. Crystalyn was trying to find her.

Fury vibrated through the tendrils outside her barrier. Several detached from her shield. One large tendril split from the dark mass to strike at the image center.

The image winked out.

Crystalyn!

Furious arrogance rippled throughout her dome. The tendrils clamped on her dome and lifted; feelers snaked underneath, squeezing from the inside and out. The barrier buckled, collapsing. Suddenly she felt a much greater over mind attached to the intelligence by an ancient, maternal link. The over mind was not yet fully awake, but it was *aware*. Its offspring reached for her, the dark tendrils writhing.

Terrified, Jade hastily installed a wall of resistance, this time severing the sense of the over mind. Gathering her will, she pushed the wall forward. Confused, the offspring fell back from her wall in leaps as the bubble dissolved. Gaining momentum, Jade shoved harder, stopping only when she sensed the edge of her mind.

Screeching with defiance, the intelligence now resisted, snapping at the edge of her awareness.

Determined, Jade brought the full weight of that determination bearing down upon it.

Reverberating deafeningly through the cold recesses of her mind, the malevolence shrieked once with a long, drawn-out wail of fury. Then pure, sweet silence settled in. Jade could no longer sense it anywhere. A different blackness encompassed her mind then. One she welcomed.

DARK IMAGE

Crystalyn shook Lore Rayna, her anxiety adding force to her arms.

The scream severed in mid-shriek. Startled, Crystalyn let go. Lore Rayna rocked backward and then slumped forward, her head bouncing against her drawn-up knees. She toppled to the side.

An inhuman wail pierced the room. The dark image shrank into the orbs.

Sliding from the bed, the Lore Mother thudded to the floor beside her pupil. How was she to know which one was hurt worse?

The bedroom door crashed into the wall with a thunderous bang. Cudgel charged inside, an iron-tipped club as thick as a man's arm gripped in one hand. Spotting the comatose women lying on the floor, rage twisted his features.

Crystalyn rose to her feet.

Cudgel leapt, landing in front of her.

"Cudgel, good, I—" Cudgel's big hands clamped around her biceps and lifted her off the floor. She sailed across the room as if she weighed less than one of her stuffed animals. She managed to throw her hands out just before her body hit the wall. Even so, her arms folded. Striking her head into the wall, she dropped to the floor. Her legs slipped out from under her, and she landed on her side in a heap. Pain ripped through her head and hip.

"Blast you, Dark User! What did you do to them?" Cudgel shouted. Dropping to his knees beside Lore Rayna, he placed two thick fingers against her neck. "She's alive but unconscious," he snarled, his brown eyes glinting with the promise of violence. "If she fails to wake, today will be your last. Tell me what you've done to them!"

Crystalyn couldn't reply. Her side throbbed in time to the burgeoning pain inside her head. Biting back a moan, she waited for it to recede. After a time, she struggled to sit, checking for broken bones. Other than the painful twinges in her hip, she seemed intact.

Planting her back to the wall, Crystalyn stood, keeping an eye on the big warrior as he squatted beside the Lore Mother. Bringing out the black knockdown symbol she'd used on Atoi, she let it hover in the air before her. Combining it with the two other aggression symbols from the black-lettered book, she recreated her enhanced symbol. Circular in design, the pattern that formed inside the circle had three-sided squares running upward from the center and then down from the top, repeating when it met a horizontal centerline. Underneath the broad line, the pattern stayed the same but switched to a horizontal direction. It was the same one she'd destroyed the crates with, nearly crushing her lungs as it flattened her in the alley. She hadn't dared use it on Atoi for fear of killing her. With Cudgel, she was afraid the original knockdown wouldn't be enough. If it killed him, he'd made his choice when he'd laid hands on her.

Cradling her head, the Lore Mother abruptly sat up.

Relief shone in Cudgel's brown eyes.

The Lore Mother moaned.

Cudgel glanced at Crystalyn. His eyes narrowed as he regarded her symbol. Leveling his thick club, he pointed with it. "So, I was correct. You're as filthy dark as a pit of adders. Not even trying to hide it now, eh?"

Turning, the Lore Mother's hands dropped to her side. "How extraordinary..."

Furious, Crystalyn glared at Cudgel. Killing again was not her first choice, but she would if the man ventured close. "I don't want to hurt anyone, not even a brute like you. But know this, I won't allow you to put your hands on me again. Do you *hear* me?"

Atoi poked her head through the shattered doorway. "What happened here?"

Silence reigned.

Crystalyn met Cudgel's darkening glare with resolve. She meant what she said. No one would touch her without permission again.

Sounding oddly supernatural, Atoi's hollow laughter pealed throughout the room, ringing with a wickedness that belied her youth as it somehow insinuated violence and pleasure in the same tone. A shudder of revulsion gave Crystalyn a shiver, but the girl looked her normal, unsmiling self. "It was not long before your Using popped up again. I'm glad it's not pointed at me this time." Strolling across the room to stand beside her, Atoi brought her dagger out. "I told you not to trust them. Did you kill the leaf woman? Which one shall I slay?"

"Enough!" the Lore Mother bellowed. The effect was diminished slightly by her wince, as her hands went to her head. "No one's going to kill anyone. All of you, put your weapons and magic away!" Swaying, the Lore Mother frowned, rubbing her head.

Ignoring the pain from her shoulder and hip, Crystalyn kept her symbol in place. The brute with the big stick would have to disarm first.

Arms rigid, Cudgel held the pole like a great sword, one steel-tipped end forward. His dark eyes smoldered.

Crystalyn wanted to sigh but held it inside. As much as she hated to, she'd have to make the first move toward peace. It was the way of it.

Allowing the symbol to dissipate, she kept the pattern fresh in her mind, just in case. Her hip twinged, but she refused to rub it. Showing signs of weakness to the man would only make him bolder. She couldn't help but wince, though, as her head pounded anew like a blacksmith, just out of sight, working an anvil.

Cudgel rested the weapon's tip on a boot, suspicion twisting his features a different, but still ugly, way. He wasn't going to accept her offer. Fine. She owed him, anyway. Perhaps she could goad him into taking one step closer. He'd have to move around Lore Rayna, putting him in line with the window. One step and her symbol would take him from there. What floor were they on?

Cudgel took a step closer.

No goad required. She began to form the symbol.

The Lore Mother's hands went to her hips. "Cudgel, sheathe your weapon and stop acting the fool!" Several heartbeats passed. Finally, he stabbed his weapon into the sheath on his back. "Good boy. Now, go fix the door before someone uninvited strolls in. This girl did nothing to harm us. I swear, sometimes your warrior instincts muddle your ability to reason beyond comprehension." Turning her back on him, she stooped over Lore Rayna. After a moment, the old woman drew a sharp breath. "Crystalyn, you were able to heal yourself, is that not right? Rayna's hurt beyond my capability to mend. Will you help her?"

Crystalyn hobbled beside the Lore Mother, giving Cudgel a wide berth. The man may have sheathed his weapon, but he'd made no move for the door. "I can try. I'm not sure if the symbol I used on myself will work on anyone else, though."

The Lore Mother's voice sounded strained. "Please, make the attempt. Lore Rayna's our only healer, though I fear her injury is beyond her own skill."

"What do you mean?"

"Will you see to my student? We can discuss it at length, soon."

Crystalyn pictured the white-and-silver spider-webbed pentagram pattern, majestic in its simplicity. Combining it again with the one she'd read under the heading dilutions in the white-lettered book, the symbol reformed. Intricate silver and gold lines, winding back and forth, filled the symbol, a hedge maze with no beginning or end. The symbol now glowing faintly silver and gold in color, she positioned it horizontally above Lore Rayna's comatose form.

"No! We can't trust her, good Mother!" Cudgel pleaded, going to Lore Rayna's opposite side. "She has to be a Dark User masquerading as Light. You saw the black symbol hovering in the air!"

"Hush, my son," the Lore Mother hissed. "You do not have to trust her. Trust me."

Cudgel grunted but remained silent.

Crystalyn's concentration wavered from the exchange; even though she tried to close her mind to it, the symbol thinned to transparency. As she gathered her will, the symbol brightened, taking on its surreal shades of white, gold, and silver. The symbol sank into the big woman's skin, glowing briefly before vanishing.

Crystalyn's perspective of her body mass changed. Attuned to the symbol, she was startled when it took her deep into Lore Rayna's nerve pathways. Suddenly, there were many new neural connections different from her own, all linked to a body as powerful as anything she could have conceived. Wary of the immenseness of it, she nearly severed the link. Nevertheless, she was here. She wouldn't give up without trying. Lore Rayna needed help.

Willing the symbol to climb toward the brain and increase in speed, Crystalyn searched Lore Rayna's neural pathways for anything abnormal. Picking up speed, her gold and silver symbol zoomed faster than she thought possible, rocketing down dozens upon dozens of fibers, hunting for anything unhealthy. One branch led into another or sent her zooming back to the trunk. Methodically, she sped down pathway after pathway, however small, only to find nothing wrong. Not a trace anywhere; every nerve appeared healthy and functional.

Confused, she slowed, as a thought took hold. From her present position, she had access to Lore Rayna's spinal network leading to her brain. She could take control of Lore Rayna's motor functions to see if her ailment would manifest as she moved. At least then, she'd know if the link from the woman's mind to her body was still intact. Perhaps she could even see through Lore Rayna's strange, milky eyes.

But was it worth the cost? She could only drive one body at a time. Splitting her consciousness between two bodies would be complicated, not to mention dangerous. There was the very real danger of damaging Lore Rayna worse than she was, by forcing a seemingly innocent movement upon the big woman's body that Lore Rayna couldn't handle where a smaller person would be able to perform it easily.

Yet Lore Rayna must be injured somewhere. Perhaps another person's wounds were beyond her abilities to heal after all. Why was she traipsing about Lore Rayna's insides as if she was strolling around the Farm—?

At the edge of her awareness, something dark flitted along a main neural branch.

Willing her symbol to go faster and faster, she chased the dark abnormality until her awareness of the region blurred. Still she approached no closer than a vague feeling of something wrong just ahead. Slowing, she drifted to a stop. Perhaps she'd imagined it, or possibly, it was a reflection of her intrusion. Perhaps, but she doubted it. There was *something*.

Had she been going about the whole thing the wrong way? The wound may not be physical.

Casting about, she realized gray matter surrounded her; she'd stopped inside the big woman's brain. *Perfect*. Stretching her symbol, Crystalyn added a link from it to the gray matter while maintaining her tenuous hold.

Gibbering terror flooded her mind.

Crystalyn recoiled. Some of the terror was her intrusion. Lore Rayna *must* sense her presence on a subconscious level, if nothing else. *Blast it*. She must use delicacy. Adding a feeling of warmth and overall well-being, she restored the link.

This time, Lore Rayna's presence swarmed to her symbol. Ambitions, determination, spunk, enrapture, steadfastness, bitterness, and a multitude of other sensations flowed through. An almost overpowering empathy for growing things made up the end, gusting into Crystalyn's mind with abandon. Gust after gust, the empathy windstorm assaulted her, pulling at her self-awareness, ripping at her sense of herself. Crystalyn held on.

At the back of a final gust, she felt a foulness slipping away. Inflating her symbol, she shot it after the shadow on the off chance she might use it as a net. The symbol folded around the foulness, dissolving much of the mass before unraveling, severing her link.

Thrown back into own cognizance, Crystalyn reeled, fighting to adjust her internal awareness of a body much smaller in scale. Dizziness assaulted her, bringing on a debilitating weakness she couldn't attribute to a toss across the room.

Wiry arms wrapped around her shoulders as she began to slip away. She struggled through the sensation. After a time—how long she couldn't say—the dizziness subsided.

Crystalyn relished the feel of her own body. Even Lore Rayna's neural pathways had seemed large. The woman's empathy for living, growing things was much bigger than any other she'd known. Crystalyn smiled with a newfound respect as she gazed at the big woman. Her convictions were remarkable.

Lore Rayna's eyelids fluttered open. Luminous eyes stared up at Crystalyn. A beatific smile lit her face.

"Thank Onan!" Cudgel shouted, moving to Lore Rayna's side, nearly bowling Atoi over. Atoi bounded onto the foot of the bed with ease, her knife nowhere in sight. Moving with a gentleness belying his blocky stature, Cudgel helped Lore Rayna sit up.

Disengaging from the Lore Mother's arms, Crystalyn sat on the bed, away from Atoi. She felt weak and nauseated; her migraine flared. Closing her eyes, she leaned back on the down pillow, willing the pain to dissipate to no avail.

"Before anyone asks, I do not know what occurred," the Lore Mother's soft raspy voice drifted down to her from above. "We shall discuss it on the way."

Crystalyn's eyes snapped open. She winced. "Are you going somewhere?"

"We all are, dear. You and Atoi are coming too."

Atoi bounded off the bed. "What makes you think we would go anywhere with you?"

Crystalyn bit back a cry. Did the girl have to bounce the bed? "What are you planning?" she managed to ask the Lore Mother.

"We shall all go to Surbo. I worry the Circle of Light are the only ones who can penetrate the dark veil surrounding your sister, though I am not certain even they shall be successful. I have never encountered anything as strong in all my years contacting. By the way, that was quick thinking on your part to disrupt the focal point, Crystalyn. I could not have done it. I was committed to keeping the conduit open. Had I stopped, the creature would have overcome Lore Rayna instantly, overriding her mind with its foulness. As it was, I believe we had seconds, or less, before we both would have been beyond help."

Silence descended after the old woman's statement—made eerily starker by her matter-of-fact delivery.

Crystalyn swallowed. "When do we leave?" she asked.

The Lore Mother's shoulders seemed hunched when she stood. Life's burdens, her age, recent events; it all must weigh heavy upon her.

"As soon as you're packed, meet us at the stables. The Child of Dark can show you the way. It is going to be a long road. We shall require a wagon, but I fear our chances for finding one are dismal with the Snow Melt Festival commencing. Come along you two," the Lore Mother said, motioning at Cudgel as he helped Lore Rayna to her feet. "I wish to be traveling within the hour, if Rayna is capable of it." Clasping Lore Rayna's elbow, the old woman supported her student on one side as Cudgel assisted at the other side.

Watching them leave, Crystalyn wondered if going anywhere with the three of them was a good idea, especially traveling with Cudgel. What would stop her from having another altercation with the man? Did it matter? She could take care of herself, even against all three at once. How bad could it get?

THE FINAL APEX

Peeking outside the pantry door, Crystalyn made out the tavern bar. The barmaid who'd attempted to take their order at the booth was working again, pouring drinks to robust, short-statured patrons garbed in silver armor. Perhaps the same envoy Hastel had mentioned when he'd sent the barmaid to see to them. The innkeeper was nowhere in sight. Crystalyn smiled and withdrew into the pantry.

Meat pies, apples, loaves of bread, dried meats, and blocks of cheese vanished into Atoi's leather-bound bag. Hefting the bag with one hand, the tiny girl set it back on the wooden cutting table. Rummaging through spices in the walk-in pantry, Atoi added her selections to Crystalyn's pack, not the bag.

Crystalyn's impatience flared. "You're overfilling them, just take the essentials. Give me my pack. Mr. Muddy Wagon himself could show up at any time," Crystalyn said, holding out her hand. Atoi brought it to her, going back to filling her own without comment. Putting her daypack on, Crystalyn winced. The weight of it pulled on her shoulders, yet the little girl had carried it with one hand.

Both hands gripping food accoutrements, Atoi flipped her head back and shook her long black bangs from her eyes. Potatoes, carrots, and additional meat disappeared into her bag. She spoke as she worked. "Weeping face usually wants a nap after his breakfast. At least, that's what I've heard his lazy helpers say when they think no one's listening. Look how the white flour has turned brown from the missing lid. Do you think they worry about this place?" Atoi asked. She gestured with an onion stalk toward a nondescript clay bin with its matching lid lying to the side.

"You're right. It's time to motivate the help again." Hastel's gravelly voice came from behind Crystalyn.

Crystalyn jumped. Flailing her arms, she skidded in spilled flour and grease. Gaining her balance, she turned and glared at the man.

Stepping under the doorway with room to spare, Hastel leaned a shoulder against the doorjamb, a smirk playing on his chapped lips. His brown eye narrowed, rotating between Crystalyn's taut backpack straps and Atoi's open bag, and his grin vanished. "Going somewhere, little one?"

"Yes, I am. Stop glaring at me," Atoi said. "I'll pay you well for the supplies, you know I have coin." Hefting her bag, Atoi pursed her lips. "Where are the sweet tarts? I'll make the space; yours are the best around."

Hastel gestured at a woven green basket. "In the bread bin. They don't last long, so we make them daily." He folded his beefy arms across his broad chest. "You're changing the subject. I don't care about the fare. What's important is where you're going."

Crystalyn was amazed. "Why would we tell you? We don't want to get ambushed a few miles from here."

Lifting the brown rag draped on his shoulder, Hastel daubed at his jagged wound. Ignoring her question, he scowled in silence, his eye fixed on Atoi. Crystalyn glanced at her protégé, wondering if it was the right way to consider her. She did feel responsible for the little girl, even though Atoi had attempted to kill her—twice—and steal the black crystal candle.

The little girl was an enigma. She'd shown a fierce independence but lacked the basic social skills, yet she seemed knowledgeable well beyond her ten seasons. And, there was the other voice that kept showing up; she couldn't forget that. Perhaps on the road, she'd have the opportunity to delve deeper into Atoi's psyche, which should provide a clue into why the little girl was so murderous at times and perhaps bring the other tone into the open.

Her list of things to accomplish was growing. Three items were clear priorities: discovering the motives behind the giant trio, learning about the war and Darwin's part in it, and locating her sister—not necessarily in that order. Somewhere in the list would be figuring out a way to get home. "Pay him what he wants, Atoi. We need to be at the stable soon."

Atoi lifted the lid on the long rectangular basket and set it to the side. Tossing the leather bag beside the basket, she wrapped the pastries separately in waxy leaves and put them in a small, urn-like basket, which she placed in her bulging bag. "The demanding woman will wait for us. I do not think she's found what she's after."

Hastel straightened, his voice taking on a pleading tone. "You don't mean those bloody naturists, do you? Tell me you're not leaving with the old mother and her giant student, are you? They never go anywhere without the warrior Cudgel. He thinks he's the greatest swinging stick alive. At some point, I'm going to *splinter* that belief. You can't trust them. The naturists follow some master plan known only to them. They force anyone they deem necessary to the plan to adhere to it too, by coercion or trickery, sometimes both." Swinging his head back and forth between the two of them, he waited for a reply. When none came immediately, he went on. "What are you after at the stables? Tell me, please?"

Neither girl spoke. Finally, Crystalyn looked at Atoi. "I don't trust him. Let's be on our way. Pay him in full. Leaving debts behind is like setting a snare and forgetting it's there. Eventually you'll pass that way again and get caught in it, as my dad would say if he were here."

Shrugging, Atoi tightened her drawstring and then slung it over her head. A smaller bag, tied at her waist, clinked, when she tugged it free from her tiny waist. "One silver should cover this as well as my remaining tabs, leaving you with a handsome tip."

Crystalyn had no idea what she could buy for gold or silver, let alone copper, on Astura. She hoped to figure it out before having to use it.

Hastel's one eye gazed at them like a bird of prey waiting for a varmint to break cover. "Fine," he said. Don't tell me then. You won't find a wagon during the festival, anyway. They're at least a week out."

Crystalyn regarded the one-eyed man. "We never mentioned a wagon."

"It doesn't take much of a presumption on my part to figure out what those three would need at the stable. Some of them are too big for most horses," Hastel said bluntly. "I have a wagon I'll fully provision at no cost to you."

Crystalyn was surprised. "What do you want?"

"Not a thing. It will all be free, including your tabs. However, there is one condition," Hastel replied, pausing to draw a deep breath. *There's always a condition,* Crystalyn thought. "You have to take me with you or no deal for anything. I won't sell you the wagon *or* the foodstuffs you have in the bag. You'll have to get them somewhere else. And, your room fee will now be ten times greater. I doubt Atoi has the coin to cover that." Hastel folded his arms at his chest and fixed his eye on Crystalyn, making no move to wipe at his oozing wound.

Crystalyn's surprise grew. "Are you serious? How do I know I can trust you?"

"You don't. Nevertheless, I have what you need. Besides, I can be a big asset around camp. I am a horseman, I handle myself well in a fight, and I can cook."

"Battle expert, huh? Yet, you lost your eye and gained a wicked wound."

Hastel frowned. "Perhaps, your young friend will tell you about my wound on our journey. Dabbing at the putrid flow once again, his scowl softened. "Are you going to accept my offer? Think carefully, someone else on your side against the three naturists wouldn't hurt."

Crystalyn glanced at Atoi, wondering what the girl knew about the man's wound, though it would have to wait. She envisioned a divine clock winding down in her search for Jade. "What do you think? Should I let him come?"

Atoi shrugged. "It's not I that wants the wagon; I can run to Surbo with little effort. I have the coin, either way." Shifting the bag on her shoulder, the little girl strode through the opposite door in which Hastel stood without another word.

A thought occurred to Crystalyn. "Why risk leaving your inn behind to travel with us?"

Staring at the doorway Atoi had left through, Hastel answered with no hesitation. "She needs watched over, someone to care for her."

"Then you don't know her that well. Atoi can handle herself better than anyone I've met, so far."

Hastel's one eye fixed on her, but he kept his silence.

Crystalyn was at a quandary. She could use some help, but his coming along as a travel companion left little in the way of desire; the man was a smelly eyesore. But he had a wagon. With a little luck, perhaps they could slip away from town without him after picking up his wagon or get him to change his mind and stay behind. If not, another person around to keep an eye on Miss Dagger wouldn't hurt. "You guessed right about my travel companions. Tell me, can you get along?"

"What choice do I have?"

"None, if you want to come."

"Then I'm coming for Atoi. And you, as long as you're with her."

Crystalyn gaped, it almost sounded noble in a way. "You do know, she's maybe ten seasons of age and appears to hate the very sight of you."

"Appearance is an illusion some learn to project with skill. I can live with it."

"Don't be cryptic; I've already decided you can come as long as you do what I say. The first time you don't, you're on your way. Is that clear?"

Eye gleaming, Hastel permitted a brief half-smile to show. He gave a deep nod. "You're in charge. I'll need to order my affairs here. Could I meet you at the stables in one bell with your assurance you won't leave without me?"

Crystalyn kept her face smooth, though she wanted to roll her eyes. "Very well, you have my word."

Grinning, Hastel spun, slipping back the way he'd entered.

Turning away, Crystalyn began her journey. Somehow, she'd make it all work. Hastel had a wagon. She wouldn't hesitate to use whoever and whatever useful items she could, if it meant locating Jade faster, though she found it hard to trust the man. With luck, the Lore Mother had located a wagon by now, and they could leave without him.

Atoi waited for her inside the main kitchen, her green eyes brightening briefly. It was the only indication her pale companion was excited to begin a journey. As she motioned for Atoi to lead the way, Crystalyn wondered how far to trust her. Though the young girl had stabbed her, Atoi still seemed like her oldest companion. She was the first person Crystalyn had met upon arriving on Astura.

It was hard to believe she was stuck on another world. So was Jade. Dad must be beside himself with worry. A sharp pang of remorse struck her. It was her own doing; she'd colossally blown it this time. Tears blurred her vision. She was glad Atoi wasn't looking back. Rounding water basins, prep counters, and bread racks, Atoi led her through the deserted kitchen to the rear. Crystalyn dabbed her eyes and then pinched her nostrils closed. Strong spice smells made her want to sneeze. "Where's the kitchen help?"

Pushing open an iron-banded wooden door in the rear, Atoi paused, holding it cracked open as she peered outside. "They're eating with the overnight boarders in the tavern. Do you want something before we go?"

"I'm not a morning eater."

They entered a side alley between the tavern and another brown stone building the same length as the Muddy Wagon Inn. Rancid refuse piles lined both walls. Choosing her footing, she stayed near Atoi. Scanning the area ahead and behind, the little girl kept an observant vigil on their route, her tiny head in constant motion. Crystalyn looked around. With all the barrels and wooden crates stacked along both sides, the alley could hide those seeking to do harm. Little Miss Dagger might prove to be a useful companion.

The alley opened to a noisy red clay thoroughfare. At early mid-morning, the hard-packed road was crowded. Townspeople garbed in plain leather hurried past occasional armed guards patrolling in front and behind merchants dressed in bright silks. The merchants called back and forth to each other across the busy street as gaudy caravan wagons pulled by teams of horses rambled past open-bed wagons harnessed to sturdy draft horses. Mounted riders threaded their way among the wagons. Each claimed their portion of the street.

Setting a brisk pace, Atoi stepped onto a walkway built from rough-hewn lumber worn smooth from muddied feet. Townspeople strolled past in groups, some loitered near a chandlery storefront or mixed with the crowd, shouldering their way in and out of establishments displaying produce out front. Nearby, a barbershop promoting women's hairstyling squatted next to a mercantile store advertising items ranging from saddles to clothing in window displays.

Slender and small, Atoi flitted through the crowd like a dragonfly buzzing past a pond of reeds. Flashing a heel or an elbow now and then, she danced away before most knew she'd passed. Ignoring the new sights, Crystalyn concentrated on keeping up. Even so, many storefronts and dozens of nameless faces filtered through from the periphery. The culture on Astura varied beyond anything she'd ever experienced.

Slipping past a finely dressed couple, Crystalyn approached her guide, who waited at the entrance to a side street. "The axle master's yard is at the edge of town this way, though the others won't be there for a time," Atoi said. "Do you want to go to the town square and look around the festival?"

Crystalyn looked farther along the packed street. A writhing wall of congestion became noticeably worse closer to what she guessed was the town's center. "What is the Snow Melt Festival?"

"Every new spring, when the mountain passes melt enough to allow merchants, ranchers, farmers, and outlying villages safe passage to a crossroads city like the Four Bridges, there's a festival. It is an opportunity for buying seed for planting, purchasing depleted winter supplies, and bartering for Kell fur from winter traps, but it also permits the young women to put their wrist ring on the grappling pole. The pole, a hewn tree really, is always a spectacle holding everyone's attention. It will start soon, and we can always use the coin. Shall we go?"

Crystalyn detested crowds, but she was curious about the culture. If not for Atoi's reference to coin and something about holding the townspeople's attention, she might've been tempted. She probably didn't want to know how Atoi had come by the credits—coinage here, she seemed to have. Atoi wasn't above frisking a corpse; she could attest to that. "Not today. Let's find a place to wait near the wagon builders. I want to get going."

Atoi's countenance flushed slightly. "Very well, follow me." Charging into the side street without a backward glance, she dashed ahead.

Forced to trot around a group of sturdy-dressed men strolling arm in arm beside women wearing bright dresses, she passed several young men in a group. Wide grins lined their faces when they noticed her. Striving to keep pace with her guide, she resisted the urge to look back to see if they followed her progress with their eyes; most certainly would.

The crowd thinned, permitting her to come abreast of her tiny companion. Atoi kept her eyes to the front, striding forward at a strict pace. "Is it always this busy here or only during the festival?" Crystalyn asked, shading her eyes from the bright sun rising.

"The Snow Melt Festival is popular. It brings whole families in town to celebrate, but the Four Bridges is a crossroads. It's active year-round."

"What's the festival about? I mean, besides the obvious seasonal change."

"Trading, as I mentioned. The biggest event is the grappling pole. The townsfolk carve a tall, smoothed, many-limbed pole, where the young women hang wrist rings unique to them on it. The pole is greased and then raised. Every young man ready to wed competes against other locals and outlying villages to reach the desired wrist ring first. Whoever is successful in retrieving it becomes the woman's betrothed."

Crystalyn's skin ran cold. The custom sounded barbaric to her. What happened when the wrong person got the ring?

"Hatchet throwing, log racing, archery, starlight fires, and mercantile booths are but a few activities happening throughout the fifteen-day period." Atoi said. Shifting her bulging leather bag to the opposite hip without slowing down, she sidestepped a man leading a furred pig the size of a wolf. Crystalyn followed her example.

"Wait. Didn't you say locals? Aren't you from here?"

Atoi stopped.

Crystalyn's momentum carried her a few steps beyond the girl. Glancing over her shoulder, Crystalyn regarded her guide. Atoi's green eyes smoldered, counteracting her smooth face, though her compressed lips spoke otherwise. "What? Did I say something to offend you?"

Atoi said nothing for a long while, and then, without warning, she charged past, her tiny head held high.

Crystalyn wanted to sigh. Apparently, there were questions one wasn't supposed to ask in this odd world. What other blunders was she going to make?

Content to follow, Crystalyn noted a grand, barn-like structure looming beyond the next intersection, marking their destination. The structure loomed over a good portion of the street's far side. A fenced field, the grass cropped short, surrounded one side, vanishing behind.

Atoi strode halfway across the busy street, taking a direct route toward the monstrous building. Glancing both ways, Crystalyn dashed behind a cart harnessed to a white ox. Sea-green melons filled the cart to the rails, stacked high in the center. By the time it passed and she crossed the thoroughfare, Atoi sat on one side of a pair of shady wooden benches.

The benches faced each other near a set of wide doors chained open. Haggard grooms mucked nearby stalls inside, while liveried men hurried in and out, going about errands. Atoi stared at her feet, so

Crystalyn sat and waited for the others.

Eventually, she meant to drag Atoi's background out in the open even if the girl glared until her eyes bled. Knowing whether she could depend on all of her companions in a scrape usually began with a person's upbringing. A thorough knowledge of individuals under your leadership could be the difference between dying and living, as Dad had stated many times. She meant to live long enough to find Jade and send her home. No little girl's dark past was going to keep her from it.

The three larger travel companions appeared along the road making their way toward them. Trailing the Lore Mother on each side like armed guards—that, Crystalyn supposed they were—Lore Rayna and Cudgel made an impressive pair. The big warrior had donned a thick-linked chain mail shirt. His conspicuous blunt weapon protruded skyward beyond his left shoulder, though Lore Rayna's longbow—taller than some warriors—drew the eye. A fat quiver, burgeoning with green-fletched arrows peeked over her shoulder. The leafy dress adjusted around her body with each step. Crystalyn wasn't happy with the male side of the trio, but there was no help for it now; she'd agreed to travel with them.

Mounted or not, the crowd parted before them, possibly having something to do with Cudgel's fierce scowl, apparent from yards away, and Lore Rayna's tall, muscular stature. Remarkably, the Lore Mother was the one setting the pace. Crystalyn hoped she moved as well as the Lore Mother when her lifespan began the final apex.

"Stay with the girls, Rayna," the Lore Mother commanded, hastening through the double doors. Cudgel followed close behind, staring everywhere but at Crystalyn, though his eyes did linger on Lore Rayna before he stepped inside.

Atoi jumped to her feet. Leaning back on her heels, she looked up at Lore Rayna. "She won't find a wagon."

The big woman's lips thinned. "She has to try, little one."

"Why?" Crystalyn asked. "She looks like she travels on her own two feet better than any wagon I've ever seen."

Lore Rayna turned toward her. "You may be right. However, we have…gear…that would be difficult to transport on two feet."

"Is it too big for a large pack horse?" Crystalyn asked.

"We believe so. Though, we may attempt it if Mother is unsuccessful here," Lore Rayna admitted. Raking her golden hair behind her waist, she went on. "Even so, ensuring the contents remain intact on a pack animal would be difficult."

Crystalyn let the matter drop. Lore Rayna's recovery from the attempted contacting appeared complete, yet one never knew. The big woman could collapse at any time.

They sat in silence.

Crystalyn's gaze followed the road beyond the stables. An arched bridge spanned a wide river not far from them. Their path would take them over the wood-planked bridge like the many travelers arriving from out of town who crossed with new energy, knowing their journey was nearing its end. Hers was about to begin with new companions she knew little about, as soon as Hastel arrived. She half-hoped he wouldn't show, but she wanted to get started. The midday heat approached, and the shade provided by the wagon master's warehouse was beginning to recede.

The Lore Mother stomped out of the warehouse with Cudgel on her heels. "Blast it!" she swore.

"Mother!" Lore Rayna said, shocked.

"This whole blasted town shuts down for that bloody festival," Cudgel growled.

"Cudgel!" Lore Rayna exclaimed. "Now I know where Mother gets her unladylike words."

The Lore Mother ignored Lore Rayna's outburst. Hands clasped behind her back, she paced in and out of the double doorway. "I'm at a loss on what to do now," she moaned. "I don't want to resort to horseback."

"I guess we're stuck with *his* wagon after all," Crystalyn said, crestfallen.

The Lore Mother halted in her tracks. "What wagon?"

"That one," Crystalyn said, pointing.

Pulled by a huge Shire horse, Hastel sat on the front seat of a sturdy, wooden wagon, gripping stout leather reins. Tethered to the rear gate, a palomino horse tossed a magnificent tan mane.

The Lore Mother and Cudgel swore again.

For better or worse, her journey was about to start.

.

LURE

As the wagon bucked its way through the shallow creek bed, Crystalyn stoically endured every rough bounce. The next one proved particularly bad, nearly throwing her onto the wagon's tongue when a rear wheel collided with a boulder the front wheels had steered past. The sturdy wagon careened over it and up the far bank, where the road mercifully leveled out. The Lore Mother pulled on the reins, bringing them to a standstill. Setting the wheel clamps, she turned to the biggest piece of cargo, the coffin-sized crate, resting on the wagon's rear gate at a precarious angle.

Cudgel sprinted up and pushed Hastel's two chests back to the front. Lore Rayna eased the crate into the wagon's bed and began to repack the straw around it.

Crystalyn rubbed the small of her back. "Other than a broken tailbone, I'm fine. Thanks for checking, though."

Cudgel and Lore Rayna glared, or at least Cudgel did. Lore Rayna's luminous eyes brightened, which usually meant a glare when the big woman felt one was appropriate for the situation.

"You should be well enough. If you manage to break a limb, you could always mend yourself. Our…cargo won't have that option," the Lore Mother said, not bothering to look up from her inspection. Lifting each of the four handles in turn, she made sure the lid was intact. Satisfied, the old woman faced forward and released the brake, but she didn't immediately signal for Drumn to move as Lore Rayna still worked the straw.

Atoi spoke from the ground beside Crystalyn. "What's in your precious crate?" Steadfast with her refusal to ride, Atoi had jogged the entire climb up the mountain. The girl's stamina was spectacular; she didn't sound the least bit winded. No one bothered to acknowledge the girl's question.

Hastel brought the palomino to a standstill on the wagon's other side. "We've lugged your cargo over some tough terrain. Is it really that fragile?"

"One tiny crack would be enough to destroy its value. Other than that, I cannot say," the Lore Mother replied.

"You'd better open it and check. We'll help," Atoi said, her white face impassive.

The Lore Mother's impassive face did not turn toward the young girl. "I'll take my chances."

Crystalyn studied the shortest of the three larger companions. Cudgel leaned against the wagon rail and dropped his hands to his side, a scowl fixed between his bushy brown eyebrows. Though he'd avoided making eye contact or speaking to her the whole way, which was fine with her, his body language gave him away. He was anxious about something. "We should know what we're carrying," Crystalyn said.

Lore Rayna looked away, into the tree line, but her voice was loud. "What's inside *our* cargo is business of *ours*. Desist from your inquiries," the big woman hissed. Agitated, her green dress shifted back and forth on her backside, as if her skin now secreted poison.

"Rayna's right. All of you go about your own business," Cudgel said.

Hastel's frown darkened his face. Pulling a cloth from his vest pocket, he daubed at his wound. "We're traveling together. It *is* our business."

The naturists went to a great deal of trouble keeping the crate's contents to themselves, and Crystalyn didn't like it. They could be hauling around an unstable hydro bomb for all she knew. "Is it dangerous?" she asked the Lore Mother, ignoring the others.

Atoi spoke before anyone could answer. "Is it valuable?"

Lore Rayna spun, her face flushed with heat. "Didn't I just say you don't need to know?"

Cudgel reached over his shoulder to grip his pole weapon, but he left it sheathed. "And *I* said to go about your business."

Hastel fingered one of the dual axes, hanging on each hip, he'd strapped on immediately after leaving the bridge crossing the Even Flow River, along with a crossbow slung on his back. "We don't take orders from you, flame beard. The horse and wagon are mine. Tell me what we're hauling around in that crate of yours or I'll dump it out, right here."

"You'll do what?" Crystalyn raised an eyebrow.

"Dump it with your permission, Miss Crystalyn, of course," Hastel added hastily.

Crystalyn kept her face smooth. "Of course, permission granted. I think we all deserve to know what's inside or we'll leave it here."

"Enough!" The Lore Mother shouted, her voice booming throughout the small meadow. "Cudgel, cease your threats. Rayna, show some respect for our fellow travelers. As for the cargo, know this: it may play a pivotal role to all of our well-being, but it is our burden to endure. Further, I will not say! Please, clear it from your thoughts."

If it affected their well-being, Crystalyn wanted to know about it. Before she could voice her thoughts, the old woman snapped the reins, throwing her back into her seat and leaving Lore Rayna with straw in her hands. With three powerful jumps, the big Shire horse, Drumn, brought the wagon to a breakneck speed.

Crystalyn gripped the front handrail. Even a small bump could catapult her from the wagon. Slinging mud in all directions, they thundered along the trail, the wind knifing through her hair. Despite the danger of overturning at such a reckless speed—or perhaps due to it—Crystalyn felt exhilarated. The roan was magnificent horseflesh in his prime. Strong and energetic, even after a short day's climb, Drumn galloped as if unaware that wide leather straps harnessed him to a heavy wagon. Head and neck stretched forward, the big horse flexed his powerful loins with joyous abandon.

Their headlong rush was short-lived. The level ground ended at a steep incline, and at the last possible second, the Lore Mother drew hard on the reins. Drumn lowered his haunches and straightened his front legs, plowing furrows in the soft ground. The wagon slowed enough to bounce uphill, creaking loudly in protest. The crate slammed into the wooden tailgate with a sharp bang. Crystalyn shot her best glare at the Lore Mother. "Keep driving like that and we'll get see what's inside your precious package, or what's left of it."

The Lore Mother kept her luminous eyes forward, slowing the Shire to a slow walk. "I did not expect such speed from a work horse," she admitted, her voice barely audible. "Truly, remarkable, Hastel has done well for one of his station. I do owe you an apology, however. That was…reckless of me."

Crystalyn raised an eyebrow. "Oh? Words like downright foolish, immature, bloody juvenile…are closer to the truth to me."

The Lore Mother scowled. "Enough! What's done is done!"

Crystalyn clamped her mouth shut. She didn't trust herself to speak. The woman could've killed them both. Nearly as bad, she could've broken one of Drumn's legs, yet she was acting as if she'd had a momentary lapse in judgment. What would she do if the Lore Mother "lapsed" near a cliff edge? As wonderful as the big horse was, Crystalyn was certain he wouldn't be able to fly. They'd die screaming at each other all the way to the bottom. With luck, she'd get the last scream. Unfortunately, the old woman had proven to be better at handling the wagon than anyone, save Hastel. Perhaps she'd let the matter drop for now. She doubted she could drive the wagon half as well.

The climb lessened as the afternoon wore on. Crystalyn slouched in her seat, gazing at red sandstone cliffs rising above pine trees that towered over green, fern-like plants, eking a shaded existence out from under them. Orange and red leaves, shed from deciduous trees last autumn, littered the ground.

The wagon rolled onto a tranquil path through a grassy meadow dotted with sage and clumps of scrub oak. Patches of snow clung to north faces wherever shade allowed.

Crystalyn marveled at the vibrant world around her. It was so much better to be experiencing it in the wild instead of at the Farm or watching one of Dad's holographs illustrating the way the landmasses used to stretch before the Breaking at family evening—until he got so busy with the Administration. She and Jade had envied their father living in the time before there was the Mountain.

Their mom, too, had lived beside an ocean she could swim in without exposure before her parents were married. How would it have been to go for a walk through the forest, enjoying the outdoors without glancing once at an oxygen meter? Or swim in an ocean without fear of flesh rot?

A small black woodland creature slipped into the underbrush. Alert at once, she kept a sharp eye out for further movement. She'd only ever seen the poor, decrepit creatures left in the Administration's zoo and the holo images in school. Her excitement rose.

As hard as she tried, Crystalyn failed to get a good look at the black flashes. They moved too fast. Giving up, she looked around and gathered her bearings. The wagon wound around a small rockslide half-buried with mud, still following a gentle upward slope. She was glad. Such steep rises pressed the small of her back against the wooden backrest, making her sore. "What are those black-colored creatures?" she asked as she eyed another dark flash. It vanished behind some blue-green lichen-covered rocks on the Lore Mother's side of the trail.

The Lore Mother's luminous gaze swung her direction. "What black creatures?"

"Beside the trail, they dart into bushes or behind rocks."

The old woman frowned, deepening the furrows there. "I have not noticed anything, though my diligence in keeping watch beyond the road immediately ahead has been lax. My mind has been engrossed with…other things."

Crystalyn dredged up a few phrases from her psychology module, adapting it to the situation, though she doubted it would work. The woman was proving to be harder than steel when it came to giving direct answers. "Let's talk about what's troubling you. Perhaps I can provide a different perspective."

The Lore Mother hesitated, her luminous eyes unreadable. Was the old woman considering how much to reveal? Crystalyn couldn't tell. The Lore Mother and Lore Rayna would make an unbeatable duo in a game of D-cards where reading your opponents' eyes for a hint of what cards they held was a major part of the game. "I've been meaning to speak with you at some length about our Astura. I believe you have many questions. Atoi can be…reticent in those matters. Regrettably, this war has preoccupied me. From the reports I have received, it is not going as hoped."

"You say that like there's been several."

"Sadly, yes. This one is the youngest in a long line of them, dating back as far as The Ruination, possibly even further. The Surbon Codex begins with the appearance of the flying beasts and land wraiths and their rise to dominate the world. It had succeeded until something happened we do not—"

"Hold it! What is the Surbon Codex? The Ruination?"

"The codex is a set of ancient scrolls prophesying events throughout many ages, written by a man who—as far as we can determine—had no history here. About all we have is a name and vague description. He went by the name of Jornas Surbo, though no one knows if it is a real designation or not. Much of his early work consisted of indecipherable ramblings, but almost all of what is decoded so far has come to pass. We are only now touching on some of his earlier writings, which relate to our present time. In his madness—or incomprehensible foresight—he wrote the future from forward to backward. The Ruination is as far back as our records go. About all we can gather is something alien to this world nearly destroyed Astura and humankind. It has been an epic struggle to repopulate and get to where we are now."

Crystalyn was fascinated. "Please, continue." There was no such thing as prophecy as the Lore Mother spoke of in the codex, but as long as she related history, Crystalyn wanted to hear it, prophecy or not. She was happy to hear some of Astura's history. What could possibly be strong enough to all but wipe out a whole planet? History always provided an invaluable and fascinating insight into the way things worked now. *Wait.* Jornas Surbo wrote the *future?* Surely, she'd meant Jornas Surbo had jotted down the events of history. How could he write history forward to backward when tomorrow hadn't happened yet?

"For instance, Jornas predicted the present war and the races involved. Sadly, it has been among Dark and Light Users, once allies against the great terror and the wraiths of long ago—or so it reads in the codex. This war has dragged on for too long. Suffice to say, a century has passed."

Crystalyn gasped. "You've been fighting for a *century?* How can you live like that? How could anyone? Undoubtedly, one side or the other would've gained dominance by now."

"Perhaps, if it had only been between Users, it would have finished some time ago," the Lore Mother mused. "But too many who don't Use are involved after all these years. At least, everyone follows the Aftermath Edicts—or the AM Edicts for short—which states that the losing side, the one with the most casualties, has to reforest the area but are not obligated to rebuild the cities. To each their own on that issue."

"Isn't one side good, the other evil? You know, the age-old battle of light against dark?"

The Lore Mother laughed without mirth. "There is not much distinction between good and evil these days. All races have committed their share of atrocities. With so many sects warring, it has been too much for those of us in the Vibrant Vale to restore peace, though we will not give up on it yet. Those are just the ones who war openly. I am aware of three other sects slinking around the outskirts, content to bide their time while their numbers grow. Some allies change almost seasonally."

Though the early evening sun cast its warm light full upon her, Crystalyn shivered. With five races and three slinkers struggling against each other, the chance of staying away from warfare altogether must be slim to nonexistent. The odds were, Jade had already stumbled into one…but she mustn't think that way. Jade was safe. She *would* find her sister, even if it meant wading through the entrails of every bloody army and every blasted sect on this war-mongering world. It was enough to make her want to send her symbols flying in all directions.

Whoa! The last thing she needed was to make herself mad…even a small argument could easily lead to actions, at least, for her, it could. Now that she had powerful symbols to hurl around, she couldn't afford a tantrum. Augmented by the black crystal candle and driven by her mind affliction anger, her symbols made for an unstable, though powerful, force. One she'd better keep in check, for at the back of her mind—waiting for her will to slacken but a moment—her anxieties roamed, stronger than ever. She could sense them now in the way she'd terra-screwed everything up this time, trapping herself and Jade on a violent world with no path home. Jade may have already paid for that mistake if the sapphire obelisks had deposited her near an army. *No, please!*

The absence of motion brought Crystalyn out of her thoughts. Drumn stood tall and immobile in a clearing covered in grass, his beautiful bronze head held high. The Lore Mother stood taller still, her feet splayed on the top rung of the wagon's dismount ladder. Her luminous eyes, slightly sunken into her wizened face, looked down at Crystalyn. "We'll make camp beside this stream. Come, there is little time for slack. Help the others with the setup."

Crystalyn bristled a little at the command but said nothing. Doing something besides sitting on a hard bench would help ease her mind. Besides, it would help exercise her muscles far better than arguing with the old woman. Of course, the time to broach the subject of who would command *whom* was fast approaching.

Once her feet hit the ground, she went to the stunted tree where Hastel was tying the palomino. "I'll take care of this one. Drumn would be a handful as big as he is, until he gets used to someone like me grooming him."

Planting an affectionate pat on the tan horse's neck, Hastel eyed her with his one good eye. "His name is Ferral. He's been with me longer than Drumn, but he's every bit as temperamental as the Shire. I can groom them both, soon enough. Are you sure you want the job?"

"Yes, I do. I need to move around. You know, work the cramps out."

Hastel eyed her in silence for a long moment. "You're in charge," he finally said. Giving Ferral another affectionate pat, he walked away, leaving an admonishment behind. "Let me know if he gets too feisty; I'll lend a hand. Don't try and handle him yourself."

Crystalyn waited until the innkeeper was far enough away to be no influence to the horse and then gripped Ferral's halter under his chin. Pulling his head close to hers, she gazed into his huge, almond eyes. "I won't need your master's help, will I, Ferral? You and I are going to get along fine, aren't we?"

Ferral's unblinking gaze matched hers for a short while before pulling away.

"So that's how it's going to be for now," she said, smiling. "I can live with it." Releasing the halter, Crystalyn unbuckled the front shoulder strap. The strap under Ferral's belly was next, allowing her to roll the saddle into her arms. The saddle was heavy, but she managed to straddle it over a decayed log. Rummaging through a saddlebag, she found a rub cloth and brush.

Ferral stood placid during her brisk rubdown, only sidestepping a couple of times when she brushed his coat dry. The summers spent gallivanting about the administration's farm on horseback—the farm, the designation given by the king's administration—was paying off big now.

"I was going to say I would take it from here, except you didn't leave me much to do," Hastel said from behind her.

Crystalyn spun to find him holding a partial bag of oats. "You've already seen to Drumn? You're much faster than I am."

"Hitched to the wagon, the big brute didn't need for much except a brief rub. All he wanted was some oats and a drink from the stream."

The mention of water caught Crystalyn's attention, drawing her eyes to it. Splashing along its small banks, the brisk stream looked inviting after many hours traveling in the hot sun. "A trip upstream wouldn't hurt me either. I could stand a brief wash."

"As could I," Atoi said. Strolling around the wagon, she carried a brown washcloth clasped in one hand.

Hastel folded the oat bag's edges down and then hung it on Ferral's neck. "You two go ahead. I can finish up here."

Spotting a well-used animal trail, Crystalyn headed for it, nodding for Atoi to follow. From the start, the trail followed the tiny stream as it wound around bushes, boulders, aspen tree clumps, and under many enormous trees. They looked like evergreens but weren't. Their leaves resembled ferns, something she couldn't recall the big trees in the holographic at school or at the farm having, though it didn't mean much. The holograms only trained them on what the administration wanted them to learn.

She'd never traveled to the Lower Realm, though her dad was originally from there. Her home on Mid Realm was the farthest they'd gone, and it was still relatively high on the Mountain. She wasn't certain a tree *could* survive in Low Realm or even in the lower part of Mid Realm with all the pollution. Dad had promised to mask them with breathing cylinders and give them a brief tour outside a hover of the place where he grew up, but that was before losing his service indenture as head of the administration's security.

Now everyone was missing—her mother, her father, and her little sister, all of them separated—as if a family digi portrait was stuck on one frame without them all in it. Crystalyn's stomach burned thinking of it.

The trail ended at a tiny clearing nestled at the foot of a steep ravine. Overrun with deadfall and choking grasses on three sides, several flat rocks ringed a clear pool glistening at the mouth. "This looks perfect," Crystalyn said.

Stripping down to her undergarments, she waded into the pool, rinsing off her dusty clothes first, the water cold but refreshing.

Wringing her jeans and tee dry as best she could, she left them on a rock to dry, while she scrubbed the dust caked on her arms. It refused to budge. She missed her synthetic body scrub; one drop would restore and moisturize her body.

Stringing her wet dress on a branch, Atoi waded into the pool. "Here, use this." Somewhere along the way, the little girl had picked a fern leaf from one of the huge trees.

Taking the fern and the washrag from Atoi, she looked at her young companion, raising an eyebrow.

Atoi demonstrated with a leaf of her own. "First, get it wet. Then rub it fast in your palms."

Crystalyn rubbed the leaf briskly between her palms, breaking open the stalk. A clear gel bled onto one palm. Discarding the unused fiber, Crystalyn brought the gel to her nose. Lavender tinged with a faint pine scent caressed her nostrils. "This is wonderful!" Lathering it on the sweat-stained parts of her body, she reveled in the cleanliness, but she hesitated when she got to her head. "Will it damage my hair?"

"The falun trees properties are particularly good for hair. Nothing else need be used."

Atoi's shiny black hair added weight to the firm statement. "You don't have to tell me twice." Crystalyn dunked her head. The frigid water stole her breath. Shaking her head, she cleared the water from her eyes, gasping.

Atoi was frowning. "I don't understand. Why would you require a second telling?"

"Never mind, I'm not even going to try and explain." Smiling, she kneaded the gel through her auburn hair from the roots to the ends as fast as she could. Bracing herself, she took a second, longer plunge, submerging to rinse her long hair in a flurry of splashes.

Once finished, she hurried from the pool, making a conscious effort not to shiver as she stepped into the clearing's center where the sun was the brightest. As she raked her fingers through her hair, the only drawback to the bath besides the cold water was the fact she'd left her brush in her pack back at the wagon. The falun tree gel felt better than the synthetic on her skin.

The sun and a slight breeze soon dried her skin, taking the pond's icy bite away. Her hair and undergarments dried to a pleasant dampness; she needed a few additional minutes to dress, but sunlight was receding fast. "As much as I'd like to stay here, we should start back. I imagine it may get cold in these trees when the sun goes down."

Twisting her jet-black hair tight against her scalp, Atoi surged from the pool. "It will. The temperature will fall with the sun. Methinks I shouldn't have wet my hair."

"We needed it, I can't stand the dust. We'll just have to carry our clothes until we get closer to camp. They'll be almost dry by then." Gathering her jeans and shirt, Crystalyn slung them over a shoulder and then squeezed the excess water from her socks. Satisfied she'd had the best wash possible under the circumstances, she slipped on her boots and started for camp.

At the clearing's edge, a small shape bolted into a thick copse next to the trail. This time she sprinted after it, hoping to get a good look.

Atoi's call echoed through the trees behind her. "Where are you going?"

Crystalyn didn't answer. The small woodland creature darted in spurts through thick underbrush. She didn't want to frighten it away or lose sight of it. Moving through the thicket proved difficult, but she managed to break through to another opening running parallel to the stream.

She froze. A man stood next to a black horse not far from where she'd emerged. Someone she recognized from town.

Confused, Crystalyn sorted through the names in her mind. "Darwin Darkwind, what are you doing here?"

Darwin smiled. "Why, looking for you, of course. You're a hard one to entice away from your companions. I nearly depleted my reserves casting my lure creation so many times."

"I don't understand."

Darwin frowned. "Surely you've cast a medium creation in some form, by now. You'd have to be a fairly strong to knock someone unconscious like you did in the alley." His tanned face relaxed. "It does not matter. There's aspects to you to find each time we meet. You are as intriguing as you are beautiful."

Crystalyn ignored the compliment, if it was one. She'd best not dwell on them. The first shards of cold had begun to seep in raising her anxiety level; when that happened, her ire rose with it. "You still haven't answered my question. Why are you here?"

Darwin's face clouded. "As I mentioned when first we met, our side could use someone such as you. I hoped to discuss this at length."

"So you followed me up the mountain? I find it hard to believe."

Darwin's frown cleared. "So you're not native to Four Bridges, as I suspected. You wouldn't know then. The wagon trail you're on is one of only two ways to cross Wannabe Pass. The other is a horse trail that only a goat would be comfortable traversing in some places. From time to time, the trails intersect from past travelers avoiding the worst spots. I was making my way on such a place when you passed in the wagon. Acting on the chance to entice you away from your companions, I sent the lure out when opportunities allowed."

Crystalyn felt a twinge of remorse. Perhaps she was being too hard on him, but she couldn't shake her wariness. Too much had happened. "Why not ride into our camp and ask for me?"

Darwin looked pained. "There are some in your party who would not want me anywhere close to you. In fact, there is a strong possibility they'd attack before I could speak your name."

Crystalyn gaped. Was he trying to make her wary? "Who would want to attack you?"

Darwin grinned, lighting up his deep blue eyes. "There are three in the company you keep who harbor no love for me. The old woman, the plant woman, and the red beast are sworn enemies to the Greater Power, though I know not why they are against it so. As for your other two, the axe man will do whatever the Dark Child commands, which may or may not be to my benefit. I don't believe the child has met me in the past, so she harbors no ill will."

"You lost me, I'm afraid. What Dark Child?"

Atoi stepped out of the thicket to stand beside her. "You are mistaken. I am not a Dark Child." Atoi had put her dress on. Crystalyn's face heated. She'd been conversing with Darwin the whole time in her undergarments.

Crystalyn slipped her shirt over her head. "What does he mean by it, Atoi? What is a Dark Child?"

Darwin interrupted. "Let me ask you this: have you ever seen her sleep?"

Crystalyn glanced at Atoi while struggling into her damp pants. The girl's too-white face remained impassive, gazing unblinking at Darwin. Holding herself erect, she said nothing. Crystalyn turned to Darwin. "I don't understand, am I supposed to know if she sleeps?"

Darwin climbed upon his mare. "The Dark Child may confide in you, in time. For now, I must go. The path ahead is too steep for a horse in the dark. I must take to the trail ahead of your party. We will meet again. Farewell." He slapped the reins, and the mare leapt forward, trotting for the clearing's far end.

"Wait!" Crystalyn called. "Why do you keep calling her a Dark Child?" For an answer, Darwin spurred his dark horse into a gallop, vanishing around an outcropping of aspen trees. Rounding on Atoi, Crystalyn frowned. "What did he mean by that? Is there something I should know about you?"

Atoi's expression remained impassive. "Come, we have to find our path to camp in the dark. I am capable of this, but it will require you to stay close." Turning away, she melted into the thicket.

Crystalyn stamped her foot in frustration. Just when she was beginning to find things out, sunlight gave way to the darkness.

Shouldering aside scrub oak, Crystalyn followed Atoi's footsteps. The darkness was deeper as soon as they broke through to the trail. Crystalyn strode as fast as she dared, scrambling to keep the pace Atoi set. The tiny girl moved ahead each time she got close enough to ask the question reverberating through her mind. *What was a Dark Child?*

She would find out, whether Atoi wanted to talk about it or not.

DARK USER, DARK CHILD

Beheld from such a high vantage point, Crystalyn could see how different Astura's land compared to the Mountain back home. For one thing, it was green—or soon would be—and it *sprawled*. Trees, bushes, and plant life spread far, adding to the oxygen-rich air. Growing things thrived, absorbing golden sunlight instead of gray polluted air.

Taking up a large portion of the land below, the mighty Lake Ever Cold reflected its white-capped lovely blue all the way back up to where she stood at the cliff's edge. From so high up, it was easy to see how Four Bridges had gotten the name. Four arched, wooden bridges, each similar in construction, provided a trade route across the rivers to the rest of Astura.

Three major tributaries fed into it from the north, east, and west. Wider than she'd expected, the great lake seemed a freshwater sea. The eastern side allowed an escape path for the snaking Even Flow River, the southernmost end draining away into swamplands.

Taking a last look at the tiny speck Hastel had assured her was the Muddy Wagon Inn, Crystalyn turned away from the overlook she'd demanded they stop at. The time they'd spent climbing the mountain had been almost intolerable. She already had a low tolerance for bickering—brought on by the mind affliction, her irritation was quick to flare up.

The side remarks, lashing tongues, and grating commands had begun with the first time they'd mired in mud and continued with every bog the Lore Mother always seemed to drive into afterward. The companions had bickered over being stuck and then every little thing after that.

The Lore Mother snipped at everyone but Lore Rayna and Cudgel, though she did bark orders at them like everyone else.

Cudgel went out of his way to provoke Hastel. The two had to be broken apart almost every bell—as everyone called an hour here. Atoi usually joined in those encounters, brandishing her dagger too often.

Lore Rayna hissed at everyone, including her precious Lore Mother, showing signs of disrespect enough times Cudgel had shown signs of his shock, though each of the naturists was quick to side with each other against the rest of them. Crystalyn was about ready to leave them buried in the next wheel rut and continue alone. As it was, she'd had to medicate several times.

Stepping around the softer patches of earth, she went to where the Lore Mother stood near the cliff's edge, presumably looking down. It was hard to tell exactly where the old woman stared. She fought off a flash of annoyance for the Lore Mother's glowing eyes, quelling such irrational behavior. "From here, it looks like Four Bridges is still growing. The houses around the southern swamplands, the ones with stilts, look newer. Am I reading the layout of the town right?" she asked to take her mind off the woman's unnerving eyes.

"You are observant for one so young."

Crystalyn flushed. A compliment from the white-haired woman meant quite a bit since she didn't part with many. In fact, Crystalyn couldn't recall even one. "My dad has a saying—'Failing to take the time to look at the lay of the land will cost you a longer road with a high probability of added hardship.'"

The Lore Mother chuckled. "Your dad seems knowledgeable. He is still on your home world, I presume?"

"Yes, probably worried sick by now." The thought of her dad brought homesickness barreling to the forefront, but she needed to stay focused. "I've wanted to ask you something."

"Yes, what is it?"

"Have you ever heard of anyone named Darkwind?"

The Lore Mother's wizened face swung her direction, her long white hair billowing behind her. "I know the name too well. How is it someone new to this world has heard it?"

As soon as she'd asked the question, Crystalyn recalled how Darkwind had mentioned the naturists dislike for him. "Someone in the Muddy Wagon Inn used the name. He sounded scared," she said, surprised at how comfortable the lie felt. Her reply seemed to placate the old woman.

"As well he should be. Darkwind is a Dark User of some renown, he holds great power. He is not far under Lord Charn."

"Lord Charn?"

"The current great lord leading Virun's dark army."

"Virun is a place?"

"Yes it is. Virun encompasses the easternmost lands. Claimed ages ago by Dark Users, Virun's main city has been carved into a formidable fortress called the Dark Citadel by Light and Dark Users alike, back when they still got along. Over half is underground, hewn through hard stone by use of the Flow."

A thought occurred to Crystalyn, brought on by something Darkwind had said about choosing sides. "Is the war here with Virun? How long has it been going on?"

The Lore Mother hesitated, her luminous eyes flashing brighter. "The threat from the east has been known for many an age. The darkness dwelling there seeks to swell its ranks; all it asks for is servitude—to the death. You cannot change your mind. The Flow binds you, once sworn. It is the same if you commune with the Light, which prevents spying to an extent. A Dark User would not be able to manipulate both sides, so eventually any pretense would come into the open. Likely sooner than later, someone would surely notice the pulses of dark color flecks in their eyes after their strength grew."

"The Flow is different for Dark Users?"

"Yes. Theirs has a distinct shadow within the Flow, and the color prism throughout it is limited. Black, red, orange, and most times brown, this can be confusing, since monks wear brown robes. It can be difficult to distinguish between the two."

Crystalyn shook her head to clear it. She had so much to learn. "I don't know of these flecks you speak of."

"Every User gets pulse flecks over time. It becomes prominent the longer they've been Using."

"You say that like it's an addiction or something."

"Oh, but it is. No one is immune, even the most powerful. In fact, the corruption runs deeper the stronger you are. You will know in time, I doubt even you are immune. As I was saying, in some ages, the eastern darkness is the strongest. During those times, the rest of Astura bands together to hold it at bay. This age has been...different. Many powerful foes have spewed forth from the dark lands. Darkness is encroaching faster than any have ever known. There are new factors involved from each side. Some have been foretold, some have not."

Crystalyn was intrigued and concerned at the same time. "What new factors?"

"Your sister is one. I believe this Darkwind to be one, though I had not seen it until recent events. He has advanced through the Dark User ranks in a short amount of time at a young age. Darkwind has held the high station of the Onyx Sword insignia for over four seasons now. Most do not last one."

"Why don't they?"

"Not only does one have to be a powerful Dark User, supreme efficiency with a weapon is required. Not just any weapon: it has to be the weapon the insignia brand signifies, the Onyx Sword in this case, which normally requires two decades or longer to master."

"So Darkwind mastered this Onyx Sword in less than the twenty seasons that it usually takes? Don't some people have a natural ability with certain weapons?"

"Permit me a better example. Most who believe they are ready to challenge a weapon master have gone through a well-disciplined course of training. Only then will any utter the challenge, for there can only be but one outcome. It is a duel to the death. Every other challenger that is, except Darkwind. He defeated a master swordsman who had over fifty seasons of experience with the magically infused weapon." The Lore Mother paused, presumably, gauging her reaction.

Crystalyn had already gotten the impression Darkwind had greater abilities than he let on, though hearing about him in such a manner sent a thrill racing through her for reasons she couldn't fathom. She motioned for the Lore Mother to go on.

"Darwin used the Flow during the battle, so did the weapon master—he *was* considered strong as far as Dark Users go. Darkwind won without injury in what many believe was a short battle. He has held the Onyx Sword for six seasons, even though he has had to accept many challenges for the sword and the general's position that comes with it in the Dark Citadel. Most commanders do not bother with acceptance, though. Instead, a hired assassin ends any potential challengers. Darkwind killed the assassins, the Onyx Sword's former owner, *and* he's accepted each challenge for it, so far. Strangely, he refrains from donning a full helm to disguise his identity from assassins or the plate armor for protection against a dagger. He uses chain mail and rarely wears a helm like the rest of their lords and generals."

Crystalyn wondered why Darkwind would want to live such a violent life. He didn't seem like the type to relish violence when she talked to him. "Why are people afraid of Darkwind if Lord Charn is the leader?"

"Darkwind is a decent tactician and a strong opponent in his own right against the White Lands. He is a powerful Dark User. I have heard reports that he is much different than any other Dark User on the battlefield."

"Why?"

"He has shown considerable mercy. There are reports of times when he could have ordered the survivors killed after their surrender. The usual Dark User method is to round them up and burn them alive with their corrupted dark Flow. Instead, Darkwind ordered his troops back to the citadel."

Burn them alive! Crystalyn shuddered. The mercy part sounded like the Darkwind she had met. Crystalyn opened her mouth to ask about the corruption, but Atoi came up beside her.

"Hastel claims the horses are getting antsy," Atoi said without preamble. Not sparing a single glance below, Atoi flitted toward the others. How long had the girl lived in Four Bridges? She knew next to nothing about her companion, about any of them for that matter. She waited for Atoi to hop out of earshot before changing her line of questioning. "What is a Dark Child? What does it have to do with Atoi?"

"So, she let it slip, eh? I am beginning to believe the Dark Child does it intentionally, though only to a select few. Come; let us take a walk as we speak." Without waiting for her to acquiesce, the old woman followed the top of the cliff face along the hillside.

Crystalyn caught her after a few steps, staying back from the edge. "What *is* a Dark Child?" she asked again. Why was it so hard to get a straight answer? *What was wrong with these people*? Probably nothing, she realized. She must be getting irritable; she hadn't given the woman much time to respond. Perhaps it was time for another med.

The Lore Mother's luminous eyes regarded her as they walked. "So it did not reveal much. It is typical of the entity, I am afraid. Very well, I shall summarize what we know. Be warned, you may not think of Atoi in the same light as you have. Do you still wish to know further?"

Crystalyn replied without hesitation. "Yes." Everyone else in her little band seemed to know.

Taking a deep breath, the Lore Mother began. "As you wish, Atoi is…unique…in many—"

Thinking about Darkwind's comment, Crystalyn interrupted. "Such as, she never seems to sleep." After the conversation, Crystalyn had stayed up as long as she could that night. Atoi was the last one at the campfire, poking the fire with a sharp stick; the little girl had looked forlorn but wide-awake.

The Lore Mother nodded. "So you have noticed. Let me begin another way. There is a race of…I do not think race is the right word. Perhaps entities would suffice, though that may not be right either.

Alas, we do not know much about them."

"Who are we?"

"We naturists—others have called us druids, some call us Valens, though that is a name for only those with lineages like Lore Rayna and myself, use whichever you prefer. A select few of us are part of an ancient order known as the Green Writhe. However, that is another discussion. The race of entities associated with the Child of Dark has been on this world long before humans' arrived, or so we believe. Most reside in dark areas like the Dark Citadel, flitting from eon to eon, existing away from sunlight in cold, lonely places, going about matters known only to them. That is what we used to believe. As of late, we've had reports of Dark Users collaborating with them—or taken by them, we do not know which. In any case, Atoi's possession originated many years earlier."

"Are you referring to a demonic possession?"

"Not quite. Demonic is a term from your world, I think. Shade or dark spirit would be an applicable description here."

"So Atoi is possessed by a shade?"

"She has a Dark Child attached to her soul; her body is the host. The Dark Child gives her certain…abilities, but one never knows whether the Dark Child has control or Atoi."

"Why do you call it a Dark Child?"

"We believe it to be one of the shade's young, only the fledglings ever claim a host. The Ancient Ones leave other races to their own devices. At least, they have as far as we know."

Crystalyn grappled with the concept. Atoi was a *host.*

The Lore Mother went on. "We of the Green Writhe only know of three subversions involving humans in the past. In every known incident save one, the host's mind and motor functions dissolved, two of our strongest held out mere minutes before succumbing. Those two were honored with *Terra' a morn,* their blood returned to where life began. The third has been lost to us for some time."

"Terra, huh…what?"

"*Terra' a morn* is from the old tongue. Roughly translated, it means *Replenish the life bosom*."

"I don't understand. What's it got to do with Atoi?"

The Lore Mother stepped upon a large boulder, jumping to the dirt below it with barely a pause. Crystalyn went around. They circled two minor rock beds before the Lore Mother slowed, continuing where she'd left off. "Some of my race has conjectured Atoi is the Lost One. I reserve judgment; I will decide judgment after sound observation only. Particularly now that she seems to have attached herself to you, but that is enough talk for now. Behold, Glacier Ladders." Raising a weathered arm, she pointed to some rock ledges on the side of the mountain. Steps of flat stone, gigantic and squared, fell gently for thousands of feet before a final long fall of hundreds into the raging Glacier River. Awed by the sheer beauty of the natural phenomenon, Crystalyn gawked, her questions forgotten.

They stood in silence, the view bringing wonder to her heart. Why didn't her world have such spectacular beauty? Finally, the Lore Mother stirred. "Come, the horses shall have rested by now." The Lore Mother strode away, slogging through mud that sloped too close to the cliffside for Crystalyn's liking. The old woman didn't seem to care that her bare feet had blackened beyond her calves.

Crystalyn lingered for a last look at the magnificent falls and the town where she'd first arrived. Given the opportunity, she would've liked to spend time exploring the town, discovering its culture, and making new friends. She sighed. It was time for her to get the party moving, though she had to wonder what the Lore Mother meant about Jade being a "new factor." Why wasn't she herself a new factor? There were too many questions and not enough time.

Locating Jade was her only concern, yet thoughts of Atoi crept inside her mind. Atoi was host to a Dark Child that she knew nothing about. Even so, the little girl still needed watching over.

Hugging the hillside, she hiked back to the trail, making a promise to herself to wheedle additional information from everyone. Everything about this new world added a new question to the countless others clogging her mind. Would she ever sort it out?

TAKE IT BACK

The palomino's saddle was vacant when Crystalyn arrived back at the semi-dry wagon trail. Hastel's blue eye twinkled, though his wounded face remained neutral. "Want to take a break from the bone-jarring axles of a wagon for the rear-mashing hooves of Ferral?"

Ferral's huge, almond eyes fixed on her from where he stood behind Hastel. Crystalyn could almost swear the horse's lips twitched, matching the glint in his eyes. She decided the golden-skinned horse and she were going to become friends. "I've not ridden a horse since I was younger than Atoi, but I'll give it a try."

Hastel's bushy brown eyebrows rose. "How do you know you were younger? Never mind. Do you want me to help you mount?"

Crystalyn climbed into the wagon's front seat. "No. For now, bring him closer. Eventually I'll learn to use the…stirrups?"

"Yes, that's what they're called, and you're right, you're going to have to learn to mount before we reach Surbo. Once we're there, we won't be able to ride, so I wouldn't be able to train you." He led the horse to the front. Ferral snorted, leaning his broad back close to the wagon.

Swinging a leg over the horse's back, Crystalyn eased into the saddle. "How many days travel to Surbo?"

Hastel passed the reins up to her. "Ten to twelve if no problems arise. Something always happens though. I call it the law of chaos. Use firm knee pressure and the reins to guide him. He will 'listen' for your signals; he is quite intelligent. Why don't you wander up the road for a bit? He needs to become used to you. It may take a while, since I'm the only one he's let sit on his back for many seasons."

"What? Now you tell me!"

Chuckling, Hastel patted Ferral on the rump as if the horse had made a joke.

Clucking softly, Crystalyn convinced the palomino to step away from the wagon. Acknowledging Drumn by tossing his white mane high, Ferral cantered past. Crystalyn smiled despite the sensation of feeling like a mouse allowed riding privileges on a wolfhound; it was good to ride. Ferral seemed to sense her lack of expertise and slowed to a walk moving up the gentle incline the road followed.

The early afternoon sun warmed her face and baked the mud to dirt in splotchy patches. Ferral clopped through it all, dry or soggy, keeping his head pointed slightly to the ground in search of horse delicacies, preferably something green with grass-like qualities. The strong scent of alfalfa and the distinct smell of horseflesh and manure filled her nostrils, bringing back memories of Dad and Mom at the farm. The other adults stationed there, security personnel like her parents, animal and flora caretakers, and the haughty, lab-coated scientists, all called it the farm without fail.

She'd spent two summers there with her family. While the adults worked, the young ones had the run of the place. So many exhilarating horse rides with Jade rushed into memory. The tingle of excitement she'd experienced right before sneaking away with Jade to explore acres of rolling fields on foot or wandering through the single forest from horseback below the ever-growing mountainside resurfaced. It was a strong memory. Crystalyn found herself blinking the mists of nostalgia from her eyes.

Atoi's casual question jarred her. "How far are you planning on leaving them behind?" Wiping at her eyes, Crystalyn was surprised to find Atoi maintaining Ferral's pace with ease, as she loped beside the trail.

She shouldn't have been, not after the first day beyond Four Bridges. Atoi had surprised her then, running up Glacier Mountain trail beside the wagon for hours at a time, only stopping when the wagon did. The little girl never appeared the slightest bit winded. "I don't see any reason to head back quite yet. It feels good to get away from the wagon. How anyone can last for hours riding in a wagon is beyond me. By the way, should the opportunity arise, I want you to find out what's so important about that crate we've lugged all the way up here."

"To do that, I'll have to get a look inside."

"Yes. Don't get caught either. Abort if there's the slightest possibility of being seen."

"I'll do what I can."

They rode and ran on in silence for a while, the ambient air cool and clear. The trail straightened out, heading for a small meadow, a good indication they must be nearing the pass for the great Glacier Mountain. Wildflowers bloomed in clusters, sprinkling the bright green landscape with varying shades of blues, whites, reds, and yellows shaped like little bells or delicate daisies. Crystalyn felt a rush of elation. The area was so beautiful there was no way she could pass without stopping. Besides, they had some time while they waited for the infernally slow wagon.

Reining in at a small copse of aspen trees next to the trail, she slipped her leg over Ferral's golden back and dropped to the ground while holding onto the saddle pommel for support. Overall, she was happy with her dismount. Ferral gazed in approval, standing placid afterward.

Tying the reins on a wrist-sized branch, Crystalyn went to where Atoi had stopped near some brush. The little girl kicked at an anthill with the toe of her boot. "You do know they're going to relay what you're doing to every ant generation that ever lived, don't you? They will all attack you on sight from now on."

Atoi looked startled. "They will?"

Crystalyn laughed. "Just kidding, but it does make them angry to have their home destroyed." Leaving her to the anthill, Crystalyn strode to a nearby cluster of flowers resembling wild bluebells she'd found growing fitfully in Mid Realm once. Stooping, she plucked a small bouquet, holding the beautiful flowers to her nose, inhaling deeply. As she thought, the lilac-like fragrance was faint.

Wondering if her companion would like a smell, Crystalyn glanced at Atoi. The lithe, young girl stood immobile, staring at the anthill, her lips thin and her green eyes round. '"Don't hold back just because they intend to ambush you later," Crystalyn said with a giggle, unable to stop herself.

A rough masculine voice spoke from behind Crystalyn. "Ambush is right."

Crystalyn spun toward the voice.

A man, medium-sized, stood in the road not far from her, clad in a patched vest over a dirty, gray tunic, along with ragged pants a size or two short. Greasy, shoulder-length black hair framed a narrow face sporting a scraggly beard. The man's mirthless, dark eyes appraised her as if she was one of the farm's cows shivering before the slaughter master. Contrary to the scientists' beliefs there, the cows weren't stupid; they knew what was about to happen.

The man's dull gray eyes glinted. "Though I don't know how you knew. He told us you'd be surprised. Don't bother to answer, it was rhetorical anyway." His hand gripped the handle of an ugly-looking whip coiled at his hip. "Now! Take care to pin the tall one's arms!"

Grabbed roughly from behind, Crystalyn struggled to move as two smelly arms encircled her chest, pinning her arms to the side. A third hand, tasting foul, pressed against her mouth squelching the scream forming on her lips, clamping her in place.

Scowling, the man in front of her bellowed, "Look out, you stupid skreevils! She's got a knife!" The man's whip snapped out, a blur of motion.

"Blast you!" Atoi yelled. From the edge of her vision, Crystalyn caught a flash of her tan dress disappearing into the scrub brush.

The face of the man with the ugly whip reddened. "Don't just stand there, you brainless rull! Go after her!" He strode toward Crystalyn. Stopping a hand's width away, he glared, eye to eye. "My man will find her soon enough. He's the best tracker I've had. We've been watching you, pretty one. I still don't know if our benefactor knows what he's talking about; we haven't seen you Use once. But it doesn't matter much now, does it, my beauty? You're helpless once those delicate hands of yours are bound, you can't access the Flow. You can't even screech for help, can you? You're as helpless as a babe. I can do whatever I like to you." His eyes took on a leering cast. "Do you want to know what I like?"

She shook her head; the hand at her mouth moved with her. *They've done this before,* she thought, revulsion rising in her stomach.

"No? Too bad, I'm going to show you anyway. And I'll make it last a long, long time. After that, my boys will show you too."

Several deep voices chuckled.

Crystalyn cringed.

Spotting her reaction, the leering man smiled. "Go ahead and fight, it'll make it all the sweeter."

Crystalyn was frightened, but her anger grew beside the fear. What was he suggesting? That she not struggle? Blast that. She wasn't going for the victim scenario again, especially not with men like him.

Grinning with excitement, the grungy man reached for her, tearing at her hoody.

Many of the symbols she'd read in the *Tiered Tome of Symbols* scrolled through her thoughts, and she selected a splintery feeling one out of the multi-aggression chapter. Next, she chose an airy one from the pushbacks chapter. Her third and final selection was a lovely white snowflake one from "decent defenses. Unraveling all three in her mind, she combined them, creating a compact one, black on one side, white on the other. Octagonal in shape, the pattern inside, drawn with thin, stick-like lines, formed a myriad of pinwheels tipped with round spikes at the points.

Keeping the white side pointed toward her as she brought it out, she released the symbol, only to wish she could take it back.

Black icicle-like spikes shot from the symbol, exploding outward in multiple directions, with one quick, deadly burst.

The leering grin dissolved, along with the face behind it.

A mushy red gel sank to the ground with an ugly sloshing sound where the man had once been.

Crystalyn's stomach heaved.

The hands holding her disengaged. Crystalyn turned around, her symbol revolving with her. Two men stood close by, eyes shiny with terror.

"What kind of User *are* you?" a bald brute of a man whispered. "I had you locked down."

"*He* said you couldn't…hurt…us," his companion said. He was smaller, but not by much, with his dull brown hair that stood on end.

"What do you mean? *Who* said?"

The bald brute began backing away, his gaze fixed on her symbol. "You're going to have to figure out how to kill her if you answer that, Skarn. I want nothing to do with this now."

His eyes flitting from her face to her symbol and back again, Skarn scuttled backward in line with his companion. "Look, lady, we just want to leave."

Crystalyn's ire rose. She *would* have answers. "Not until you tell me who *he* is. Why did *he* send you to attack me?"

"He promised you'd be helpless with your arms pinned; you weren't supposed to be able to reach your blasted User magic," Skarn whined. His tone grated on her ears. Her ire grew, but she kept focused. Slipping his hand behind his back, the skinny, bedraggled man touched something there. Relief flitted across his grizzled features. Emboldened, his nasal tone dripped with added confidence. "That's all you're going to get out of me. We're leaving now." Ignoring the symbol, he looked pointedly at her, his face hardening as his hands shifted to his hips. He backed toward the trees.

"Thom's the one that set us waylaying you, miss. You've kilt him, so we'll be on our way. We don't want any trouble," the bald man said. Moving backward beside his companion, he slid his right hand under the opposite sleeve of his tunic.

"Who hired this Thom of yours?"

Jumping backward, Skarn reached over his shoulder. Something metallic flashed at the bald man's sleeve.

Crystalyn activated the symbol. Rotating as fast as a hover turbine, it shot forth a multitude of dark splinters, shredding tree branches and humans alike. The two men dropped into piles without a single scream. A pitted throwing knife and broken crossbow lay on the ground beside them.

Crystalyn dissolved the symbol.

Stumbling through wagon wheel ruts, she ran to Ferral, bile rising in her throat, her eyes stinging. A bent aspen sapling took shape near the horse. She fell across it, retching in earnest, until there was nothing left.

After a while, she sat with her back to a tree, wiping at her mouth. Weak, she glanced at Ferral, wondering if her legs would hold her long enough to go to him. Tossing his head up and down, the palomino stepped back and forth in agitation. She couldn't blame him. With everything that had just happened, she'd be nervous about her too.

Forcing her legs under her, Crystalyn went to him. Stroking his white mane, she spoke softly in a soothing tone without words. Finally, he stood still, quivering occasionally. It would have to be good enough. She wanted so much to leave this horrid place of death.

Glancing at the scrub oak, her heart sank. There was no getting away just yet. Atoi was still missing. The girl's gleaming dagger lay on the anthill as a stark reminder.

SELF-PRESERVATION

Crystalyn's head throbbed loud in her ears, matching her heartbeat. Gripping Ferral's saddle by the pommel, she hoisted her sickened body onto the palomino's back only to nearly fall off the opposite side. Swaying, she retched again, but there wasn't anything left inside to expel. Ferral stood stoic and solid, as if he sensed her frailty. *What a dismal sight I must be,* she thought.

After a while—how long she couldn't say—she looked up to see Atoi trotting around a bend in the trail only mildly surprised by the girl's sudden appearance; Atoi had a way of surviving. Yet she still wondered how the little girl had managed to stay alive on a world where the simple act of enjoying flowers in the warm sunlight could turn so violent so fast. Perhaps, the entity inside her had something to do with her survival. Perhaps, she'd simply learned how to handle herself over the seasons.

Skidding to a halt, Atoi gazed up at her, a strange expression on her face. "How bad are your wounds? Are you going to meet The Maker, Onan?" Her interest seemed genuine.

Crystalyn blinked. Then she realized what her companion meant. "I'm not going to die for a while, at least I hope not. The blood isn't mine, so don't be too disappointed."

Jumping over a tree root, Atoi picked up her dagger, then hesitated, her wide eyes suddenly wary. "I won't ask how you escaped, as long as you don't ask me," she said, putting her left arm behind her back and hiding the angry red welt half-encircling her wrist.

Crystalyn's reply was immediate. "It's a deal." She didn't want to know about it or the welt. Nor did she want to talk about the mess steaming on the wagon trail. "Let's go. I need to find a stream." Coaxing Ferral to a slow trot required minimal pressure; the palomino seemed to want to leave the place as much as she did. As they went around the bend Atoi had so gracefully sprinted from moments ago, her stomach protested Ferral's swaying motion and her head protested every jolt of his long legs. She kept going, clamping her jaw to the pain.

Running beside the horse with the elegance of a wild deer able to look graceful in any terrain, Atoi gestured to a small grove of evergreens below a decline. "There's water on the other side of those trees. After this, the wagon trail begins heading downhill."

Crystalyn didn't care what the trail was doing. She wanted to get to the water. The blood was beginning to dry, becoming uncomfortably sticky. Easing Ferral into a canter, she covered the distance to the stream swiftly.

A tug on the reins brought the horse to a standstill beside the clear running water that cut through the wagon trail. Crystalyn jumped to the ground with a grimace, her head still tender. Wordlessly, Atoi handed her a falun leaf.

Crystalyn waded to the stream's center and splashed frigid water wherever her skin was bare, scrubbing furiously with the aid of the marvelous gel. Most of the blood and gore washed away from her skin, but her clothes would need something else besides her fingers to clean them. She worked on the bigger stains anyway.

When her blood began to congeal in her veins, she trudged through the frigid water to stand beside Ferral. Head down, the reins floating in the stream, Ferral drank noisily, making no move to shy away. "I'm surprised he's still here," she mused.

Atoi squatted upstream, holding a leather bladder underwater until the air bubbles no longer rose to the surface. "Are you speaking of Hastel's big horse? It must like you. Weeping Face complains of its tendency to bolt and run."

As if the mention of their companion brought them, the wagon rounded the bend, Hastel driving this time. Whipping the reins, he coaxed the enormous Shire horse faster. The Lore Mother bounced on the bench beside him. Lore Rayna and Cudgel ran fanning out beside it, one on each side, scanning the terrain away from the trail. Cudgel sprinted with his iron-tipped weapon in hand, while Lore Rayna ran with her bow. "Speak of the devil, here he comes," Crystalyn said.

"I don't understand. What is a devil?"

"Forget it."

Rumbling thunderously, horse, wagon, and runners bore down on them. Hastel wrenched the reins at the last minute. The Shire's hooves dug in, plowing furrows to the water's edge as the horse brought the wagon to a standstill. Snorting in protest, Drumn whipped his head around to throw an accusing glare at Hastel before swinging his thick neck to the stream.

The Lore Mother climbed from the wagon and marched toward Crystalyn. "Is anyone hurt?"

Hastel scrutinized Atoi. "What did they do to you?" Without waiting for an answer, he looked at Crystalyn. "What about my horse? Has he come to harm?"

Resting his pole weapon on his shoulder, Cudgel's broad head swung back and forth, searching the horizon. "How many were there?"

Lore Rayna stood shoulder to shoulder with Cudgel, her golden-haired head turned toward the opposite tree line, her bow half-raised. "Did any get away?"

Crystalyn held up a hand. "Wait! Everyone calm down. I don't think any got away, but I can't be sure. Cudgel, will you and Lore Rayna check the area from here back to the meadow?"

Exchanging a quick glance with each other and then the Lore Mother, they nodded. As one, they trotted back along the road a few yards. Separating in opposite directions, each melted into the trees.

Hastel sprang from the bottom step. "I'll see to my horse."

Jerking his head from the stream, Ferral shied into the water, clomping upstream a few steps.

Hastel's hands went to his hips. "What's gotten into you?" Frowning, he plodded into the stream after the horse.

Ferral clomped over to Crystalyn, eyeing Hastel with suspicion.

Hastel froze, standing in water above his ankles, a dumbfounded look on his face. "What's this? Have you stolen my best horse?"

Crystalyn bit back a smile. "*Your* horse and I have an understanding. Could you let him be until the others come back?"

"Blast me! I suppose so, but I don't like it much," Hastel said. He floundered to the bank and stomped to the wagon. As he rested an arm on Drumn, his one eye shot traitorous glares at Ferral.

Crystalyn put him from her thoughts. Instead she regarded the Lore Mother, who'd come to her aid as fast as any of the others. She felt a flush of guilt for arguing with her so much. *Perhaps I should adhere to their ways while on their world.* She'd refused to use the older woman's reverent title ever since Lore Rayna had commanded her to do so back at the Muddy Wagon Inn, but she needed the Lore Mother's support right now. "The blood's not mine…Mother."

The Lore Mother beamed. "I am much heartened to hear it…my daughter. Will you tell me what transpired? My concern and curiosity has been piqued since we found the gore piles."

The matter-of-fact description of her bloody handiwork made Crystalyn's stomach lurch. "There's not much to tell, but I'll do my best." Beckoning Atoi to join her, Crystalyn described the encounter without mentioning Atoi's escape. She ended with a quick description of their arrival at the stream.

Hoping to gauge the Lore Mother's reaction, she'd studied the woman's lined face and glowing eyes through it all, but she was disappointed. The Lore Mother's face was a mask of serenity. "Your symbol use fascinates me, daughter. Your ability to destroy your attackers without the use of your hands is astounding. Any other User on our world would have been in a crisis. Our ability to Use requires a direct path to the Flow, usually by establishing a conduit from the Flow to our hands, so to speak. Humans and most intelligent beings use their hands to create, to build, to replenish, so it is fitting. It is our strongest path for the least resistance to the Flow, which is why the conduit focuses through the palm in most cases. Did you know this?"

"I didn't. But, you mentioned the palm of a hand is the path of least resistance; are there other places on one's body the Flow can be drawn through?"

The Lore Mother nodded. "There are a few. With difficulty, a strong User could pull a measurable amount of the Flow through their feet, if they're unshod. A person's eyes have the potential with great risk; the probability to burn through into one's brain is substantial. Other…conduit paths…don't apply to humans."

"So, what the cutthroats' employer told them wasn't entirely true when they pinned my arms. A User could've still zapped them without the use of their hands."

"Almost all Users would have been in dire trouble, my dear. Your symbol use, though, seems to function outside normal laws of Using. Not only did you decimate all seeking you harm, you managed to do so without killing your horse or your companion. The whole incident is rather remarkable. I've seen a small example when you healed Lore Rayna, but that was only for a short moment before it vanished inside her. I don't suppose you'd care to demonstrate the symbol you used in the meadow?"

Crystalyn recalled the octagon symbol, letting it hover in the air for a short while. Interestingly, her nausea remained the same. Bringing it out without activating it had no effect on her.

The Lore Mother stood rigid. "Your symbol use is truly remarkable. You seem to have picked up much on your own, which is remarkable in itself. Though, I believe, there is something else to the story you are not relating. I cannot help you fully unless you fill in every gap. Hold nothing back."

Atoi fidgeted, shifting her weight from one foot to the other.

Gripping Atoi's shoulder, Crystalyn met the Lore Mother's glowing gaze. "I don't know what you mean. I told you the relevant details. Isn't that right, Atoi?"

"She did, old one," Atoi said.

"I see. What matters most is you have both escaped intact. Shall we begin your instruction?"

"Huh, you're sure this is a good time?" Crystalyn asked.

"What better time than while we're waiting for your scouting report? Besides, I now believe I should have started during the climb up here. It is taxing, but possible, to interrupt the Flow while moving as long as the User has a strong ability."

"Okay, what do you want me to do?"

"Simply tell me what you see. Do nothing else." As she extended her arm palm down, the Lore Mother's eyes burst into a brighter white and then dimmed.

The ground beneath Crystalyn's feet melted into transparency. Pulsating with starkness mixed with colorful flashes, the stormy river raged beneath her, treating her eyes to a precipitous rainbow of vivid color, this time. Every hue known to her flashed intermittently throughout the pulsing, silvery flow. Wanting to look everywhere at once, Crystalyn noted the barrier holding her above the storm seemed pliable to the touch, though not from the touch of flesh, from the touch of a compatible mind. She reached out to it with her will. A barrier different than the one holding her above the storm stood in the way, but she pushed through, stretching her awareness out to the Flow like she had when she'd attached herself to her golden healing symbol.

A myriad of blinding colors flashed before her eyes.

Blinking rapidly, she found herself on the ground staring up at her three companions' faces. Hastel, Atoi, and the Lore Mother knelt over her. The Lore Mother's concerned expression flickered to annoyance.

"Is she going to live?" Atoi asked calmly. Her interest seemed genuine. "I've never seen a User with so many colors in their eyes. I don't see how her body can take it."

The old woman pushed herself to her feet. "She will live, but she may need to be sent through a child's training camp: she does not seem to understand the simplest of instructions. You can help her stand now, Hastel."

Hastel lifted her to her feet, easily. As he released her from his strong grip, a kaleidoscope of colors danced before her eyes. Slowly, the colors faded into some sense of normalcy. The familiar outline of her surroundings merged into view. "What did I just do?" Her voice sounded older than the Lore Mother's to her ears.

"Apparently you tried to destroy yourself and those around you," Hastel said, dryly. "You've been out cold for some time."

The Lore Mother lifted a thin white eyebrow. "I told you to describe what you could see, not to interrupt the Flow. I take it you tried?"

"I suppose I did."

Hastel whistled softly.

The old mother hesitated, the lines on her forehead deepening. "I thought as much. You are fortunate to have such a strong self-preservation instinct. Anyone else would have burst into an inferno of uncontrollable power. I have seen it happen twice in my lifetime. Several of my colleagues died extinguishing the remains of those unfortunate pupils."

"How did they die, extinguishing?" Atoi asked.

"The students had flashed into a raging pillar of the Flow. While attempting to sever them from the source, it jumped to my colleagues. Destroying the conduit, they burned with them."

"Why not let the Flow burn down to something manageable?" Hastel asked in the silence that followed. "The two students were dead by that time, anyway."

"We couldn't; there was enough potential inside the inferno at the time to blow apart an entire city on both occasions."

Hastel's face whitened. "I suppose that would do it."

The Lore Mother's shoulders slumped, her voice, quieter. "My friends died because the students failed to exercise the protections we believed were instilled in their minds. I blame myself. I should have stressed a welfare partner. We do this now, even before they are fully accepted. Had the two students known, perhaps they would have brought at least one User strong in the power to their unsanctioned and unsupervised session. I tell you this, now—had they brought a standby User with them, they would have lived."

"How would someone standing by have helped them?" Crystalyn asked.

"When the draw of the Flow proved too much, they could have fed it into the standby User, who then could have severed the link to the Flow."

Hastel's sunburned face had whitened. Even Atoi's normally passive face looked as if she'd eaten something rancid. "Are you saying your students opened a source of power they couldn't close?"

"Not opened, interrupted. They were not training to become Users. They were training to become Interrupters. There *is* a difference, a critical one. In basic terms, the two students interrupted a trickle of the Flow and then redirected it...to themselves. That in itself is a vast mistake. One of the first things we teach is that an Interrupter's *only* purpose is to provide a conduit of the Flow to a User at a rate appropriate to the User's strength. The Interrupter's internal matrix is the conduit, so a great danger exists for uncontrolled flow. With the proper training, the risks remain minimized. Unfortunately, those two up-and-coming Interrupters believed they could handle the Flow without having the ability to use. It cost them dearly."

Crystalyn was hesitant, but she still had to ask. "Could I have pillared, Mother?"

Two glowing eyes regarded her for a long moment. "There was a possibility. I installed a block in case you should try, but you wiped it away as one would remove dust coating a window. I could not stop you, but your innate instinct, or your ability, perhaps the Flow itself, repelled you before you could draw from it. In any case, I do not believe you shall ever be able to interrupt the Flow. Your self-preservation or your own power will prevent it. The two are tied rather close together, anyway."

Crystalyn was disappointed that she might not be able to use but not much. "I don't really need to be an Interrupter or a User, do I?"

Cocking her head to one side, the Lore Mother's mouth pinched, deepening the lines in her cheeks, "I suppose not, with your...symbol magic. One other thing you should know, Crystalyn. I am a strong

Interrupter. Not many come stronger. Yet as I said, I could not open a conduit to the Flow to you or stop you from attempting to access it on your own. You must be very strong, possibly stronger than anyone I have met." The Lore Mother clamped her mouth closed with a grimace, as if the admission pained her.

Crystalyn gazed at her companions' faces, musing aloud. "I may still be able to access the Flow using a tentative approach. Now that I know—"

The Lore Mother exhaled an explosive breath. "No! Did you not hear me? I cannot do it alone. You are too strong if something happens."

The protest on Crystalyn's lips dissolved as Lore Rayna and Cudgel sprinted around the bend. Cudgel gripped a long rope trailing behind him. Horses galloped into view. Running side by side at a ground-eating pace, the pair covered the distance, coming to a halt before Crystalyn, breathing easily. The horses thudded to a stop as soon as the pair did, bunching together as far away from the man and woman as the rope permitted.

Lore Rayna spoke first. Head held high, the big woman seemed to be in one of her better moods. "We found where your attackers left their mounts."

Crystalyn looked over a mare and two stallions, automatically performing a count and noting the differences, part of her list-ordered mind from her mind affliction, she knew. She couldn't change it, even if she wanted to. The horses' front shoulders had lathered from hard use, save one. A magnificent black mare with dark, wary eyes showed no signs of a hard ride. "Those poor animals! Look at them! Are they going to make it?" she asked no one in particular. "Why would anyone destroy their transportation?"

"I believe the brigands rode them hard to stay ahead of us," Lore Rayna said. Her face flushed at the Lore Mother's nod of approval.

Crystalyn nodded too; it made sense. She was about to say as much when Cudgel's bass voice spoke with a rumble. "There's something else we discovered: two sets of horse tracks headed east toward Misty Gorge. These horses," he said, raising the lead rope, "were tied on the path to mill about and obscure tracking. Beyond them, the trail had been raked with branches. Someone knows what they're doing."

"Blast!" Hastel said. Moving behind Atoi, he stared out at the surrounding trees, his head swiveling back and forth.

Atoi's wide, green eyes narrowed, shifting from face to face.

Even the Lore Mother looked around.

Crystalyn stared at her companions. So there it was. Someone wanted her buried, for some unknown reason. Perhaps they didn't want her going to Surbo or finding her sister. Well, she was going anyway; it was her best shot at finding Jade.

Setting her pack on the ground, she squatted, rummaging inside. Where were her blasted meds? Her headache had officially pillared.

SHIVERS

Following the stream farther down, they set up camp in an inviting copse of trees someone else had used in the past. A ring of river rock surrounded a fire pit made for cooking, though big enough to provide heat in case of need. Crystalyn's shivers provided the need. The whole group gathered enough wood to last as Hastel got a fire crackling. Sitting on a rock beside the growing warmth, she willed her bloodstained pants to dry faster as the rest of her companions set up camp for the night.

Crystalyn envied them their movements. At least they would stay warm going about their tasks, but her instructions, from everyone except Atoi, were to stay put by the fire. Crystalyn wasn't about to argue with the Lore Mother about it—not after disregarding her warning with the Flow—nor would she any of the others. They all meant well on her behalf.

Rummaging around in one of the chests on the wagon, Hastel pulled some material out and strode to the fire, passing by Atoi as the girl took a seat on the opposite side of the fire. "Here, put these on," he said, tossing some leather garments to Crystalyn. "The pants may be too short and the shirt too big, but at least they're dry."

Crystalyn jumped to her feet, delighted. "Oh, Hastel! I could kiss you. No one thought to purchase me something at Four Bridges," she said, giving Atoi the eye as she peeled off her shirt. The tiny girl gazed back unblinking, her face void of compassion.

Hastel pivoted on one heel, concentrating on the tree line. "Well, you can keep them if they fit well enough." His voice sounded a little strangled.

Crystalyn pealed with shivery laughter. "You don't have to look away. I still have my undergarments on."

"Uh, the leather…outer garments…is made from Kell. They will retain the heat from your, uh…body better, allowing your…your undergarments to dry faster than the clothes you're…removing," Hastel said, his voice sounding further strained with each syllable.

Crystalyn laughed, pulling the drawstring snug at her waist, a simple tie-knot secured it in place. "Oh!" Thank you so much!" The fit was about what Hastel thought. The pants hung above her ankles, and the shirt was baggy when cinched tight, though the overall look was tolerable. She did feel warmer, and the leather was much suppler than it looked. It was almost like wearing leather made from silk if there was such a thing. One thing she did know, there was no way Hastel was going to get them back.

Mumbling, Hastel strode off in the rapidly falling darkness in the direction of the horses. Draping her bloodstained clothes on the rock to dry, Crystalyn moved to a stump, which was farther away from the growing heat of the fire.

The rest of her little band of travelers soon joined her as the darkness fell beyond the firelight, accelerated by the sun sinking behind the mountain. The temperature dropped as the stars came out. Sitting on logs, rocks, or the ground, all of her band sat in companionable silence.

Lore Rayna had sat cross-legged on the ground. "We should keep moving. The air will chill after sunset. The farther down Glacier Mountain we travel, the warmer it will be."

The Lore Mother's wizened face swung toward her student from her place on a wide rock. She frowned. "We would not get far before losing light, and you know it. Or did you want to stumble around in the dark?"

Atoi's callous voice spoke up. "Has your memory lapsed? Crystalyn was soaked; she needs to dry."

Lore Rayna pulled her knees up. "I shall make torches and lead you all. Toss the outlander in the wagon with a blanket. We shall keep moving."

Atoi folded her tiny arms at her waist. "The *outlander* is the one in charge here. We halt when she says so."

Hastel rose to his feet from where he'd sat behind Atoi, his voice stiff with irritation. "Even a Valen like you would have to know we'd risk breaking one of the horses' legs with all the ruts up here."

"What's the hurry, Rayna?" Cudgel asked, sitting on a log behind the big woman. "We all could use a good rest. We'll make better time at first light."

"My words are for the Mother, no one else," Lore Rayna said.

"The 'Mother' has already spoken, my daughter," The Lore Mother said. "Though I would like to climb down from this mountain, you shall not change my mind this evening."

"Crystalyn will decide when we go, *no one else*," Hastel said, mimicking Lore Rayna's tone as he moved into the firelight.

"I don't think I like what your inferring, friend," Cudgel said.

"You don't have to like it, but you do have to do what she wants," Hastel said, his voice low but clear.

Cudgel stood. "Perhaps you and I ought to settle this, right now."

"Stomp him, then toss him in the wagon beside the outlander, Cudgel. We need to get moving," Lore Rayna said.

"Now, now, everyone, I'm certain this is not the best way—" the Lore Mother began.

Enough was enough. Crystalyn shouted, not looking at anyone in particular, "Stop it, all of you! No one's tossing me anywhere. We leave, when I'm ready!" Couldn't they all just get along?

Lore Rayna jumped to her feet, towering over Cudgel and everyone else. "We have to keep moving. Why do you all not know this?" Turning, she vanished into the dark.

Cudgel raced into the darkness behind her. "Rayna, what's wrong? Talk to me!"

Crystalyn's ire grew. "What's gotten into her, again?"

The Lore Mother shrugged. "Her moods have shifted as much as a child denied a time of play on this journey. I have not known Lore

Rayna to be this petulant, not even during her moon cycle. I shall be speaking with her about it... at length."

"She should not be allowed—" Atoi began.

A piercing growl severed her words. The horses screamed.

Hastel charged off into the darkness, bellowing. "There's a dragon lion after the horses!"

Yanking a branch from the fire, Crystalyn raced after Hastel, following the sound of his bellows, as they moved away. Bushes loomed from the darkness. As she dashed between them, the shadow of trees rose higher than her branch light. A high-pitched roar close by broke the stillness. She slid to a halt, waving the meager light back and forth. There. Two amber eyes glowed in the dark, regarding her. A low-pitched growl sent a sudden chill up her spine as the eyes approached. Standing immobile, she shuffled through patterns in her mind trying to recall their use.

A broad head appeared behind the yellow eyes, followed by a sleek, scaly body. As tall as a horse, the creature stalked into her wavering light; a cougar's fierce, tawny head directed a reptilian body. Lips pulled back in a snarl, its whiskered muzzle displayed the many menacing teeth underneath. The dragon lion circled, amber eyes fixed her direction. Turning in place, Crystalyn kept the creature within her dwindling light. An errant gust of wind fanned the flame wildly, matching her thumping heart. The beast halted, facing her, its front shoulders tensed. *Prepare a symbol,* her mind screamed. But the patterns eluded her. Her branch light wavered.

Suddenly an arrow bloomed from the creature's side, penetrating a gap in its armor. Staggered slightly, the lion roared with rage and leapt.

Barreling out of the darkness, Cudgel slammed bodily into the dragon lion's front shoulder, knocking it over onto one side, almost at her feet. His club already in motion, he hammered on the beast's brow above an eye. His resounding thwacks filled the air. The dragon lion roared again, blood dripping from the powerful jaws that snapped at the big man. Cudgel slipped his club in the beast's mouth. The beast gnashed at it, clawing to regain its footing. Another arrow sank beside the first. The creature succeeded in getting a front and rear shoulder on the ground, beginning to right itself.

From the edge of her meager light, Hastel's axe fell, sinking into the thick, brown fur of the dragon lion's unarmored neck. Its legs stiffened and retracted, shaking once. Then it went still.

Breathing deep, Cudgel regarded her. "Did it injure you?"

She shook her head.

He released an explosive breath. "That is well. It was quick thinking to bring light for Rayna's arrows, but I was nearly too late to assist. Please don't push it so close in the future." Pulling his bludgeon from the dragon lion's mouth, he poked at it, making sure it wouldn't suddenly return to life. With each stab, blood dripped from three jagged gashes on his arm.

"You're injured!"

Cudgel bent over the downed creature, looking at the scaly armor of the dragon portion of its inert body. "It will wait until we've harvested the scales on this dragon. It is a rare creature and worth much to armorers," he said without glancing up.

Crystalyn hung back, not certain those yellow eyes wouldn't suddenly fix upon her from where the head lay, the shadowed, darkened orbs facing toward her, the snarl fixed forever upon its lips. Atoi appeared in front of it. Blocking her view, the little girl bent over it, a dagger in her hand.

At Cudgel's gesture, Hastel wiped his axe on the ground and then sheathed it. "The bloody thing killed two of the bandit horses."

Crystalyn's stomach tightened. She could've been the big cat's victim—no, would've—if not for her companions. They'd kept the thing's claws from her with their killing blows, and Cudgel had blocked its attack with little regard for his personal safety. Next time— and she was positive there would be one—she may not have her friends around. She shivered. From now on, she couldn't let her symbols flit away in the heat of danger. Something she would work on. Right after she'd seen to Cudgel's wounds.

MISTY GORGE

Crystalyn dropped to the ground from Ferral's broad back, splattering mud in all directions. Her backside protested the move with a twinge. She groaned, even though the saddle soreness was getting markedly better. At least, it was on the insides of her thighs.

Atoi slid from the back of the black mare easily. "Didn't I say you should take a break from horseback to ride in the wagon? Now we're way ahead of it. What's so important about Misty Gorge that it couldn't wait for the rest of your people?"

Crystalyn envied Atoi her durability. No amount of physical activity, or anything else for that matter, seemed to faze the little girl. "That's the point. I had to get away from them. Their constant bickering is fraying my limited self-control. For a while after the dragon lion's attack, I thought things were going to go smoothly, but it didn't last. Why does Lore Rayna have to be so hateful? I thought for a moment back there the Lore Mother was going to leave her behind, and it's the first time I've seen Cudgel side with her against her. Besides, I've wanted to see the gorge everyone's been mentioning, and it's been taking forever for the bloody wagon to get here. I wish we could leave it behind."

Atoi stretched, pushing her chest out to straighten her back. Perhaps the ride had gotten to her a little. "Why can't we leave it? Hastel follows your orders, and it's his wagon. He wouldn't like it, but he'd leave it behind if you told him to do it. Myself, I'd prefer to run the entire way rather than subjecting my bottom to horse or wagon."

"The big crate the giant trio insists on hauling around, remember? Which reminds me, have you found out what's inside?"

"No, they guard it day and night. Like they're afraid it might suddenly stand up and slink off into the dark."

Crystalyn laughed and then with a smile said, "Why, Atoi, I do believe you've made a joke. Did it hurt much?"

Atoi's green eyes glinted as she changed the subject. "To be candid, I was surprised you wanted to ride off alone after those…men attacked us. Two of them escaped. We know they headed this way."

"They *seemed* to be going this way. My turn to be candid: I've decided to give them another chance at us."

Atoi goggled at her.

Crystalyn kept her voice steady with difficulty, biting back a smile. Atoi could be so adult-like at times; sometimes it was easy to forget she was child. "I want to find out who sent them after us; perhaps he's one of the two who came this way. Not to mention, it doesn't make sense why they didn't go after the bigger fish in the wagon if they were brigands. That's a lot of high credit cargo in there."

Atoi pondered her words, her tiny face taking on an endearing innocence. "I don't think they would come here to fish. It's too far down," she replied solemnly.

Crystalyn giggled. "You're too cute, sometimes."

Atoi smiled faintly and then shrugged her shoulders. "Perhaps they just wanted to ride you and had no desire for big fish in the wagon. What do you have in mind while we're here?" She tied her horse's reins on a low-hanging branch of an evergreen tree. The mare snorted, and then lowering her black head, she grazed on the delicate grass shoots growing at the roots.

Crystalyn watched the horse eat. The black mare had been skittish at first, but now that she'd grown familiar with them, she'd gotten much better. Ferral seemed to like her as long as she followed them and didn't try to take the lead. At some point, she'd have to get the mare a name.

Leading Ferral to a nearby meadow surrounded by evergreens on three sides, Crystalyn released the reins, leaving him to graze on his own. "I'm not expecting much here. I love waterfalls and I heard this one is quite spectacular. Besides, it lets us get away. Shall we engorge our eyes on the gorge?"

Atoi's fine black eyebrows rose. "What do you mean?"

"Forget it, bad pun. I know you led me here, but I've never asked if you've actually seen it. Have you?"

"Yes, many times."

"Good. Now you can show me. Let's get going, shall we?"

Atoi set off at an easy pace. Once again, Crystalyn followed the agile little girl with the quiet but violent demeanor. Though she hadn't told her, Atoi was a part of the reason she'd chosen to come here without the others. She wanted to spend some time with her, perhaps get her to talking about her background. Where had she come from? What was her story? Crystalyn was certain it would be exceptional. Since Darkwind had mentioned it, and again, after her conversation with the Lore Mother, she'd paid attention to Atoi's sleeping habits, which amounted to none. The little girl never slept.

Taking a winding path around some blocky, amethyst-colored rocks, Atoi strode toward a gap in the land. The rocks changed from granite to beige sandstone. The sound of the Even Flow River increased in volume, as if a conference of water sprites waited for a siren keynote speaker. Crystalyn grew excited. Perhaps there was a conference. On this world, anything seemed possible.

Rounding a dirt and rock outcropping, she drank in her first close view of the chasm, reminded yet again of the power of God's handiwork. Or Onan, or The Maker, as this world's occupants called the Great Spirit, or simply, the One. *He has many names, even here,* she thought, awed by her realization.

They made their way toward the great chasm, a vast, open gap filling the horizon. A higher plateau loomed far beyond it. A fine mist soon beaded on the silky leather clothes Hastel had given her, dripping from the ends of her sleeves.

The dampness was refreshing in the hot afternoon air. Her skin luxuriated in the moisture on her face. Doubtless, upon her leaving the sun- and wind-burned areas of her exposed skin would protest upon drying. For now, she relished the moisturizing caress, though it brought fervent wishes for a heated bath.

Aptly named, a palpable mist hung everywhere over Misty Gorge forming a humid curtain that Crystalyn parted behind her lithe guide. She stepped upon a large flat rock overhanging the gorge, halting at the brink. The ledge jutted toward the monumental waterfall that plunged past on the far side, roaring with the rage of a caged tsunami. Instilling a profound sense of awe, the waterfall dwarfed her, leaving her feeling small and insignificant.

Crystalyn glanced at Atoi, though the din of the falling water made conversation difficult, if not impossible. Gazing downward, Atoi's green eyes sparkled; a half-smile splashed across her lips. So, her companion felt the magnificence of the place. There was hope for her yet.

Concentrating on ignoring the dizzying drop before her and the eye-catching plunge of the Even Flow River above, she crept to the edge. Looking down, she stared into the maw of a water dragon. Roaring into a black hole from the long drop above, the river crashed against something hard she couldn't see, belching up spray from the throat of darkness below, higher than her ledge. The spouting jets of mist broadened into shining bands of clear blue water that took on a new shape as it fell back toward the gaping maw. Entranced, Crystalyn stared with wonder as a spout near her fanned into a pair of giant wings, beating faster than a hummingbird, forming with startling clarity in the spray.

In another, not far from the wings, an enormous bee-like body accommodated a hand-sized stinger. Darker bands of blue striped the body in two places, but she was still able to see through them to the emptiness inside. A third—hanging in stasis very near her—revealed the fluttering wings and bee body were attached to eight hollow, spider-like legs where a white mist swirled, most noticeable in the two longer forelegs.

Enraptured by it, Crystalyn was confused when the apparition's two forelegs suddenly clamped on her shoulders. She heard the sickening sound of bones cracking. A scream gurgled from her lips, hampered by something rigid impaling her stomach. Frigid cold exploded inside her, blowing the pain away. The fleeting moment of relief dissolved with blackness.

*****

A great weariness fogged Crystalyn's mind. Coherent thought required great effort, like the time she'd taken too many synth pops. As then, she was determined to try. Gathering her will, she punched through the lethargy. Three words flashed in her mind: *Open your eyes.*

Thunderous roaring filled her hearing; blackness faded to gray. She blinked. The grayness flickered away, revealing the dim light of a fair-sized hollow. Light-brown sandstone formed a cavern the size of a meeting hall. A stone's throw away, a turbulent wall of water boomed beyond an oval opening. Transparent…spiderbees flitted in and out of the opening. Many hovered near light-blue candy-roll pillars attached to the floor and ceiling in orchard rows.

Nearby, a stag deer struggled, suspended within the pillar. As she watched, a spiderbee buzzed up, extended its stinger, and impaled the poor creature in its midsection. Red liquid flowed into the stinger, filling the bee with the dark substance, though it maintained its odd blue outline.

Rotating in midair, the spiderbee flew sluggishly beyond her sight with its macabre payload. The deer had ceased its struggle, hanging limp. The clinical brutality of the creature chilled Crystalyn, and sadness washed through her for the noble stag, bringing a cramp to her legs. Her extremities were regaining feeling at an alarming rate. Knots in her upper arms and the back of her neck made their presence known, the puncture wound flamed, and her shoulders burned with white-hot agony. The paralysis was draining away.

Ignoring the pain required as great an effort as regaining consciousness had, but she managed. She'd lived with pain in her head her whole life, though it was never easy. Twisting her head slowly back and forth, she worked the knots from her neck muscles, reveled in the thought of being able to move something, the only part of her free. As if dipped in plasicrete, the same clear blue gel that made up the spiderbees coated her from the neck down, confining her.

She focused on the stag's drooping head. Encased in the gel—except for its majestic head—the animal hung limp, rocking from side to side. She froze. Had the poor creature attracted the spiderbee with its struggles?

Something wet and warm splattered on her cheek. Tilting her head back as far as she could, Crystalyn looked upward, her body going cold. The hapless deer wasn't the only creature caught in the pillar of gel besides her. She counted four life forms suspended above before she couldn't see any higher. Hidden by a limp form above, the three highest were vague outlines. She studied the shape below them. Curly brown hair covered the head of a small man sporting a large mustache, the black hood of his robes pulled back. The man's eyes were pinched shut, and pink fluid bubbled from the lowest part of his compressed lips.

A transparent foreleg appeared over the man's shoulder, followed by a bee's head. The spiderbee's many-faceted eyes regarded her with a clinical, alien intelligence. Wings fluttering faster than her eyes could follow, the two-toned creature took flight and sped silently away with only half its macabre load. It was going, she presumed, to report on her alert condition.

The man suspended above moaned.

Another feeling of cold crept from deep within her, the coldness of fear. Harvested for the spiderbees' macabre use, the man's blood drained from his body while he was still alive.

One thought rose in her mind, overriding all the rest.

She was next.

MULTICOLORED LIGHT

Cursing the Dragon Lady under his breath, Garnet rubbed the bruise her stiletto heel had left on his back. His suit coat had kept it from being worse, but still there was one mother of a bruise blooming. He supposed he should feel thankful Ruena Day hadn't punctured his liver or some other important internal organ. Of course, from what he'd seen so far, a simple infection on this world could be fatal. He'd seen no med facilities. It was as primitive and brutal as Low Realm.

Wandering around the town through the night, he'd witnessed three slayings. Two were for the coin the victim might carry, and the third was marked from the moment he stepped from a tavern. The well-dressed man met his demise when he passed the mouth of a dark alley: two figures in dark clothing pushed him inside. Staying to the shadows, Garn investigated as the two silent assassins padded away, not bothering to remove the victim's fat coin bag. Garn could see no good reason to leave it there. The merchant—or whatever he'd been in life—had no use for it now.

Making use of the first faint rays of sunlight, Garn crossed the hard-packed street of dirt, returning to the storefront where he'd first found himself. He sat on a rough wooden bench placed beside the entrance, wondering what to do next. There was no obvious way back. Covering almost every street by the waning moonlight, he'd found no sign of the gateway, doorway, portal, or whatever it was, that had brought him here.

There was nothing similar in design in any of the stores. Perusing the few that had remained open late had gotten him a few suspicious stares from merchant and customer alike, but he'd ignored them. What he would do when he found the sapphire obelisks, he had no idea. With luck, he'd be able to figure out how to use them.

Now, perhaps it was time to question the locals. Though how he was going to ask without raising curiosity about his place of origin was beyond him. The whole town had to wonder since he was dressed in outlander clothes. He felt it in the way their eyes followed when he walked past. Hostility to outlanders was common with cultures everywhere. How well he knew. He'd spent many seasons interrogating the administration's political dissenters and escapees from the Lower Realms, easy to spot by their lack of high-credit clothes.

So what was his holdup now? He had no idea *what* to ask. He wasn't certain how the obelisks worked or even what to call them, though he was convinced it was how the Dragon Lady had brought him here.

He'd find out soon enough what the townspeople might think. There was no getting around the questioning. His daughters' disappearances had him more worried than his own predicament. He could take care of himself. His girls, on the other hand, still needed watching over. There was any number of hardcore personages on this world to conflict with; he'd witnessed it with his own two eyes.

A woman wearing a fine blue embroidered dress and a wide, matching hat with lush golden blonde hair falling out from under it strolled past his bench at a demure pace. She was without accompaniment. Not that she needed it; the blue and white parasol she twirled would make a decent weapon in a pinch. Her confident white-gloved grip on her sunshade gave him the impression she was comfortable with her present company and would know how to handle anyone disturbing it.

Gazing his direction, the woman's eyes lingered for a heartbeat before moving on. Not one to let an opportunity flit away, Garn stood. "Excuse me, Miss. May I have a word with you?"

The woman halted but didn't immediately look in his direction. "Are you dangerous?" she asked, her voice soft and melodious. "You appear…very dangerous, dressed as you are."

"No, Miss, I'm not dangerous. Not unless I'm threatened."

"Do you not feel threatened by me?"

"Not right now," Garn said, playing along. He didn't know what her game was, but at least she hadn't run from him. *So far,* he thought.

"Perhaps you should be," she said, gazing at him coyly. Her long black eyelashes fluttered above her russet eyes. "I am called Corteezsha," she added with a smile.

"Most everyone calls me Garn. It will do."

"Very well, Garn. What word would you have from me?"

"Please, may I ask a few questions to aid me in my search for someone? Actually, I'm searching for two someones. I'm not as familiar with this area as I should be, so my search has been fruitless. I'm looking for two young women dressed in outlander clothes, like mine. The girls may be near a set of tall, sapphire obelisks. Have you seen them?"

The woman's eyes flickered at his mention of the obelisks, though her face remained smooth. "Nay, My Lord Garn, had I seen anyone attired as you are, rest assured I would recall. However, I do have contacts who will aid you in your search," she replied, casting a quick glance along the street. "Would you care for an introduction?"

Garn gazed deep in her eyes. He wondered what motivated such a beautiful woman like her to help an out-of-shape, middle-aged man like him. Perhaps she felt sorry for him or she was just being gracious. It didn't matter; bringing his girls home safe was all that did. He could almost hear their excited chatter now. His chest constricted enough he missed a breath. "My Lady, I would regard any assistance you're willing to give with the highest gratitude. I do find myself in need of enlisted support."

Corteezsha eyed him for a moment. Then she chuckled, soft and deliberate. "Oh my, Garn, you do speak well, and your outlander clothes have the look of a high station beyond most of the rabble in this part of Gray Water. One could almost expect you to execute an exquisite bow, right now. All right then, please consider me as enlisted support. I accept the position."

Garn didn't know about the exquisite part, but he felt certain he could pull off a respectable bow, though he was hard-pressed to recall where or when he'd learned the proper form for it. It bothered him that he couldn't remember. Was this a sign of old age? The odds were high. "Should my lady wish it, a bow will be hers."

Corteezsha tinkled with laughter. Then she pursed her full lips, looking him up and down. "I think when given time, I will wish it. For now, I'll be content to hold you to a place and time suited for the occasion. Come, Lord Garn, walk with me, so that we may become better acquainted on our way to my…contacts."

Garn walked alongside the younger woman, feeling old and awkward. His forties had nearly fled, and now he strolled with a woman fifteen seasons his junior, on a world with customs he knew nothing about. How could he ask about simple customs likely taught in childhood, without her believing he'd lost his mind?

No one traveled between his world and this one on a regular basis or he wouldn't have received the inquisitive looks he had. Perhaps losing his mind wasn't the right analogy. Perhaps he'd created a world within his mind. Could he change things with a single thought? No, he'd attempted—and discarded—that scenario early on. One fact remained: his back still ached from the Dragon Lady's heels.

The sun reached its zenith, sidling downward behind them, and heat radiated against the back of his neck, as they strode along a clay roadway. His escort followed the main thoroughfare due east at a brisk pace. Garn glanced sidelong her direction. Face smooth and unreadable, Corteezsha stared ahead, hat tilted slightly back, the parasol tilted slightly forward, making her oblivious to the sun's rays. Or was she? He had a feeling he'd never see her bothered by anything if she didn't want it to be seen.

He paused at a gilded storefront. Patrons bustled in and out, garbed in various clothing ranging from gaudy silks to serviceable leather to embroidered robes and dresses. Intricate carvings, painted dark yellow with gold trim, portrayed the sun, moon, and stars in various stages above differing landmasses. They covered every visible trim surface. The trim stood out in stark contrast to the weathered wooden entrance.

Corteezsha collapsed her parasol, frowning. "My Lord, why do you delay? I cannot say how long my contacts will tarry. Come, we must make haste."

Garn inclined his head toward the store. "What is this place?"

Corteezsha's fine auburn eyebrows scrunched. "Surely you recognize the signs for glimmer infusion?"

"I believed so," he said, quickly. He had no clue what she meant, but he intended to find out. "I require but a moment inside."

Corteezsha regarded him. Her face had smoothed, but her eyes smoldered. "Very well, as you require. However, I cannot ensure my contacts will still be around should your delay lengthen."

"It will not, my lady."

"See that it doesn't. I'll accompany you inside."

Garn led the way into a crowded yet dimly lit room. Thousands of crystal shards lined shelves and glass display cases or swung in a leisurely rotation hung from fine thread. Their brilliant colors flashed through the room dampened by an amber hue everywhere he looked. He tried not to gawk. Tried and failed.

GLIMMER SHARD

Garn found the pulsating effect of the room disconcerting. The room flooded with pale amber light one moment and plummeted to darkness the next. It switched with a synchronous precision, as if every shard synchronized to an alien heartbeat somewhere. His excitement rose. The room sported many crystals. The obelisks the Dragon Lady had booted him through appeared crafted from crystal. With luck, he'd stumbled on the right place.

Four counters, overseen by attendants—two on each side of the room—assisted with perusing the shards. A small crowd milled around the back of the store. He shouldered his way there. After he pushed past the first few, the rest moved aside; his height and weight outmatched anyone else in the room.

The crowd gathered around an entrance to a small back room where a white-robed, gray-bearded man appeared in the doorway during the bright peak of a pulse. "Here you go, Diera," the man said, handing a leather-wrapped bundle to a robust woman in a red lace dress as darkness swallowed the room. "Who's next?" the man's disembodied voice asked, drifting out of the darkness.

No one spoke up, so Garn did. "I will be."

The white robe's hooded face turned toward him, shadowed in the quickening light. "Where's your shard, outlander?"

"I would like to discuss the matter with you in private, if I may," Garn said.

The old man hesitated. The light brightened. His deep gray eyes regarded Garn from within the white cowl. "Very well, follow me." Turning, he shuffled into the room.

Garn scrambled to stay near the man. Behind him, the room plunged into darkness again but not before he made out Corteezsha following.

The robe the old man wore stood out in the dim amber glow from somewhere unseen. The low light made it hard to make out details other than some dim thresholds indicating side rooms. He was grateful for stable light, however dim. The pulsating light in the shard room would be hard to take.

As he stepped into a large, windowed room, his gratefulness grew for the light of midday. The robed man stood at the doorway, waiting to close it behind Garn. The old man hesitated when his escort followed him inside. A deep frown furrowed his wrinkled brow. "What in the name of Great Onan are you doing here?"

Corteezsha's smile was smug. "You may close the door, Jard. I'm with the outlander."

Jard looked at Garn, one bushy eyebrow raised. "The young lady has been gracious enough to offer aid."

"So it would seem. Yet it would behoove one to be wary of assistance unsought," Jard said. Closing the wooden door, he crossed the room to stand before a small, low table. Two porcelain pitchers and four plain cups resided on an ornate tray there. Several cushions surrounded the table. "Please, sit."

Garn sat on the largest cushion with some struggle. Placing his hands on the floor, he shifted his girth as close to the center of the overstuffed thing as he could, but he still had the pressure of his weight on his back and knees. He wouldn't be able to sit this way for long. Why had he let himself get so far out of shape? He knew the answer. It had been easy to quit worrying about his own health after Sureen's disappearance. The only thing keeping him going was his girls.

Once his escort, knees placed firmly together, settled in beside him, Jard settled on a cushion across the table with practiced ease. "Would either of you care for a taste of Surbon White or a cup of chilled water?"

Corteezsha's reply was quick. "The Surbon White, if you

please."

Garn didn't know what the Surbon White was, but it sounded like something made from grapes. It'd be too easy to fall into that trap again, and he needed to keep his head clear. "Chilled water will suffice, thank you."

Jard poured Garn's water first and then half-filled two cups of Surbon White for himself and Corteezsha, his hands steady and true. Garn took a sip from his cup, pleasantly surprised. Chilled to perfection, the water provided a small burst of energy to his overtaxed body and sleep-deprived mind. Searching a deadly and unfamiliar town the whole night through was beginning to catch up to him. He was getting too old for trials like this; soon what hair he had left would turn as gray as Jard's, or worse, fade to pure white. Upending the cup, he tossed every drop down his throat.

Gray eyes bright, Jard set his cup on the tray, pulled his cowl back, and leaned forward, his silvery hair dully accented from the late afternoon window light. "Now tell me, what merits disrupting my flourishing business at this hour? Do you seek an infusion from one of the exotic glimmer shards? Where is it?"

Garn slipped forward on the cushion. The pressure alleviated, a little. "Nothing as involved as that, I'm afraid. I simply require information."

Jard frowned, sitting up straight. "Anyone can give you information. Corteezsha should be able to supply you with whatever you require from her...chosen profession. What malice is this, outlander?"

Garn held up a placating hand. "None, I assure you, Master Jard. Please, allow me to explain." The old man's frown lessened considerably. Why had he used the word master? He didn't know, but for some reason, it had seemed like the right thing to say. "You have many of these crystal shards on display, Master Jard. However, I would venture to say not all are out front. Is this correct?"

Jard sat back on his cushion. "I may have others."

Corteezsha snorted with laughter. "By others, Jard means he

keeps his best stock in the back, does it not, *Master* Jardy?"

Jard looked sidelong at the blonde woman. "Do you think I'd be so foolish to tell you, Corteezsha?"

Corteezsha laughed. "You don't have to, my dear sweet Master Infuser. I've suspected for some time. You have confirmed it."

Jard's face reddened.

Garn didn't care whatever history was between the two, but if he didn't control the conversation from the start, he'd lose any hope of eliciting the old man's help. "Do not let her get to you, Master Jard. You're not doing business with her. You *are* with me, however."

Jard regarded him in rigid silence for long enough Garn began to think about trying a different tack. Finally, Jard stirred and stood.

Garn fought to his feet. Corteezsha beat him there.

Jard pointedly avoided looking in Corteezsha's direction, and she laughed. "What shard are you after, outlander?" Jard asked, his face flushing deeper from the woman's laughter, though he refrained from saying anything to her.

"Not just one. I'm looking for a pair of shards, a hand taller than my own height, of a particular color."

Corteezsha's laughter ended abruptly.

Jard's eyes widened. "Would that I had such a pair, outlander, I'd want for little. Nothing I carry will reach beyond your hand to mid-forearm."

Garn's heart sank, his trepidation rising. What if there wasn't anything comparable to the obelisks on this world? What would he do then? He shied from thinking about it. "Do you stock anything shaped like an obelisk, perhaps blue in color?"

Jard spoke softly. "Blue, you say? Sapphire is one of the rarer shards. The Circle of Light in Surbo, the Brown Recluse monks, or members of the Obsidian Table in the Dark Citadel may have a little, but that is only a guess. I've never actually seen them. Perhaps you can enlighten me, outlander. Is sapphire crystal common to your area? Where do you hail from?"

Garn didn't like the change in subject. Corteezsha's russet eyes focused on him as much as Jard's gray ones. "Where I hail from is irrelevant. I am at this place at this moment, searching for two young women. Have you seen any other outlanders, Master Jard?"

"I can't say that I have. I am sorry…what are you called?"

Jard's question indicated the man didn't have additional information he could use, and it was best to take their leave. "Excuse me for not mentioning it earlier, Master Jard. My full name is Garnet Creek; call me Garn. Thank you for taking the time to talk with me. Shall we finalize our business? I would like to purchase one of your best shards…from the back."

Jard beamed. "Shall I infuse it with glimmer light, Master Garn?"

Corteezsha suddenly spoke. "Address him as my lord, *Master Jard*,"

"Oh? He must be of high station then. Did you want it infused, My Lord?"

"Are you going to include it with the purchase of the shard?"

Jard frowned. "That is not normally done. Infusion is always an extra cost. It requires greater skill manipulating the Flow the less flawed the crystal is. A high quality shard could drain an adept User for a week, perhaps longer."

"Show us your wares, Jard, then we shall decide," Corteezsha said.

Garn nodded when Jard looked to him, wondering what the man meant by User and the Flow, though he suspected it didn't matter. One positive thing at least, he'd have a crystal of some sort to compare against the sapphire obelisks.

Jard left the room through a door at the rear, returning a short while later bearing a wooden tray. Corteezsha removed the tray with the pitcher and cups, setting it aside. Jard set the new tray in its place.

Covered with a golden velvet-like material, the tray was soft to the touch when Garn rubbed it between his fingers.

Four amber-colored shards lay in separate cushioned partitions. Each glowed with a dim light that faded to its natural amber color at the same time. The largest, slightly bigger than a large tankard of ale, cut in the shape of a triangle, took up most of the tray's center. A hand-sized rectangle, circle, and a cone shard filled up the rest, similar in dimensions. The rectangle had something about it, something he couldn't quite fathom. Picking it up, Garn stared at its multifaceted features. Being careful not to drop it to the hardwood floor, he flipped it over in both hands. Both sides were identical. Glowing bright and then dimming, the shard felt powerful and oddly alive.

"I see you have a good eye, Lord Garn," Jard said. "You are holding my best crystal."

"What is your price?" Corteezsha asked. Garn looked up at the sound of her voice. He'd almost forgotten she was there.

"Two gold marks," Jard said without hesitation.

"Infused?" Corteezsha asked.

Jard sighed. "Yes, I'll include the infusion for two gold marks."

Garn looked at his beautiful companion. Corteezsha nodded. "It is a fair price. He'll have to turn the rest of his customers away for the remainder of the sun's golden light. Is this not so, Master Jard?"

"Longer, I'd say. I shall be drained until tomorrow evening, at least," he said, his aging face morose.

Garn tossed Corteezsha the leather purse he found on the assassins' victim. The last thing he wanted was for them to see him fumble around with the wrong coins, raising their suspicions further. Corteezsha's eyes widened when she loosened the drawstrings and glanced inside. Deftly fishing out two finger-sized gold rectangles, she placed them on the cloth where the shard had lain. "Give him two of the silver, as well," Garn said, seeing them in the bag.

Jard made a strangled noise, sputtering. "What? No need, no need..." he trailed off. His words said no, but his gray eyes were wistful.

Corteezsha glanced at him sharply. "Why would you give him twenty times the amount he asked for? Are you attempting to impress me, My Lord?"

Garn smiled, trying to hide his discomfiture. "Am I so

transparent? Give him the appropriate amount as you will, then."

Corteezsha's smile was wide, brightening her blue eyes. She placed two lead squares beside the gold without comment, keeping her eyes on Jard.

Sweeping the coins from the table, the older man smiled. "I thank you both. After the process is complete, I would ask you both leave by the rear door. My assistants will inform those inside of our early close. Are you ready?" He stretched his hand out.

Garn looked at the proffered hand. With reluctance, he placed the rectangle shard in it.

Jard clamped his hand around it. At first, nothing happened. The pulsating light leaking from around his hand remained the same. After a time, the light dimmed and stayed dark. Garn's chest tightened. He'd never wanted the shard's light to go out; that wasn't what he sought, at all. What had he done in his ignorance? He reached for it.

The shard burst into blazing brilliance, painful to look at.

Jard slumped on the cushion. "Here, take it," he said, his voice weak.

Garn took it, hands shaky. He hated when his body betrayed him. Seemed like he only shook when he was trying his best not to. Pleasant warmth emanated from the crystal.

Corteezsha tossed him the soft material that had originally covered the crystals. "Wrap it snugly. The light will stay brighter the longer you keep it covered. How long will the infusion last, Master Jard?"

"I am uncertain. Lesser amber shards have lasted over a year, even with extreme use," Jard said, his voice weaker. "Now if you please, the back door there leads to a hallway, then to an exterior door that will lock behind you." Shaking with the effort, he pointed to an unadorned door in the rear. "I'm too drained to escort you."

"Thank you for your service," Garn said. Stuffing the covered crystal in the front pocket of his slacks, he strode to the door, waiting for his guide. If she found even a hint of his daughters, he would tip her well.

Corteezsha gestured at the tray on the table. "I *could* take what you've got left. You're too weak to do anything about it."

Jard stared at her in silence, his tired face unreadable.

"Yet, you know I will not. You've done a great service, *Master* Jard. Your skill has grown." Corteezsha crossed the room to stand beside Garn.

He pulled the door open.

"Outlander, Garn?" Jard called, his voice barely audible.

"Yes?"

"I kind of like you, so I put a bit extra into this infusion. May it help you with your search."

Garn nodded. Pushing through the second door, Garn found they were halfway down a narrow street. The dimming sunlight fought the first skirmishes against the invading shadows of evening.

Corteezsha smiled. "I know where we are. Come, this street isn't far from my contacts' meeting place." Breaking into a fast stride, she splashed through mud and water alike, oblivious to the brown stains accumulating on her blue dress.

Glad to be back into the search for his girls, Garn hurried after his beautiful guide. With the crystal shard, he had something to show by comparison to the sapphire obelisks, though he was uncertain how much it would help. It was looking like the two different crystals had two vastly different functions.

FLOW THREADS

Fear rooted Jade in place. Something dark and monstrous was coming. She heard the scraping of its scaly, elongated body against the cave walls and the roof, grinding stalactites and stalagmites alike into mineral dust. Inexorably, the monstrosity slithered her way. The cave shook and groaned in protest, as oily black dust sprinkled down. The mountain boomed and lurched sideways. Dust avalanched. Sucking in a breath, her nose clogged. Rubbing desperately at her nasal passages, she fought for air, her fear mounting as primitive emotions assaulted her in torrents; a hunger for soft, organic meat came first. Assimilate. Rend flesh, succulent bones to crack open and slurp the marrow inside. Assimilate. There would be sweet, oily gray matter to digest, to absorb, as its own. Assimilate. Become one being. Anticipation strong, the end was near. There was no way out, no chance to run. It had locked onto her scent. *It was coming.*

A voice intruded into her hearing, a harsh voice she struggled to recognize.

The cave dissipated, though blackness reigned.

"Put her down, you bloody mop handle! Thank Onan, she's coming around. Gently, blast you! If you add to her wounds, I shall burn you where you stand!"

White-hot pain flared inside her skull. She winced, wanting to cry out, but her throat was too raw; a lump clogged her airway. The pain in her head surged stronger, forcing a whimper to escape through her aching throat, loosening the clog enough that she was able to swallow. At least now, she could breathe.

The pain in her skull receded enough to let her flick her eyelids open.

Dispassionate yellow-orange eyes regarded her from inches away. She blinked.

The strange eyes withdrew, replaced by two ice-blue ones set in a hard, weather-beaten face, looking concerned but also resolute. "I shall ask you a question of some significance. You have mere moments to respond," the face said. Taking a deep breath, he spoke quickly. "What is my name?"

What was he jabbering on about? Why would she know his name?

His blue eyes bled into gray and hardened. A frown creased the weathered face.

She glanced below the hard facade of his face, looking at the strange supple leather she'd seen him wearing in his image when she first met him. One hand held a torch; the other wrapped around the hilt of a familiar, long knife, beginning to rise.

Memories flooded in. The sapphire gate, how she'd arrived here. What else could she call it? The obelisks *had* been a gate to another world, hadn't they? They had stranded her on a world prone to decisive violence with a silver-haired man who'd saved her on occasion.

"Camoe, wait!"

The knife halted but stayed suspended above her chest. "State my full name!"

"Camoe…Camoe Shadoe, why? I don't understand." Relief flashed across his weathered face so fast, Jade wasn't certain it had ever been there. The long knife vanished into the sheath on his side. Face stoic as usual, he moved the torch close, peering down at her with his intense, now blue, eyes. "Are you injured physically or mentally, in any way?" His voice was neutral, but his eyes gauged her like a starving bird of prey waiting for a rodent to break cover.

"What do you mean?"

He gazed at her, unblinking. "Those dark creatures delve deep into the mind. All memories and thought processes erased. Domination is total and permanent. No cure has ever been found, at least, nothing the Green Writhe has ever heard about."

Jade gaped at her druid friend, essence druid, to be precise. Her memory was still leaking tidbits into her mind, but one sentence from his quiet statement caught her attention. There was no cure, none at all. "I don't understand. If there's no cure, will I die soon?" Something sharp bit into her back, and she squirmed away from it, realizing she was resting on the rocky cave floor near a boulder-strewn dead end. She must've been out of it for a while. How far had they come through the sewers?

Camoe shook his head. "It does not work that way. There is no disease, viral or otherwise, associated with the attack. It is a malevolent dark creature, as ancient as it is rare. The vile thing uses a single magical ability, albeit an extremely powerful one. We call it a dominion wraith. Dropping a paralyzing blanket of evil on its intended victim, the creature feeds on neural processes as far as we can tell. The host's mind and willpower subvert to its evil. Three of our strongest held out a quarter of a bell before succumbing. Two of those three were honored with *terra' a morn* and their blood returned to Onan. The third is somewhat alive, yet lost."

Cold filled Jade. "What happened to the two? I don't understand your phrasing for it."

"*Terra' a morn* is a complex rite of passage to the afterlife we druids hold for the honorable. First, you must know Onan formed Astura from the blood of a son, freely given. In return for oxygen and sustenance, we sprinkle the blood of our fallen upon the feet of flora. It's the highest honor among our people."

"Supplying oxygen? So, you mean plants?"

Camoe offered his weathered hand. "Yes, but flora is way beyond that. We'll talk later on the subject. Can you stand?"

Jade accepted the offer and pulled herself to her feet. Disoriented, she staggered backward. Camoe stepped close, his grip shifting to her elbow. Grateful to find his broad shoulder near, she hung on until the feeling passed.

"Are you well enough to keep moving, young seer? We should

be going."

"Why did you call me that?"

"There are so many aspects to you, far more than you know. We shall discuss it when there's less pressing matters gaining on us; we need to flee our pursuit," Camoe said.

"What's pursuing us? How long has it been?" Jade asked.

"Six bells, surely, you considered that stealing a Dark User's creature and then killing those guards would bring the Dark Citadel after us in force? I am uncertain if it is the soldiers or the Dark Users, perhaps both."

Wow, six hours, Jade thought. She found it hard to believe. "I never thought about pursuit."

"That is now apparent. Come, we have wasted too much time as it is. Can you walk?" There was a sense of urgency, mixed with exhaustion flowing from her guide. Camoe must be too weary or too worried to keep it from leaking out. He looked over his shoulder with greater frequency, and his booted feet scraped on rocks often whenever he shifted his stance.

She'd have to find the strength from somewhere to keep going. She *would* stay on her own two feet. She wasn't about to be the one to get them caught. "Yes, I can walk, as long as you keep it slow to begin with."

Camoe moved away, his shadow grossly elongated from the torch's meager light. Jade followed, her stomach growing more nauseated with each step taken. Lightheaded and weak, she stumbled along. Soon, she worried she was going to lose consciousness again. The last thing her friends needed was a girl-sized log to carry. *Just keep moving.*

After an interminable time, nausea loosened its clamp on her stomach and her head cleared a little, though she still fought weakness. She breathed a silent prayer of thanks to the One. She may yet live, after all.

Glancing over her shoulder, Burl's glowing yellow-orange eyes trailed them like a supernatural being following behind in the darkness.

Had they always been so bright? She couldn't recall. The name she'd chosen for him fit—she was happy with it—though what he thought about it, she'd never know. It was too bad the Dark User who created him hadn't bothered to give him a voice, but it wasn't surprising. An arrogant master wouldn't want a servant voicing complaints.

Thinking about her first meeting with Camoe, and then Burl, brought back memories of how she'd arrived. One instant she was touching the dark curtain in Ruena Day's office, the next she was in a room full of armor, and she'd stumbled upon the druid in the hall after.

Camoe had saved her life when they ran and when he'd forced her to crawl through the smoke ventilation to find Burl at work in the kitchens. Without her druidic guide, she would've been soul food for the horrible flickers. Now he admitted to being part of a druidic order known as the Green Writhe. Who was he, really? Thinking back, she noticed that Camoe never spoke much about himself. Most of what she knew she got from reading his aura, but there was no reason not to trust him. He'd gotten her this far.

Camoe halted at an intersection. She made out the dark faces of four foreboding tunnels leading away as she moved beside him.

"This is where we discovered the side shaft. I am uncertain of the way out from here since we had to run from the dominion wraith and our pursuit. Your friend may know. We shall have to follow him."

"I thought you didn't trust Burl."

"I do not, but I shall not let you die in this Onan-forsaken hole underground. When the wraith attacked, I was struck by the strongest foreboding." He paused. "I keep forgetting you are unfamiliar with our ways. I suppose I should offer a brief explanation. Some claim I am blessed. I attract Flow threads riddled with possible futures. Most would say I am cursed. The threads are just that, only a thread…a primitive sense of what may happen, a foreboding, or foretelling, if you will. Most do not believe in it. How you decide for yourself is of little consequence. What matters is that I never ignore a foreboding. When the thread struck, I believed it was too strong for me, but I had accepted it. It was then a vision of a desolate Astura hit me, except where you traveled. Where you went, the flora thrived. My mind began to slip beyond my control, which can happen, has happened, in the past. I fought back. It was a near thing, but I regained it. I live. As do you. I now believe you are to have a large part to play in Astura's future. What that role shall be, I cannot say."

Jade frowned. "I don't understand. Tell me something else about this…this…foreboding. You mentioned it happens from Flow threads, but you didn't say what you mean by Flow."

"Blast me! I have failed to tell you about the Flow. Why have I not? Perhaps it is because you remind me so much of…never mind. That is in the past," Camoe said, his voice cracking. "For now, you need to know how the Flow works here, at least for most of us. I am uncertain how yours works, though I do have some ideas about it. Well, we have to start with it, or you will not understand a lot of what I am about to tell you. The Flow derives from—"

A burlap bag stepped between them. Jade felt a pang of guilt. Burl's muteness had almost made her forget they traveled with someone else. Tugging on her tee, he gestured farther along the tunnel. Moving toward them in the distance, dozens of dim specks of light hovered in the darkness, held by unseen hands.

"Blast it!" Camoe swore. "How did they get ahead of us? No matter now, they are coming from the only way I know to escape this rock. There is no hope but to battle our way through. I hope your friend will fight, Jade. There is too many to take alone. What is it doing?"

Burl had removed the soiled rope he carried around his waist. He slipped it through Camoe's sword belt and around her waist. Coiling the center of the rope around one tree-bark wrist, the raggedy man reached out and smothered the torch. A soft hiss preluded a plunge into total darkness.

The darkness vividly reminded Jade of a cave outing with her family many seasons ago. The administration guide had switched off her light to demonstrate the complete absence of light deep underground. She'd appreciated the woman's action back then—

though it had only been for a few moments—as much as she liked what Burl had done now; she hated it. Only now, Jade knew it would be longer. As back then, a scream built in the back of her mind.

A sharp tug sidelined her tension. She had to walk. Or be dragged.

Camoe's whispered voice spoke from close by. "Blessed Onan, your stick man must be able to see in the dark! No wonder it stayed back from the torch! I thought it afraid. I am a fool for not noticing sooner. Pray it knows another way out, or we are doomed to wander in here for an eternity."

She'd been relieved to hear Burl could see in the dark, but the rest of Camoe's words brought panic to the forefront again. Jade walked blindly into the nothingness ahead. However long an eternity would turn out to be, it was already far too long for her liking.

OLD HEART

Having slipped out of the side street, Garn's guide deftly maneuvered through a dense crowd of townsfolk heading the opposite direction. Dropping farther behind, he struggled to keep her in sight. Though blue dresses abounded within the crowd, Corteezsha seemed to be the only one with a blue hat with a widened brim. He was thankful for that, particularly when she crossed the main thoroughfare.

The roadway was crowded with riders on horseback threading their way past horse-drawn carriages and townsfolk pulling handcarts loaded with bulk goods. Corteezsha weaved between them deftly, at last darting into the maw of a dark alley.

Garn halted at the street's center, his wind gone. Gasping for breath, he waited for a troop of pike men in burnished plate armor to file past while keeping the alley his guide had vanished into firmly in his sight. What was wrong with her? At this rate, she'd lose him before long.

The hard eyes of the pike men fixed on him to a man, as they marched past within arm's reach. A soldier wearing a plumed headpiece marched in time beside his troops at the center row. "Make way, outlander!" the plumed soldier snarled, closing the gap between them. Garn fell backward, narrowly avoiding being bowled over. Glaring with open animosity, the officer stomped past without a single glance back. Giving them a wide berth, Garn waited until the last one moved past.

The shadowed alley began at a decent width but soon narrowed to less than four men abreast. Corteezsha was nowhere in sight. There was only one path forward, so she must have ventured deeper inside.

Striding behind dismal stone and wooden buildings, Garn rounded some storage barrels and stacked crates cluttering the path on both sides.

He was uneasy about the whole situation. He knew well how dangerous an alley could be in this place after witnessing two deaths in alleyways, so far, in Gray Water. He didn't know what Corteezsha was up to coming in here, but he hoped she wasn't putting herself in danger.

Garn slowed, glancing over his shoulder. Shadowy figures slipped into the alley along each side. *Damn!* What a fool he was! He should've seen the situation for what it was before he'd sprung the trap. The trap Corteezsha had deftly maneuvered him toward the moment she walked by.

On higher alert now, Garn continued moving the only way open to him, the swiftly darkening alley. If only he could see well enough to find a weapon of some sort to make a fitting end for himself. And it was all for what? Not the coin he carried. The traitorous woman hadn't given it back. What could she possibly want then? He was missing something crucial. There had to be something she wanted from him. Something with enough worth she'd deal with the messiness of dispatching him when she could've just vanished with his coin.

Then he had it.

Corteezsha wanted the glimmer shard. Slipping his hand in his front pocket, Garn glanced over his shoulder, surreptitiously this time. The shadowy figures kept the same distance behind him, obstructing the way back with a wall of bodies, destroying any thoughts of escape. Not that he had harbored any.

The rectangular shard felt noticeably warmer, though it was still wrapped in the soft leather, as if it anticipated what he was about to do. First, he needed a weapon. Removing the wrap from a tiny spot in the crystal's center, Garn let a pinpoint of light escape. His focused light beam shot forth from his palm, illuminating an area the size of his hand.

He searched quickly; if his attackers spotted his makeshift light, it may force them to act sooner than they—or he—would like. He shielded the light the best he could with his bulk. Sweeping the beam back and forth along the debris on both sides revealed a thick wooden board, which he picked up. It would have to do.

The light winked out when he covered the crystal. Letting his eyes adjust to the growing dark, he assessed the situation. Two shadowy rows—one behind the other—each three men wide, made an effective human barricade against fleeing to the relative safety of the street, as he'd thought. Well, they'd not find him as easy a mark as most. Defending against a thrown dagger or crossbow would be tricky, though. He'd have to watch for that.

The human wall made no move toward him. They stood in silence, staring at him with unseen eyes. He didn't know what the delay was, but he was relieved for the moment. He would prefer to find room to swing his makeshift weapon.

He moved deeper within. The alley opened onto a cul-de-sac overlooked by buildings and high wooden fences. He approached the area with caution, wishing he had some of his men—former men, now—for backup. Twilight leaked into the area from the waning sun, enough for him to distinguish a life-sized shape standing in the center. A few steps closer revealed a female form wearing a wide-brimmed hat and bright parasol, now open.

So, this is the place.

Abandoning his pretense at caution, Garn strode openly to the cul-de-sac's center. Halting a board length from Corteezsha, he studied his surroundings. Several men sat on crates placed to one side, while both men's and women's shadowy forms stood in front of a wall on the other. The men behind him filled the path back to the street four rows deep. The first two rows now had enough light he could make out individual features on many a grizzled face. Committing them to memory was pointless. They wouldn't allow him to leave the cul-de-sac unscathed.

Corteezsha spoke as soon as he strode near. "I suppose you kept coming for your coin. I hoped you wouldn't follow me here."

"To be honest, I never considered the coin until too late. My desire to find my daughters has made me a blind fool to one of the oldest traps there is, I should've known you'd have a prearranged signal to alert your cohorts of the mark following you. My guess would be that whenever you enter here with your parasol open, your cronies get a signal as blatant as any flag. I can't believe I trusted you enough to fall for it."

Corteezsha's face turned pouty. "You're not serious, are you? No one trusts me." The woman's rue sounded almost genuine.

A new voice spoke. "You're right, Cor. No one should trust you long enough to for you to throw your net, not even a dried, old fish like him. There are too many holes in it." Several voices, male and female, laughed.

A man hooded and robed in a dark color emerged from the shadows to stand beside Corteezsha. The man's features were indiscernible to Garn. No weapon was visible, for which Garn was thankful. Perhaps he could come to some agreement with the man. "What do you want with me? You may keep the coin. I ask only for information in return," Garn said, keeping his voice even.

The dark-robed man cackled without mirth. "You ask me for information? I am a *Flow Master*. Yet you have the audacity to ask me?"

Corteezsha retracted the parasol sharply. "Can't you see how he's clothed, Malkor? He's an outlander searching for his missing daughters; he's ignorant to our ways. Why don't you let the outlander go? We have his coin."

Malkor sneered. "Go?" No one *goes* here. You know well."

"Malkor doesn't have any say in the matter. *I* decide who lives and dies here, *no one else*," a quiet but commanding voice said behind him.

Garn spun. A stocky, hooded man garbed in the same velvety leather covering the shard—only black in color—slipped past him. The hood covered his shoulders and fell to his midsection, leaving his stomach and most of his arms bare. Made from some soft metal, two silver bands fit snug on his biceps. The light was fading too fast to identify it.

Anxiety rose in the pit of Garn's stomach, which he ignored. The situation had gone from life threatening to no way out alive. So be it. He was dying from heart disease anyway. Failing his daughters was the worst of it. Part of him begged to negotiate with this den of murderers for a chance, however small, to stay alive long enough to see them home. Yet he knew with the mob watching on, it would do no good. Still, he had to try. His daughters depended on him.

Corteezsha turned away, confirming his fears. He tightened his grip on the shard.

The dark shape of the hooded man stepped beside Corteezsha, swinging her around, forcing her to look in Garn's direction. "Malkor does have a point, however. No one *goes*. Kill him!"

Wait!" Garn shouted, and thinking furiously, he raised the shard high. He required a little additional time. Not a lot, the alley was rapidly darkening. "I'll break this into a thousand pieces. Then what use will it be to you?"

The hooded man's soft voice dripped disdain. "What is it you hold that you believe *I* would care about?"

"Tell him, Corteezsha," Garn said.

Corteezsha's reply was immediate. "He has a glimmer shard, one of the best I've seen in Gray Water."

"Infused?" the hooded man asked.

"Yes, quite a masterful infusion, so it could be fused with something else," Corteezsha said.

The hooded man's dark shape hesitated, his voice soft but malevolent. "That is useful. But I think I'll just take it from you, intact or not. Malkor, burn him where he stands, mind the shard."

As darkness fell, Malkor's hands illuminated with a dark red glow.

Garn sprang into action. Covering the distance with three running steps, he vaulted into the air; his right booted foot connected somewhere near Malkor's face. Malkor's glowing hands winked out.

Landing on his feet, Garn swept the board toward the dark outline of the hooded man and Corteezsha, but he encountered only air. Following through with a spin, he released his grip on the cloth, and the glimmer shard blazed with a bonfire light.

Charging back the way he arrived, he stretched his palm out before him. The shard's brilliant light illuminated the wall of humans. Tossing the board out front, he caught it near the center, braced it at his waist, and plowed into the wall at his top speed. Though he prepared for it, the impact sent a shock reverberating through his bones, nearly doubling him over.

Caught with hands shielding eyes, most in the front row flew into the row behind. Staggering through tumbling bodies, Garn bounded forward, pushing with all his might, using his momentum to stay on his feet. The board snapped, dropping away. He punched and kicked, fighting with his elbows and knees as he'd trained, smashing into all who stood in his way.

Suddenly, there was no resistance, and he shot forward, the way ahead clear. Sprinting to the corner, he careened off a stack of wood barrels on the far side. Righting himself, he could see the busy street ahead.

Something was wrong. His breath came in ragged gasps, forcing him to slow. The sweat on his skin turned cold and clammy. His chest thrummed with pain. Forward movement ceased to a standstill.

He toppled. The pain fogged his mind, and darkness closed in. Dully, he heard booted feet drawing near, but it no longer mattered. *My old heart picked a bad time to give out,* he thought, his sadness acute. He'd failed his girls. Remorse settled in with the darkness enveloping him.

FEAR

Fear is an unproductive emotion. It doesn't aid blood flow, it doesn't clean tear ducts, and it doesn't increase euphoria. Therefore, it's useless. Succumb at your own detriment. Crystalyn clearly recalled the dispassionate nasal tone the med instructor had lectured the class with after interrupting a holo presentation of dissected body parts. Even now—seasons later—she could still see his sneer of disdain when buff-bodied Jake had fainted at the beginning. *Fear is an unproductive emotion. Succumb at your own detriment.* Crystalyn silently repeated each sentence over and over until her fear slid away, replaced by rage.

Now she could function. She was *through* with giving away blood, *through* with the helplessness of hanging in a macabre candy-roll pillar, *through* with providing the protein drink for spiderbees. She'd make the bloody creatures pay; blast her, if she wouldn't! Anger *was* a productive emotion.

How well she knew. There were many days where only anger kept her going. Most times, she didn't know why or where it had come from, only that at any given moment, she'd shift from euphoric to livid for no apparent reason.

She'd learned to focus that anger into a kind of manic energy, to make it work for her. She welcomed that energy now, letting it fill her. Now things would get messy, and she didn't care if she destroyed the entire bloody hive.

Sorting through the *Tiered Tome of Symbols* stored in her memory, Crystalyn selected a black net-looking one under the ominous title group aggression. As the symbol hovered before her, the anger inside burned away her doubts and anxieties. She felt no need to combine it into something new. It should suffice for rounding the spiderbees up and popping them like repulsive, overfilled leeches.

Tilting back, she found a spiderbee above her, finishing its grisly work. Pushing away from the ashen man, the blood-laden creature dropped a few feet toward her before its silent beating wings halted its downward fall. Hovering slightly above her, it provided a decent target.

She took it.

Releasing the net symbol, it sailed toward the spiderbee, unfolding to triple its original size. Black, pole-length spikes sprang from every knot on its octagon shape and snowflake center. The spikes were longer and sharper than the black icicles on the splintery one she'd used at the meadow on Glacier Mountain.

Floating straight and true, the symbol enveloped the creature…and passed through. Unimpeded, it struck the cavern roof and shattered, dissipating as smoke would against a solid surface.

The spiderbee spun to face her, regarding her with its many-faceted eyes.

Crystalyn gaped.

How could she have missed? Gathering her will, Crystalyn selected the knockback symbol with its concentric circles, the surefire one she'd used in the alley, which now seemed so long ago. Quickly, she redrew it into her own design, the one she'd feared to use on Atoi. There was no such compunction now.

A second spiderbee appeared beside the one carrying the payload. It too paused, regarding her. Taking advantage of the delay, she sent the symbol gliding toward the new creature just as it flew toward her. Without deviating, the spiderbee flew through her pattern, dispersing it.

Crystalyn gawked, unable to believe her eyes.

When the spiderbee landed with its forelegs on her shoulder, she felt the stab of its stinger for a moment, but only for a moment. Thankfully, the paralysis was fast. *What happened?* she wondered.

Perhaps she wasn't as strong as the Lore Mother had believed. Already, she felt much weaker. The spiderbee was wasting no time draining her lifeblood.

An image of her pale corpse swinging inert as the spiderbee suckled its hungry offspring sprang up with a disquieting clarity in her mind. Perhaps she had a vision of the near future. Or, her oxygen-deprived brain had conjured the scene to make sense of her life siphoning away.

Her death would be painless, but it was small consolation. She'd much prefer leaving this world screaming in agony than to die not knowing what happened to Jade. Had a similar fate befallen her sister? Did little sister cross through the dark curtain of the Sapphire Gate only to cross over to the afterlife?

Cold seeped into her extremities, replacing the blood siphoning away. Seconds passed. A great weariness pressed upon her. The strength to keep her eyes open fled with each drop of blood stolen. It wouldn't be long. The Great Sleep would end her weariness.

Happily, her last sight comprised a beautiful banyan-like tree coming her way swinging its many arm-like branches in all directions, flanked by its smaller sister shadow trees.

Where had she seen banyan trees? Oh, yes, on an island surrounded by a wondrous ocean in a holo image. She'd longed to see an ocean before she died. It was one of the few things the farm hadn't been able to terraform. They'd managed several ponds and a large lake but not an ocean: land was too scarce, too precious. Now, she'd never view a sea with a vibrant ecosystem still intact.

Spiderbees swarmed around the tree, popping wetly. Crystalyn tried to smile but lacked the strength. The struggle to hold weariness away grew too great. Closing her eyes, she succumbed to it, saddened to the core. In the end, her symbol magic had failed when she needed it most.

*****

Crystalyn struggled to surface. A bright light beckoned above. Stoical and enduring, the light radiated supreme compassion, tinged with knowledge so vast, her mind shied away from it lest she be lost for an eternity. At any moment she'd break through the surface, fling her head into the wonderful radiance, know the secrets of creation, and be filled with utter joy. Only a few kicks left.

Stretching to full length, she extended her fingers. She could almost reach; thrusting a fingernail into the light would be all she required. This close, Crystalyn felt warmth bathe her face, bringing a profound, unadulterated love from within the light. Just one additional kick.

Something cold and firm wrapped around her ankle, pulling her away.

No!

Flailing her arms and legs, she fought with everything in her, sapping strength from deep inside. She'd been *so* close!

The light held, growing brighter and beaming jets of brilliance to the surface's edge, seeming to reach out to her, to offer encouragement, to be there in her time of need. So close, so close! She stretched her arm out.

She couldn't hold on. Her strength collapsed. The light receded.

Nooooo!

She kicked feebly. The light faded to a slit and vanished. Despair, dark and deep, replaced her joy. She looked far into the gloom about her and despaired, to the point of not caring. Let the gloom swallow her.

A great weight settled into the part of her she knew as her body.

The world shifted from darkness to gray and brown. Gray cirrus clouds floated lazily above brown treetops. Confused, Crystalyn forced her eyes wider. Blurred, colorful images bled into her vision.

A female voice spoke from nearby. "She's coming around." The voice seemed familiar, but her mind refused to provide the facial image. "I wonder if she'll live," the voice mused, expressing much interest.

A new voice, heavy with fatigue, spoke from somewhere close. "Move away, child. I am uncertain of the effects so much healing will have on her perceptions. I would not want her to destroy you and everyone here before the mistake could be explained." Again, Crystalyn felt she should recognize the voice, but she found it hard to care. *Where was the lovely light?* She'd been so close.

A third voice drifted to her hearing. "Is she blind now? Look at her eyes." This voice, a low masculine rumble, carried an inflection of imminent harm.

A melodious fourth voice spoke above. "Who can say for certain? She's been through great trauma. The leechers had nearly drained her life fluid. Perhaps her eye fluids dried beyond recovery. Our strange young User is alive, that's what counts. We need to get moving." Crystalyn strained her eyes as wide as she could, but the images refused to form. Gray and brown blurred together, but there was a tiny flicker of color, up high, in a corner.

An abysmal tremor vibrated her very core. Darkness nearly swallowed her.

"Blast you, Hastel! I told you to keep the horses still!"

"I'm sorry, Lore Mother, but standing in the open like this has them spooked. Can she make it to those trees, do you think?"

The Lore Mother's voice was dry. "Why not ask her to sit up and take the reins herself?"

Her memory returned in a vivid torrent. A white-haired old woman and a face-wounded man wearing an eye patch flooded in. Images flashed through her mind, faster and faster. Some scenes she didn't want to recall, so she shuffled through them as if she was forwarding a bad dream, such as killing her attackers in the meadow and meeting the Hartwig kid.

Others, she lingered on—the rare outings the family had went on together where her mother's laughter, her father's joy, Jade's constant smile, and the feelings of love sent an ache deep inside, begging her to release it and relive those precious times.

Hastel's raspy voice intruded. "I am truly sorry. I'll do what I can to be gentle, but I'll have to go to those trees. The horses want the grass growing there. It will keep them settled."

Shifting from one side to the other, a shocking pain coursed through Crystalyn's body. A moan escaped her lips. For the second time, she nearly gave in to the blackness that welled up in her mind. Pushing it away with great effort, she swallowed, wanting to beg for it to stop, but a tiny moan gurgled outward instead.

She was so weak. The simple act of drawing breath required great effort; her arms and legs were leaden and unresponsive. She recalled incidents of nursing duties. A few patients had gotten miraculously better for a while, only to crash hard afterward.

She wasn't about to let that happen. *I'm going to live if it kills me*, she thought. Such a stray oxymoronic thought would have brought a smile to her lips at any other time. Not now, she was much too weak. Perhaps her mind was shying from her condition, or worse, she could be crashing in reality but her mind was shielding her until it couldn't any longer.

The Lore Mother's voice was heavy with concern. "Go with care; she shall feel every single motion. Rayna, go help steady the horses. This is critical, we may yet lose her!"

Another flicker higher up alerted her to a shadow detaching from the distortion. As she tracked the shadow, details trickled in. Bushy hair beyond shoulder length, leafy shapes covering a large upper torso, spots of green. Dare she hope her vision was returning?

Colors bled in from all directions, creating a bizarre kaleidoscope of twisted, broken landscape. A jagged blue line interspersed with blacks, grays, and browns. Dull, washed-out whites formed twisted shapes. But shapes they were. Seeing them, her excitement rose. She couldn't wait to view her surroundings in the normal light and color.

Grayish wagon railing turned slowly brown, growing recognizable, adding grainy wood texture the longer she stared.

From some distance away, Atoi's voice rang out. "Something's coming!"

Cudgel's booming voice blared in her ears. "Where?"

Atoi called again. "Behind us."

Lore Rayna screamed. "It's frightening the horses!"

A dreadful wrench slung Crystalyn toward the back of the wagon. Her last vision was of the gray meadow grass bleeding green before blackness rose up to swallow her.

*****

A voice called to Crystalyn. Complacent, yet hinting at urgency, it pleaded for a response. *"Are you there, Do'brieni? Come to me. We've much to discuss and little time. Are you there, Do'brieni? Please, answer."*

"Where are you?"

A surge of elation, tinged with hope, washed through her. *"I am near. You will have to find the way."*

Darkness blocked the way. It wasn't going to be easy. When had anything she set out to do her whole life been easy? Moving blindly in a general outward direction, she froze. Had the darkness just moved back? Not daring to believe, she traveled a short distance in three quick spurts. The darkness vaulted away three times, each time the same distance from her. Elated, she raced into the darkness, sweeping it before her. She called out to the voice, *"Am I going the right way?"*

"All ways end the same."

What did he mean by that? She couldn't say for certain, but she felt the voice was male. Lacking any feminine or masculine tonal inflections, there was no way of knowing if she was right about it. Except "voice" wasn't the right word. It was a *sense* of a voice, except…*except*…she heard it as she would her own thoughts. Distinguishing between her thoughts and the voice was a *distinction* her mind sorted with ease.

How that could be was beyond her. Nor did she care. She liked the support she sensed emanating from the feeling.

Pushing the darkness back, she moved until she found a corner.

Without slowing, she swept down it to find another, then another, coming to a halt at a fourth, which had to be the beginning.

"Where are you? Are you hiding from me? I've searched everywhere."

Joy tinged with amusement washed over her. *"Open your eyes, my Do'brieni!"*

Her eyes flew open.

Light flooded in. Squinting, she searched for the voice. The glowing-eyed Lore Mother was kneeling at her side, concern wrinkling her wizened face. Huge Lore Rayna and one-eyed Hastel hovered behind her.

The Lore Mother cackled with glee. "By Onan, she is coming around! She's made of sterner stuff than I ever imagined. How do you feel, child?"

"Where is he?" Crystalyn asked, her voice small.

The Lore Mother frowned. "Where is who, dear?"

"I don't know. I heard a voice; he called me his Do...Do'brieni. Didn't you guys hear him?"

The Lore Mother sat back, exchanging a look with Lore Rayna before fixing on her again. "Do you know what the word means? I was not aware you could speak the ancient tongue."

"I don't know what it means, and I'm too weak to think about it. Please, just tell me where he is. I want to see him."

The Lore Mother pursed her cracked lips. "I cannot tell you where he is, though I suspect he is near. But the meaning matters considerably."

Groggy, Crystalyn was suddenly alert. "What do you mean?"

"Do'brieni is the ancient word for link mate. It appears you have been linked."

"Blessed Onan—" Lore Rayna breathed.

Crystalyn squinted at the Lore Mother. The light of day was so bright. "That means nothing to me. I still don't have any idea what you mean. I'm too tired and too weak to think about it."

"Connected, dear, it means you're connected. A warden offered an empathic link to you. You must have accepted. The warden has to be fairly close for the link to happen; it is likely the cause of the horses' jitters."

A familiar throb began to build behind Crystalyn's eyes. "You're giving me a headache. You'll have to tell me some other time."

The Lore Mother's tone filled with awe. "Do not inquire of me, dear. Ask your Do'brieni."

"My link mate? How would you suggest I do that?" Crystalyn asked. She was beginning to get irritated with the old woman. The Lore Mother acted as if she should know how to do everything from the start. What was she going to do with these people? Sometimes she wanted to give them all a tongue-lashing. Especially the Lore Mother, when she was being cryptic. What was she supposed to do? *Search around with her inner vision, reach out with her mind, or perhaps, lash out in silence?*

An almost overpowering sense of wonder flowed into Crystalyn's mind. *"You have discovered how to open your inner being sooner than expected, faster than any passed down through our lore! I am pleased, yet I am confused. What has raised your ire, Do'brieni?"*

The voice sounded so near and so intimate that it frightened her. At the same time, a single thought stood out, stronger than terror. She clung to it. *The voice hadn't come from the world outside.* It derived from within, as if the speaker behind it shared her mind somehow. It frightened her that she received sensations from the other mind too, feeling it in the physical sense as if it were a disembodied brain floating in the half of her mind that it had claimed for its own.

Except she knew where the voice's body was; pinpointing it was simply a matter of following the sensations back to their source, which she did. A dried stream bank lined with cedar trees, south of the wagon road, formed in her memory. *"Why do you stay hidden in the old streambed? Come to me,"* she thought, concentrating on the link.

A response tinged with surprise slipped into her mind. *You must make your companions aware of me.* An image of an arrow protruding from a sienna-furred shoulder followed the thought.

Suddenly, she was groggy, way beyond tired. *"Stay where you are. I'll come to you soon."*

The Lore Mother's voice intruded, echoing the way she felt. "I'm very tired. Is it safe to set up camp?"

Cudgel answered from the opposite side of the wagon. "We should be far enough from the hive by now."

At least she thought it was he. Sometimes he sounded like Hastel or the one-eyed warrior sounded like him. She didn't bother to look. Looking required energy, something she was severely short on now. Allowing her eyes to flutter closed, she gave herself to the blackness waiting to engulf her in its healing embrace, secure in the knowledge her newfound friend was watching out for her not far away.

VOICES IN THE DARK

The odd, guttural voices had steadily encroached upon Jade's darkened world. The first sounds of pursuit had drifted down from above after Burl had led her and Cam down a steep ramp and crossed an immense cavern. Then, they were only a faint echo from time to time. Now, the voices in the dark grew louder, drifting across the cavern behind them. They called out with grunts and clipped, raspy sounds, foreign and familiar at the same time, though she didn't recognize a single word. The unfamiliar language worried her, worse than the hours of dogged pursuit. How would she communicate if the voices caught them?

She'd trade every possession she owned to wake in her small bedroom, with its single dim light and tiny window, shared with Crystalyn. Led around by a Dark User's creation through suffocating darkness as the voices came ever closer brought home the reality she may never see that wonderful room again, nor her sister. Something she shied away from thinking about.

Camoe and Jade were completely dependent on Burl. Without his ability to see in absolute dark, they would wander until falling to their deaths in a hole. They might *still* be falling, their hoarse screams echoing back to them with cold mockery.

Little of the harrowing flight through blackness had seemed real until the voices had reached her. She'd simply walked where led for hours, taking it on faith that the enemy followed only because Burl hadn't stopped tugging the rope.

As soon as the thought crossed her mind, the rope fell slack around her waist. Too late, it struck her the raggedy man had come to a standstill; her shoulder and chin took the brunt of the impact. Jarred, she bit her tongue. Though she tried to hold it back, a small cry slipped through her lips.

Camoe's voice, low and drawn, followed her cry. "Blast you, dark creation. Give proper warning before stopping to smell the rock flowers! Our eyes were not born from blackness, as yours."

Pulling the rope taut, Burl's dark outline moved to one side without a sound. A dull flicker caught Jade's eye. "Camoe, wait! Isn't it getting lighter ahead?"

"By the One God, I think it is!"

Brushing past her, he moved to take the lead. He made it about a half step before a sharp tug pulled them together.

"Ouch. I think he wants us to go this way," Jade said, rubbing her hip she'd banged against Camoe's. Despite his many seasons, the druid's body was solid as a tree.

"What is it doing, now?" Camoe asked, his voice hoarse. "I had thought to believe your creature may actually want to lead us safely from this cesspit. Now I am not so certain. There is light ahead. With light, there is the possibility we can find our way out of this rock. I have been here too long; I *need* sunlight."

"Burl's done well this far. He could've led us right into those voices trailing us a long time ago. In case you haven't noticed, they're getting awful close." A sharp tug on her waist emphasized Burl's impatience.

Camoe's reply was grudging. "Fine, we shall do it your way this time. However, should I get a single hint your Burl has led us astray, I shall kill it first." Turning away from the dim light, he vanished from sight. She knew he was still close by the rigid sound of his boots moving away.

Jade followed, concentrating on not banging into him again, no easy feat with the length of the rope being so short and having to do it by feel. She understood Camoe's need. Light with which to see the way forward would be divine.

Burl forced them into a near run for perhaps a minute, before she felt his hand press against her shoulder slowing them to a cautious walk. Loose rocks, mingled with larger boulders, loomed out of the darkness. Jade discovered some only when she scraped her knees or shins on them. The greatest terror of anyone living without vision must be the not knowing what lay in wait ahead, especially navigating through terrain like these caves. Small rocks waited to cause the unwary an abrasive stumble, and rock walls stood ready to bash them to a halt. Worse, the path ahead might drop away to nothingness.

Stop it! Jade admonished. Stumbling around in the dark must be getting to her, though it had given her new respect for the blind. When she returned home, she vowed to help someone with it, somehow. Perhaps she could study to become an administration ophthalmologist. If she ever got back. No! She had to stop thinking like that. Despair would claim her.

She couldn't help wondering where Crystalyn was right now. Her sister searched for her; she'd seen it during the dominion wraith's attack. Or had she imagined it? Had the wraith provided the image as some sort of tactic to break through her protection?

Her musings cut short when a weight descended upon her head. Startled, she quelled her rising panic when she realized Burl's rough hand rested there. Following his urgent—but gentle—pushes, she went down on her knees, feeling her way into a small opening.

Great, yet another crawl in the dark, when would it end? "Watch your head, Cam. I think Burl's taking us into a vent again."

"All right, but leave the rope where it is, untie only if the shaft climbs too steeply, do not follow. We shall then find another route," Camoe whispered.

They hadn't gotten far when Burl halted without warning again. This time, a rough-textured heel smacked her chin.

"That's it! Burl, you've got to stop—"

"Quiet!" Camoe hissed into her ear. "They are close."

Jade had almost forgotten the voices. Clear and distinct, one guttural, echoed about in clipped tones, a stone's throw too close.

Sounding loud in her ears, Jade quieted her ragged breaths, and moments passed in stark silence. She wondered how her companions managed to keep silent—not even a drawn breath from Camoe—with danger so near.

Camoe must be very brave. Jade wished she could be, but her legs had cramped painfully, and she couldn't stay still. She leaned back on her hands slowly.

Light bloomed at the shaft's entrance.

Her heart thumped against her chest. Surely, the entire citadel could hear it hammering, giving them away. Now they'd die violently. They'd come so far, been through so much, and now they were all going to be killed. The entire harrowing escape trek had all been for nothing. A scream of frustration reverberated in her mind. And stayed there, echoing back and forth.

The light had withdrawn.

Camoe inched close, releasing a small hot breath at her ear. "Keep moving and stay quiet."

She didn't trust herself for a reply with her heart still racing. Pushing against Burl's legs, Jade got him to continue. Again, she thought of Burl in the masculine sense, but how would she ever know? She couldn't ask him, since he was so profoundly mute. Not once had he produced the smallest sound.

This time the crawl seemed endless, though the shaft stayed straight and true to its gentle upward slope. An hour passed at most, but she couldn't go on. The last of her energy had burned away. Opening her mouth to call for a rest, she stopped, but her forward progress never ceased.

Burl pulled her along with apparent ease. Jade held on, grateful for the reprieve on leaden legs, though she did feel guilty for not pulling her own weight.

Relying on others to carry you through life will leave dependencies.

Sounding a bit like she recalled Mom had, Crystalyn had told her those words often enough, usually finishing by telling her to be strong for Dad's sake. Sometimes Jade got the impression Crystalyn blamed her—but mostly Mom, for not being there—for the troubles at home.

Jade reached for the rope, but her arms had grown as heavy as the smooth rock Burl pulled her over.

The darkness seemed darker than it had a moment ago. Had her eyes closed? How would she see where they were going?

PONDEROUS MOUNTAIN

The heat on Jade's cheek and the light leaking in under her eyelids told her the auto tint adjust for the window had drifted out of calibration again. Crystalyn would be mad she hadn't checked the solar sensor for particle buildup before going to sleep.

Filled with trepidation, Jade opened her eyes. The blazing light of midday stabbed her vision. Bright spots danced before her eyes. She blinked and rolled on her side. Harsh, brown shrubs sprang into focus, growing reluctantly through sickly, gray-colored sand. Two legs and feet, the color and look of tree branches, stepped into view, halting beside her head.

For a moment, she was frightened until she recalled whose they were. Jade sat up. Burl's yellow-orange eyes gazed at her dispassionately. Going with an impulse, Jade clasped the raggedy man's wrist, and pulled herself upright, feeling the bark-like texture of his skin. Burl never budged from her unexpected added weight. *How strong was he?*

Camoe stepped from behind some enormous dark gray rocks surrounding them. "Good. You're finally awake. You had me concerned."

Jade glanced around. A boulder big enough to flatten her dad's hover cycle lay at the base of the cliff face, marking their exit route. Well, perhaps cliff and face weren't the exact words she wanted. Tilting her head back, she gazed upward until falling over was a real danger. Dark, ponderous mountain was apt. It was a wonder such a thing had allowed them to escape. The mountain brooded overhead with a palpable sense of malice exuding a presence so strong she was afraid it was going to somehow reach out and pull her back inside.

Lest its malevolence swallow her, Jade turned her back on the forbidding stone, suppressing a shudder. She never wanted to look at it again. "I'm alive, thanks to you both."

"You will feel stronger once you have eaten," Camoe assured her. He handed her a bowl of soup, two slices of bread, and a water flask.

A pleasant aroma wafted from the soup. Parched, she took a long pull from the damp flask first, pleasantly surprised at the chilled temperature. Her benefactor must have discovered fresh water from somewhere nearby. A glance at the soup revealed unknown sprouts mixed with carrots and potatoes. Tentatively, she dipped a small portion of her bread into the tin bowl and tried it. The sprouts gave it a satisfying, robust flavor, bringing to mind a protein cube. Before she knew it, her spoon was scraping the bottom. "Oh, that was very good! What are those sprouts you used?"

"They are called meat sprouts, since they have a similar flavor. But I did not make it." He glanced sidelong in Burl's direction.

Her mute friend was busy packing her and Camoe's bags, utilizing a waist-high rock, flat on top. Not only was Burl a huge help, but he seemed able to perform tasks with relative intelligence. "Do you know where we are?" she asked the druid.

Camoe shook his head, his blue eyes wide. "I think we have somehow crawled out of the southern end of the Dark Citadel. Until now, I would not have thought there was anything but this ugly gray granite on this side. No one in my order knew of any way in or out of the citadel here, not even the most traveled. Many have sacrificed a lifetime studying the citadel's defenses, searching for some small chink in its dark stone, though no one looked behind this boulder field, it seems. Of course, if one did happen to trudge by, the opening is small enough it would not have merited a second glance."

Jade slung the water flask over her shoulder along with her bag. "Why bother searching? A place this size must have a large front door somewhere. Surely, someone could muster enough troops to take it by force. Why not storm the main entrance?"

Camoe's icy blue eyes stared at her, stretching the moment into two. "Do not think there has not been an attempt. This age—along with some that passed before—has seen many attempts to cull the dark threat. Permit me a brief description of the most recent. The Dark Users swarmed from the Dark Citadel pushing their slaves before them and whipping their dark creation creatures frenzy high. The allied armies of the White Lands withstood the hordes of darkness this time, even pushing them back to their stronghold, back to the Dark Gate. There, they fled inside and the great gate closed behind them. Deterred, the allied armies could only hurl their magic at the great gate. It stood, dark, powerful, and scarcely marked. Appalling, flying creations disgorged from the cliffs above then. While battling those evil things, burning oil, catapulted boulders, and barbed cross bolts as thick as poles flew from the cliff face. A multitude of dark flame balls, funnel cones, and acidic rain, conjured by the Dark Users to name but a few, harrowed the armies from high. Eventually the commanders realized the futility of such a siege and returned home defeated, but at least Astura had peace for a time.

"But that's what I mean. Why let them regroup and destroy your world? Take their base and they won't be able to come at you again, infiltrate it first if you must."

Camoe's blue eyes lightened as he scowled. "I was able to infiltrate the Dark Citadel by the pretense of paying homage to their *great lord*, but it wouldn't work for a large group. In order to accomplish my mission, I spent seasons making them think that I believe theirs is the greater power as I trained their elite with advanced sword and warfare tactics. Discreetly, I dispatched some of their promising young magic Users. In the name of my task, I have shown the enemy a greater provision than I care to admit, I have sworn service to their great lord, bound to serve as long as Lord Charn lives, but it was necessary to convince them of my loyalty. Many have thought as you throughout the ages. Some have even tried a frontal assault or infiltration. All have failed. Come, I shall let you see for yourself. I know a place where you can view the grand west entrance, the dark hole in the rock." Slipping around a rock shaped like a giant stairway, Camoe vanished into a thicket of stunted trees.

Stunted, yes, but trees all the same, *living* trees. Jade stared with reverence. It didn't matter should they serve no purpose other than fuel wood or shade, or as only a supplier of precious oxygen, trees were majestic at any size. A memory of Dad showing her and Crystalyn the first fruit trees preserved under the dome of the farm, back when she'd barely been old enough to speak, flashed through her mind.

The fruit trees had been the beginning research for the citrus and nutrients. If it weren't for the dome, the trees wouldn't have survived the radiation, and the farm wouldn't have been able to synthetically manufacture citrus and stave off the palsy. The king's administration now provided the daily requirements in a capsule, if one had the credits to buy it.

Diminutive fields sown for certain vegetables too stubborn to synthesize on Mid Realm and above won a spot under the dome, but there was no place for average trees without fruit. Gazing at the living wall made her realize just how great a loss it was.

A bit of searching revealed the obscure animal trail Camoe used. Ducking under a branch, she caught sight of a boot heel where he waited for her. As she hurried to catch up, her feet crunching on the drier twigs, the boot spun around. Camoe stood silent as she clomped up beside him.

"We are still striving for silence, Jade. Your created friend does not do too badly and it cannot bend at the knee," he said. "Your legs work like they should, yet birds are taking flight for leagues."

"I don't know how to be quieter."

Camoe sighed. "I thought you would say that. You were louder than I liked underground, but there was no help for it. I suppose I should begin your training. First lesson—watch where I step from now on; second, put your foot down from toe to heel, like this. Let your toes take the weight as you roll your foot to the heel so that most of your foot never touches the ground at the same time. Do it with both feet with each step." Exaggerating each foot placement, he stepped forward several paces. "You can also go from heel to toe, depending on the terrain and situation, but not that often. Now you try it."

Jade did so. It was much harder than the druid made it appear.

"Not like that! I told you, toe to heel. Visualize it. Imagine you're walking on hot rocks. Try to keep as much of your flesh away from the heat as you can, for the barest amount of time. Try again." Not waiting for her second attempt, he stalked silently off into the forest.

Jade sucked in her lower lip but then spit it out. Left alone, it would heal, but it was hard with Camoe's impatience to deal with. She *was* trying her best. Following his advice, she imagined the heat emanating through her boots. Stepping gingerly, toe to heel, she concentrated on keeping the red-hot rocks from burning into her soles.

When traveling on an incline, it was hard to walk that way, but she kept at it. After a time, her leg muscles loosened, making the hike easier. The forest quietness, bright patches of sunlight, and pungent smells of fresh pine needles mixed with an underlying moist hint of moss exhilarated her. Vibrancy grew all around, instilling a keen sense of renewal, making her feel alive. It was good to be outdoors.

The path continued much the same way for a good portion of the day until she rounded a small ridge top to find Camoe waiting in front of a thicket. He flashed a partial smile. "Well, that was much better. Keep it up and we may live through this." Turning his back to her, he slipped into a withered patch of tangled scrub oak without a sound.

Jade stared at the living wall for a long moment. How was she supposed to watch where he stepped, or where she was *stepping*, through that dying mess? Sucking in her lip, she went after him.

Once she fought beyond the first few dry brambles, the scrub oak thinned, revealing sagebrush mixed with tall meadow grass. Jade drew in a lungful of the sage. The farm had specialized in it; she'd never gotten tired of the scent. The sage made it markedly easier to move through since it grew in small, short clumps, but Camoe made for the thickets.

Forging ahead, he slipped into a thick stand of unfamiliar, evergreen-like trees, far bushier and taller than any trees she'd seen on the farm or viewed in holos. Not even the great sequoia or redwoods compared. Farther than she could see, the thick fern-leaves and massive gray-brown trunks lorded over their surroundings from great heights. Dwarfing everything around them, they stood as stoic testaments to a land lush and vibrant.

As she advanced on the stand, she noticed the lodgepole pines trying to grow under the great branches were in danger of perishing, if they hadn't already. Caught in the behemoth's shade, lack of direct sunlight had turned their needles brown, while the bark had faded to a repulsive rust color. Dense carpets of moss, ferns, and sprawling crabgrass grew up the great trunks, adding to the mess she'd have to work her way past. The whole forest appeared to be dying, even the great trees.

A thought occurred to her. Burl didn't have knees. Something his dark creator had deigned unnecessary or lacked the skill to finish. In the Dark Citadel, the only time they'd had to crawl was the last vent shaft, but it was too dark for her to see how he accomplished it. Well, that and she'd fallen asleep. But outdoors, away from the citadel, it looked like crawling was going to be required often. How did he do it? She stopped and looked back.

A moment later, her curiosity was sated. Falling deftly to the ground as if commanded to perform Dad's morning ritual of pushups before her mom's disappearance, Burl crawled forward on his hands and toes like a bug going under tree limbs and deadfall. When the debris became lower still, he simply went down to his elbows with apparent ease. Thankfully, he did have elbows. Burl made a bit louder noise than she cared for, but at least he seemed to be able to keep up.

Jade put her concerns aside for the time being: slipping through the brambles quietly took all her concentration. Perspiration beaded her brow. With any luck, she was getting better at it: Their lives depended on it. If only she could make Burl understand the need for stealth. She paused. Why couldn't she? Burl had already proven he was capable of understanding her to a degree, even if he couldn't speak.

Crawling near her, Burl paused, too, looking up like an obedient pet waiting for a signal from his master. Jade immediately felt guilty for the comparison. She wasn't his master. Only the rich kept pets, with most of them connected to the king's administration in some way. Besides, a pet would have emotion visible in the eyes, such as devotion.

Burl's yellow-orange eyes were devoid of *any* emotion, as impassioned as a wind-up doll. Yet, his eyes glinted with an inner fire. How was she going to convey to her mute friend the need for silence? *Now there's a paradox,* Jade thought and then pushed it from her mind. Camoe was widening the distance between them every second that passed.

An idea occurred to her to hold a finger to her lips. Except Burl didn't have lips, or a mouth, for that matter. Putting her hands over her ears wouldn't do any good either. Burl had no ears, not even charcoal drawn ones. He did respond to her commands well enough through either intuitive sight reasoning or signal recognition—likely, some form of both. She was at a loss what to do. *Wait!*

Eager, Jade motioned Burl to keep his eyes on her, and then using exaggerated motions, she performed her best imitation of a feline stalking prey. Three times, she went through the routine, making sure Burl kept his gaze locked on her.

Satisfied the raggedy man had at least wondered if she was losing her mind—if he knew what one was—she continued after Camoe, concentrating on stalking like a feline but only on two feet. Either Burl got the message or he didn't. Before she'd gone very far, she found that stalking worked well with the toe-to-heel walking, making it easier to be quiet, particularly when navigating thicker areas for some reason.

Contorting around several entwined branches and deadfall a few hours later—the forest was looking further desiccated the farther they went—she was surprised to emerge in a small meadow. Relief flooded through her. The small clearing would provide sanctuary from the arduous task of quiet walking, at least for a time. Camoe lay on his stomach, peering over a rock ledge below a cliff face. She crossed the clearing, hunching over when the edge popped into view.

Camoe's voice came to her, barely audible. "You will need to be prone. Keep your body outline hidden and your movements minimal."

Avoiding the bigger rocks and thorny shrubbery, Jade flattened out and crawled beside the druid. "What is it?" she whispered.

"Any other time I would not have come this close: there are safer places to keep an eye on the Dark Citadel's front door. However, I wanted you to see what we spoke about this morning. Behold, the Dark Gate."

Glancing over the edge, Jade hugged the ground. The Dark Gate was close, too close for her liking. A three-story drop would land her on top of the gate wall looming darkly below. She stared in awe. A hundred meters wide, the gate curved outward at its center a half kilometer away, back to span a narrow canyon.

Built with the same dark gray granite as the brooding mountain, the gate defied her imagination by its sheer size. Except "built" didn't seem like the right word. No stonework seams were visible, as if the gate had been sliced from the stone. Two gigantic, black iron doors stood closed halfway along each side of the center arc, hung on massive poles bored through the wall.

On the top of the wall, two huge gears lay immobile above the doors. Crenelated turrets lined the outer edge with many squat, sturdy-looking catapults placed behind them. Again, there were no seams or visible mortar lines on the turrets. Jade gazed wildly around. The gate, the gate wall, and even the massive gears appeared *carved out of the mountain*. The enormity of the task was staggering. How many years of backbreaking slave labor and slave lives had been lost in the construction of such a monstrosity?

Camoe gestured for her to look farther behind the gate. Raising her neck at an awkward angle, she looked up to see a second wall towered above the one below.

Jade wanted to sink into the ground. How had she missed it? Or had she? Not entirely, she'd thought of it as a cliff face when she'd first seen it, but it wasn't. It was a major fortification of the Dark Citadel proper. Four great doors were spaced evenly with room to slide open on one side. Gigantic stark reminders of the dreadful flying things Camoe had mentioned. He'd taken an awful chance in coming here. Anyone or any…*thing* was sure to spot them from high.

Pushing back from the edge, Jade crawled, her cheek touching the ground. Lifting her head only when necessary to clear rocks or debris, she snaked methodically around shrubs and higher deadfall, vaguely noting Burl standing at meadow's edge like a tree stump long forgotten. Oblivious to the sharp rocks and broken deadfall, she crawled until shelter behind a rock at the foot of one of the big desiccated trees enclosed her. Safe from hostile eyes, she sat with her back on the far side of the wide trunk. Pulling her knees up, she wrapped her arms around them and lowered her head to still her racing heart and shortness of breath.

She wanted to cry. How could anyone expect to survive on a world where evil had a stronghold of such magnitude as the Dark Citadel? It was too powerful. How would she survive, even with Camoe's help? After all, he'd lost the girl in the image. Why should she expect it to be any different for her?

Astura was much too dangerous. Sometime, somewhere in her travels searching for Crystalyn or the way home, she was bound to make a mistake, a critical mistake. One stupid, simple slipup was all it'd take. She'd die, violently.

The worst part was she was clueless as to how to stack the odds in her favor. This dark and violent world wasn't going to give her enough time to learn its ways. Her only defense was the ability to read images floating around a person. What good was that going to do?

The crack of breaking wood startled her. Camoe was bending small branches between his fists until they broke at a length he wanted. Burl stood close by.

Sounding as loud as a scream, at least to her it did, Camoe

snapped another twig. "Come, we forced our luck too much here. I want to put some distance between us and this place before dark fall." Content he'd made enough to start a fire at some future point, he tied them into a bundle and then tied the bundle to Burl's back.

"Camoe, can I ask you something? You've never told me about the girl in the image. Who was she?"

Reaching for his leather bag he'd hung on a lower tree branch, Camoe stiffened. His arm fell limp to his side. Moments passed. She was about to tell him never mind when he suddenly snatched the bag and stalked into the forest. "She was my daughter" hung in the air after him.

Jade scrambled after him. Compassion, respect for his privacy, and questions about all of it warred in her mind.

DO'BRIENI

Two short steps and Crystalyn would be beyond going back. Two small fir tree branches stood between her and the voice she had heard in her mind. Two short breaths and she'd finally come face to face with the warden who waited in the small meadow ringed with trees. She knew the precise layout of the clearing; the image was still vivid in her mind, yet she had apprehension. The being that had projected the image remained a mystery.

She sensed the impatience from the warden, who'd kept a patient vigil while she'd regained strength for days, maintaining a self-inflicted silence, telepathic or otherwise. The spiderbees had taken a toll on her. Much natural and magical healing had been required to keep her alive. The Lore Mother had done what she could, but the wound refused to close.

She'd kept it from the others, letting them believe she was on the mend so as not to further delay the search for Jade. If not for the spiderbees' weakness to *wood,* of all things, she wouldn't be here, at least not in the corporeal sense. Every living thing has to have a weakness—as her dad would say—or it would take over the world. The natural makeup of the spiderbees—or leechers, as the natives called the creatures—apparently had a resistance to magic, since they were an aberration to the Flow. At some point in the past, they'd fed from the Flow or a User had created them.

Either way, it made them magical creatures that had proliferated on their own, and they were not unique. The Lore Mother had warned there were other species. Had it not been for Lore Rayna's Terra magic and Cudgel's wooden weapon, she would've been lost. Or would she?

The memory of the beautiful, beckoning light was fading, but she'd carry the sense of great loss from not reaching the golden light with her from now on. She'd been so close to having all the trials of her past life stripped from her, as if they'd never been. Such things didn't exist there in the light.

Shouldering through prickly—yet green and soft—pine needle branches, she took a few steps forward and then paused. She was close enough she didn't need the link to sense the excitement bubbling from the being nearby. Doubts assailed her. What if the warden didn't realize who she was and attacked? Should she have a symbol ready? After all, there was only the assurance of a voice in her mind that no harm would befall her.

No, she was creating fears where none should be. There was no animosity from the warden, only excitement tinged with its own apprehension.

It was time to get on with it.

Brushing past a final tree branch, she slipped into the clearing and then paused, gaping in awe.

Lying sedately, a huge canine-like being sprawled on top of a patch of meadow grass, reminding her of the great mastiff statue she had catalogued once for Ruena. The short and glossy sienna fur was similar to the fur of a golden Labrador the farm scientists had retained, but any resemblance ended there. Four massive paws supported thick claws.

The being's broad back and wide head bore a set of powerful jaws that stood out on a trim face, which reminded her of the holographic of the northern wolf. The eyes—hourglass in shape—were a vivid amber, gazing at her with a vast and somber intelligence. Otherworldly and beautiful, it was beyond what she could have imagined.

Love blended with joy bombarded her mind. Coming in torrents faster and faster, it built to a crescendo too pure to absorb, too pure not to try, yet too strong to grasp, and she let it flow past. It was too intense. Torrent after torrent slammed into her mind with no pause between. Stronger and stronger they washed over her self-awareness. Soon, there was only joy and an unabashed love.

Crystalyn relished the love. She opened herself fully to it. The torrent swept her up. A profound joy frolicked around her, beside her, with her. For the first time in her life, there wasn't a thing wrong, no doubts from the past, no anxieties of the current situation, and no frets for a better future. Not one worry, only unadulterated joy.

It frightened her. There were always anxieties. Instinctively, she slowed the flow to a trickle by reducing the size of the link to her. The clearing sprang into clarity. She was on her knees looking into the yellow, hourglass eyes of the warden an arm's length before her. Was it truly from this mortal dimension? Or was it astral by nature?

Either way it didn't matter. She couldn't take such a strong, emotion-laden assault; she was afraid her individual emotions would be laid bare, and she'd revert to her preadolescent state where anyone could see what was happening inside her mind by the expressions on her face...before she'd had her barriers in place, when life wasn't so complicated. Worse, be wiped clean. *"Please, don't do that again. Your feelings are quite strong and a bit...overpowering."*

Bemusement flowed through the link, gaining in intensity. Now she knew how to handle it. Gathering her will, she reduced the link and slowed the flow substantially. Bemusement switched to one of respect and a sense of something else...awe, perhaps, tinged with worry.

"I meant no harm, Do'brieni. I was simply overjoyed to find my link mate so soon. Please, accept my apologies. I'm still considered young by my people. I erroneously allowed my exuberance to get the better of me. Will you allow me to make amends?"

"You can start by telling me how we are able to communicate without words."

Confusion flowed in. *"You and I share a link."*

"I've gathered that," Crystalyn thought, climbing to her feet. A twinge from her stomach brought her hand down to cover the wound. Many days and nights would be required for the spiderbee's puncture to heal. The wound should have stopped oozing blood by now. Perhaps

when she felt stronger, she would see to it herself instead of relying on Lore Rayna.

Right now, questions for the lovely creature in front of her burned laser-deep in her mind. *"Why don't you speak normally, using your voice? Why don't I?"*

"You would not comprehend my voice, as I would not understand you. The link converts human words to familiar images for me."

Now it was her turn to be confused. How could she be hearing *images?* It didn't matter. As long as they could communicate, she was glad. *"Are there many who live on this world such as you?"*

"We are dwindling...too few...too few. I am one of only two dozen males that remain. Females do not link."

"What happened to all of you?"

Savage anger and deep sadness flowed through in a rush. *"Users have hunted our males for ages. They hope to duplicate the telepathic links we establish with humans so they will not have the limitation of having to perform a contacting. The Flow drain on the person using the Flow is substantial, so as a rule, they are short in length and only used when necessary. They have done this by attempting to forge an unnatural link with us by torture, or magical coercion, or both, in the hopes of gaining the ability to use it for their own ends. Thankfully, they seem to have given up such attempts recently. That coupled with our low birth rate has taken a toll."*

Crystalyn felt the sadness down to her core for the being. Life must have been so hard. On an impulse, she sent a feeling of empathy through the link. Gratitude flowed back. *"I should've asked this first. Where do you hail from? The Lore Mother hasn't spoken much about you. What do I call you?"*

"As your ancient Valen female mentioned, I belong to a solitary race known as wardens. I am from the oldest clan. For longer than the eldest of the White Fur clan remembers, we've held vigil against evil, whether it derives from light or dark. As for my designation, it's entirely too long for a human to pronounce since it contains much

ancestral lineage. I've shortened it to Broth for you. In time, you may learn my full name."

Crystalyn tried the name aloud. "Broth it is, then. I like it very much. It suits you." Something Broth had said earlier, coupled with his last statement, clicked together. "Wait! You know what the Lore Mother spoke? You understand what I'm saying when I say it aloud? You can hear what others say to me?"

Amusement and affection brushed her mind. *"Of course, I understand. I can hear quite well, actually. As I send, the link converts human words into images I comprehend."*

"So I'm not limited to communicating with you through the link?"

Additional amusement touched her mind. *"No, only I am 'limited' to communicating this way since you would not understand my language."*

"Can't you use your thought projection on others?" she said, trying it aloud.

"Thought projection? That's an astute way of putting it." A warm feeling of approval mixed with pride flowed through her mind. *"We males link once in a lifetime. In time, we shall be so heavily linked it would be devastating to us both. I would not survive it, but you may, should I go to meet my ancestors. Humans have adaptive minds and, as such, fare better."*

Crystalyn smiled with affection. A thought occurred to her. "So that means no one can really tell you to do something except me? You could simply ignore it as if you didn't understand." The Lore Mother had raised her ire for much of the past few days with her increasing commands to eat and rest. Even Lore Rayna had begun to throw words out intended for her compliance. As if she ever would comply.

"I suppose so. You would have to be within hearing of the command, though. It's through you that the link converts the images."

"Come, I'll introduce you to the others. The Lore Mother and Lore Rayna are not going to like it when you don't respond to their commands. This should be interesting."

"Why would they take an interest in commanding me?"

"It's what females of any race do when they get together. They'll be angry when you listen only to me. This should be fun!"

"I don't understand. What is the advantage to making them angry?"

"Never mind, they're anxious to meet you. Let's go."

Flexing powerful front shoulders and massive rear haunches, Broth sprang to his feet. A twinge of fear passed through her: Broth's powerful jaws were suddenly close. She inhaled his warm, sour breath. Her eyes fell on a patch of white that stood out from his sleek sienna fur under his jaws. She touched it, feeling the soft silky fur, short enough she almost thought of it as skin.

Wrapping her arms around Broth's thick neck, she pressed her head against his, holding him in a fierce embrace. As if cementing a bond, a heady, unrestricted love flowed. Things were right for once; she'd found a friend she could trust without reservation.

How long they stood that way, she couldn't tell. Finally, she pulled her arms free and stepped back. Broth shook, muscles rippling. As he bounded to her side, they began the trek toward camp in silence. For a time, nothing else conveyed or projected was required; contentment laced with excitement flowed through the link, giving her a great sense of comfort. For the first time since stepping through the Sapphire Gate, she was glad to be on this world.

The camp's occupants arose to their feet as she strode to the small cooking fire with the warden trailing close behind. The Lore Mother and Lore Rayna each uttered a small cry. Cudgel and Hastel cursed. Atoi stood, silent and impassive.

Crystalyn halted near the fire. Broth pushed his broad head over her shoulder. She smiled. The action seemed so puppyish but completely natural at the same time. Scratching under the warden's offered jaw, she regarded her little group.

Cudgel's right hand reached over his shoulder to grip the iron-tipped club strapped to his back. By contrast, Hastel appeared calm, standing in his customary spot slightly behind Atoi; both of his battle axes hung in the two leather sheaths at each hip, and the crossbow straps crisscrossed diagonally across his broad chest. Atoi stood gazing back at her with those overlarge almond-shaped green eyes, oblivious to the big canine head hovering above her shoulder.

The Lore Mother stepped out from behind Lore Rayna. "A little advance notice before trotting a warden into camp would have been respectful, daughter," she said.

Crystalyn turned her head to regard the canine head plopped over her shoulder. Perhaps she was imagining things, but Crystalyn could almost swear Broth's canine jaws lifted for a wide grin.

"Please, My Lord, how may we serve you in our meager camp?" the Lore Mother asked.

"Lord? Why do you address him as lord, Mother?" Crystalyn asked. The mother-daughter way of speaking was hard for her to get used to; she wasn't at all certain how well it was working.

Lore Rayna stood in front of the Lore Mother, her green dress gyrating in distress, revealing too much, again. "How can you not know? The color of his fur denotes him as a warden noble, or higher. A link with a warden is a rare and precious occurrence, but you should be aware of your linking to someone of high station. Nobles have only linked once or twice through their history."

"Is this true?" Crystalyn sent.

"It is part of our ways, yes."

"Why didn't you tell me?"

"It is of the smallest importance. We are link mates. Nothing else need be significant."

Crystalyn felt a slight letdown. It was doubtful the Lore Mother or Lore Rayna would try to boss nobility around. What else had Broth failed to mention?

Her stomach rumbled. The time for food was drawing near; eating and sleeping would help with the healing. Tomorrow, she'd insist on continuing toward Surbo, recovered or not. Her newfound companion would aid greatly in her search for Jade, royalty or not.

QUIET FOOTSTEPS

Jade gazed at the horizon from high on the mountainside. The twilight of first light failed to overrun the brightest eastern stars still clinging stubbornly to the gray sky. Sunlight would eventually win; each star would wink out one by stubborn one. Perhaps one or two of them would be a planet reflecting the sun, in which case they'd hang around longer. Possibly. Astronomy had never been her passion. Only those living on High Realm bothered with it at all.

Turning her back on the eastern sky, she searched for Camoe, marveling how he was able to wrap the terrain around him. Be it dark, or full light, it never seemed to matter; he vanished without a sound, not even a sigh of wind left whispering behind wherever he moved.

The frigid predawn air smelled fresh with the scents of evergreens and ferns that mixed with a dewy, rich soil. They'd made camp at one of the few areas still vibrant with life. Her stiff muscles welcomed the movement, loosening with each step. She felt alert and invigorated after a night spent slumbering on a bed of soft pine needles.

Burl fell in behind her, stepping from the deep shadows of one of the monstrous green trees. His presence failed to surprise her now since the raggedy man never slept. She knew he watched over her while she slept, though she wasn't sure if the thought comforted her or not.

She was positive he wasn't inherently evil, though the Dark User who had created him in all probability was, and Camoe was likely correct about that. So far, the Green Writhe druid had rarely been wrong. The dark creation might still be under the control of its creator.

How could she know Burl wouldn't bludgeon her to death in her sleep?

He wouldn't. What was wrong with her this morning? She'd been over it before in her mind. Running from death, or worse, the past three full days was bringing out her morbid tendencies again. Why not? This whole world was turning out morbid.

She found Camoe by accident. Waiting for brighter light to emerge from behind the Dark Citadel, she paused beside a rock she was thinking about sitting on. The rock decided to stand. Camoe's quiet, raspy voice broke through the brisk air, leaving a trail of icy vapor behind. "It is good I did not have to wake you. We should be pressing onward. I want to speak with the monks at Brown Recluse before three days have passed."

Her ears perked at the mention of a destination. "You haven't spoken much about the place. Why are we going there, again?"

Camoe blew a soft breath. "The monks are knowledgeable in many things. Brown Recluse has nurtured many scholars. Only the Vibrant Vale lore masters have bested them with their knowledge base in written form. Besides, the monks hear things…they may have heard of your sister, but I make no promise of their aid. They can be…temperamental, at times."

Jade grew excited. As bossy as Crystalyn was, Jade couldn't wait to see her. Her stomach burned as she thought about her big sister. She missed her so much. And Dad, it would be wonderful to see him soon. "Okay, we should get going then. It's getting light enough. I think I can move faster with less noise now."

Camoe's silver head swung toward her. She hated not being able to see his eyes. Were they blue or gray? "As I said, I make no promises. The monks owe me, but that does not mean they will help us. They are a solitary lot and view visitors with disdain and suspicion. Even so, I have strong ties there, enough we can gather information about your sister. Someone surely has heard about her on this world. The monks pride themselves on keeping up with most Users."

"I don't know if she is a User. Just like I don't know if I am. I'll have to accept your opinion on that, since you keep saying so."

"Your sister brought you here by reading symbols in a book, did she not?" Camoe asked. Jade didn't need to see a frown crease his forehead to know it was there. "Those symbols are conduits leading back to a User, they have to be. It takes someone quite strong in accessing the Flow, or something with similar magical properties, to invoke one in the first place."

Jade hesitated. Could Crystalyn be a User? It hadn't seemed that way, not even when she touched the gateway Crystalyn had brought to life. Did that fact alone mean her sister was a User? Did her own visions make her a User? No. It didn't feel right. Crystalyn's and her powers were different in some profound way. Exactly how, she wasn't certain. She wasn't going to disagree, though. The last thing she wanted was to alienate Camoe. He'd saved her several times, like Burl. A chill swept up her spine, leaving a shudder in its wake. Without her two companions, this new world of Astura would've ended her life in a matter of hours, or sooner. All she wanted was to find her sister and go home.

Camoe ended their conversation by walking off into the trees. Jade followed. Once again, she concentrated on keeping up and staying quiet. Before going very far, she could tell she was getting better at it. After spending days crashing through one forest or another, stealth was becoming second nature.

Insidious shale rockslides, lichen-covered boulder fields, and fire-starter-dry pine needles all lay soundlessly behind them as she slipped through yet another pocket of pines, only to pull up short. Spreading steeply downhill, blackened, splintered trees, many times thicker than her waist, rested on massive boulders, mixed with muddy dirt mounds.

The deadfall, varying from sticks to log-sized branches, jutted from the mix or lay crisscrossed like giant, forgotten beaver dams filling a great gully, like the many desolate ones on the farm. The farm terraformers had recreated the dams since the industrious animals that'd once made them were long extinct. She still felt sadness for the woodland creatures.

Sickly willows and thick brown grasses pushed up through the debris field, adding to the chaos. Water burbled somewhere underneath it all. Camoe had led them to the top of a massive avalanche area, recent from the looks of it. Jade studied the slide with dread. Dark holes, large enough to swallow a man, gaped wide. Smaller holes, wide enough to break a leg, dotted the area. Camoe could not possibly want to climb down it, could he? Rappelling down a cliff might be less dangerous. Besides, the sun had nearly sunk down to the western slope.

The druid stood on a small animal trail, looking left and right. The woodland creatures had begun to adapt to the slide by veering to either side, but Camoe looked unhappy with either choice.

"What is it?"

"The path used to step down this ravine. The slope was a gentle, easy climb down, yet thick enough to provide good cover. It was also the last good source of drinking water for a long while. Now I am uncertain of our next course of action."

"How are we doing with water?"

"Used with care, we should be able to stretch it through two sunsets."

"Why don't we go around it then? Surely two will be enough."

"Two days will not see us at the bottom of the plateau. Worse than that, it would expose us to the Dark Road for much of the passage. I would hate to chance it, yet I see no other way. We cannot take the left path: the Molting River feeding Fetid Fume Swamp lies in our way. Most creatures living beside the river are carnivorous along with a few in the swamps. Almost all creatures and flora in both areas are poisonous to consume; sustenance is scarce. Those ways are not a choice I care to take."

"Well, what then? We can't go back."

"No, there is no going back, but the Dark Road is risky, even with darkness as cover—" He grew quiet, staring into the distance.

Jade followed his gaze, her breath skipping a heartbeat and then two. The mountainside changed drastically not far downhill from where the druid stood. The trees grew sparse and stunted. The blackened trees clung defiantly to a bald, rocky hillside sloping ever steeper, toward a treacherous cliffside. The rocks looked like the same type of black stone as the Dark Citadel's exterior. Her stomach sank. Even after grueling days of sneaking through an overgrown, dying forest, they still hadn't cleared the Dark Lands. How far did they have to go to leave this dreadful place? The hillside was steep without anything resembling a trail. How would they ever make it down intact?

The sharp crack of a branch breaking brought Jade out of her reverie.

"Blast your creature! What is it doing now? We cannot go that way!"

Marching to the debris field's edge, Burl high-stepped over a large mound of overhanging deadfall and vanished.

"Burl!" Jade screamed. She ran to the edge of the debris mound on the heels of the druid.

Pausing on an overhang long enough to glance down, Camoe dropped over the edge and then reappeared at the far side of a narrow ledge below. He knelt, looking down from there. "Your creature lives. He is climbing down some rubble."

Jade slowed, choosing her route to the overhanging edge with care. There was a drop of over twice her height onto the narrow ledge the druid stood on. Beyond it, hundreds of feet of open space awaited. There wasn't much space on the ledge, so she'd have to pick her landing with care. Selecting a spot with fewer branches buried in dirt, she bent her knees and then stepped from the overhang.

Missing the mark slightly, she landed hard, staggering to maintain her footing. A loose branch snapped under her foot, tearing a slash in her jeans. Something warm trickled down her leg. Choosing to ignore it, she joined her companion looking over the edge.

Facing the mountainside, Burl was sliding down the debris-filled ravine by gripping deadfall and rocks and even digging into the mountainside with one hand to support his dangling legs and slow his descent.

Jade marveled anew at Burl's strength and his ingenuity in working around his inflexible legs.

Burl reached a small boulder-filled ledge after a few minutes. Dropping his arms to the side, he stood immobile, gazing at the hillside.

"I suppose your creature wants us to go down there. Who is leading whom here? I do not like it," Camoe said, starting to climb down. "This could not have been here long. Something is not right."

"What do you mean?" Jade asked. She followed Burl's example, using logs and half-buried branches as a makeshift ladder to work her way down to the next big ledge. After a short while, her arms and legs ached from the effort.

Camoe reached for a handhold below her, climbing down with the same expert skill with which he did nearly everything. "No talking. Concentrate on maintaining a firm grip. If you slip, you'll take us both. I do not wish to be impaled on some of those sharper branches."

The druid was right. Much of the jagged deadfall below was sharp enough to puncture flesh or gash a leg.

Sunlight wore into twilight with much the same repetitive action; Jade stuck with three points of contact, though it forced her companions to wait at every landing. She wasn't about to be the one to cause an impalement. As careful as she was, there were still incidents where a rock failed to hold her weight or a branch wasn't as strong as it looked. Each time she had to scramble for another hold to keep from falling, each one caused her to expend her dwindling energy and left her clinging to the mountain like an insect caught in a strong wind.

In the late afternoon, she stretched to full length, reaching for a root. The rock supporting her feet tore away from the mountainside. She dangled for a moment by the root before it too pulled free. She began to slide. Frantically, she looked for something to grab, but there was nothing. Dirt and rock carried her down the slope on her hands and knees, gaining speed. Twisting, she landed on her backside in time to finish the slide with a gentle stop on the widest debris ledge they'd encountered so far. Camoe rested, while Burl stood stoically in the waning sunlight, gazing her direction, his orange eyes revealing nothing.

Camoe's blue eyes twinkled. "Nice arrival, wish I had thought of it. But it makes a lot of clatter."

Jade dusted off her bottom, throwing the druid a quick glare, though she'd have rather been immature and stuck her tongue out at him. "Are we near the bottom yet? I'm thirsty and I need to eat something."

"I should think. Well over two-thirds, I would estimate," Camoe said, passing her a flask of water. "It has been rough, but I think your friend may have helped us out by taking off this way. The Dark Road is dangerous, doubly so at the fall of darkness."

"So you said before. What is the Dark Road?" Jade tilted her head back. She squeezed the flask, taking a long drink. Warm and tepid, the water was still refreshing. Camoe motioned for her to open her bag. She removed two meat pies along with two generous slices of the cheeses taken from the citadel's kitchen. Well, Burl's kitchen, as she liked to think of it. Passing Camoe his share, she chewed her pie, waiting for him to continue.

The druid swallowed the last of his food before continuing. "We have been traveling across a plateau the size of a small continent since leaving the Dark Citadel. I doubt you have anything as large on your home world."

"I don't know about that. You've never seen the Mountain," Jade said, nibbling on her cheese. *Our greatest failed achievement,* she thought.

Camoe's eyes flickered at her comment, but he went on as if it was of no consequence. "There is something I do not believe you realize. The plateau *is* the Dark Citadel."

Jade almost choked on her pie. She grappled with the enormity of his statement. "So we're still on the Dark Citadel after all this time? Does that mean there could be an entrance to it nearby?"

"Yes or an exit. For all I know, there is one hidden around here.

But there are some things much older and far worse than the citadel nearby, and we have many days of travel left to get through the dark land of Virun after we reach the plateau's bottom." Camoe dusted crumbs off his leather tunic. "The Fetid Fume Swamps *and* some of Brown Recluse are part of it."

"So the Dark Road is the main thoroughfare to and from the Dark Citadel?" Jade popped the last bite of cheese in her mouth savoring its rich flavor, though she wasn't happy with what she was hearing. The Dark Citadel's reach was long. She'd hoped that once they escaped the caverns the worst was over. Now she wasn't so certain.

"Yes, it extends the length of Virun. Caught on or near the road is certain death, they would know immediately we are not in service to the great lord. After dispatching those guards, they are pursuing us. Our best hope is they believe us still in the tunnels underneath the citadel with no way out."

The cheese grew bitter in her mouth. Chewing slowly, she forced it down. *He mentions violence so casually,* she thought. "Do we really have a chance of escaping this?" she asked quietly.

He gazed at her for a moment, his weathered face stoic. "We have been doing okay so far, but we have still got some distance to go. We had better get moving. It will be dark before long." Pushing away from the mountain, he began the trek across the debris mound. He hesitated. "One other thing—"

"Yes?"

"You have done well, in fact, very well, so far."

Jade sat a minute longer, watching him spring from rock to rock across the mound. Had he just given her a compliment? It certainly sounded like one, yet she must've not heard him right. She most definitely hadn't done well since her arrival. The flickers had almost claimed her, not to mention the dominion wraith. Burl had twice had to carry her or she wouldn't have made it this far.

She climbed to her feet, starting across the mound, keeping to the few grassy spots with soil underneath, following Camoe's example.

She felt much better after the short rest, and the unexpected conversation that ensued. It was nice to have the taciturn druid's approval; she relied on him beyond what she cared to admit.

Burl, too, even without a voice, was a comforting and rock-steady companion to have near her. Perhaps together, they'd make it out of Virun alive. Right now, she didn't want anything else. She was anxious to begin the search for her sister, but to do that, they had to escape from Virun's apparent long reach.

Camoe paused at yet another edge. Going to one knee, he studied the path of descent with care. Jade jumped to the next mound of soil.

There was just enough time to let out a yelp of surprise before the world fell out from under her.

Plummeting into darkness, she slammed into frigid water.

NOT RUN BACK

Broth padded behind Crystalyn as she rounded the fire pit, making her way to the naturists' camp by the wagon. The camp was set away from the rest of them for reasons not given, though she suspected they wanted privacy for the mysterious contents of the crate. Something she was ready to discuss, among other things.

The Lore Mother stirred a simmering pot over a fire, not looking up from the task when Crystalyn halted opposite her. Settling in for a wait, Crystalyn gazed around the naturists' orderly camp. Lore Rayna sat rigid on a log nearby, her face a thundercloud. Cudgel slathered something dark on one side of the hub of the wagon wheel while glancing surreptitiously now and then at Lore Rayna. There was trouble between nature's children, it seemed.

Stirring the pot a final time, the Lore Mother removed the spoon and lifted it away from the fire, setting it on a rock to let it cool. Satisfied it would remain where she wanted, the old woman acknowledged her presence with a frown, her hands going to her hips. "What is it?"

"What are you cooking?" Crystalyn asked. She'd get around to the significant part soon enough; besides, she did want to know what the wizened woman had made. It smelled…exotic.

Her brow smoothing, the Lore Mother looked abashed. "Something I should have taken the time to make once we climbed higher into these wild lands—a poultice to rub on the horses. Carnivores do not like the smell of it, though it should deter the smaller ones simply by having your young prince around." She inclined her head toward Broth.

Broth sat on his rear haunches beside her, and Crystalyn smiled at him, sending a query laced with amusement through the link. *"Are your princely duties going to take you away from me?"*

Embarrassment tinged with…apprehension flowed back to her. *"There are many females searching for me to perform my…duty. My sire has sent them after me to ensure a continuing bloodline. Please do not reveal this to anyone. Ask the Valen to refrain from naming me prince outside of your clan here, please."*

Crystalyn was mildly shocked. She'd meant the question as a jest. *"Your secret is safe with me for now. However—"*

"Yes, my Do'brieni?"

"There may come a time when I will ask you to fulfill your sire's wish."

An image of Broth racing away from camp flowed briefly through the link.

Crystalyn sent an image of her standing in the way of his escape path with her hands on her hips.

Broth's next image showed the warden skidding to a halt, surprise dropping his jaw.

Crystalyn laughed.

The Lore Mother glanced at her sharply, and then her glowing eyes settled on Broth, her lips pursed. Finally, she set the wooden ladle on a rock and stretched. Crystalyn heard the crack of several bones shifting into place. "Though you carry a smile, I am certain you did not seek me out to learn solely of my concoctions, my daughter."

Crystalyn's amusement faded. "I want to know about the spiderbees, I mean, leechers. Are they native to Astura? Will we encounter others? I suppose I most want to know about those that are unaffected by my symbols, Mother."

The Lore Mother pulled a rag from her white dress to dab at her sweat- and ash-stained face. "I am afraid so. Most we know how to combat, as we did with the…spiderbees—I like your word for them better. However, a few seem impervious to any damage. Those we have learned to avoid."

Lore Rayna's face had flushed deeper with every word throughout the conversation. "Stop your foolishness, outlander. Avoid unfamiliar creatures altogether."

Crystalyn ignored her, as they had come to do in both camps. Lore Rayna's scathing remarks had gotten to everyone. Either the surliness was worse since the warden's arrival or no one had noticed how bad it was before. Whichever the case, Lore Rayna grew agitated when Broth was close, and her harsh words would bite at everyone but him, for reasons known only to the big naturist. Lore Rayna completely ignored the warden as if he were an apparition she refused to acknowledge. Crystalyn was getting tired of arguing with her—so was everyone else in her little group.

The Lore Mother continued the conversation. "For instance, let us talk about the krell. It requires steel or lead to dispatch the krell, the Flow has no effect on them. Some are dark creations that have destroyed their creator to gain freedom, but that is another discussion. For now, you should be aware when passing through known areas, it is advisable for a User to travel with soldiers if the User has not trained with a weapon, which most do not. The sand krell are the worst; only an infused weapon of some sort will damage one. As bad as those— while rare—are the tree dragons. Their teeth and claws are so poisonous men have died from the mere threat of being slashed by them when spotting them among their habitat, but any weapon or magic may damage them."

"What? Are you serious?" Crystalyn asked.

Roaring with mirth, Cudgel laughed.

The Lore Mother smiled. "No, but I did want to lighten the tone a little. The tree dragon's poison will kill a strong man in twelve heartbeats or less, they are quite deadly. There are many other menaces on Astura; all are region specific. For now, I shall speak only of those dangers we may encounter on our journey to the White Lands, as we make our way to Surbo."

"That's another thing: I know you're concerned with me healing a while longer, but we should be moving on. I have to find my sister,"

Crystalyn said.

"Yes, yes, we should get moving, to Surbo. We have to go," Lore Rayna interjected.

The Lore Mother turned to her student, a frown creasing her forehead. "Your constant interruptions are going too far, daughter. We have been over this not long ago, yet there you are doing it again. You will desist at once."

Lore Rayna's full lips compressed to a thin line, but she said nothing.

Cudgel's deep voice rumbled through the cool evening air. "Why do you persist with that, Rayne? What's the big hurry? We will get there in good time."

Drawing a deep breath, Lore Rayna's face looked ready to burst. "Now who is interrupting when he should be repairing the wagon? No one permitted you to speak. You take too long. Do not dawdle or I will do it for you." Her voice gained in intensity with the last word.

Cudgel stiffened. Reaching for a gob of the black substance, he growled a reply, his words as rigid as his body. "I'm going as fast as the job allows. You can work on the other side if you think you can do better."

"I'll get the other side as soon as I've watered the horses," Hastel called. His raspy voice came from out of the trees on the far side of camp, a stark testament to how far their words carried.

"Stop it, Rayna, that is enough! We've spoken of this far too much as it is. I will decide when Crystalyn is travel ready. Only then will we continue our journey." The Lore Mother's harsh words rang through the camp.

Lore Rayna's lips curled. "And when shall that be? Do we leave tomorrow, the next day, or the two after that? Why has the child burdened us by choosing to fight everything that moves? Even our youngest know better than to stray too close to misted water. We have to keep moving."

Beyond what the situation probably merited, Crystalyn was angry. Nevertheless, she'd had it with their squabbles. "Hold on, all of you! *I* decide when *I'm* good enough to travel, no one else. *We* leave at first light, with or without the three of you." Folding her arms at her waist, she glanced around the camp.

"Yes, let us leave. We have to keep moving," Lore Rayna agreed.

The whole conversation made Crystalyn querulous. As her eyes fell upon the crate beside the Lore Mother's tent, her anger grew. "As I said, we leave in the morning. Now you're either going to tell me, *the rest of us,* what's in the bloody crate, or you can pack it on your back from here on. We're taking the wagon and horses, they're ours."

The camp stilled, even Lore Rayna quieted. The Lore Mother faced her in stony silence for many moments. Crystalyn's anger lessened, she wondered if she'd gone too far. Finally, the Lore Mother looked away. "I suppose it is time you knew. It is taxing keeping the Child of Dark away from it, anyway. Or do you prefer the challenge, Atoi?" she asked, turning toward the crate.

Atoi looked up from where she squatted beside the crate. Pulling a lock pick from the keyhole, she straightened.

The Lore Mother's long stride brought her beside Atoi before she could step back from the crate.

Crystalyn hurried to Atoi's side, and Broth padded over with her.

Removing an iron key on a chain from her bosom and around her neck, the Lore Mother's head swiveled between those in view. "I want everyone's word you will not speak of what you see until I say it is safe to do so. Do we all agree on this?"

"Of course, we do," Crystalyn said, eager to get on with it. Finally, they were getting somewhere.

"Do not do it, Mother!" Lore Rayna exclaimed.

Cudgel stood up from the wagon's hub. "Are you sure about this, Old Mother?"

"Of course, I'm not," the Lore Mother said. "But you cannot carry it on your shoulders the rest of the way to Surbo, strong as they may be." Bending, she prepared to insert the key.

"It's unlocked," Atoi said, quietly.

The Lore Mother frowned sharply at Atoi. Without another word, she slipped the key's chain over her head and snapped the lock downward with a loud chink. Removing it from its hasp, she flung the hinged door against the tent.

Crystalyn gasped. Packed with wood chips, a pair of topaz crystal obelisks gleamed inside. She glared at the Lore Mother. "You had these this whole time and never told me?"

The Lore Mother shrugged. "That was the idea, dear. The fewer privy to the gate's existence, the safer for the obelisks, they are quite valuable. This set alone would purchase a duke's keep and the servants to maintain them, along with the mercenary cost to hold a besieging border kingdom at bay."

"Can I use them to return to my world, Mother?"

"I am afraid not, dear. This gate is attuned to one location, a location best kept secret." Crystalyn opened her mouth to ask where, but the Lore Mother held up her hand. "I know you will never be satisfied to leave it at that, but you will have to for now. In time, you may gain additional knowledge, but right now, I cannot, and will not, speak of it without guarded walls."

Gazing at the crystals, Crystalyn frowned. If they wouldn't help her return home after she'd found Jade, what good were they?

Atoi's tone was dispassionate. "I am not surprised by their subterfuge, Crystalyn. The three of them wear secrets like a favorite shawl they fear to lend."

Hastel took up a position behind Atoi. "We don't want your shawls."

At least Hastel and Atoi seemed to be part of her team. She was grateful for that. "Yes, we do, Hastel. I don't expect to know all their secrets, but I do expect some respect, and I will have it. This secret would've been safe with us from the start. Their…the Lore Mother's lack of trust is misguided."

Lore Rayna jumped to her feet. Drawing an arrow to her bow in one fluid motion, she leveled the razor-sharp tip at Crystalyn's breast. "What we and the Lore Mother do is for our discretion. You *will* show the Lore Mother *respect* before your own. I have warned you for the last time," she said, pulling the bowstring to her bosom.

Crystalyn was astounded. After all she'd done, Lore Rayna drew on her?

Without warning, Broth leapt. Stretching out a front paw, his great claws raked the bow, slicing the string. A loud twang split the air, as the warden dropped to the ground, dragging the bow with him.

Grunting in surprise, Lore Rayna's forearms thickened, taking on a wooden, branch-like quality, her fingers forming pointed stakes. Without pause, the big woman swung at the warden.

"Broth!" Crystalyn screamed.

Front shoulders tangled in the longbow, the warden leapt backward on his two rear legs but didn't get far. Lore Rayna charged, executing another swing. "No!" Crystalyn screamed again.

Cudgel leapt between the two, his club taking the brunt of Lore Rayna's swing. "Rayne! What are you doing? You're attacking a *warden*!" he yelled, his tone aghast.

Ignoring him, Lore Rayna rained blow after blow upon Cudgel's weapon.

His hands centered on the iron-tipped club, Cudgel spun the ends back and forth, blocking every blow with expert skill.

"Daughter!" the Lore Mother shouted, her voice a boom. "Cease this immediately!"

Lore Rayna snarled. Her arms doubled in size and elongated as her stake fingers branched tree-like outward, seeking a way around the club to the man behind it. Thick, root-like vines formed from her feet; ripping through the humus ground, they circled around the warrior, making for the one he protected.

Crystalyn released her knockback symbol. The three silver concentric rings smashed into the big woman, pushed her back across the meadow, and thumped her to the ground. The leaves on Lore Rayna's dress rippled as the concussive wave passed over, blowing soil, plants, and small rocks high in the air, forming a dense cloud of debris. At the meadow's edge, the rings broke apart, raining twigs and soil around the base of a falun tree.

Gasping for breath, Lore Rayna slowly regained her feet and stood gazing across the meadow in silence.

Though the big woman appeared calmer, Cudgel made no move to go to her.

Broth slipped from behind the big man, taking a position at his side.

Crystalyn was relieved. The warden appeared to be unharmed.

Slowing her breaths, Lore Rayna's bark-like arms and branching fingers shrank rapidly, reforming into her normal tanned skin. "You are right, beloved, what am I doing?" she asked softly.

Behind her, Atoi crept close.

Crystalyn's anxiety tripled. "No, Atoi! Get away from her!"

Atoi froze, her dagger gleaming in the sunlight. Face impassive, she stepped away from Lore Rayna, giving her a wide berth. Slipping the jeweled dagger through the slit in her dress, she resumed her customary position by Crystalyn's side, keeping her emerald gaze fixed on Lore Rayna.

Crystalyn brought out a symbol from the black-lettered book, one nested under the heading elemental style. A glowing, green circle, half the size of the Shire horse Drumn, hovered before her. The white, maze-like pattern wound around circles of various sizes. Though it felt airy to her, she was unsure of the symbol's effect. She'd not used it, nor did she want to use Lore Rayna as the test subject, but she had to have something visible to defuse the situation.

Or end it.

Keeping her face smooth and her body rigid, Crystalyn donned her emperor mask. "Make a move to attack me or my companions again and I'll not hold back. I *will* destroy you," she promised, using her firmest tone.

Lore Rayna's skin flushed, and her green-leafed dress shifted back and forth around her body, expanding and receding in agitation. "That won't be necessary…I owe…I owe you all an apology…" Lore Rayna said, her words barely audible.

The Lore Mother's angry tone filled the silence after. "I would say an apology is but a mockery of what you *shall* do. You have brought great shame upon your race. My utter disappointment knows no bounds. How could you attack your companions?" The Lore Mother held up an unsteady hand when Lore Rayna opened her mouth. "Do not bother to reply. I have had enough of your childishness. You will do penance for it. One other outburst between here and Surbo and you shall be sent back to the vale with the mark of high dishonor infused in your forehead, do you understand?"

Cudgel inhaled sharply.

"Yes, Mother. It is no less than I deserve," Lore Rayna said softly, her glowing eyes downcast.

"Oh, Rayne," Cudgel said, sadly. Shaking his broad head, he tromped back to the wagon.

"You can put that away now, Crystalyn. You too, Hastel; Lore Rayna won't be troubling anyone this journey," the Lore Mother said.

Hastel sheathed his two axes. "Troubling? You make it sound like a petty argument. Well, the fire needs to be built for supper anyway," he said, moving off.

Crystalyn was loath to let the symbol go. A latent power resonated through its intricate, almost transparent design. It pulsed brighter in the center in a straight line, giving her the feeling of a wide horizontal swath, for some reason.

"Does it drain you the longer you hold onto it?" the Lore Mother asked, her raspy voice intruding on her concentration.

Disinclined to answer, Crystalyn let the symbol fade. She was getting a headache, anyway, though probably not from the symbol. "I meant what I said, Lore Rayna. I can't let that happen again."

Lore Rayna's brow furrowed, but she remained silent. Tossing her head back, she shifted her golden hair from in front of her breasts as if a reply was beneath her.

Glancing away before her anger could set in again, Crystalyn spotted a small cliff face overlooking the campsite. She motioned to Atoi and Broth. "Come on. I feel the need for a walk." Setting a fast pace, she made for the trees guarding the way higher. Crossing inside, she felt the Lore Mother's luminous gaze fixed on her, but she wasn't about to look back. She might decide to destroy the lot of them.

The climb wasn't as bad as she expected. A well-beaten path angled up a gradual slope circling away, then winding back, where it topped out above and behind the rocky ledges she'd seen from camp. As she'd expected, her anger dissipated with exertion.

The explanation for such a nice path became clear when they caught tantalizing glimpses of a pond glinting with sapphire brilliance through open patches of the birch trees.

A vivid image flowed into the link, startling her. A tent-like structure constructed from deadfall overlooked the pond. *"We are not alone,"* Broth sent. The perspective was from the trees beside the path where he'd wandered off to keep watch.

Crystalyn thought about turning back but decided to keep going; she wanted to see the full extent of the pond. The path paused at the mouth of the pond's gurgling outlet, as did she. Swallowing the better part of the small upper valley, clear blue water supported budding lily pads floating on three sides of the pond. They continued toward a lean-to where a familiar figure lounged on a boulder.

"Are you certain you're not following me, Darwin Darkwind?" she asked, as soon as she drew close. "I *am* starting to wonder."

A look she couldn't identify flitted across his tanned face, but then he grinned. "I believe you're following *me,* since you wandered into my camp. Nevertheless, it is fortuitous. I was about to dine. I would be honored if you and the Dark Child would join me for my humble repast," he said, motioning toward three rectangular bundles wrapped with broad, green leaves and placed on a nearby rock. "They should be cooled by now."

"There are three of us now," Crystalyn said, glancing at the wall of trees at her right. "Broth, come here, please."

Slipping from beneath an evergreen, Broth meandered around the small camp's perimeter, sniffing at rocks and the makeshift tent.

"How remarkable," Darwin said. "You've managed to get linked since last we met. You are beyond exceptional…" Gazing at Broth, his expression grew wistful.

Crystalyn flushed at the compliment. "I don't know about that, but I do know he is extraordinary. His name is Broth. He's a warden." Her flush deepened. What was she babbling? Darwin would know Broth was a warden.

Darwin nodded as if it was the most natural comment on Astura. "Please sit wherever you find the most comfort," he said, gesturing at the area nearby.

Atoi plopped on the grass with a boulder against her back, silent as usual. Crystalyn selected a rock the right height for her knees.

Though cut from a different pattern than hers, Darwin wore Kell leather. The leather rustled softly when he moved to hand her one of the leaf-wrapped bundles. It was warm to the touch like his long-fingered hand, which she learned when her fingers brushed his. She peeled back the leaf with care, exposing a red-spotted fish surrounded by steaming vegetables.

"Please, allow me," Darwin offered. Bending over her lap, he pinned the tail with a finger and pulled the head toward it, lifting the skeletal frame out of the orange meat. Discarding the bones, he rewrapped the leaf with a deft hand, leaving it on her lap. "Go ahead, try it," he said with a smile.

Looking up at his dark, shiny eyes, Crystalyn smiled. She took a small nibble from a corner. The leaf was a pleasant surprise. Tasting faintly of apples, the flavor of it brought to mind the farm's romaine lettuce, though it had a much softer texture. Her next bite was larger. The vegetables combined with fish oil, meat, and some spices went well with the leaf. Crystalyn gave a nod of approval as she swallowed.

Darwin beamed, placing one in Atoi's lap and setting the third in front of Broth.

"My palate is not used to heating out the flavoring, Do'brieni."

"He likes it raw," Crystalyn said.

Darwin picked up the leaf and replaced it with a large, raw, spotted fish he retrieved from the shade of a boulder beside him. "It's a good thing I never make much then," he said, settling on a smaller rock to debone his own meal.

Broth swallowed the fish in a few gulps.

Savoring the taste, Crystalyn chewed, looking around. Darwin had chosen his campsite well. A boulder, the size of a small boat, protected the area from a west wind. A lean-to was propped against it. The site was sheltered on the eastern side by the northern cliffs, which left the south side open for a prime view of the pond. She did notice something missing. "Where's your fire pit?"

Darwin grinned. "That's the beauty of it. I don't have one."

Atoi sat forward. "You have minute control over your using?"

Darwin smiled cryptically. "Anyone can make a fireball. Generating a precise amount of heat at a certain point, however, that takes skill. One not easily mastered, I daresay."

Crystalyn stopped chewing, surprised to find only a couple bites left of the wrap. "Go on, you have my interest."

Setting his uneaten leaf wrap beside him, he stood. "I've been experimenting for some years on my own. Shall I demonstrate?"

She nodded, keeping her eyes on the leaf-wrapped bundle. At first, nothing happened. Then slowly, with increasing rapidity, the rock *under* the wrap began to glow red. Darwin turned the leaf over as the rock faded to its normal color, poking a finger gingerly at it a few moments later. "It'll be a while before I can sit down, but the food's warm," he said with a smile.

Crystalyn was impressed. "You used the rock as a stove. I wouldn't have thought of that."

Darwin grinned. "It is harder than it looks. No one else I know has learned how to trickle the Flow, as I call it. The stone melts or starts on fire, or it explodes. I'll bet you can, though. Allow me to show you," he said, taking her hand. "I shall help you direct your energy in small increments."

Darwin's hand was callused, which surprised her. She'd thought of him as a noble as well as a high-ranking commander. Most in his position would insist that someone else do the menial work for them. A pleasant tingle raced along her spine from his touch adding a distraction to her sorting through the symbols she'd used in the past. Not one she could recall had any fire or flame associated with it.

Darwin spoke, his tone implying impatience and excitement at the same time. "Go on; draw upon the Flow's energy. I shall let you know when you have enough, keep siphoning until I tell you to stop."

"His heartbeat has increased, Do'brieni; I can hear it. Interact with care. I do not believe this one can be trusted."

Darwin seemed so sincere, and his beautiful brown eyes glinted with an inner fire. "If you don't want to try the stone, use the pond. It will soak up any excess. Go ahead, access the Flow. What are you waiting for?"

Perhaps she could try the airy one in miniature form to rub the rock's molecules together. It should heat up then.

"His heartbeat has accelerated again. What does he wish of you?"

Crystalyn pulled her hand free. "I, we…have to get going. The others will be worried. Thank you for sharing your meal with us."

Surprise shone in his eyes as his jaw worked. "No! Please, you do not have to go. Stay here, the Dark Child and your warden will inform the rest of your party that you will rejoin them with the rising sun."

Crystalyn gazed long at him. He was so handsome even when worried, as he looked now. It was tempting to spend the setting of the sun strolling along the pond getting to know him, perhaps training with some of her unknown symbols under his gentle guidance. After, as the sun began to fade, they would retire to the warmth of his blankets. Would it be such a bad thing?

"I would object to such an arrangement, Mistress," Atoi said, her declaration only slightly undermined by her passionless tone.

Darwin reached for her hand again. Squeezing it gently, he flashed a confident smile. Making up her mind, Crystalyn pulled her hand free a second time. "There will be no need for any objection, little one. Let's go. I don't wish to walk down to camp in the dark."

Standing, she moved onto the trail.

Broth leapt in front. *"My relief is great, Do'brieni. Leaving you alone would cause anguish."*

"Eventually we may have to separate for a while, Broth, but not now."

Looking over her shoulder, she paused to motion Atoi ahead of her. Though the young girl could likely defend herself in almost every situation, Crystalyn preferred to keep her in the safer position of the middle, where she could keep an eye on the Dark Child within her.

Darwin stood silent and unmoving, his face unreadable.

As she rounded the pond's outlet where the path began its descent, it took all of the restraint she'd developed to keep herself in check and not run back.

SMOKY GARLANDS

Crystalyn's leg muscles protested every step. Miles of stomping across dry, arid soil and then some hopping from rock to rock on a talus field as the wagon rolled through a dry creek bed had ruined her knees. *Only twenty-two with worn-out kneecaps, how do I get myself into things like this?* Her companions never revealed any such difficulty. They'd all trekked longer than she had throughout the day and every day before this one.

Still, she stuck by her decision to give Ferral a rest, though Hastel had insisted the horse was fine to ride. There was no way she'd be able to handle the stallion's canter when her injury was seeping worse than ever. Her attempts at healing with the golden symbol helped but only until she stretched the wrong way, stepped the wrong way, or sat down the wrong way. It didn't matter what she did. It wouldn't heal or be healed.

Finally, she'd resorted to the old, low-magic way. Going off alone in the trees, she'd sacrificed her old undershirt, tearing it into strips. She now had a few spare bandages to sop up the leakage whenever she exerted too much. Trooping through rough terrain certainly qualified as excessive exertion.

Perhaps with Broth's stamina, she would handle it better. The warden padded tirelessly, moving side to side, covering twice the distance as anyone.

Cudgel and Lore Rayna kept a steady lope a few paces ahead of the wagon with ease. After Lore Rayna's attack, the big woman had remained sullen, but she seemed to want to make amends by helping everyone with camp and travel tasks.

The Lore Mother maneuvered the laden wagon along the narrow, beaten path; Drumn pulled it with vigor still, his magnificent head high and his gait long. Tied to the wagon's side rail, the palomino and the black mare kept pace with ease despite the long ride she and Atoi had hit them with the past few days. Hastel trooped behind the wagon's right flank, his two axes, one on each side, not hampering him in the least. Atoi also kept up easily, running beside her. Everyone in her little group looked as fresh as new morning, not her.

Crystalyn tried to maintain some semblance of vigilance as she plodded alongside Hastel, but most of her attention went to hauling her wooden legs over shrubbery, around boulders and bushes, and through dry and near-dry creeks beds as they made their descent from Glacier Mountain. Another stumble on a ground squirrel burrow and she would scream. Or, at least protest under her breath, vigorously.

Atoi seemed to have the most endless supply of energy. The little girl flitted ahead and then slowed to allow Crystalyn time to clomp near, her tiny feet barely scratching the terrain.

The wagon trail narrowed, diving into a muddy ravine. The Lore Mother slowed but didn't hesitate to drive the Shire inside. From the rear, Crystalyn had a disconcerting image of the horse, rider, and wagon vanishing into a sinkhole, swallowed without a sound.

A few aching footsteps later, she was relieved to know her fears were groundless. The Lore Mother popped out of the far end of the ravine. As she sat vigilantly on the front seat, the woman's white hair stood out starkly against a day overcast with clouds.

Crystalyn trudged into the ravine with Atoi at her side. Passing crumbling ledges jutting outward, Atoi stayed near for a while in companionable silence. Then she suddenly bolted ahead to the ledge wall.

Crystalyn watched her go; too tired to tell her to watch her step, she moved forward only because her companions did. Not long ago, she would have jumped at the chance for a hike in real mountains with clean air to breathe while exercising her cardiovascular system, burning calories. Not that she needed it; weight had never been an issue for her or Jade. One of the many good things handed down from their mom.

A twinge reminded her again of her failure to heal the spiderbee punctures, something she hadn't told her companions. The last thing she wanted was for the search to stall longer as she healed. Broth knew, but he'd simply voiced his concern—well, *expressed* his concern—and moved on.

Using cracks as handholds and tiny toeholds for support, Atoi sprang onto a smaller ledge as the trail widened. Peering down, the little girl kept pace as Crystalyn marched by trying not to hold her palm on her stomach. So far, the seepage had stabilized.

"How does one survive on your world?" Atoi asked.

"What do you mean?"

"You stumble after a short hike on easy terrain. Do your people all rely on horses to pack them around?"

Crystalyn regarded the girl, who'd been ten seasons for more than four hundred seasons, in silence. How long could one host an alien entity and retain some semblance of oneself? Was she dealing with the host now or the Dark Child? One instant she was an amiable companion, and the next, she seemed to want to instigate an argument.

Hopefully, her day-to-day experience with the girl from now on would provide the clues she needed to make an accurate judgment. For now, she'd send the girl off on her own; she didn't feel too companionable now. All she wanted was rest.

Slipping around a jagged outcropping of brown stone, Atoi dropped onto a narrower ledge without adjusting a single stride.

"While you're listening to the naturists' conversations," Crystalyn said, ignoring the girl's opening comment, "find out where those bloody obelisks are attuned to, like I asked. I would've thought you'd gathered something by now. Do you need to hone your skills?"

A flicker of annoyance crinkled Atoi's youthful face. She vaulted from the ledge, landing softly in the rocky grass. Sprinting away, she passed Lore Rayna and then Broth, disappearing around a bend in the steep canyon.

Crystalyn sniffed. It served the entity, or Atoi, right for making fun of her. Granted, she was out of shape, but that didn't mean she had to have a reminder of it. It was likely not one of her companions would know what it was to fight an irrepressible illness while being the sole earner of credits for their family. What debts could they possibly have? Cudgel seemed to be the financial man for Lore Rayna and the Lore Mother; he'd paid Hastel with a gold coin for their stay at the Muddy Wagon Inn. Atoi had yet to pay for anything, but Hastel seemed to believe she was loaded.

Broth would have no use for coin or credits living away from humans. He would simply take what he needed from Astura by hunting wild creatures and drinking the plentiful water. She hated to think of it, but he did have to eat. He wasn't a grazer; therefore, he was a carnivore, and likely, a proficient one. His sleek body and boundless energy indicated a healthy diet.

Thinking of her companion, her eye sought him, Broth loped around a sharp bend in the trail, vanishing from sight, as the ravine leveled out to open mountainside again. A pebble caught at Crystalyn's boot. She stumbled. Would she make it until they rested? *Think positive and make it through the day. Think positive…make it through.* Another litany from lockdown blossomed from her memory. What worked before should work again.

Technically, she could call for a halt at any time since she was running the show, but it was not worth an exchange of words with the Lore Mother. Crystalyn could hear her now, asking if she was ill or grouching about how far they still had to travel. Perhaps there would be a nice stream flowing through a vibrant meadow with a watering hole around the bend. She could then justify it on the pretense of refilling water and…

"Take cover, Do'brieni, ambush!"

Broth's urgency flowed through the link, bringing a powerful image of dark funnels of swirling energy arcing through the sky above a bowl-shaped green meadow.

Crystalyn fought for equilibrium as the image widened,

encompassing a larger field of view, the rim of the bowl springing into focus. Black-armored soldiers stood in an ominous shoulder-to-shoulder line across the farthest side.

Crossing a stream, Atoi hopped from rock to rock, oblivious to the dark power arcing toward her in the sky. Crystalyn drew a full breath to shout a warning only to find herself back with the rest of her companions. "Everyone, prepare for battle! Someone is attacking at the next bend!"

Hastel glanced sharply in her direction and then sped for the horses. Cudgel and Lore Rayna fell back to the wagon, protecting it on both sides. The Lore Mother allowed Hastel the time it took to untie Ferral and then whipped the reins. Drumn leapt ahead.

As she raced behind the wagon, Crystalyn's rising anxiety bled away, leaving behind a rigid calmness, two sentences resounded in her mind. *Atoi's just a kid. She needs protection.*

Aching knees and seeping wound shunted aside, she ran. Rounding the bend, Crystalyn drew up short. She'd read the link image wrong. Or Broth had sent it with his perception. The trail descended into an ancient crater overgrown with grass and littered with tumbleweeds. A stream cut through the center. Two small copses of aspen trees blossomed on two sides. From her higher vantage point, Crystalyn could see Broth had been right about the ambush but wrong about the target. Atoi wasn't the target, though she was running toward them.

A man and a woman stood alone in the meadow, hands locked together. The woman's free palm stretched to the sky, the man's at the ground. A glowing, transparent bubble encompassed her and her companion. A barrage of black cones flew toward the bubble, launched from three directions by black-robed figures hiding in the midst of black-armored soldiers. Like miniature, swirling black holes, the cones swallowed light as they went, trailing a wake of darkness through the sky. Drilling in upon impact, the cones left behind raging maelstroms as big as a wagon wheel. The black maelstroms deflected off the couple's shield bubble, boring small craters around it, before losing energy and disseminating into wisps of smoke. In the forefront of the dark army, black-armored men and women fought silver-armored figures.

Atoi popped out of the wide gully, still on the wagon trail. Sprinting in a zigzag pattern, the young girl's tiny, swift-moving legs closed the distance between her and the two holding hands under the shrinking dome. *What was she doing?* Crystalyn wondered.

Exposing another group of ambushers, a black cone streaked toward Atoi from the copse of cedar trees at the bowl's rim on her left side. Thinking furiously, Crystalyn entwined three black aggression symbols into one shadowy offensive symbol. Hexagram in shape, the symbol, with its intertwining lines and black rose shapes, writhed like constrictor vines caught in a burning garden of roses. Beautiful and powerful, the symbol streaked toward the cedar trees, trailing smoky garlands of its pattern, her most intricate yet.

But she was already too late: the cone would reach Atoi first.

Oblivious to the danger from above, Atoi dashed behind a large granite boulder next to the road. The swirling cone slammed into the rock. A thunderous *crack* rent the day, and dust and rock chips mushroomed into the air.

Crystalyn's lucidity changed to the surreal. The dust cloud slowed, rolling upward and outward languidly. Broth raced slowly into view, loping frame by frame from a distant tree line, moving toward the cloud. The wagon driven by the Lore Mother descended into the small ravine of the creek bed, both front wheels leaving the ground. Cudgel and Lore Rayna sprinted away from the gully, their ground-eating strides looking like giant leaps. Reins flapping ever so slowly, Hastel sailed past the Lore Mother on Ferral, heedless of the two cones arcing toward him from atop the bowl.

Wrenched back to normalcy, Crystalyn's mind sped up, allowing her to assess the situation with stark, split-second clarity. The barrage on the dome continued. With each hit, it inched closer to the couple, collapsing slowly inward. Strewn beyond them, armored, robed, and some odd-skinned bodies lay crumpled beside splintered wagons, some still burning. A sickly-sweet odor wafted through the air.

Crystalyn's eyes slid from the carnage at the bottom of the bowl to the attacking forces positioned on three sides at the top. Whoever had planned the ambush had set the trap well—perhaps too well for her little group to handle careening headlong into it as they had. There was no choice but to battle on, as strung out as everyone was now.

The main enemy force stood guarding a company of black- and red-robed Users where the wagon trail climbed from the bowl. Beyond them, Crystalyn made out a contingent of bows. On the left and right, she spotted additional robed enemies using a copse of cedar trees for cover on each side, though some had lost their cover. Her symbol had ripped through most of the left side, leaving the fifteen or so Dark Users still standing but exposed.

Surprisingly, Atoi exploded from the dust cloud at full speed.

Three oblong projectiles shot from the trees on the right, almost as soon as the little girl did, leaving angry red glows trailing in their wake. Each projectile turned as one, arcing toward Atoi as she ran.

Working as fast as she could, Crystalyn sent the first symbol she thought about on an intercept course toward the bolts of energy. Expanding into concentric circles as it went, her knockback symbol struck the first two missiles, exploding them on contact. The third wavered slightly but continued on, striking Atoi in the chest.

No! She'd been so close. Preparing a symbol—bigger this time—she sent her smoky garland into the trees on the right. For one beat of her fearful heart, the enormous hexagram symbol hung in stasis above the trees, imprinting its intricate rose design in fiery red in the sky.

Then it imploded inward. The area inside the pattern rippled the fabric of the sky, turning it as black as an impending storm. Building to an immense pressure, it drew from the air trapped within the hexagon; she could hear and feel it, even over the screams of the battle. Once charged, the symbol released a booming concussive ring downward, flattening anything caught inside its diameter. In its wake, tattered robes fluttered above shattered rocks and splintered wood floating above a dense cloud of dust.

Averting her eyes from the former copse, she spotted Atoi lying crumpled on her side. The bolt had hurled her yards across the meadow. A wisp of smoke spiraled up from an ugly burn on her tiny chest.

Anxiety for her little companion arose from the familiar place in her stomach. Atoi was badly hurt. Crystalyn panicked, looking wildly around at the devastation. Pocked with craters big and small, the shattered landscape, littered with torn and bloody corpses wearing white robes and gleaming armor, angered her. Had the enemy ambushed them too? Crystalyn chose to believe so, fueling her anger. She reveled in the anger, which cut through her panic like a flaming sword, calming her with an almost boiling clarity.

The enemy would seek her next.

A beautiful white symbol bloomed in her mind in the shape of a cross. The weave of the pattern was long. It twisted and turned, weaving around and under itself, back and forth, up and down, until finally coming back to its point of origin. Unraveling it in her mind's eye, Crystalyn combined it with three other white ones. On an impulse, she redrew them all and centered the whole within a circular, black pattern where the white crosses flowed along an intricate, swirling design.

The now dark symbol felt rubbery but durable, almost plasicrete in consistency. Releasing the new symbol, Crystalyn floated it outward a few feet from her, stretching it to the ground while expanding it sideways and upward, visualizing a wall. Separating an end of the symbol, she secured it to her movements just as a barrage of black cones and red bolts struck. Every hit felt like the biting gnats that gathered around ponds at the farm, but her symbol held. The bombardment deflected from the symbol and detonated around her. Dirt and pebbles rained down on her head.

A wave of weakness washed through her. The ground rose up to meet her; suddenly she was on her hands and knees. The wall wavered violently.

"You are strong, Do'brieni. Do not falter!"

Clutching strength from the link, Crystalyn tightened her will on the wall, drawing a roof on it, expanding it over her head.

Blackness welled in her mind, overtaking the headache. A great weariness permeated her to the core. She needed rest. A couple minutes would do it. She was *so* tired. With her symbol sheltering her, nothing could hurt her. Five quick minutes, what would it harm?

No. Atoi was down. She needed to keep going. What would her dad say? He'd want her to do whatever it took to save a life; the Great Father knew he'd protected many throughout his lifetime. She had to try, even if the life in need had nearly killed her upon her arrival. A persistent memory of her first encounter with Atoi—one of her first on Astura—nagged at her. She reached into her pack.

The pall of weariness lifted. Physically touching the black candle made the difference; clarity bloomed sharp and vibrant, bringing with it a sense of surprise and chagrin from many minds.

Getting angrier by the moment, Crystalyn realized the Dark Users had changed tactics and stepped up their attack. While some Users had rained dark cones and projectiles on her wall, others had made a concerted effort to dismantle the symbol by attacking the mind behind it.

The parasitic link was easy to find. Where Broth's link was a bright and shiny beacon in her mind, the new one strove for a sense of nothingness. That—in itself—was a mistake. There was never "nothing" in her mind. Something was always happening; her thoughts and emotions whirled about in constant activity. She'd never been able to control it, and even though she was constantly telling herself to find her inner calmness, she never had.

Gathering her pent-up rage, Crystalyn concentrated on the intrusion and flowed into the dark link. Many minds hastily joined the ones there, expecting to sweep away her anger and lock her inside herself, alone with her wrath.

Crystalyn snarled aloud as if she were an animal trapped in a den, its place of sanctuary. Forcing further into the link, she brought her rage to the forefront. The dark link shrank away from her gnashing fury of affliction.

Crystalyn let go, lashing out unconstrained. Constricted to a single tube, her storm of fury roared along the violating link reaching the minds in an instant. Without slowing, it gusted through cerebrums like a vehement gale of neurotic wind. As one, the minds collapsed in gibbering terror.

Crystalyn closed the foul link with the same technique she'd used on Broth when his exuberance had gotten too strong. She diminished it, but this time, she compressed it down to a speck, and then she squeezed it with a thought until it burst to nothing. Revenge took its place, fueled from a new desire to build a barrier no one would get through without consent.

"Broth, are you there?"

His response was immediate. *"I am coming, Do'brieni, almost there."*

"No! You'll only draw their fire. They cannot hurt me for now. Try to circle around and attack them from behind." She added an image of the warden stalking from out of the trees by the upper trail.

"As you wish," Broth sent. She could sense his reluctance intermixed with a desire to please. He veered away, moving in the opposite direction of her attackers.

Though her mind was now clear, her body felt drained. She forced herself to stand and stumble to Atoi, thankful the physical attack had lessened. The mental assault could no longer cause her harm. Falling to her knees, she scooped the little girl up in her arms.

On her feet again, she reeled from the weight. For a girl of only ten seasons, Atoi was heavy. What had she expected? She had a mere twelve seasons on Atoi and likely outweighed her only by fifty or sixty pounds. Leaning back, she draped Atoi's head over one shoulder, carrying her like a toddler. The simple act brought tears to her eyes, reminding her of when a young Jade had fallen asleep in her arms. It also freed one hand for carrying the black candle. Pushing her tears aside, she blinked her vision clear and focused on the back side of the clear dome. Shuffling toward it, she kept an eye on the rest of her companions.

Not far away, Hastel winced as his crossbow and an axe smacked a rock when he dismounted in the gully. He flattened himself against the stream's western bank. A black cone slammed into the rocky eastern bank behind him. Rocks clattered like a giant game of throw stones played by powerful beings. Many medium-sized chunks thumped against his torso armor, but somehow his head and legs escaped damage.

Another cone slammed into the western bank a yard ahead of him. Gathering his legs under him, he bolted to the spot, staying hunched over and hugging the bow to his waist, betting another cone wouldn't land in the same crater. Seconds later, he bolted upstream. With a start, Crystalyn realized he was drawing the enemy fire away from the others, away from her and Atoi.

Explosions left both sides of the upstream banks pocked; some landed close enough to rain mud and water down on him. Hastel slowed to wipe his eye clear and then sprinted to a place where the stream had carved banks tall enough for him to stand.

He made better time upright, splashing upstream through ankle-deep water, holding to the western edge. As he rounded a rocky bend, Crystalyn almost lost sight of him as he barreled into stunted trees growing along the banks, but then he slowed, realizing at some point the barrage had ended. Scrambling atop the stream bank, he pulled an arrow tipped with a glass vial from the quiver on his back.

Satisfied of his safety for the moment, Crystalyn searched for the others.

Lore Rayna's great size made her easy to spot. Positioned near the top of the left side hill, the big woman fired arrows into two ranks of Dark Users stationed behind the armored main force. The Users appeared to be attempting to create a shield as they died.

One of Lore Rayna's arrows broke apart on a smoky translucence inches from a figure in a black robe, disintegrating in midair. The next arrow dropped the Interrupter standing behind him. A third arrow sank into the black-robed being's upper torso, her original target. Two out of every three thinned their numbers, but eventually she would run out of arrows. Lore Rayna ignored the armored ones and picked off the robed ones making the shadowy translucence of the magical barrier spotty, but even so, it was growing rapidly.

Cudgel stood below the big woman, battering a company of black-armored soldiers working their way up the hill. A pile of corpses ringed him. The two of them had likely garnered many of the Dark Users' attention away from Hastel, for which she was grateful yet fearful at the same time. Cudgel was tiring. He would soon be in big trouble. Hastel couldn't reach him with his crossbow, even if he was an expert shot, which she doubted.

Movement behind the User ranks caught Crystalyn's eye. Lore Rayna was decimating the Dark Users with her long arrows though it hadn't escaped notice. A bow infantry mobilized at the main front lines.

Fear grew in the pit of Crystalyn's stomach.

Lore Rayna and Cudgel couldn't withstand a contingent of arrows.

Crystalyn sent two of her wall symbols speeding to her companions. Stretching them to protect her friends while maintaining her own shield was taxing; she wasn't certain how long they would last. Without the black candle, it wouldn't have happened at all. Thrumming with a faint vibration, the candle warmed in her hand.

With two of her largest companions safe from projectiles for the time being, Crystalyn looked for the oldest. The Lore Mother stood behind the wagon, Drumn unharnessed next to her.

Beyond her, the protection dome of the couple holding hands had thinned to the point of bursting, shrinking to nearly the top of the woman's long, auburn hair. The woman held one hand toward the dome's peak while bending at both knees, as if she could strengthen the collapse by sheer force of will.

The Lore Mother's eyes burst with light, shining brighter. A glowing bubble matching her orbs of radiance sprang up around her, moving outward. A moment later, the glowing dome encapsulated the thinning bubble surrounding the couple.

Crystalyn staggered onward. The Dark Users' attack progressed with thundering bursts, bombarding her roofed wall with abandon. The black candle vibrated, growing warmer in her hand.

Hastel had five of the glass vial-tipped arrows lined on the bank near him as he poured a thick, brown liquid from a well-padded flask into a sixth. Cable already cranked back, he set the shorter but thicker arrow in the crossbow's channel. Deliberately, he raised the tip to the sky, aiming for the right side group of Dark Users, untouched as of yet.

He pulled the trigger. Streaking toward the target, the arrow struck near the group's center, detonating with a thunderous boom. Black smoke and red flames balled outward, burning trees and humans alike.

Stunned, she looked away, toward the main force at the bowl's exit. So much destruction on the hillside had to cause a reaction. A commotion broke out at the rear. Broth tore through the back row, flinging Users high in the air with his powerful jaws and massive neck. Surprise enabled the warden to take down many, but they were seasoned soldiers. The rear lines immediately began to close ranks, surrounding him.

Crystalyn reached the wagon. Under the shelter of the Lore Mother's dome, she sat on the ground, cradling Atoi's head in her lap. The black candle cooled slightly. Dissolving her wall, she focused on aiding her companions.

The shield wall the black-robed Users had died to raise was in place, protecting the longbow archers.

Lore Rayna fired upon the front row of soldiers.

Cudgel had moved below her hillside vantage point, but his swings were slowing.

Surrounded on all sides, six rows deep, Broth's escape path had closed behind his enraged attack.

A concussive wave rippled through the middle front two lines. Crystalyn had only a moment to marvel before Hastel's third arrow struck. Falling slightly short, the arrow landed near the center of the right rear, thankfully far enough from Broth to save him from damage. Fully half the leftmost line blew apart, hurling bodies high in the air. The black shield wall in front of the longbows winked out.

Crystalyn struck as the focus of the battle shifted toward Hastel. Her smoky garland symbol ripped apart a wide, fiery circle where the shield had been moments ago.

A hailstorm of arrows, dark cones, and missiles fell toward the one-eyed man. Hastily launching a final arrow, Hastel vanished in a cloud of dirt and debris.

Hastel!

Preparing another symbol and then another, in rapid succession, Crystalyn sent one into the enemy force toward the hailstorm's origination and one behind where she'd seen her *Do'brieni* last. Her vision dimmed with each release, and the throb inside her head boomed.

"Broth? Do'brieni? Are you there?" No response. She wondered if she could even hear her link mate over the throbs in her head. It required some of her dwindling energy to maintain the link, so she dropped it, feeling like she was abandoning him. A weak sense of betrayal echoed through her mind.

Her anxieties rising as high as her fear for her companions, Crystalyn tripled the size of her garland symbols, sending two others into the midst of the army attacking Lore Rayna and Cudgel.

The black candle flared with heat, strong enough she felt her hand burn through the raging torrent of pain in her head. She dropped the artifact as Drumn galloped by, carrying a rider. Who would be riding the horse?

Crystalyn found she was sedentary on the ground, Atoi draped across her knees. Looking down at the small, innocent face of the four hundred seasons old girl lying cold in her lap, Crystalyn's heart jolted. "I'm sorry, little one. I should've been stronger," she said.

Atoi's open, glazed eyes stared up at her as the last of her strength fled.

NO MIRTH

Light surrounded Garn. Gratified, he absorbed some of its pure white luminance, drawing it deep within him with one long pull. Details emerged from around the light's ragged edges: a pale, shaved log beam overhead, a glassless window cross-trimmed with bars, and a sanded bedpost. Wood joists spotted with dark brown stains designated leaks from above, the source of a stale moldy scent. Mold wasn't good. He'd break out in hives if forced to be around fungi too long.

He pulled light in, imbibing deeper. With each pull, his thoughts took on coherence, establishing a firmer link to his sense of who he'd been, who he was, who he strove to be. He had a mission.

He sat up, looking for the way out. The small room was barren except for the large bed, a small vanity, and a matching wardrobe. A rough-cut wooden door with an oval, iron-barred window was the room's sole exit.

The flight from the alley flooded into memory. Briefly, he wondered how he could still be alive, but it didn't matter. He had a mission.

He stood. Gripping the door latch, he twisted until he met resistance. The door was locked; no surprise there. In the room adjacent to his, two men sat in silence at the far end of a long, scarred table, sipping tankards filled to the brim with an amber liquid. Two men he recognized. One wore a red-robe, the other, a leather hood ending at the sternum. A woman joined them, taking a seat demurely next to the black-hooded man sitting at the table's head. The woman, too, was familiar.

"How long is *he* going to be here?" Corteezsha asked. Setting a delicate glass on the table, she poured a red liquid from a bronze-colored bottle.

"When you refer to *he,* I assume you mean me," Malkor said. He took a long pull from the tankard, wiping foam from his goatee with the back of his bronzed hand. Plopping the tankard down, he belched. "I would've departed hours ago, if not for you."

The blonde curls draping under Corteezsha's chin shook slightly as she locked eyes with the red-robed man. "Me? I would be the last person to detain your departure. You may go now, if you'd like."

Malkor scowled, narrowing his oval brown eyes. "I delayed to attempt a final heal to your pet mark for you. I've expended much effort to provide the Flow for a rapid heal. The fool won't draw upon it. Perhaps I shouldn't have repaired his blood circulator. His death would have come quickly, and I wouldn't be here expending my energies for *you.* It's not as if I do not have other duties elsewhere."

Slamming his tankard on the table with enough force foam rose to the top and spilled over the sides, the hooded man leaned forward, his voice soft and ominous. "You healed him at *my* command, not hers. You would do well to remember that."

Malkor quavered. "Yes, Great One. May I ask, why have the fool healed?"

The black hood swung slowly toward Garn. Their eyes locked. Garn's breath caught in his throat. Dark amber, feline eyes glinted from underneath the hood. "The *fool* tore through seventeen of my strongest, nearly escaping the alley trap," the hooded man said, still looking at Garn. "No, he *would* have escaped if not for the defect in his heart. I shall decide if there is merit to this or merely desperation providing undue strength. Should there be potential, a place with us shall be found." The hourglass eyes under the hood glinted brighter. "Provided, such a one as him can be trained to the higher quality. If not, you may remove his circulator for your own dark experiments, Malkor. At present, you may continue your other duties. The *fool*…has accepted your heal."

Corteezsha glanced at the hooded man before turning to look at

Garn. Her large blue eyes glinted as a smile tugged at her lips before vanishing so fast he wasn't sure it'd ever been there.

Malkor was slower. "I checked on him before we sat down," he said, frowning. "As I tried to say, the blasted fool won't take what's placed right inside his..." He spun toward Garn so fast the red hood on his shoulders flapped. "Oh! Blast you!"

Springing to his feet, Malkor strode across the room, kicking two chairs aside as he went, and halted at the door's threshold. His brown eyes glared through the bars. Garn could have punched him in one of those eyes had he wanted to, but the situation hadn't fully developed yet. "How long have you been standing there? Do you know who your benefactor is, *fool?*" Malkor asked. His hot breath smelled of stale ale.

Garn said nothing. He'd come across men of Malkor's type somewhere in his past, though he couldn't recall where. Short and spoiling for a fight, Malkor believed he had something to prove. The shorter man was looking for any provocation, however small, to take on someone bigger than he. Such men were dangerous. Sureen had called it short man's syndrome, but then she'd been a psychology instructor.

There had been supplements to the conversation, but he couldn't recall the specifics. Large gaps in his memory had been with him much of his adult life—particularly when he tried to recall some tiny detail involving his wife or his life before he met her—and he hated it.

He had only vague memories of his parents in Low Realm, but he did retain a vast knowledge of certain survival skills there. Sureen had never pressed him on it, though she'd had him see one of her doctors every few months, though nothing had come from it. Now he was past caring of that life. The most important was retaining memories of his wife. His newly repaired heart lurched.

Malkor pressed his narrow face close to the barred window, blocking Garn's view of the room outside, his thin lips pulled back into a practiced sneer. "Well, fool? Have you nothing to say to your benefactor?"

Garn spoke loud enough for those in the other room to hear.

"Yes, I do."

Malkor raised his smug, haughty face.

Garn straightened to his full height, looking down at the red-robed man. "My benefactor…won't be disappointed with my training."

Thrusting his face against the bars, Malkor snarled, his beady eyes wild.

Garn held his ground, keeping his gaze steady on the shorter man.

A low laugh sounded from the room beyond. "There you have it. What do you think of your fool now, Malkor?" the hooded man asked, his voice soft. "He has passed his first test well by showing how much you are feared."

Giving the bars a final shake and a hard glare, Malkor turned and stalked from the room, raising his hood as he went.

The hooded man laughed softly again, his teeth bright and uniform under the hood's shadow. "You shall reclaim your room, Corteezsha. Go inform Codar he has a new…volunteer for his…loving ministrations."

"Codar is too brutal, Great One. I don't think he likes training. There are far too many 'accidents' under his tutelage. Won't you command Braith to do it? He's quite good."

The hooded man's voice was softer still. "Go. Do as I say."

Corteezsha rose and left the room gracefully without a backward glance.

Sliding sinuously to his feet, the hooded man regarded Garn with his yellow eyes. "Continue to prove your worth to me by mastering what Codar has to offer quickly. Monumental…events are about to happen. Do so, and you may yet survive your…apprenticeship," he said, his voice low enough Garn had to delay drawing a breath to hear. The man's vibrant, hourglass eyes regarded him for a while in silence, and then he left the room through the same wide door the two others had used. Garn suspected it was the only way in or out, though he could see a door to his left. It likely led to a storage closet or pantry.

His suspicion was confirmed when a beefy man shouldering a

monstrous hammer entered through the door a short time later. Inserting a key into Garn's door, he swung it open, using his broad frame to block any chance to run past. "Pay attention, you learn; give trouble, you die," the man, presumably Codar, said. His language was comprehensible, though he spoke with a thick, unrecognizable accent.

Garn detected the arrogance of confidence in his words but no malice. Still, he planned to watch for an accident since Corteezsha had warned about it, should he decide to go along with his captors. The big man was alone. He could kill him and take his weapon. But he suspected such a move to be...expected. Besides, the inhabitants of this world had shown him they were capable of healing by some sort of magical source. What other powers might they have? "Perhaps you'll find it relevant to inform me what you consider trouble before it comes to that," Garn said.

Codar blinked. "Do not speak to me, or anyone, unless I give permission. Or you die. You follow me. Do not stray or you die."

Garn followed, electing to not speak or stray. Discovering how things worked was his best course of action for now.

The area outside the two small rooms wasn't what he expected. Codar led them into a hallway with dirt flooring. Rooms branched from each side, four on the right, and three on the left. Barrels crowded the rooms, with the exception of the first one where racks of dark bottles gleamed. A musty fragrance wafted up as they climbed a single story of wide, rough-cut wooden stairs.

At the top, Codar set a steady pace across a large warehouse buzzing with activity. Men and women in leather aprons sweated over fires built under metal bands that ringed curved slats of wood soaked in water. As they went along, another group of workers pounded the top band over the slats' upper portion. Using wooden mallets, they worked wide iron bands around the slats in a circular pattern and then pounded end caps in place on both ends. Other workers marked finished barrels with an inked stamp. Many others in the busy warehouse carried empty barrels to storage or rolled full casks through a massive set of doors to a dock where wagons waited to be loaded.

The workers kept to themselves or worked in small teams, going about their business in silence. Every eye he tried to meet slid past without a hint of curiosity on each sullen face.

He followed Codar down a side stair that passed a windowed room built to the dock's end while providing a panoramic view of the warehouse inside. The guards inside the room wore dark plate armor and stood with weapons drawn, keeping watch both inside and outside of the bustling warehouse.

Garn glanced through the largest window facing out onto the docks. Seated behind a counter, he thought he glimpsed a dark hood and the glint of a gold band clamped around a muscular arm, but he couldn't be certain. A second look wasn't worth the risk of being cut down, well, bludgeoned down, in this case. Codar's hammer was massive, and the big man would know the instant he slowed. Now wasn't the day to die. He had to bide his time until he discovered enough to move out on his own.

From the dock, Codar set a fast pace through a jumble of back alleyways. Climbing over fences using wooden crates stacked into makeshift staircases, he suddenly veered into a decrepit shack without slowing, and then popped out into another back street lined with ominous-looking shanties.

After many such ventures, Garn supposed Codar didn't want him to find his way back to the warehouse or his ultimate destination, likely both. The broad-shouldered man had done a masterful job so far. For a man his size, Codar strode easily at the pace he set, which was one step shy of a run.

Garn concentrated on maintaining the same pace as the taller man, managing a furtive glance to one side now and then. They marched past bustling smoke-filled back entrances to two different smithies, away from a seedy tavern, and beyond several busy structures with no obvious clues revealing the types of services they provided for the community, good or bad.

A brightly painted house sported several women in scanty lace, leaning provocatively from a second-story deck railing. The women refused to look in his direction upon noticing the brute he followed. Codar was obviously notorious in Gray Water, which meant the hooded man must run much of the place, if not all. Things were not looking good for him, so far.

The worn, wooden buildings gradually improved to stone. The structures grew more immense with each one passed and sprawled right up to a brown rock mountain flecked with gray, the same color as the buildings.

Codar veered from the back streets only when a huge coliseum blocked the way forward, which proved to be their destination. Cradling his hammer on a shoulder, Codar swung onto a wide walkway lined with tall, robed statues keeping a stern eye on those bold enough to pass below. Male or female, the carved, stern faces displayed no mirth.

Garn found their dour moods fitting. He had no mirth lurking inside him either.

GROTTO

Jade pushed upward when she felt something solid beneath her feet. Breaking the surface, she blew water from her mouth, gulping a ragged breath. A fit of coughing forced her lungs clear, giving her eyes time to adjust to the dim light. Large boulders loomed on both sides. Nearby, water swirled shoulder-deep around a massive rock before draining away gurgling, as if someone had pulled a huge plug.

A loud clatter caused her to turn. A hole was opening up above a series of benched rocks stacked like an uneven staircase, meeting the hole she fell through. Clumps of rocks and grass splashed in front of her, and twilight flowed in. Hopping tranquilly down, Burl moved from bench to bench, stopping at the bottommost one to peer at her with his yellow-orange eyes. She smiled at him.

Camoe shoved his head into the hole upside down. "Are you injured?"

"I don't think so. I'm thoroughly soaked, though."

"Can you get to your creature? I am coming down."

She pushed through the frigid water, discovering an underwater slope, which made it easy to climb beside Burl. How could Camoe still call him a creature? He'd been so lifesaving to have close by.

Burl made as if to pull her bag from her shoulder with his surprisingly dexterous hands. Curious to see what he wanted with it, Jade didn't resist. Lifting it gently away from her, he set the bag on the edge of a dry, flat rock and then hopped into the subterranean pool, twisting to flip the black bag open. Removing the nearly empty water flask, he set about submerging it underwater.

Camoe climbed down in the hole, stopping beside her. "Would

you look at that? Your dark creation does not drink—there is no mouth—yet it fills your flask."

"He's not a creature."

"Have it your way," Camoe said cheerfully. Squatting, he began to fill his own water bag. "He certainly found the best way down to you after bringing it to my attention you had vanished. Check for wounds; the water is cold enough you may not feel anything right away. The drop is longer than I had first thought."

Close by, a tall rock beckoned as a good place to take the weight from her tired legs. Sitting, she felt what she could of her wet body. Nothing seemed to be broken or bleeding, not even where the branch had ripped her jeans. "No wounds but I'm freezing."

"Yes, that is going to become a problem. We do not have enough sunlight to risk climbing down the next ridge. Perhaps we should remain here for tonight. It is well hidden and protected from the wind, though the humidity is high. Starting a fire may prove to be difficult, but it is critical to get you warm. We have to risk it. Hopefully the smoke will not be spotted before full dark has fallen."

Jade wasn't about to argue. Cold, wet, and weary, a fire did sound critical. "Where do we get the wood?"

Camoe set his bag and bulging water flask next to a rocky bank of debris. "It is closer than you think. With luck, I can dig out enough." Climbing partway to the surface, he pulled several wrist-sized branches from the tangled mess around them. Dropping the armful in front of her, he returned to pick through it for dry flower tops and splintered wood chips.

Watching his every move, she shivered. *Can't he move faster?* Sometimes he could be too methodical.

Camoe balled up a mass of long, dry weed stems, pressing down on one side to resemble a bird's nest. Breaking several smaller sticks to length, he set them to one side.

Her teeth began to chatter. Jade opened her mouth to keep from vibrating her skull and everything it enclosed. *I'm going to die of exposure while he builds the perfect fire,* she thought. "Can I help?"

"I do not believe so. The first part is tricky; I have to cultivate the right ember." Removing a flinty stone, a rounded piece of metal, and a charred cloth from a tin in his bag, he carefully placed the cloth in the center of the nest. Striking the metal against the flint, a spark flicked downward. After the third pass, he leaned in close and blew on the nest.

A tiny flame sprang to life. Adding a twig at a time, the druid coaxed the flame higher. The flame joined others, feeding on the wrist-sized branches. Camoe sat back, satisfied with his handiwork. "You did well in finding this place. I would have sauntered past without ever knowing this underground hut was here," he said, a soft smile playing at his lips.

She managed to flash a quick smile though her teeth clattered as soon as they touched. Any other time she might have laughed at his dry humor, for it didn't come very often. Right now though, she was convinced she was going to freeze solid where she lay.

The little underground grotto soon heated. Jade's soaked body warmed quickly, but her clothes stayed moist. Though he stayed back from the flames, Burl brought enough wood in one load that Camoe didn't have to do anything but keep it going. To her, the fire felt better than the heat of the midday sun.

Before long, her eyes felt as heavy as her sodden clothes, so she lay on her side with her bag under her head, giving in to her fatigue.

Jade woke in the gray darkness of predawn light. The fire had burned down to tiny embers, glowing with a last stubborn light. Her clothes had dried except for a few persistent damp spots on the seams of her jeans. The grotto still radiated warmth, but it was cold on the side of her body farthest from the fire. Camoe would need to rebuild it soon.

Though still sore, she decided to do it herself. The heat would do them good. Stifling a groan, she sat up. A sound made her freeze. Snuffling drifted down from the entrance hole above and echoed softly throughout the grotto. Fear stole through her.

Suddenly, the tiny embers seemed terribly bright.

Animalistic by the sound of it, the snuffling grew louder. Jade heard heavy breaths mixed with guttural grunts and then the sound of padded feet coming to a standstill straight above them.

A hand gripped her elbow. Jade stiffened, too frightened to cry out or gasp with relief when she realized it belonged to the druid.

After an interminable time, the padded feet moved to the cliff edge Camoe had looked over. A commotion of snuffles intermixed with soft whines floated down. *There are several of them,* she realized. Milling back and forth, the whines mixed with deep-throated growls. Amid savage snarls, and without warning, the sound of padded feet faded rapidly into the distance.

They sat in silence, Jade scarcely recalling the need to breathe. Finally, Camoe spoke, his voice low enough she strained to hear. "I believe they are gone. At least, I hope so. I have no idea what manner of species the Dark Citadel has sent to track us. From the sounds of them, I have never encountered their like in my seasons of infiltration. Nor would I want to. We shall have to use caution from this point on, keeping a sharp lookout and making no noise."

Jade was numb. How could she hope to travel quieter? She was already putting forth her best effort. "I thought we'd been careful."

Camoe stood. "We have to keep better watch from now on; I have been too lax in favor of keeping our strength up. Come, the night is drawing to an end."

He was right. The outer edges of the stepped ledges peeked out of the darkness, but something was missing. "Where's Burl?"

"Blast it!" Camoe swore. "Your bloody dark creation has run off, gone back to his dark master. He shall bring enemies upon us!"

"Burl!" she called, a bit louder than they'd been speaking.

"Jade!" Camoe said, his voice hoarse. "We must be quieter. Those animals—or whatever evil creations they are—could still lurk close by. Let them get some distance away before we get moving. The best we can hope for is to avoid them and stay ahead of the pursuit."

Jade didn't trust herself to speak. She grappled with Burl's disappearance. He'd been watching over her without fail for days.

Why would he leave now?

"Drink your fill of water; it will become scarce from here," Camoe whispered, unstopping his leather flask. "I want our water flasks topped off, too."

She glanced around the grotto. "Where's my bag?"

Camoe lowered the flask from his mouth, glancing around. "Blast it all to dust! Now we only have one pack and one water bag. The fault is mine for allowing us to sleep at the same time and trusting that creature to wake you at the sign of trouble. I am a bloody fool! Here, drink this until you feel sick." He thrust his flask in her direction.

Despite her worry, she did as instructed, draining two-thirds of the flask in one pull, surprised at her thirst. She upended it again. Finally, she couldn't swallow another drop and handed the nearly empty vessel back.

The druid submerged it in the flowing water. Then, slipping the flask over a shoulder he stood and moved as close as he could. "What was in your bag?"

Jade thought about it. "My water and quite a bit of food; it will hurt us not to have it."

"We can make do without the food. The water is far worse."

Suddenly, Jade felt sick to her stomach. "The water isn't the worst of it. The white candle is. It's important. I know it! I felt *something* whenever I've touched it. Crystalyn will be so mad that I lost her Indenture Service Provider's artifact."

Camoe drew a sharp breath, made intense by its low volume. "You had a white candle, a white *crystal* candle? Why did you not tell me?"

Jade was indignant. "When have I had the chance? It's not as if we've had much leisure time around a warm campfire. Besides, I had to know I could trust you."

"Can you?"

"Yes, I know that now."

Camoe's blue-gray eyes glinted in the dimness of first light. "I would have given much to study the candle. You are correct believing it an artifact. All the crystal candles are, though I have never heard of the white one. Perhaps it is one of the rarer ones. Infused with Greater Flow, it could augment a User's ability, limited only by the User. Infused with any Flow at all, it is still a great loss. It is likely the candle is what the dark creation's master wanted all along. If it *is* of the higher class, it's a strong possibility your creature's master was able to perceive it by the creature's proximity to the artifact. Our side has taken a great blow."

Jade wasn't thinking about sides, but she did feel bad about losing the candle. *And* for losing Burl, she missed him already. She couldn't believe he would take the candle and run off, not him. A thought occurred to her. "Your daughter had a blue one. Was it an artifact? Did it have power, this Flow you mentioned, infused in it?

Camoe paused. "I have not had time to assess the strength of your...ability. It is stronger than I knew. Yes, Maialene had a blue crystal candle, one that augmented her ability quite a lot, though it was not one infused with Greater Flow. Some of those great artifacts can negate the need for an Interrupter, but they are extremely rare."

"What's an Interrupter? Have we talked about this?"

"I do not believe so. We shall but not here. Come, we have allowed them to move far enough away by now, I do not wish to give them time to come back if whatever scent led them away fades."

The rock stairway brought them to the debris mound's surface where Jade glanced around. Nothing seemed out of the ordinary. In fact, nothing moved at all. Not a single bird took flight. That in itself was disturbing. Now that accessible water was exposed, some woodland creatures should have crept out of the forest to investigate.

Halting at the cliff's edge, Camoe looked around. Jade chose not to think what they would do if the pack of creatures circled back; they were too exposed once they moved beyond the grotto.

Silent, the druid began the long climb down the last cliff.

Automatically now, Jade let him get far enough ahead to shout a warning in case she kicked a rock loose. Then, concentrating on the descent, she descended, avoiding looking below except where required to map out the next step of the path.

She'd learned that a glance downward might invite vertigo, the last thing anyone wanted while hanging on a cliff face. Testing the next handhold, she wondered how Burl fared, wherever he had gone. Without him, her new world had become harsher and lonelier than ever before.

Jade wanted to cry.

NOT HER WORLD

A bright, hot light lanced into Crystalyn's eyes when she tried to open them, adding to the pain inside her head. Squeezing them closed lessened it, though not as much as she wished. Still, it was some relief. Now, if only the wind would stop rocking the bed.

A woman's melodious, yet commanding, voice cursed. "Blast you, fools! Keep her shaded until you get to her inside! Do you want her blinded as she comes around?"

A paler shade of gray enveloped her as the weight of her flesh descending upon her exoskeleton crashed upon her awareness. Slowly at first, then with a frightening rapidity, she felt everything as freshly dropped into her own body. It was like the time she had controlled Lore Rayna's motor facilities and then returned to her own. Except this time, pinpricks of the white-hot pain burned under her skin, and she moaned. Was this the price for her callous use of her symbols? She *hurt!*

"Do'brieni, are you here?" Concern flowed through the link, and surprisingly, much of the pain lessened.

"Yes, my dear, sweet Broth, I'm here again. I'm so sorry for cutting you off. I don't wish it again." Crystalyn sent love and affection.

Agitation and fear flowed in. *"I have searched long; nowhere in my race's memory has this occurred. I would not have believed it possible. I, too, do not wish it to occur again. It is a very troubling and aberrant behavior."*

Her affection grew. *"You should know by now, my dear Broth, nothing about me is normal, not in the slightest way."* Her pain lessened substantially. *"Are you doing something with my pain?"*

Smugness tinged with pain flowed through. *"I also have found an ability which is not normal; in fact, I am certain no Do'brieni has accomplished it in the past. Your hurt is great. I've mirrored half of what you have so you do not bear the full brunt. The link will not allow any additional support. It will dissolve as yours does or worsen."*

Crystalyn sent gratitude along with concern of her own. *"I am in awe, Broth, but do not be so noble to draw in too much. I cannot have anything bad happen to you."*

"It is a new ability. I will be cautious, my Do'brieni."

The rocking motion ended, replaced by a firm feeling under her back.

"Leave us," the melodious voice commanded. "Not you, Leven. I need your healing abilities."

Crystalyn's eyelids snapped open.

An interior sparsely furnished with multicolored cushions laid out purposefully upon the floor. A small writing desk sat underneath a squared, clear section sewn into the tent's roof, which provided the strongest luminance. A yellow crystal candle beckoned to her from atop the desk, identical in height to her black crystal candle, though differing in design. A woman's slender fingers cupped a clear orb, made of the same material as Jade's white candle. The orb exuded a subtle sense of chaste feminine vitality she sensed through her pain. Unique symbols ringed its base.

A woman's tall, slender form stepped from the side to block her view of the candle. Opening the desk's single drawer, the auburn-haired woman busied herself with something. Sliding the drawer closed, the woman turned to face her, slipping a key into the front pocket of her yellow dress. The yellow candle had vanished from atop the desk. "The dim light of my tent will help stave off the pain," the woman said.

The woman's voice was the melodious one she'd heard. Now she had a face to match it. Wide-set, dark green eyes regarded her from a rounded face. Red lips pursed, the woman clasped her hands to the front with the patient air of someone waiting for a child's response to some unasked question.

Crystalyn wasn't confident the two of them would get along. "I still feel awful, but the shade most definitely helps. Will someone tell me what happened? How many did I lose, besides…Atoi?" Crystalyn asked though she feared the answer.

A middle-aged man dressed in stark white robes stepped beside the regal woman. "Your little friend is alive…well, not deceased," he amended. The dark-eyed man was devoid of hair. Scalp, facial, or otherwise, not even a single eyebrow defined his features. "As for the others, two had severe enough wounds I was forced to draw some strength from those without injury in order to complete the healing process…by their own request. They will require added rest."

Crystalyn was relieved yet confused. "So, no one died? How can that be?"

The woman raised a broad eyebrow, a half-smile flitting across her lips. "No, Crystalyn, as impossible as it sounds, you and your companions chased a regiment of Dark Users away. My reinforcements showed up, but you'd already forced them to begin withdrawing with your final two…detonations."

"You know my name. I don't know yours," Crystalyn blurted.

The woman's face smoothed. "So, you do not. I am Kara Laurel. This is my companion, Leven," she added, gesturing toward the man beside her.

Crystalyn nodded and then grimaced, as pain flashed inside her skull. Looking down, she pressed her palms over her eyes, waiting for it to subside. She refused to add further to Broth's pain; he already carried a lot.

When she could, she looked up to find the man and woman had moved close, one to each side.

"Your headaches," Leven asked, without preamble, "when did they begin?" His dispassionate face gave no indication as to why he'd asked.

"I'm not sure, but I think they began when I started using my symbols."

Kara Laurel's eyes flickered. "Tell me about these symbols. When you create them, do you pull the Flow from around you, or do you think about what you want to accomplish?"

She thought for a moment. "I put them together by concentrating on the patterns themselves. Most of the time I redraw them the way I want. There's no pulling and no Flow involved, I don't believe. Why do you ask?"

Ignoring her question, Kara Laurel met Leven's eyes. After exchanging a long look, the reddish-brown-haired woman fixed her startling green eyes on her again. "Have you had ailments after using, such as nausea, vomiting, or acute weakness? Perhaps nosebleeds?" she asked intently.

"I seem to be acquiring nosebleeds. How did you know?"

Kara Laurel's eyes widened slightly. "How severe are they?"

Instead of ignoring what was happening, Crystalyn decided to be honest with herself for a change. They *were* getting worse. "Bad enough they're becoming harder to staunch. The migraines come after every symbol creation, though."

Staring into the slightly older woman's like-colored eyes, Crystalyn recalled Jade. A vivid image of her sister chewing her lip flashed into her mind along with a powerful desire to find her. She would.

Crystalyn pushed her emotions away by concentrating on the middle-seasoned woman's eyes. A lovely deep green, they held a vibrant intelligence and something else Crystalyn couldn't define.

"I see," Kara Laurel said softly. Moving close enough for her to inhale the woman's scent, Kara Laurel gazed at her unblinking.

"Well? Do you know what causes it?" Crystalyn asked.

"Yes, to an extent. There is a power within you that you are using incorrectly. You are exacting too high a price on yourself. At the rate you are going, you'll likely have destroyed your cognitive mind within a few months, a year at the most. That is, providing you don't cease what you're doing today. You'll still be able to eat, sleep, and possibly see to your own bodily functions, but that will be all."

Crystalyn frowned, fighting her anxiety down. When had she taken her meds last? "How can I stop? Without it, I'm defenseless." Trapped on a world where magic use was commonplace and evil lurked everywhere, stopping would be the same as suicide.

Kara Laurel moved closer still, until she was mere inches away, saying nothing.

Drawn to the woman's eyes, a flicker of white mist, mixed with light blue, pulsed across each of the older woman's corneas. Transfixed, she stared. Regular pulses flickered there, reminiscent of blood cells flowing through capillaries.

A flash of memory bloomed in her mind. In the image, Atoi casually mentioned that Users had colors associated with their magic use. She wondered why she never noticed before, but then she recalled she hadn't met anyone with the phenomena yet. Lore Rayna's and the Lore Mother's eyes glowed. There was no way to see into theirs, even if they had corneas, which she doubted.

Kara Laurel's regal face hardened. She drew back.

Crystalyn spoke without thinking. "The pulses in your eyes are white and blue, such beautiful colors."

A sharp intake of breath arose from Leven's direction.

Kara Laurel's eyebrows rose, her eyes widening with surprise.

"Is she right? Are your colors white-blue? Is your addiction deep enough she can see them?" Leven asked.

"Yes," Kara Laurel replied, without looking away. "I'm afraid I owe you an apology, Crystalyn. I was within a moment of destroying you."

Anger rose from deep inside her. "Why would you do that? Didn't I just help you against those Dark Users? You may not find me as easy to destroy as you think." A variation of the black and gray knockback symbol formed in her mind.

Kara Laurel smiled warmly. "Stay your anger, my feisty one. There are some strange things about you, but I no longer believe you to be a Dark User. Such a User could not see my colors, nor I theirs. You must understand, I'd first thought so of you. I can detect no colors in those magnificent blue eyes of yours, yet you see mine. Perhaps you haven't been using long enough for the addiction level to show? Or is there another, darker reason for it?" she asked, her eyes hardening.

The conversation was beginning to irritate her, along with the two other people involved in it. All of her companions had fought bravely for them. They didn't deserve their suspicion. "I have no idea. Either I'm not a User at all or I'm not a conventional one. You pick which one you want, it's time we continued our journey." Expecting the worst, she sat up. Thankfully, her head didn't protest too much. "Where are the others?"

"They're outside where I sent them. Your friends wanted to be here, but I for—" Kara Laurel started but then a commotion at the tent's entrance flap gave her pause.

Broth charged through with Atoi in tow. Halting one to each side, both her companions faced the couple interrogating her. Hastel pushed through right after, tilting his head to favor his good eye. Taking in the situation at a glance, he stood relaxed yet attentive by the flap.

"I am with you, Do'brieni."

"I know you are."

A frown marred Leven's smooth forehead. "What is this? Did my lady not command you to wait outside her tent? Leave at once!"

"I am going to wait here," Atoi said.

Hastel thumbed the edge of one of his axes. "I kind of like the shade in here."

Broth made a show of sitting on his rear haunches.

Crystalyn draped an arm over his broad front shoulders, pulling the warden close for a quick squeeze. "I prefer they remain," she said, visualizing the knockback symbol again. If Kara Laurel was telling the truth, she was destroying her mind with every symbol she used. Yet what choice did she have? The tent was beginning to feel like a prison instead of a place of healing.

Kara Laurel moved away from Broth, sweeping the room with a

stony glance. Smoothing her face with a visible effort, the red-haired woman leaned on her writing desk. "Your recovery should proceed quickly without the distraction of your friends, however well meant," she said, her words clipped. Straightening, she left her hands behind her back.

"I'll decide what's best for me. Besides, my affliction is related to my symbol use, is it not?" Crystalyn asked.

"Yes," Kara Laurel admitted, moving a step away from the dresser.

"Well, it stands to reason then, my friends won't delay the recovery. Only using symbols will. Like this one," she said, producing the knockback symbol. As lovely as a black-and-white king butterfly, the symbol hung majestically in the air before her, beautiful yet ominous.

Leven shuffled to Kara Laurel's side. "What is this? I told you she was a blasted Dark User, Kara!"

Kara Laurel's eyes narrowed. "In your weakened state, you won't be able to hold it long."

"Wrong! It doesn't take anything from me to have it here. I won't pay the price until *after* I've used it. I don't want to, but you get to decide if I'm going to by your next actions," Crystalyn said, proud that her voice stayed steady. "And, Kara, your yellow candle won't help you much."

Leven gasped.

Kara Laurel's shoulders slumped. "This has escalated beyond what I expected. What is it you wish?" She sat the exquisite candle atop the writing desk.

Hastel expelled a low whistle.

Leven's tanned face whitened. "What are you doing, Kara? Prepare! She'll destroy us both!"

Crystalyn's anger at both of them suddenly flared. It would serve them right if she let the symbol knock the consciousness out of both of them. "I will do no such thing! Well, not unless you attack my friends or me, first. What I want to know is what you two hope to gain. We helped you, but you're treating me like some bloody monster you've never encountered before."

Kara Laurel nodded. "You are correct. I am shamed beyond measure. In our quest for answers for something new, we went too far. We are indebted to you and your companions for coming to our aid. What can I do to make amends?"

"Can you heal her?" Atoi asked, raising an eyebrow at Crystalyn.

Leven frowned, looking to Kara Laurel for guidance.

Kara Laurel nodded, slowly. "Do what you can, even though it won't be enough."

Scowling deeper, Leven stepped beside Atoi.

The tone of Hastel's voice was incredulous. "You're not going to trust him, are you?"

Crystalyn kept her eyes on Kara Laurel. "I am, but the symbol will remain in place for a while. Go get the others ready, Hastel. If this works, we'll leave as soon as he's finished."

"Yes, Mistress," Hastel said. Taking his time, he backed to the door and then vanished outside.

Clasping Crystalyn's hand, Leven hesitated, glancing at Kara Laurel.

"Have a care, Leven. You've seen the magnitude of her power."

Crystalyn had scant time to wonder what the woman meant. Leven's hand, while soft and smooth at first, had become rock solid, painfully constricting her delicate hand.

She was about to cry out when the pain dissolved into sweet energy.

Flowing into her bloodstream like the warmth of the new spring sun after a fell winter, energy swept through her extremities, ending with severe abruptness at her neck. The overall effect was shocking. Her body felt young and vigorous, yet her head throbbed with a dull pain beyond her years. Her symbol sickness, as she now thought of it, must be beyond a simple heal.

Leven sat back, fatigue riddling his face. "I cannot heal mental injuries," he said wearily, confirming her fear. "And the wound of a spiderbee can only be healed by a naturist druid. You have one in your company capable of it, I believe."

"Do your wounds still bother you?" Atoi asked.

Gathering her legs under her, she climbed to her feet, wincing as the puncture tore a little. She nodded to Atoi as something wet flowed down her abdomen. The two puncture wounds weren't going away soon. Clutching Broth's back for support, she kept a firm tie to her symbol. She wasn't ready to put it away just yet. The throbbing in her head had lessened, but she still felt like she did after she'd used synth for too long. But that was seasons ago, after the Hartwig kid, when she'd been a total mess. Except this time, there was no nausea.

"You are by no means cured," Leven said with a scowl. "A week of bed rest is the minimal amount for your long road to recovery."

"Is it even possible to cure my symbol sickness?" For now, her symbols were her concern. She'd worry about the spiderbee wounds later.

Leven hesitated. "I am uncertain. Only the Circle of Light in Surbo would have the expertise to attempt such a complicated healing. I suppose it's possible. Even if it isn't, they should be able to teach you how to use without so much drain. Kara Laurel could train you as well."

Hastel's grizzled head popped inside the tent. "Everyone is prepared, Mistress."

Crystalyn dissolved her symbol. "Excellent." She slipped past Kara Laurel. "Come on everybody, let's get going."

The bright afternoon sunlight struck her in the eyes like an errant laser some negligent gearhead engineer had left powered on; her hand sprang to her forehead for shade almost of its own accord.

Kara Laurel was the first to step out of the tent behind her, followed by Broth, Atoi, and Leven.

The bowl was abuzz with activity. Kara Laurel's soldiers worked at identifying corpses as they laid them side by side or stood vigilantly guarding the perimeter. Several scouts rode in and out of camp on fleet horses. Spotting the wagon next to a picket line of horses, she strode toward it.

Kara Laurel stuck by her. "Will you give me seven days of your time, Crystalyn? I could train you on the basic procedures to *grounding* yourself. Doing so will protect you from drawing too much of your own energy without losing any of your considerable strength. In fact, you might gain power with the right performance teachings."

Crystalyn thought about it. "Is that what it's called? You could show me in a week?" Then she reached a decision. "No, I cannot, I have…much to accomplish and so little time. I'll just have to chance it."

"It is a bigger risk than you know."

"Such is the way of my life," Crystalyn said. She was relieved to note all three of her Valen companions moved around the wagon. They performed the little last-minute tasks that needed doing—with thankfully, all their limbs intact. But being alive didn't mean the battle hadn't changed them in some significant way.

"It is most unfortunate you feel that way," Kara Laurel said. Glancing at the three naturists, Kara waited for the Lore Mother to catch her gaze. When the old woman did, she spoke up. "I am dismayed to hear the news filtering out of Vibrant Vale. Surbo will respond, if they are aware. When I file my report on the attack here, I will make a point of mentioning it. I now believe this attack was meant as a distraction to what the enemy is doing in your vale."

Dropping Drumn's rear hoof, which she'd been inspecting, Lore Rayna spun to face the auburn-haired woman. "What do you mean?" A big part of the living dress covering her chest was brown, as if some of the leaves had perished. A closer look revealed it was dried blood, perhaps hers.

Kara Laurel turned to the big woman, her manner reserved. "Hasn't one of your runners arrived yet? The Vibrant Vale is under concerted attack by several companies of Dark Users."

Cudgel balanced a large food sack slung over a shoulder. Both of his arms sustained clean bandages from wrist to shoulder. Crystalyn wondered why he hadn't healed fully and then she recalled Leven and possibly Lore Rayna only had the strength for severe wounds. "No! By Onan, how can this be? We've kept a constant vigil on Virun for ages. An advance warning has always given us plentiful time to prepare."

Leven walked past Atoi and Broth to stand beside Kara Laurel. "Not this time. They stole down the Serpent Gorge by the cover of darkness and crept into the dark alleys of Silent Blade to wait until their force had grown sufficient to assault the vale from the south during the dark of night."

The Lore Mother started, stiffening on the wagon's seat as if stabbed. Perhaps she had been in a way. "No! Surely one of our scouts would have noticed!"

"I'm afraid not," Kara Laurel said. "Our last report read the southern half of the vale was ablaze."

The Lore Mother's face drained of color. "Virgin Mother! I am truly sorry, Crystalyn, but my people have great need of me, of us! We have to go." Without another word, she slapped the reins on the front board, clucking her tongue unnecessarily. Drumn was already moving, and the crate banged against the rear gate. Lore Rayna and Cudgel broke into a run beside her.

"Don't worry about us, we'll be fine," Crystalyn called. "See to your people."

Threading around craters, piled debris, and the grisly remains in the field, the trio soon vanished from sight. Crystalyn turned to Hastel. He stood watching the trail the wagon had taken. "Where are the rest of the horses?"

"I know he'll be taken care of, but Drumn's going to be cranky when he figures out we're not with him. I hope the Lore Mother can manage." Hastel shrugged. "The horses are tied to a post around the side. For a wonder, we only lost one in the battle."

Kara Laurel stepped in front of her. "We could learn much from each other. Are you certain you won't stay with us?"

"I have given you my decision," Crystalyn said. She followed Hastel behind Kara Laurel's tent to where Ferral stood saddled and waiting. Mounting, she waited for her two companions to climb in the saddles of their own steeds, letting Kara Laurel wait for her answer. "Perhaps another time, we have much to accomplish before I'll have the luxury of seeing to my own safety."

"Then allow me to assign two of the reinforcements to escort you to…what is your destination?" Kara Laurel asked, raising her eyebrows.

Crystalyn ignored the question. Trusting the woman with a location was the same as inviting her to meddle. "Your men are needed here. There's a lot left to do with treating the wounded and burying the deceased. We'll be fine; these two are seasoned travelers."

Kara Laurel kept her face smooth with only a slight difficulty. "As you wish. I do hope we meet again."

Crystalyn met Kara Laurel's brilliant emerald eyes. "I don't doubt we will." Coaxing Ferral around, she urged the stallion into an easy gallop. Averting her eyes from most of the carnage—some likely hers—they topped a small hill at the bowl's end. Halting Ferral to one side of the trail, she allowed Hastel to take the lead as he passed by on the appaloosa mare. Glancing back, she reflected on how Kara Laurel's tent, while appearing small and forlorn amidst the village of tents, stood defiant, facing a field of gore. Something she was likely to see again on a world ripe with violence. Turning her back on the scene, she urged Ferral into a thick falun tree forest.

Astura was not her world, but its viciousness had blooded her. There was more in store for her. Of that, she was certain.

HOW BROKEN HER MIND

The forest shade cooled the dull ache inside Crystalyn's head to something negligible. Sitting back in the saddle, she began to enjoy the ride, feeling almost normal again. But she was far from normal, as she'd sent to Broth. How could she be? A mind affliction, with a bad habit of pulling her own energy from deep inside in order to use her magic symbols, wasn't normal. How long before one or the other destroyed her mind and rent her body beyond repair?

Crystalyn sighed. There wasn't a lot she could do about it. After all, she wasn't using her symbols to start the evening campfire or create the morning meal. She used them only when danger threatened or when healing was required to save a life. Though she wouldn't hesitate to use them if the situation merited it, the best she could do was try not to use until she'd completed training to help prevent the life-draining effect they had on her.

Astura may not allow her to play it safe. Since her arrival on the planet, there'd been few days of no danger, so she might as well enjoy the morning ride of late spring. It would get hotter as the day progressed.

Hastel set a steady pace through the behemoth trees of the Falun Forest, keeping to the wagon trail even though Drumn and the wagon had left with the naturists. The trees grew sparsely enough in the outskirts for wild meadow flowers to bloom with strong scents and vibrant colors. Some bloomed so bright and fragrant Crystalyn had to resist the urge to stop and commit the scents to memory.

She missed not having the time to experiment with new smells, especially on living things. Those days had fled, chased away by her mom's disappearance and the responsibilities of her indenture to Ruena Day. Now the sole focus in her life was the journey to find Jade and staying healthy enough to do it. Astura was making it difficult.

About midday, Hastel paused to rest and water the horses at a clear, sandy stream, for which Crystalyn was grateful. She still hadn't recovered fully from the battle despite Leven's healing. When she dismounted, the spiderbee wounds sent a stabbing reminder shooting through her stomach of her abysmal failures to close it.

"I shall follow the stream in search of small prey, Do'brieni."

Crystalyn grimaced. *"Ugh, please try to keep any graphic thoughts or images to a minimum."*

An image of Broth gazing at her, head tilted to one side, flowed into her mind. Crystalyn laughed. *"Never mind, my wonderful Do'brieni. Just don't go far."*

Hastel looked up from where he was digging into the appaloosa mare's saddlebags. "What's the laugh for?" Without waiting for a reply, he loaded his short beefy arms and then passed around sweetmeats, warm cheeses, and apples.

Crystalyn accepted the flask and the food Hastel offered though she chafed at the delay. The farther away from Carnage Field—her name for the site of the battle—the better. She could then work on putting the destruction behind her.

While Atoi chomped on a sweetmeat, her brilliant green eyes regarded her in silence.

Crystalyn found a rock next to where the little girl sat cross-legged on the grass. "Why did you run to help Kara Laurel and Leven? Did you know them?

Atoi froze in mid-chew, her eyes round. Her arms dropped to her side, the sweetmeat gripped in one hand, forgotten. "I didn't," she replied, her voice soft.

Crystalyn was confused. "You did. You attracted a field full of dark cones that attempted to destroy us while trying to get to those two. You must've known who they were. It's the only logical explanation for such a foolhardy act."

"I don't think that's what she meant," Hastel said. Squatting, he set his food on a cloth as he nibbled on smaller portions. For such a wide man he didn't eat much.

"Oh?" Crystalyn regarded the little girl. Atoi's big green eyes stared at her. Or, beyond her, she couldn't tell which. "Why would the Dark Child go to them?"

Atoi regarded her in silence.

Crystalyn was frustrated. When Jade was Atoi's age, it had only taken a simple tongue-lashing or two to get answers. It wouldn't work with Atoi. Perhaps at first, it might have, but they'd been through too much now. Atoi knew her too well. "How do I find out? I don't want you—or the entity inside you—flinging us into a combat zone again, or worse."

Broth joined the conversation, though she was the only one to hear. *"I am uncertain the Ancient young one can answer your inquiry."*

Suddenly, images bombarded Crystalyn's mind.

In them, a great darkness grew swiftly, swallowing a beautiful green countryside. Moving fast, a child-sized shape fled before the great darkness, running with incredible speed. The distance between the two lengthened. Three enormous shapes detached from the darkness then, forming into colossal flying beasts. Overtaking the child shape, the oblong-winged forms drew together to block the sun. Spurred to greater speeds, the child-like shape ran into the blackness created by the flyers and vanished.

Crystalyn's mind reeled. *"Oh, Broth, please, don't do that without warning."* What did it all mean?

Confusion flowed through the link. Crystalyn felt it as if it were her own. *"What have I done, Do'brieni?"*

"Overwhelmed me with those images, there were too many, too fast. Who was the shadowed child?"

An image of Broth stalking though trees in search of prey flowed in. *"I sent no images."*

"But if you didn't, who did?" Crystalyn asked aloud, her eyes still fixed on Atoi. The girl had resumed eating the sweetmeats.

Abruptly, she stood, going to the nearby stream and pulling stalks of grass from the moist ground. Bringing them back, she offered them to the black mare. The mare pulled them from her tiny hand, munching away happily.

The child shape *had* been about Atoi's size. "How did you do that? What was chasing you?" Crystalyn asked.

Atoi's large eyes regarded her. "Do what?" she asked without much interest.

"Send me those images. I'll ask again, what was that chasing you? It was you in them, wasn't it?"

Atoi's bone-white face remained smooth.

Crystalyn regarded her young companion until it was obvious she wasn't going to receive an answer.

"She won't answer if she doesn't know it," Hastel said.

Crystalyn started. Hastel had the appaloosa's reins firmly in hand, the saddlebag buckled. "You've known her a long time, haven't you?"

Hastel eyed Atoi, his face taking on an odd, tender cast unbefitting his normal gruffness. "Aye, I have indeed."

"How many years would you say?"

Hastel's scraggly brown beard tightened around his small mouth. "Since I was a babe, younger than she appears now," he said, his voice barely audible. Moving away, he climbed into the spotted mare's saddle, his axes thumping against his thighs. Shifting his weight forward, he looked back at her. "We should keep moving. The daylight left to us will barely be enough to see us camped halfway to Surbo."

Crystalyn scrambled onto Ferral's tall back. "Wait!" she called, bringing her horse around to follow. Hastel passed by Atoi as the young girl mounted the white mare. When Crystalyn caught up, she asked, "Has Atoi ever shown you images…inside your mind?"

Hastel brought the horse to such a sudden halt Crystalyn nearly rode past. "No. I didn't know she could. Are you sure it was her and not your warden?"

"I'm reasonably certain, yes."

Atoi trotted past them without expression, not glancing their way once. Hastel's face soured. "No matter, I doubt she'll ever share a vision with me," he said quietly. Kicking his heels gently to the mare's belly, the white-spotted horse jumped into motion.

"Hastel, you can't leave it like that! Why wouldn't she share with you?" Crystalyn called, loosening her hold on Ferral's reins. The big horse sprang past Atoi's mount, following the appaloosa. Hastel ignored her shout, his horse nearly at a full gallop.

Bloody stubborn man, she thought. How was she ever going to know what was going on if he wouldn't tell her anything?

Ferral needed no urging to run. At full gallop, Crystalyn hung onto the reins, recalling that Broth had wandered downstream hunting, though she could pinpoint his location without much effort. The warden was stationary downstream. *"We're on the move again. Hastel's being petulant."*

"I am aware you are moving away. I will complete my meal and join you soon. There is a peculiar darkness in the human Hastel, yet I've detected no malice toward you."

"You can do that; detect malice, I mean?"

"Only when directed toward my link mate or myself. It has limitations on the specifics of what I can sense."

"You mean someone would have to have murderous intentions."

"Yes. You continue to surprise me with your advanced grasp of our ability." She caught a flurry of emotions from him: pride, confidence, and a slight hint of arrogance.

"You expected me to notice that."

"Our link is gaining in strength."

Crystalyn didn't have the same exuberant outlook as the warden. She was afraid of a close link. Would the time come when she didn't know which emotion was hers? No. She wouldn't allow that to happen. Too much depended on her being her. No matter how broken her mind had become.

DESOLATION

Jade reveled in the mundane task of walking on level ground. Even though her arms and legs begged for the mercy of extended bed rest, she was heartened to be upright and on her own two feet, not worrying about losing her grip. At least if she fell here, it was only a short way to the ground.

Camoe preceded her, slowing whenever he noticed her lagging behind. Jade glanced back at the route down the plateau, for a moment expecting to find Burl trailing behind. An empty cliff face stared resolutely down at her like some monstrous stone leviathan. As before, at the grotto, nothing moved there. No bird flew along the towering cliff faces on gliding wings. No sure-footed animal bounced from ledge to ledge.

She'd half-hoped to see Burl climbing down a ledge, disjointed legs dangling below him. Instead, there was…desolation. On an impulse, she opened up her mind, listening for anything moving, however small.

She stumbled and nearly fell. Something else was there, a presence she didn't expect, would never have expected. Desolation wasn't so desolate. Her mouth dried. Desolation was aware. It watched. It waited. It was aware of her.

Prying her eyes away from the plateau, she closed the distance to Camoe, trying not to glance over her shoulder. The essence druid chose to take her quickened steps as an indication to pick up the pace. She was happy to comply; the urge to run raced through her to the core.

Sucking in her lip, Jade pondered the feeling she still had.

Something powerful and clinically evil had grown aware of her and sensed that she was aware of it. It wasn't certain how something could be aware of it from so great a distance, so it watched and waited. Now that she'd opened herself to it, she couldn't drive its foulness from her mind. It had the horrible reek of an army of dominion wraiths watching her, seeking her. Nothing could be that powerful, not even here, could it?

Camoe kept his grueling pace until dusk brought twilight down upon them. Rounding a fallen falun tree, he halted at a massive root system that created a natural windbreak. Setting his bag down, he began to round out a fire pit with the many flat stones nearby. Jade gazed ahead. A line of dark trees trailed black vines from most every branch. A foul smell permeated the air, wafting from their direction.

Jade turned her back on the dark trees. Gathering smaller rocks, she put them in the holes left from the bigger rocks her companion had stacked in a circle. "What's that stench? Do you smell it?"

"One would have to have cauterized nasal canals to not smell it. Behind those cypress trees are the Fetid Swamps. The only way to avoid them is to keep clear of the region altogether, which I always do as much as possible."

Jade's stomach sank. "But not this time, I suppose."

"No, not this time, it's going to provide a natural cover for us. Even the Dark Users give it a wide berth. I expect they shall not follow us in there."

"So, you think we're being followed or we will be?"

"We cannot afford rashness. Not with your little dark creation out there knowing which way we went."

Jade chose not to respond. All she knew was that he was missing and that she missed him. "When I looked back at the path we took, no one was following us, not down the cliff. It's funny though, the mountain did seem to be watching us. At least, part of it was."

Camoe froze, his hands gripping the last rock for the pit. His light blue eyes regarded her with disbelief. Or was it surprise?

Gathering kindling, Camoe spent a few moments building a fire without looking at her. "When did you get that notion?" he asked finally.

"About halfway here, after reaching the bottom of the cliff."

Camoe pulled his bag close. Rummaging inside, he began preparing the meal by setting his cooking pot on the ground. "Can you sense the direction it is coming from?"

Jade didn't need to think about it. There was a sense of watchfulness with an underlying hint of…malice, stronger south of the way they'd come. "Yes. What's to the south of us?"

Camoe's dark blue eyes regarded her. He nodded, as if he expected her to know. "A league to the south is the Stair of Despair. You have detected its malevolence."

"Oh! That doesn't sound good. In fact, it's sort of despairing," Jade said with a smile, trying not to giggle.

"No one sane would dare go near," Camoe said, his face hardening. Jade dropped the smile from her face. "It is a place of evil so ancient that no one knows how to ward against it. We have yet to discover its weakness, if it has one. Even Dark Users avoid the stair unless they have considerable power. I would rather be struck mute than go near it again."

"Yet we are near, much nearer than you would like, right? You said *again*, so you've been here before. Why come this way? Why risk the cliff ledges when you know we have to go so close to the stair?"

"Those ledges were not there a season ago. The path away from the citadel used to be a series of waterfalls with clear ponds underneath called the Plunging Chasms. The animal trails beside them provided an easy traversal with good cover. In the past, it was a way to spy on the Dark Citadel. I suspect its collapse was for this reason; some great lord somewhere figured out how good a cover it was. Our chances of passing unnoticed are still better than on the Dark Road. Both ways have eyes. By that, I mean those leaving are watched too. The great lord does not wish those held prisoner, or his creations, to escape before they are released to perform his foul bidding."

Camoe set a small pot of water to boil on an overhanging rock above the fire. "This way down from the mountain is only guarded by roving long-ranged patrols and the evil present in the Stair of Despair."

"Is having a fire a good idea with patrols about?" Jade asked. Her alarm grew thinking about it.

"It is a risk, but it is needed. What little food I have left should be heated."

"I know. My bag had most of the food we had left in it."

Camoe stood. "This will be the last fire for a while. In the morning, we shall cross into the swamps. Keep the fire as small as it is but warm enough to heat the water. I shall be gone for some time foraging for roots and leaves to add to the soup stock. I shall return as daylight wanes." Glancing into the pot once, he turned toward the blackened trees.

"And Camoe…" Jade called softly.

Camoe halted, looking back over his shoulder.

"Be careful," she said.

Tilting his head down slightly, Camoe resumed his trek across the field of stunted and overturned trees to vanish into the darkened forest.

Jade gazed at the tree line long after, willing him to hurry. She felt so exposed. But she did agree with Camoe's reasoning—a hot meal would be needed before tackling the swamp, though she hated being alone. This was a first for her since coming to this world, since the sapphire obelisks had flung her into Lord Charn's armory. Camoe had almost killed her before she'd read his aura. Viewing the image of his daughter Maialene losing her life had saved her life, she knew that now. Climbing into the smoke vent tunnel to escape the flickers had brought about the chance meeting of Burl. The mute, burlap-skinned man had saved her life—all their lives—on numerous occasions. Jade couldn't believe he'd stolen away to return to his creator. There must be some other explanation. Burl was a friend.

Moving as little as possible, Jade tended to the fire twice, gathering twigs and branches from the fallen falun tree. Many times, she gazed at the path Camoe had chosen, expecting to see him enter the clearing, his sure-footed steps quickly bringing him across the dying meadow, but nothing moved. The tree line darkened and then faded from her sight as the night cloaked them from view.

Despite her best efforts at keeping it only warm, the water began to boil. She worried that Camoe hadn't made it back before full dark set in. What if something had happened to him and he never came back? No. He would come.

If only Burl was here, at least she'd have her stoic companion to lean on. *Where is he?* she wondered again. His quiet companionship was truly a comfort. She hoped nothing awful had befallen her friend. She'd relied on him almost as much as she did Camoe. How would she survive without him?

Camoe stepped into the campfire's meager light after she'd added their precious water to the boiling pot twice. Relief flowed through her. As hard as he was to agree with at times, she was happy to see him. Being alone didn't suit her.

Setting two small rodents on a rock, Camoe began processing them with expert strokes of his wide knife. Several freshly dug roots and harvested herb leaves from his foraging appeared out of his pouch next. Scooping it all into a pile, he deftly deposited every ingredient into her boiling water. Making use of the same blade, Camoe stirred vigorously for a moment. Jade smiled when he set the knife to the side, looking her way.

He smiled back though it was quick. "I must apologize for my extended absence. I did not mean for it to take as long as it did. Game is scarce in this country, but we are in dire need of protein for the next leg of our journey. I had to stalk the outskirts of the swamps for a fleeting chance at small game. Not my preferred choice, but they will do."

He was right. If the journey to this point was any indication, extensive physical activity required energy. The last thing she wanted was for her body to start feeding off her muscles. "They will do," Jade said, suppressing a yawn. "Are the swamps going to be as bad as the Dark Citadel's tunnels or the cliff faces we climbed down?"

"The swamps could be worse; they harbor some of the most unfavorable creatures native to my world, though not many here are as bad as the dominion wraith." He paused stirring the pot, regarded her for a moment, and then returned to cooking before speaking. "I will meet with the Vibrant Elders upon my return to the vale to discuss how it could be possible for you to survive such a thing as the wraith. I need to submit a report summarizing my time at the Dark Citadel as it is."

Jade wanted to know what a Vibrant Elder could be, but a horrible thought rose in her mind. "We are not going near this Stair of Despair, are we?"

Camoe glanced at her sharply, saying nothing. Removing two tin cups from his bag, he carefully poured soup from the pot into both. Setting a cup near her, he sat with his back to a rock, sipping quietly, regarding her in silence as she sipped hers.

Just when she'd begun to believe no answer was forthcoming, he set his cup down. "I had thought to save you anxiety, yet you ask the precise question I cannot provide a vague answer to without telling something false, which I shall not do. We have to travel near the stair's beginning ascent," he admitted with a sigh. "The Fetid Swamps at this end are too wide and too deep without a portage canoe, so we shall chance the driest route I know."

Catching some of the bigger chunks in her teeth, Jade chewed. It was quite good, though she avoided dwelling on the type of rodent supplying the protein. The soup warmed her insides, helping with the chill night air. Energy returned to her extremities. Another frightening question occurred to her. "Is it guarded?" she asked softly.

Camoe blinked. "The Stair of Despair's base is guarded by wrights and something as ancient as the first Dark User lords, possibly older. The wrights have a name given them from the method they feed on any warm-blooded creature. They've learned their meals stay freshest by keeping the food alive as they feed."

"They eat their food alive?"

Camoe nodded. "Alive, for as long as they are capable; eventually a person would succumb to the loss of blood. The creatures are known as maimwrights."

A chill swept through her the hot soup wouldn't warm. Her protein energy fled before the weakness rising in her bowels, and she was suddenly tired, tired of the constant flight from danger only to race toward something just as bad. From the sound of it, a maimwright had to be as bad, or worse, than anything they'd encountered, so far.

RUINS

For the first time in days, Crystalyn's behind wasn't hurting as much after a long day in the saddle. The last four days, her stiff muscles had left her hobbling around like an old woman. Every night she'd lain on her blanket, mimicking Jade's habit of biting her lip to keep from crying out. Hastel had brought supper to her each time with many a promise it would get better.

He'd been right. Tonight she'd fetch her food herself, after she found a pond or stream, something with water for a long overdue scrubbing. A mud bath would feel cleaner than she did right now. Gathering her hand towel rolled about the falun leaves, Crystalyn headed upstream beside the little brook Hastel had selected for the night's camp spot.

"I'm coming, too," Atoi said, falling into place behind her.

Crystalyn expected as much. It had become their evening routine. At least, it had before Crystalyn had developed new rider butt, as she thought of the preceding painful affliction. Hopefully, the worst was behind her both figuratively and literally. Atoi must be pining for a wash as bad as she was.

"I shall begin the hunt alongside the path you choose, Do'brieni."

Crystalyn took comfort in the knowledge Broth would be near. The warden had proven himself a fearsome warrior at Carnage Field.

The trail was springy brown grass, easy to traverse. Crystalyn found a bathing spot after a short walk. Surrounded by conifer trees, a rocky pool big enough for one person to stand in awaited; seasons of forest creatures drinking from its shallow banks had helped pool the clear water. Crystalyn stripped down to undergarments, unwilling to wait on Atoi.

The water was cold as usual but well worth the first icy shock upon her warm skin. Scrubbing diligently with the foamy falun leaves, Crystalyn spent a few minutes washing the dust and mud from her body. The black water clouding at her feet made her wonder if it came from days in the saddle following Hastel and Atoi and then nights sleeping on the ground or if the pool's muddy bottom had been disturbed by her feet. Not that it mattered. The rest of her was clean, at least for now.

Wading to the water's edge, she found a handy log to sit on as she rinsed her feet in the brook. Raking her fingers through her hair, Crystalyn pulled the biggest tangles free, though Atoi's comb would have made it easier. Where was she?

"How far back is Atoi?"

Broth's reply wasn't immediate. Crystalyn's backside began to throb from sitting on the log. She sighed. It was time to head back anyway; she'd ask for the comb on the way. What could be taking the little girl so long?

Confusion flowed through the link. *"Strangely, the Ancient young one left the trail not far from you."*

Crystalyn understood his confusion. *"Why would she do that? No, don't answer, of course, you wouldn't know. Stay where you are, I'm coming."*

Rounding a nearby bend, Crystalyn found Broth sitting on his haunches facing an inconspicuous side trail that snaked off through the trees. "Atoi might have answered the call of nature, but so far she's let me know so we could stand guard for each other. It doesn't make sense for her to wander off on her own. Can you follow her scent?"

"Yes. No other being has a scent as old as hers."

Broth slipped into the trees without a sound. Crystalyn envied him his natural stealth. All forest creatures seemed to have the innate ability to be ghost quiet. At least she thought of him as a forest animal, but she wasn't so sure. There wasn't a thing to compare him to, certainly not with his human-like mind. She dressed quickly and slipped into the forest after him.

"The Ancient One's trail indicates she's no longer at a walk." Broth's sudden thought permeated her mind, mixed with Atoi's musky scent. Atoi was musky?

"Atoi's running?"

"Yes, I suggest we do the same."

"Agreed, I think I'm up to it. She has me quite curious now."

The knots in her muscles from a long day's ride worked loose as she ran headlong along the winding trail dotted with new tree growth still small enough to see over. Crystalyn sprinted, watching the path ahead with care so as not to trip over the many toppled trees lying horizontally across the path.

After a time, the trail widened, becoming two trails running side by side. Not two trails, one road, she realized. An old wagon road slowly encroached upon by the same forest cut down to clear the path for it long ago opened the way forward. Their pace lengthened considerably now that they didn't have to vault over so much deadfall. Sprinting under two falun trees' overhanging branches, she slid to a halt. Ahead, the forest ended. Moss-covered, bleached ruins of some ancient structure oversaw a talus-strewn clearing.

"The Ancient One is there. She is not alone."

"Who's with her?"

"I am uncertain from this distance. Perhaps when we move closer," Broth sent. *"Several vague human scents clung to the link, all smelt unwashed, some fearful. Moving near is our intention, is it not?"*

"Yes, why wouldn't we? She could be in danger."

"It may trigger an ambush."

"Then we shall keep alert. Will you do something for me, Broth?"

"Express your desire, Do'brieni. I am link sworn to follow your command."

"Should I tell you to flee, you are to do so without question."

Agitation mixed with resignation flowed through the link. *"I will endeavor to comply with my Do'brieni's command. However, I may decide the risk is too great for you alone. I cannot leave you in danger."*

Crystalyn closed her mind. She wasn't certain she liked Broth's last statement.

The ancient road ended in a circle around a broken marble statue, too worn to make out much detail. A wide, weed-grown stairway rose beyond it. Crystalyn gazed at the top of the ancient stairway as she climbed. Two hooded figures wearing brown robes stood silent and unmoving like reverent guests at a place of worship, their arms folded into their opposite sleeves.

Up they went, Broth padding easily at her side. They slowed when they reached the last few steps, hesitant, though the brown-robed figures there still hadn't shown the least bit of interest in them. A circular dais rising across the top had their fixed attention. Massive pillars supported the open sky, ringing the platform's edge. At the center, a red-robed figure stood over two kneeling brown robes. The red robe brought to mind the black robes and red robes she'd fought in the meadow.

"Dark Users, Do'brieni, be alert."

She should have known, but it mattered little. Atoi was here somewhere.

"I perceive no animosity from the brown Dark Users, Do'brieni. They do not acknowledge our presence at present. I will remain vigilant, however."

Climbing the last step, they strode between the unresisting figures clad in brown to pause partway to the center of the dais, gazing behind pillars big enough to make the brown-robed person standing in its shadow seem tiny by comparison. Twelve figures in brown robes stood in front of their own monstrosity in a half-circular formation, arms folded like the two at the steps. All seemed absorbed by the actions of the red-robed man in the center; not one glanced at them.

Walking forward, she kept her eyes on the red-robed User's back while glancing occasionally to the sides. The red robe stood with both hands resting on the heads of two Users in brown robes. Hoods pulled back, both faced her on their knees. Fine-cut golden hair topped one head, a male. The other, a woman, had strawberry hair that swirled in a delicate, aristocratic style. The expression on her face approached rapture, but her eyes matched the man's dull gaze.

Coming to a standstill behind the red robe, Crystalyn's eyes fell on Atoi at last. Her hands bound to the front and her open mouth filled with a cloth, Atoi's face was impassive as ever. She knelt between two obelisks of black crystal in the center of the dais. A spiral, black curtain wavered slowly into existence between the two obelisks. A dark storm raged within, reminding Crystalyn not only of the Sapphire Gate but also of the Flow's squally qualities, except the tempest was black, not white, with amethyst flashes.

A second red-robed Dark User stood guard behind Atoi; her jeweled dagger gleamed, thrust under the cloth belt wrapped around his waist. Green eyes large, Atoi stared at her, unblinking. Crystalyn's heart raced. She looked so young and so innocent, but somewhere…else. Had they tortured her? Briefly, she wondered why the Dark Child had allowed its host to be treated so, though it didn't matter now. She was about to fix it.

"Broth, I think you should wander behind a pillar for a while." A mental image of him hiking a leg near a pillar flashed through her mind. Had the situation not been so dire, she might have laughed. Her affliction must be flaring again; she was amusing herself in the face of danger.

"As you wish, my Do'brieni. I shall remain within striking distance, however." Selecting a pillar closest to her, the warden vanished behind it.

Satisfied he was out of harm's way, Crystalyn sifted through her memory of the last few evenings spent reading *The Tiered Tome of Symbols,* tier three. Recorded with fine black ink, the first symbol she studied under the ominous heading affliction came to mind. Once the image was fixed in her mind, she combined it with the smoky garland symbol she'd used at Carnage Field, redrawing both into one uniquely her own. Keeping the new image locked in mind, Crystalyn spoke quietly. "Untie her, please."

The red-robed man stiffened, his hood swinging to the side as he looked over his shoulder. "Ah, there you are. The thief said you would come for her."

"Please, let her go." Crystalyn kept as neutral a tone as she could muster. She'd be surprised if he did, but she did still hope for a peaceful resolution. The man's silky, self-assured tone brought to mind the Hartwig kid again, drying her mouth.

"I'm afraid I can't do that. Your little friend stole something quite precious to my lord," he said, his smile showing even white teeth above his brown goatee. The smile never reached his dark eyes. "I went to considerable trouble to entice her back here with the promise of additional powerful weapons."

"You have the poisonous dagger back now."

"Oh, so you know of its infused property?" The man's eyebrows drew together on his forehead, accenting his narrow face. The two brown robes stiffened under his hands. The image between the obelisks wavered violently.

"Yes, I know of the dagger's…magical ability. I will ask again, let Atoi go. I'll see to her punishment for the theft. She'll compensate you for your troubles, with enough to take back to your lord if you so choose."

"She has nothing monetary I require—the great lord provides all that I need—but she does have a power within her that shouldn't go unheeded. Your Atoi is already mine to use as I please, Crystalyn."

Crystalyn's patience had worn thin. Negotiations were going nowhere. "So you know my name by forcing it from a little girl. What about you, got a name?"

"Ah, hah…here we go," the red-robed Dark User said. His focus on the obelisks had resumed. A dark, misty gateway swirled between the two crystal shards. As he removed his hands from the two brown-robed figures' heads, they collapsed to the dais floor in a heap. Spinning around in a flourish, the man bowed his head, saying, "I am

Malkor, which you would do well to remember."

Crystalyn moved close. "I *might* recall it. I can say it has been…informative to watch you use, Malkor. Though I daresay most of your power came from those two on the floor. Do they live?"

Malkor's narrow eyes widened perceptibly. Bright red flecks of color interspersed with something darker pulsed across his brown corneas. "You don't use Interrupters?"

Crystalyn was surprised, but she kept it from showing. The man and woman in the brown robes had interrupted the Flow like the Lore Mother. She should have realized it from the start, even though the method was so different. Malkor appeared to have drained them completely, which seemed inefficient as well as cruel. Interrupters must be in high demand with Dark Users for there would be a shortage.

The colors pulsing in his eyes put her slightly off balance. Now that she'd noticed them there, the pulses caught at her vision as if her eyes needed reassurance she hadn't suddenly lost the ability. Looking away from his eyes, she focused on a closer look at the man. The haughty, half-smiling set of his jaw indicated arrogance. Malkor was comfortable with his own ability. He believed he had the situation well in hand, like the Hartwig kid had.

Malkor's countenance darkened the longer she remained silent. He expected immediate answers whenever he spoke. Crystalyn had never been any good with such arrogance. She was nobody's subservient. The time had come for her to set the provocation imp loose upon the arrogant man, so to speak. Malkor should be easy to provoke. Provoked foes made mistakes. "Of course, I do. I don't usually use them up, is all. One might find them useful in the future."

Malkor's small eyes bored into hers, ignoring the challenge in her words. "Your accent is strange. Where did you say you hail from?"

Crystalyn decided to try for a peaceful resolution to the situation one final time. "Suppose I tell you. Will you let us leave without harm?"

Malkor pulled his red hood over his curly brown hair, shadowing his face. "I may have other…questions," he replied, his tone thick with elation.

So. He didn't intend to let them go; the delight in his voice told her that. He thought he'd won, that she was giving in. Still, she wanted to give him a chance to do the right thing, having had her fill of battle after Carnage Field. "I'll tell you what I can as long as you give me your word you'll leave my companions and I alone."

Malkor's eyes narrowed. He scowled. "The little thief never mentioned anyone except you. Where are the rest? Command them to show themselves!"

Crystalyn's ire grew. She'd made all the concessions and received nothing in return. Negotiations had failed. Danger now loomed over Broth and possibly Hastel, initiated by her stupid, blundering mouth. It didn't matter now, had never mattered. From the start, cooperation had only stoked his brutality; Malkor's type should have been simple to read. Power was his only ambition. "My companions are my concern. Please, release Atoi. I don't want to get angry with you."

Malkor's eyes bulged. "You stupid, foolish, arrogant little girl. Allow me to inform you what happens now. You won't be enslaved, as I first intended," he said, his voice a hiss. Taking a step backward, he lowered a palm toward the ground. "Your death will, instead, be marked by cries of pain. Everyone, burn her, burn her now where she stands!"

At the edge of her vision, brown shapes removed their hands from their sleeves.

Crystalyn had anticipated anger to follow her demand, but she hadn't expected him to attack so quickly. She released her prepared symbol as Malkor's hands vanished behind a red mist. Black raindrops coalesced into the symbol as it spun in front of her. Picking up speed, the symbol spun, flinging the droplets away in a growing circle at an incredible rate. Whirling faster and faster, droplets shot forth like a sodden cloth wrung dry, though her symbol was no towel, nor were the droplets flung made of water. They were liquid, however, an unforgiving fluid, something she may not have chosen to release had she known its deadly effect.

Where the droplets landed, black smoke hissed and finger-sized holes appeared. Gray marble, clothing, or flesh, it didn't seem to matter. The black rain burned through it all. Nausea rose in her stomach, but she forced herself to continue or be overrun. Rotating her body and the symbol with it, she peppered the figures in the brown robes, their fists aglow with a tan translucence.

Some of them managed to hurl clouds of needles at her symbol. The dreadful rain steamed every needle, however small. Black, caustic drops flew at the hapless Users. Some died screaming as the droplets ate through the main artery of an arm or leg. Others dropped without a sound as the black liquid sank through tissue, bone, or some vital organ.

The left side drenched, she worked her way down the right until she faced Malkor. The red-robed Dark User had erected a transparent barrier around his body but not before one leg had taken severe damage. Lips peeled back in agony, he hopped toward the black obelisks and vanished through the gate. Crystalyn swept the symbol over the one guarding Atoi.

Broth's enraged growls broke through her methodical cleansing.

Crystalyn dissolved the symbol, feeling detached but with a growing sense of elation. She'd won. With the exception of Malkor, no Dark User had survived. She had beaten them all. No one visible was upright.

Atoi appeared intact with no open wounds in sight. Crystalyn knelt beside her oldest, yet youngest, companion. The little girl was still unconscious, though her breathing seemed normal. She wondered if it was possible to kill her. Atoi the girl might die should her little host body take damage beyond the entity's ability to heal or replenish her blood. Once the precious bodily fluid was gone, it might leave the husk behind. Perhaps. Or, perhaps, the entity shielded her from the worst damage. Who knew what it could do, or what it *would* do. How badly would it want to preserve its host?

Atoi the Dark Child was a mystery that rarely communicated. She was glad she'd met her and found a friend with the little girl. Though calling Atoi a friend was stretching her sensibilities a bit—the little imp *had* stabbed her on their first meeting—but she'd been a loyal little sociopath thereafter, even bringing help to rescue her from the spiderbees. Whether the being Atoi carried inside was a friend was still a mystery. Crystalyn suspected *friend* was as alien a concept to it as it was alien to them all.

Her eyes fell on the dagger lying beside the tattered, red-robed guard's corpse. Picking it up, Crystalyn was surprised at its weight, far less than its size suggested. The balance of the thing was flawless.

Weakness and pain flowed into her mind. *"Do'brieni!"*

"Broth! Oh no, please, don't be hurt!" Silence subdued her silent plea.

Fearful of what she would find, Crystalyn ran to the last place she'd seen Broth. Rounding a pillar, she slid in a dark red liquid, careening against a brown-robed body, flailing to keep her footing. Broth lay close by. Many brown robes lay wet and torn around her faithful companion. No one moved. Not even her *Do'brieni. No!*

Falling to her knees, Crystalyn willed her heart to slow while groping under the warden's front shoulder where his fur was thin. The area slick with his blood, Crystalyn spent a terrifying moment finding a weak pulse. It would have to be enough. *It had to.* Bringing out her golden healing symbol, Crystalyn attached herself to it as it sank into her companion.

WAIL

Sucking her bottom lip into her mouth, Jade peered in terror over Camoe's shoulder as he crouched. The terror she'd sensed, growing ever stronger since leaving their camp hours ago, had its source within the monstrous wall rising dark and ominous from where they hid. The rock and earthen pile that concealed them was small: Jade imagined two giants hiding behind a thrust cycle. Some part of her and Camoe had to be sticking out flagging the enemy.

Spread out beyond their lonely pile, a shattered talus field lay leveled, as if someone had ignited explosives throughout the area, and then dragged something heavy over it once to fill in the holes. Why had the druid brought them so close? The wall was not as high as the one above the Black Gate at the Dark Citadel, but still it was high. Someone or something was watching them cower behind these pebbles; she could feel it through every fiber of her being.

Her benefactor acted from desperation. There was no way she'd be able to do what he wanted: she couldn't step out into the open in front of the ominous thing, not even with sunlight fading. It was too barren, too open out there. Even a small lizard would have to move carefully, scurrying from rock to rock. Where was the pitted ground Camoe had described earlier?

Jade glanced at her druidic guide. His plan had seemed a bit brazen behind the cover of the short, rocky ravine that had brought them this far. He had assured her that by keeping to small drainage ditches and cratered holes left behind from ancient times; they could pass the wall undetected in daylight.

They had to do it by light of day. Nightfall, he'd claimed, would increase the danger of the guardians' detection. Now look at them, stuck behind a pile of pebbles, afraid to go forward and too wary to go back. The risk was too high they'd be spotted a second time. Yet what else could they do? Sit here and wait for the stair's denizens to slaughter them at day's end?

A winged shadow in the shape of a large man darkened the ground before them.

Camoe tensed.

Jade bit her lip to keep from crying out.

What landed a spear's throw away was no man. The back of its large, wide head had thick brown hair, but any resemblance to human ended there. Its scaled wings befitted a hatchling dragon with prominent bone spikes protruding from the membrane tips. Jade guessed without difficulty what the creature was from Camoe's earlier description.

The maimwright retracted its dragon-like wings along its spine, forming a spiked carapace that added to its already formidable armor. Shifting on splayed, three-toed feet, the maimwright pointed its head toward the swamps, showing its beaked profile.

Jade's bottom lip hung slack in her mouth, chewing forgotten as her fear grew. Thick, curved claws protruded from the end of one of its arms like a wheat scythe scissor. The claw looked strong enough to shear through an aspen tree—or her waist. Camoe's comment about maimwrights keeping food fresh blared in her mind. Its food required cutting into chunks to fit in a beak.

Jade knew she should flee, but her body failed to respond. Her eyes remained fixed on the scissor hand, watching in stark terror as the maimwright opened and closed it as though in anticipation.

A shadow passing overhead, followed by the thump of something heavy enough to vibrate the ground, heralded the arrival of a second creature. Afraid of what she would see, Jade tore her vision from the first creature to gaze at the second one.

The newcomer was a darker shade of green, yet it was similar to its partner in most every horrid detail. Its monstrous face showed wide mandibles covering the jaw where a nose should reside. Two rows of jagged, carnivorous teeth lined the beak. Above the beak, two multifaceted eyes crammed with silver octagons bulged out below its forehead like a diamond covered with a screen foil.

The green maimwright halted near the brown nightmare, opening its beak. A series of clicks and wheezes in an odd supernatural tone spewed forth, rolling over the teeth. The clicks and wheezes ended abruptly when the brown creature turned its alien head in their direction.

Camoe drew his sword with a faint rustle of air.

Jade wanted to scream at Camoe. What could he hope to accomplish against two of them? It was hopeless. The maimwrights had size and strength on their side. Camoe had only useless, helpless her. Her mind cried out a warning to run away, but terror kept her mute and frozen.

The maimwrights separated, approaching their hiding spot with surprising speed.

Camoe gripped her arm hard. He pointed with his sword, breathing a terse whisper, "Run back the way we arrived. Make for the fallen falun tree. I shall attempt to meet you there."

Jade nodded, but still her muscles refused to obey. The wrights had too few steps to go before they would be upon her, dicing her and eating her alive.

"Go!" Camoe whispered urgently. Standing, the druid faced his foes.

Both monstrosities paused, gauging the druid, but not for long. The creatures advanced.

Jade couldn't move.

The creatures were almost upon the druid and then her.

Then Burl was there, halting in front of the druid. Outstretched in one upheld hand, Jade's bag dangled, swinging back and forth by the strap.

"At least I get to destroy the betrayer," Camoe said with deadly calm, raising his long sword.

"No!" Jade croaked, finding her voice amidst her fear. "He's here to distract them!"

Four foil-covered eyes followed the sound of her voice. Each facet seemed to glisten with anticipation. Ignoring Burl, both maimwrights moved toward *her*, their scaly toes scraping rocks with metallic clicks. Why couldn't she flee?

Burl stepped behind the brown wright, wrapping the strap around the beak in one awkward, though fast, motion.

The maimwright's claw shot upward with surprising speed to grip Burl's forearm. Burl wrenched backward. A snip and a sharp cracking sound rang through Jade's hearing. The creature's head fell back at a grotesque angle. "The head is the weak spot!" Jade screamed.

Pushing off from the top of the rock pile, Camoe lunged, burying his sword halfway to the hilt in the green monstrosity's screened eye. Several inches of steel protruded from the back of the creature's head. Keeping his grip on the sword's hilt, Camoe followed it to the ground.

Burl allowed the brown maimwright to drop beside the green.

Jade drew a shaky breath, stunned; it was over as fast as it began.

Planting a booted foot on the maimwright's throat, Camoe pulled his sword out accompanied by the dull *schling* of steel against stone. Perhaps the thing was made of rock.

Holding his right arm to his side, Burl stepped toward the black wall, pointing at it with his left arm.

Jade was alarmed. "What's wrong with his other arm?"

"This isn't the place to find out," Camoe said in a loud whisper. "Come on, Burl's right. We need to move close to the wall. It shall be harder for anything without wings to spot us there." Sprinting, he caught up to the raggedy man just as he reached the wall's base.

Jade scrambled over the rock wall, avoiding the creatures. Uncertain they were actually dead, she swung wide, angling ahead of Camoe. As she ran, her mind whirled. The snipping sound must have been Burl's arm. How bad was the injury?

Burl reached the wall first. Switching direction, he ran along it toward the swamps, moving with astonishing speed.

Jade pumped her legs hard, trying to catch up. Concentrating on the layout of the ground ahead, she ran past Camoe and fell in behind Burl at the wall. There was something alien behind it, a great presence. Old when the planet was young, it was here feeding on Astura's vibrancy, growing in power, devouring a young new world with ease until making a near fatal mistake. It attempted to consume something stronger. Something its alien intelligence had never before encountered in its long history. Forced into a great slumber, it had left this world alone. Now, they'd awoken it.

Terror coursed through her veins. It was aware of her, of her ability to sense things, and it had spawned an offspring. A single brood with mobility, conceived for the sole purpose of extending the range of its dreadful wrath. For its first offspring, before the long sleep, was as helpless as it was without a host.

Onward they ran. The wall seemed to go on forever. *How big can a wall be?* Jade wondered. It was taking them too long.

The looming presence shrugged off its last vestiges of sleep.

Jade gazed wildly ahead; they must leave, but the wall stretched into eternity.

The alien awareness focused on her, unwinding one of its many tendrils. Jade's breathing grew labored, harder than her running merited. Her heart thumped in her chest. "Faster!" Jade managed to yell, not much above a croak. "We have to go faster!" She feared no one would hear her cry.

Burl somehow heard. His legs a blur, he sped away.

Behind her, the malice paused briefly where they had first contacted the wall. Slipping along the inside wall, a shapeless darkness trailed them, moving with incredible speed.

The terrain changed from loose rock to dense clay, adding traction, however small, to her flailing legs.

The dark thing on the wall's other side caught up, slowing to match her pace.

She tasted its malice, stale and thick as fog fouled with evil, and something defining, something she'd felt on this world before...boundless hunger. This hunger terrified her beyond what the flickers had, for this blackness had a timeworn, superhuman intelligence. It would first assimilate her and her ability and then feed on the threat that Camoe posed. Burl was inedible, but it would destroy him nonetheless. Running was futile. It was too fast, too strong.

Slipping up the inside of the wall, the evil within stalked the top, slowing again to match her pace.

Jade wanted to veer away, but her body refused.

All she could do was run, run until the horrible darkness consumed her, consumed them all.

Except, except, the wall was no longer beside her. She was running through a narrow path overgrown with humid, frond-like plants.

A high-pitched, inhuman wail rang through the air behind her.

AN OPPORTUNITY TO RECTIFY

The blades jabbed faster this time, coming at Garn from every direction. Daggers and throwing knives sought his eyes and torso. Brutal war axes and sharp pikes sliced through the air from the front and rear, even above, seeking to sever a femoral artery or chop his legs from under him. Curved scimitars and double-edged broadswords flashed.

Garn's dual swords whirled faster than the deadly array as he spun, pirouetting around the room in a ringing, clanging, deadly dance. He leapt constantly, his feet rarely in contact with the floor, reveling in the physical exertion of it all, but he was tiring. His toes pushed from the floor to spin him along a different trajectory than he had intended. He spun less each time.

The blades' owners had begun to notice his fatigue, attacking with renewed frenzy. The daggers and knives he simply dodged, letting them fly harmlessly over a shoulder or near an ear as he whirled. The swords that came at his waist, he blocked to a standstill or flicked away with his thick-backed swords while flowing endlessly between fighting forms. The magical attacks he blocked with the flat of his steel or dodged, letting them sail into other attackers.

All of it was tiring him, however, even with the exceptional enhancement of the sixth dose from the Alchemist. Was it his age? Or did its effect lessen with use as the Alchemist was beginning to suspect? Garn stepped up the pace, concentrating on disabling a few axes and swords to even the score. Should his age be a factor, perhaps he could mask it with skill.

Mid-pirouette, he switched his whirling long swords' direction while reversing his spin. The move nearly repaid him with a scimitar to the gut, but it worked. Expecting his flashing swords to block their weapons, the men surrounding him in the first row stumbled when their weapons met only air. Even the adept swordsmen slipped.

Garn didn't hesitate; spinning faster, he roared through the front ring with a series of ripostes designed to disarm an opponent. The sound of metal *clanging* to the floor mixed with men's cries and curses. Garn slowed, assessing the situation. The second and third ring, the one with the Users, hesitated, caution apparent in faces and body posture.

The loud *kaasoom* of the end gong sounded through the room.

The second and third ring of men lowered their weapons quickly. The first ring was down or disabled; some would need extensive internal healing. Per the unwritten rule, he'd allowed them to keep their limbs intact, this time.

Garn slowed his dance, sheathing both swords to his back as he went; it wouldn't do to have his muscles cramp, leaving him squirming in agony on the floor.

Winding down to a fast walk, he moved toward the gilded table taking up the great room's northern end. The long table was likely the Alchemist's most prized possession; at least, Garn thought of him as the Alchemist now. The hooded man spent most of his time at the table poring over maps and scrolls, settling disputes in the compound, but most often mixing together dark liquids. Black streaks on the work surface attested to the volatility of the compounds.

The Alchemist wasn't mixing at present. Instead, he was watching Garn's every move. Even though he couldn't see the feline eyes under the cowl, Garn could sense them upon him when he finally stopped moving near the table, working to keep his breathing steady.

"Tell me how you feel," the Alchemist demanded. "Are you weak? Or can you continue?"

"I could go on for some time yet but not at the pace I was setting just before you rang the gong. I'd begun to falter." Garn had learned early on to provide truthful answers to the man, nothing added, no observations, and no questions. The hooded man didn't respond to any of it. Or worse, he gave a command to have him punished. The most emotion he'd seen from the man had been the first morning back in Corteezsha's room. Or was it her cell? He was still undecided which.

Placing his elbows on the table, the hooded man leaned forward. "I have one final question. This is very important. The move used to disable the adepts—was that before or after you felt yourself tire?"

"After."

The Alchemist fell back in his chair. Silence reigned. Garn began to get uncomfortable. He needed to eat soon. After every test, his body clamored for sustenance, and waiting too long could be fatal. Soon, his body would start to feed on itself at an accelerated rate, damaging his muscles and internal organs beyond magical or potion-infused healing.

Finally, the hooded man stirred. "You are twice the age of nearly every man on the first ring, which constituted many of my best, yet you have defeated them. I have little doubt you would've beaten the second and third had I not ended it. An impressive showing, I now consider you my greatest accomplishment. You may eat."

Garn was stunned as he moved to the end of the table. Stuffing meats and fruits into his mouth, he chomped with abandon, marveling. He was the hooded man's greatest achievement, something he found hard to believe. He hadn't heard any higher praise spewing from the man's mouth, not even when he witnessed Codar best a ring of steel.

In truth, the Alchemist rarely said anything at all beyond asking questions and then making notations in a journal he always kept. The man's clinical arrogance knew no bounds.

Such arrogance helped, in a way. It would make it slightly easier when the time arose for Garn to destroy him. His disposing of evil as profound as the Alchemist's wouldn't be any different than eradicating any of the assassins who'd attempted a go at the king or one of the king's administrators. It was simply something one did to protect an innocent—or not so innocent, as it may turn out—from filth. In this case, he'd be saving tens, perhaps hundreds, of souls, innocent or not.

The Alchemist didn't care and would use any soul, male or female, good or bad, as a lab rat.

Garn had seen his type in the administration's labs. Every lab had at least one smug bastard. The difference was the Alchemist probably deserved his sense of superiority. The man was more brilliant—though dangerous—than any arrogant lab coat he'd met during his seasons of service for the administration.

Destroying him wasn't going to be easy, not by any means he possessed. So far, no opportunity had arisen, not even a poor one. Nevertheless, he wasn't about to give up or hesitate when the time arrived.

Evil as profound as the Alchemist required cleansing the way one might remove a malignant growth sucking away a person's life. Though he'd never been a surgeon, he knew how to cut away the bad parts, with force if necessary, making the hard decisions when he must. At least he had as head of the king's security, until his heart had failed and they'd replaced him.

His failing organ was now in the past. There was no sign of the slightest irregular heart rhythm. He was in better shape than he'd been back in his mid-twenties but with extra muscle mass to go with it. Whatever Malkor had done to him in the alley, he'd performed it well—perhaps too well. He was going to purge that man's malignance from this world too. During the many, many days of his imprisonment, the Alchemist had invited Malkor to join the challenge ring working to defeat him with injuries on several occasions.

The Dark User had relished hurling red cones at him. Whenever Malkor had connected, the wounds Garn received were far more excruciating than any others—Users included—requiring several healing sessions and draughts of some vile liquid. Fortunately, Malkor hadn't joined in the gauntlet for some time. The red robe seemed to have a knack for timing his cones to connect with the most painful areas of his body.

However, the last time Garn had seen the red-robed User with the Alchemist, Malkor walked with a severe limp that hadn't happened in his challenge ring. Whoever had struck the red-robed man such a devastating blow merited respect, but perhaps also, a simple admonishment to leave that particular Dark User's punishment to Garn.

Provided he ever got the opportunity. So far, opportunities for escape or retribution hadn't happened. Lined with heavy bars, every window of the sprawling one-story structure looked out upon a dismal, sand-blown landscape; each evening before night fell, the steward personally inspected each window.

There was no exterior door anywhere in the entire keep, only solid walls of granite, something he'd verified many times. The only way in or out was through the gateway Codar had brought him through. Again, the question burned through his mind: how was he going to escape to find his daughters? He *would* find a way.

His plate bare, Garn stood, ready for his next session, whatever that may be. He never knew after a bout what would occur next until the Alchemist gave an order. Besides the sparring, his schedule was set for the day or even the week. Training, then training, at least his new life was consistent.

Perhaps *too* consistent; he didn't want to get accustomed to it.

He waited before the Alchemist, watching the dainty way the hooded man ate as he chose small portions carefully and chewed slowly. The man devoted enormous amounts of time to his meals. Though shorter, he had to weigh nearly as much as Garn. Of course, outside of mixing vile brews, what else did the Alchemist have to do? Perhaps sleep, which Garn had yet to discover. Or perhaps, oversee the warehouse. Strangely, the Alchemist hadn't spent much time there since Garn came to the keep.

Pausing with silverware partway to his mouth, the hooded man looked up, his emerald hourglass eyes appraising his captive as if he'd heard Garn's thoughts. "You are free to end the evening as you choose. In the early morning, you will accompany me on an errand. It's time I put you to use. You may go," he said, waving his free hand.

Garn bowed deep. Any less would signify an act of rebellion.

Punishments were severe, sometimes fatal. Garn had seen it twice in his captivity. Both times, the hooded man had exacted the punishment personally. The first was a dagger thrown swiftly into the offending man's throat. The other, a woman, had ended with one of the Alchemist's potions forced down her throat at his command. Garn retained the image of her desiccated corpse lying where he stood now, after her lengthy struggle to live. The Alchemist had observed every nuance of her losing battle with clinical interest.

Straightening, Garn spun on his heel, striding to the end of the great room at a steady pace. The last thing he wanted was to appear anxious to be away from the Alchemist's sight. Yet he was. He didn't trust himself to be in his captor's foul presence much longer. The man was putting him *to use* tomorrow. His arrogance had no end. He was no man's slave!

But he was. Garnet Creek was the hooded man's slave as long as he was captive. The Alchemist commanded his every move, dangled his life by his dark-hooded sadistic little boy whims. He was a slave. No other word fit.

Perhaps the morrow would present an opportunity to rectify it.

BURLAP FRIEND

Jade couldn't be more miserable, but at least she lived. Groaning, she forced herself to stand. Camoe glanced at her sharply from the far side of the small clearing where he was organizing his pack for the day's march, but he kept his thoughts to himself.

Slowly, she sorted through the contents of the black bag. Everything was still intact: the food from the Dark Citadel's kitchen, the water-like vitality draught from Camoe's room, and thankfully, the white candle from Crystalyn's service. The candle thrummed when she touched it, as if it recognized her. For one anxious moment, she panicked when she couldn't find the arrowhead necklace inside, but then she recalled putting it on a lifetime ago in Burl's kitchen. Her raggedy friend hadn't lost a single item, even though the bag had some prominent gouges along the bottom. Running her fingers along the inside, she was relieved to find no gouge had punctured the reinforced leather.

"Your pet is shrewder than I believed," Camoe said.

She looked up from her inspection. "Why do you say that?"

"I suspect those marks are from dragging your bag along the ground to create a false trail for those beasts to follow."

Jade glanced at her burlap-skinned friend, surprised. Burl stood in some thick foliage, watching the back trail, his useless arm hidden inside a dense jungle of green. "I hadn't thought of that, but you must be right. It would explain why he left. I know you believe he can't feel pain, but can't we do something for the arm? Perhaps stitch it together like you did his knees?"

"I would if I could. His legs ripping at the knees has helped him run and walk faster, which was a good thing. I kept the stitches loose so he has some flexibility without them tearing further. At least, I hope so. Stitches will not hold so grievous a wound as his arm together. If you can call it a wound; there is no blood, only that black, tarry substance." Camoe gave a deep sigh. "For now, the sling is the best I can do."

Jade moved closer. A brown, double-looped rag snaked around Burl's head where his neck should be and wound around his chest to the end of his forearm. He probably didn't need to hold it with his other hand now. "Oh, Camoe!" she said. She hobbled to the druid and gave him a hug. He gave her a quick hug back. When did you do it?" Jade didn't try to keep the smile from her face.

Camoe smiled back. "He allowed me to do it this morning, while you slept."

"Well, at least it won't be flopping around. I was afraid it was going to tear the rest of the way through. Though I suppose if it did, I could carry it in my bag."

Camoe blinked.

Jade paused and then laughed. "What am I saying? I'm starting to get morbid, don't you think?"

Camoe laughed too, lighting up his blue eyes. "I don't think there's any room in your disposition for morbidity, Jade. You care too much for that." His smile faded, and his eyes grew sad. "You remind me so much of..." he added so quietly that she strained to hear. "Come, we have a full day of marching ahead of us, providing we can find a decent path through the swamps. They are the last obstacles before reaching Brown Recluse."

Shouldering her bag, Jade forced her legs into motion, grimacing. Her abused body hurt as badly as she'd expected. The dark thing on the wall had kept them running until the last failing light had made for too dangerous a trek through the swamps. Pain shot through her hips and legs, a familiar but unwanted sensation retained from the Dark Citadel. She felt like wailing as loud as the dark thing had, and then she shuddered at the thought. The worst of the journey had to be behind them. It *had* to be. Nothing could be worse than what she'd been through, what they all had.

Camoe took it easy on her for the first mile, stopping now and then to gaze ostensibly at a mossy cypress tree overgrown with black hanging vines or a clump of pale green tuber plants with dandelion heads gone to seed. Then the roots of the trees immersed in water, and the tuber plants ceased to grow. After they sloshed through brackish water at the base of a tree, Jade's boots were soon soaked, and she yearned for the dry paths of the plateau's forest.

The morning wore into afternoon, the afternoon crept into evening, and the evening ambience slid toward nightfall with the same putrid drudgery. Trudging through slime yet again, she began to hate the swamplands worst of all. Though her muscles had loosened early on, the swamps were a trial. They had to wade through knee-deep water, following what Camoe hoped was the trail. Jade hadn't the faintest idea how he knew which way to go; it all looked the same to her.

Ahead, another clump of exposed-root plants gripped the meager topsoil while floating outward from the solid frond islands they normally traversed. Camoe went toward the protrusion without deviating. Jade expected as much. They'd been using the floating sod clumps throughout the day to vault over deep but narrow waterways. Afterward, there would be phosphorescent fronds to push out of the way, as they stepped from root to root in a futile effort to stay dry.

Her soaked jeans clung to her skin, creating itchy pockets she couldn't scratch. It took an enormous effort to ignore it. As Camoe stepped on the sod island, sudden ripples and a wet plop indicated one of the swamp's denizens had noticed their passing. The ripples moved to a nearby island. Jade relaxed a bit. They were safe if the ripples moved away.

The plops with no ripples, on the other hand, held her attention for as long as she dared keep her eye on them. Most instances ended with her wondering what had made the noise. In rare cases, she'd get a flash of something green or pale white but nothing tangible enough to show her what sort of creature had made the noise.

Worse by far, was the smell. As Camoe had warned her, no one with any sense of smell would be able to ignore it. The mud they slogged through, the sickly green plants they brushed past, and the deeper dark pools of water they avoided all had a horrid stench. In terms of her most horrible conditions to travel through, the fetid smell took second only to trekking through absolute dark without a light or searching for scarce handholds and footholds on a cliffside in a storm. After a day spent in the midst of the swamp, aptly named, her natural inclination made her feel like retching every step of the way.

Camoe seemed to be afflicted much the same way. Not once had he mentioned pausing for sustenance. She was grateful for it. Eating was out of the question. Sipping the water they toted was a mistake, too, for it tasted foul in the fetid air. The druid had spit it out nearly as fast as she had. No water or food for the bulk of the day would work for her, as long as they left the swamp behind by nightfall. Camoe had assured her on a few occasions there was ample time to pass through the foul bogs with daylight to spare.

Now it looked like he was wrong.

Jade leapt the narrow stream of dark water to an island amidst the swampland sea, yet another in an endless line of islands they'd crossed. The first few times, she'd been afraid she would fall through the clumps. It was comparable to walking on a bed filled with muscle-firming gel or a giant sponge. She jumped to where the roots had grown together the thickest without thinking about it. Camoe stood on the island, gazing at a wall of tall sunflower plants. The florets encircling the head were lime green, a color she hadn't seen on the farm. Jade splashed to a halt behind him. "Now what do we do? I don't see a way past, do you?"

"Not through that mess, whatever it is. I have never seen flora like them. I do not understand, I could have sworn there were only trees around here. Trees would have meant an end to these blasted islands."

"Well, those plants are blocking the way forward. How long will it take us to go around? I don't want to be stuck on an island all night."

"We cannot be on an island at night. It is too dangerous. There are things in the water that crawl on these islands at night. Poisonous things, and worse—"

"Do I want to know what could be worse than poisonous?"

"I do not understand...I could have sworn..." Camoe said, ignoring her comment. Pulling his sword from his scabbard, he made his way to the living wall. If not for the round, black flower heads, the pale green flowers would've appeared almost transparent.

Camoe swung his sword. Slashing one direction, he mowed down a large swath. Reversing direction, he cut as big a section away on the backhand. A waist-high pile littered the ground, which he kicked to the side. The wall rippled with a tiny motion along its length. "It may not be too bad. I think I can see through to the other side. Give me a few moments." His right arm a blur, Camoe swung back and forth, stepping into the space he'd cleared.

Two steps into it, his arm fell slack to his side. His sword clanged to the ground.

"What's—" Jade began to ask.

Camoe collapsed in a heap.

A quick whoosh of air brought a sharp sting to her cheek. As she put her hand to her cheek, another sting shot through her palm. Confused, Jade had a moment to wonder why she couldn't feel the large quill sticking through her hand, but then her perspective changed.

Camoe's back loomed in her view, the wide leather strap from his bag draped over a shoulder. She reached for him. Nothing responded, her fingers, her arms, her legs...she couldn't even blink. Her eyes locked on Camoe's comatose form. Helpless, she watched as a pale vine snaked around Camoe's waist. Another slithered over his shoulder, reaching for her.

Camoe moved, the floral wall parting before him. Beyond, many disproportionately wide plants the color of blood hugged the soil around a pond of brackish water. Grouped in spotty areas around the hole, the black sunflower heads stood out in the foreground like miniature storm-warning poles broadcasting the danger lurking beyond.

Jade realized the pond was getting closer, and she too, was moving forward. Camoe was nearly to the broad, blood-colored leaves.

Burl stepped into view, the druid's sword gripped in his remaining hand. Black quills feathered his textured skin. Nearby, a group of pale sunflowers shot quills from tiny-screened holes in the florets, striking Burl in the chest with chilling accuracy. Ignoring the assault, Burl sliced through the vine pulling her. Moving to the druid, Burl chopped with the sword, severing the tether, and then cropped the group of sunflowers that had quilled him using precise swings.

At first, Jade thought he was exacting revenge until she glimpsed the blood-colored leaves flipping over into the pond. Triangular tipped with a rectangular shape, the leaves resembled jagged teeth lining an enormous maw as Burl flipped over half the plant leaves in the horrid pond. Several of the tentacle vines slithered toward him, rising up from the sides. Burl cut them away.

Swinging the sword tirelessly, Burl hacked at the remaining sunflowers.

It was soon over. The vines retreated into the water. The blood-colored leaves flipped one by one onto the dark pond, leaving a bucket-sized hole in the center.

Presenting his quill-coated back to the pond, Burl slipped Camoe's sword deftly into the druid's scabbard. Gripping the silver-haired man by the back of his shirt, Burl dragged the druid beside her. After a moment, she was moving again. This time, she moved away and off to the side of the maw. Camoe drifted in and out of view beside her.

Jade's mind boggled at her companion's strength. Burl pulled both her and Camoe with one arm. How long could he last?

Sometime later, she felt solid ground dragging against her feet. Wait. She'd *felt* it?

SURBO

Only two guards stood posted in front of the western portcullis leading into Surbo. Having heard it described as a city at war, Crystalyn had envisioned rows of spear-toting armored men stationed behind a self-important soldier who glared at the piece of paper required to enter the city. Yet neither ornate-helmed guard gave her as much as a cursory glance when she moved past them. Instead, they concentrated on the row of wagons waiting to enter behind her and Atoi.

They did exchange a look when Broth padded past, slipping under the sharp-tipped gate held high by thick, braided ropes that wound around wooden cylinders. He slowed to match her pace. Crystalyn gave the warden's front shoulder an affectionate squeeze, amazed how well he'd recovered after losing so much blood. It had taken seven days of his natural healing ability before he could move again. The first few days, she'd exhausted herself repairing him from the inside out with her symbol. Her nose bled for days, and for a while, her complexion had been nearly as white as Atoi's.

Two other guards stationed on the inside surprised her. Minus the ornate helms, the guards appeared stoic, their gazes barely meeting hers when she strode past. They seemed interested only in the steady out flux of traffic leaving the city through the gate's right-hand side.

Most of the city's multi-garbed patrons appeared to be in good spirits, adding a buzz of conversation to the clatter of boots on cobblestone, mixed with the creak of hand-drawn coaches and wagons.

Conversation slowed—or stalled altogether—when the townspeople noticed the warden strolling at her side, only to buzz louder as they moved past. Some went so far as to point or shout to a friend.

Atoi's reaction to the big city surprised Crystalyn. The young girl clung to Crystalyn's left side, head down, refusing to look up. Atoi had been sullen since her rescue, refusing to talk about it, but at least the little girl had watched where she was going. Crystalyn thought about prying the reason for the girl's sullenness from her, but paying attention to the route took precedence. Blindly following the one-eyed man was certain to leave her lost and stranded at some point, and she couldn't afford to wander in circles for days, a real threat in a city this size.

The street widened beyond the gate, thinning the crowd. Hastel quickened their pace. Crystalyn gawked as they passed carved stone structures, both commercial and residential, sharing the cobblestone street's edge with carts and pedestrians.

There was no wooden sidewalk for them to traverse as there had been in Four Bridges. The crowd of people seemed chaotic at first, but Crystalyn soon discovered the faster ones kept to the middle while the slower circulation moved along the edge of the street. Anyone not in a rush joined and departed the throng at the edge as they stepped into and out of storefronts. The left half of the center flowed toward the gate.

The right half of the center remained reserved for anyone wishing to traverse faster regardless of mode of travel. Human-borne palanquins and odd, two-seated wagons pulled by a single man mixed with solitary runners. No equestrians or animals of any sort roamed the city. It bothered her. Leaving Ferral at the stables outside the city gate hadn't sat well either. "Hastel, why couldn't we bring the horses? The streets have adequate room."

Hastel hawked and spat his reply venomously. "By order of the *supreme and infinite wisdom* of the Circle of Light, no hooved beast is allowed to mar the streets of Surbo."

"Why? They're not going to hurt the street any worse than those wagons."

"Agreed, perhaps you can ask them. They used to allow it. Then, several seasons back, the Circle constructed a stable outside each gate and posted a decree. It touted something about 'going clean.'"

"Do you know why, Atoi?" Crystalyn asked.

Atoi regarded her with haunted green eyes. "They don't like us here. Do we have to stay long?" She glanced wildly around. "Especially the animals, they don't like the animals—"

Crystalyn's thoughts sought out Broth. *"This Circle of Light wouldn't ask you to wait outside the walls, would it?"*

"Every report agrees the Circle has done well for the city, but no warden has roamed here since the decree. We shall see if they wish to gain ill favor with my race. Such a thing would not be wise."

"No, it wouldn't. I would be offended by any mention of you being left outside the walls and take it personally."

Amusement and fondness flowed. *"No concerns, my Do'brieni, I will deal with the Circle of Light should the need arise."*

Crystalyn wondered how and why the need would arise in the first place. Wasn't the Circle of Light here to help people? She should find out soon since Hastel was leading them toward the city's center. Where else would a Circle be but in the center?

In the distance, five grandiose towers topped with colored spires rose above ornate, multicolored stone buildings, all surrounded by a sandstone wall. Centered in front of the fifth and largest tower, a monstrous dome stood; its sheer size and pearly stone drew the eye.

Staying on the main thoroughfare, they finally reached the outskirt of the dome, turning onto a beautiful plaza. They passed townspeople gathered around a large fountain that gurgled with an intricate series of carved waterfalls and clever waterways lined with flowers and plants. Crystalyn wished she could join them in front of the fountain, conversing with everyone, nothing pressing going on…but it wasn't her; she'd never been much good at socializing.

Moving past, she began to feel the first stirrings of excitement. They were about to meet people who could help her locate Jade, a good step toward getting them both safely home. Perhaps then, she'd make an effort to socialize and assemble friends. Jade could use some friends too; there was no good reason for her to mope through life as a social outcast. There was so much to share with Jade, so many odd things to recount. It felt like a lifetime since they'd been together.

A hooded, yellow-robed woman stood with her arms crossed in front of her on a single-stepped, marble landing. The woman stood beside a wide stone door set flush against the dome's exterior. Hastel halted at the base of the landing, executing a small bow.

The woman acknowledged the courtesy with a slight nod, drawing Crystalyn's eyes to the smooth, white stone wrapped in a leather strap around her forehead and tucked under her thick brown hair. Lore Rayna had worn a similar stone in Atoi's room at the Muddy Wagon Inn. The woman's deep-green eyes perused each companion before fixing pointedly on Crystalyn. "What is the nature of your business with the Circle of Light?" she asked, her tone neutral.

"Our business *is* the Circle of Light," Hastel said.

The yellow-robed woman didn't respond, but her eyes hardened as she continued to gaze at Crystalyn, unblinking.

"Oh!" Crystalyn said, with a start. "I, uh, we need to speak to…to the Circle of Light."

"What is the nature of your business with the Circle of Light?" the woman asked again. "Have you come seeking aid or with an offer of assistance?"

Crystalyn frowned. What did the woman want? If only the Lore Mother or Lore Rayna could've been here to give advice. Or even Cudgel, he would know the protocol the woman required. But the naturists' homeland was threatened. She didn't blame them for leaving, not in the least. Had it been her home she would've left the journey too. "I need only small help, though I suppose we could be of assistance in some things,"

Her reply seemed to satisfy the woman. At least she asked no other questions. Instead, the white stone on her forehead burst into pearlescent brilliance, and then her eyes bled as luminous as the Lore Mother's or Lore Rayna's had, her shining emerald orbs vanishing behind the glow. The effect lasted a few short heartbeats before the stone winked out and the two deep-green eyes regarded her again. "The Circle of Light is busy with pressing matters. You are requested to call again tomorrow evening," the woman said brusquely.

Hastel expelled an explosive breath. "Blast you all!"

"Let us depart from this place," Atoi pleaded. "I told you, I told you—"

"Certainly, they do not mean as long a time as the female Contactor has stated," Broth sent, his confusion evident in the link.

Crystalyn frowned at the yellow-robed woman for many moments. Finally she stirred, her ire rising as the woman offered no further explanation. "So, you are in contact with someone inside. Please make them aware I did not make the request lightly. Delay is unacceptable. Tell them to meet with my companions and I within the hour or I may decide to tear down your city walls and let the animals inside. Keeping them out is barbaric, as it is."

The woman's eyes widened. Gathering herself, she repeated the process with the stone but not nearly as quickly. Crystalyn began to wonder if she'd have to go through with her threat when the stone winked out a second time. "The Circle has voted. You will not be put before it this day," the woman said, her tone neutral again.

Crystalyn steeled herself for a retort.

"However," the woman continued, "a high-ranking member has asked for your forbearance and wishes to meet with you within the hour…providing you leave the walls intact. Is this acceptable?"

Crystalyn nodded, unable to tell if the woman was making sport of her.

"Very well, the way is open," the yellow-robed woman intoned, gesturing behind her as the heavy door swung slowly outward on silent hinges. As soon as it was fully open, Crystalyn took the lead, not trusting herself to speak further and not knowing what to expect from the so-called Circle of Light. At least they were going inside. She'd never been any good at waiting. Besides, every minute passed was another with Jade lost on this world rife with violence.

BROWN RECLUSE

For a town of supposed monks, Brown Recluse was home to many families. Jade watched a young brown-robed mother carry a wailing child down a side street. Too tired to ask for the town's history, she kept her silence for Camoe had set a grueling pace after their paralysis had worn off. The hike out from the swamps and through the dozens of cultivated fields before Brown Recluse had sapped her energy, nearly stealing her motivation for coming to the town. A vague hope that someone would help her locate Crystalyn kept her going.

Resolutely, she followed her companion's stiff gait. Camoe had taken the pale sunflower as a personal affront to his abilities. He'd repeatedly refused to talk about it, though he did say the plant was a carnivore, so she'd been close to something else eating her again. Did she look like dessert to this whole world?

In truth, Camoe had hardly spoken during the long night of walking. When she'd asked about making camp, her question had earned her a withering look as he stabbed a finger at the full moon. He kept them moving, ignoring Burl altogether again.

Jade spent most of their brief rests removing the quills stuck in Burl and tightening the knot on her burlap friend's sling. Camoe had given her a sturdy rag to remove the quills—along with a warning to handle them delicately—but that was all.

At first, she'd been excited to reach some semblance of civilization on this world, but Camoe's coldness quickly dampened it. If one of her own companions could treat Burl like a bug carrying some possible foul disease, how would the rest of so-called civilized society react?

The druid avoided stopping at any of the many inns they'd passed this morning, though she would have loved to freshen up after their ordeal. The townspeople they trudged past must smell the swamps on them. She certainly could.

Jade hadn't prepared herself enough for the townspeople's reaction to Burl. She'd expected the dark looks they cast at the raggedy man in passing, but their outright hostility surprised her. Some of the younger crowd shouted threats, or worse, picked up stones off the street. No one dared throw the stones after a glare from Camoe, though. She tried putting Burl in the middle, but he kept turning around to walk backward, keeping a watchful eye on her. Giving up, she left him at the rear, hoping for the best.

Camoe kept a steady climb, selecting the upward slope at every intersection. After an hour trudging uphill, Jade had a good indication they'd left the town proper and entered the outskirts of the magnificent Brown Recluse Monastery.

Carved from the top of an impressive cliff overlooking the swamps, a brown granite wall ringed a cliffy mountaintop. Scraping the bottom of clouds, cathedral-like structures lurked behind the wall, each one rising higher than the one before it; as if a race of giant stonemasons had sought to reach the heavens in the distant past. Perhaps they had.

Camoe plodded on, selecting a narrow, winding road cut from the side of the cliff that lay beneath the crenelated wall. Jade's knees grew weak when she looked down. The town's horses, wagons, and people resembled an insect hive going about mindless tasks important to them.

The winding road curved beneath a massive gate built into the wall and held partway open by a chain thicker than her waist. Even with such thick iron links supporting its weight, she was glad they went under the gate without stopping, visualizing an accidental squishing should it fall.

The road climbed steeply from there to deposit them in a brown granite courtyard surrounded by the majestic cathedrals. Most of the structures displayed two statues, one to each side of their main entrances, depicting winged dragons or gargoyles.

The largest structure—the one Camoe led them toward—had non-winged statues with human forms. Two stern-faced, bald monks stared down at her from two stories above. They strode past to make their way through a set of gigantic double doors left open to the mild evening air.

At the back of the large room they entered, a carved statue of a winged woman had such lifelike detail Jade at first thought it drew breath. The statue took shape from the rock wall by cutting the stone away from top to bottom with immense skill, or at least Jade believed so. Rows of benches led to the statue, and an ornate podium stood small and insignificant below it.

Camoe trod to the podium with barely a pause. Garbed in plain yet flowing brown robes, a white-haired monk stood there, speaking in a melodic chant to his fellow monks who filled the first two rows of benches, every head bowed. No one looked up as they filed past, but the chanting monk's ice-blue eyes flicked her way, widening slightly when he noticed who trailed her. Not missing a single nuance as far as she could tell, the monk gestured to a small, inconspicuous doorway left open beyond the statue's feet. Carved with the same great skill, the door would be hard to discover once closed. Camoe followed the indicated direction, his booted feet making no sound on the rough stone floor.

The clever door led to a larger-than-expected austere room, cut from the same rock as most of the monks' residence halls. Jade would be greatly impressed with the monks' skill at carving living space from solid stone if she hadn't just escaped from the halls of the monstrous Dark Citadel. Even so, the seasons of dedicated labor required to excavate this single room was staggering.

Setting his bags on an empty shelf, Camoe sat at a small, round table with pleasant aromas wafting from bowls of steaming food. Jade put Burl beside a wooden ladder secured under a small tunnel carved—

she presumed—to provide an emergency escape from the room, since it was the only other exit.

Jade sat next to the druid, in order to keep an eye on the door, and ladled soup from a serving bowl into her cup. Camoe nodded his approval. Jade almost smiled. The weeks spent with Camoe had trained her to use caution even around civilized people. *Especially around civilized people*, he would say if she voiced her observation to him, just like her dad. Now she was content to rest her weary body and sip her soup in silence. Plain vegetables soaked in some sort of meat broth enlivened her road-weary extremities.

She'd finished the bowl before noticing a golden loaf of bread beckoning behind the serving bowl. Spooning soup, she sliced a chunk of bread to dip inside it. Soft and absorbent, the bread melted in her mouth, tasting wondrous in its simplicity. After weeks of enduring trail food—some garnered from Camoe's hunting and gathering skills—it was good to enjoy a meal and not have to eat merely to provide sustenance to keep going.

Halfway through her third bowl, the chanting monk appeared, closing the stone door behind him. Taking a seat across from Jade, he ladled a bowl of his own. Scrutinizing the three of them covertly, he finished his soup before speaking. "You continue to surprise me, Druid. Just when I was beginning to get comfortable with the idea you must have met your demise at the hands of some foul Dark User, you come dragging one of their dark creations straight down the main aisle of my cathedral in front of my brethren. Have you been forcibly converted or merely gone mad?"

The monk's voice was pleasant and conversational, his actions supporting his tone, as he calmly ladled soup with a steady hand. With his stark white hair, Jade put his age at a few seasons above her father, older than Camoe.

"Wrong on both counts, though what I shall tell you will truly have you questioning my sanity," Camoe said between mouthfuls.

The monk glanced at Camoe sharply, only to rest his gloomy blue eyes on her, speaking softly. "I am not as certain as I once was of my own sanity, my *froman'atu*. I have heard and seen much evil since you left. A great darkness is gathering strength in the southeast, faster than anyone could have foreseen. More of that later, now tell me what your part in this is, young miss. Please begin with what to call you."

The monk spoke quietly but firmly. His large eyes drooped with a great sadness, but she sensed a penetrating intelligence underlying within.

Jade swallowed some of the bread she'd just softened in the soup. "My name is Jade. I don't know if I play any 'part.' I just want to find my sister and go home."

"Well, Jade, I am known around the monastery as Prominence Shadoe. You may call me by that title or use my given name of Caven, whichever you prefer."

"Shadoe? Are you—?"

"Yes, Camoe is my younger brother," Caven finished.

Surprised, Jade looked at Camoe. The shape of the eyes and nose and the slightly rounded face was the only genetic resemblance she could see. Camoe's lighter blue eyes made him appear to be from a different family than Caven with his deep blue eyes.

But then, Camoe's eyes sometimes appeared darker than Caven's were now. Pouring water from a clear crystal decanter into a silver mug by her bowl, Jade sat back, her stomach pleasantly full for a change.

Caven sliced a generous hunk of bread from the loaf to fuel his wide frame. "I suppose it was prudent to tell your young friend our shared lineage, since you did not stop me."

"I suppose so," Camoe said, chewing on his own slice.

"Yes, well, it was a rather crude, but quick, way to discover the level of trust you have placed in her. I imagine we can speak freely now?" He lifted the bowl to his lips, hiding a fleeting look of relief that Jade noticed anyway.

Camoe confirmed with a nod. "My wards are in place, sealed when you closed the door."

"Ahhh, I had hoped as much, and your third companion?" Caven raised a bushy white eyebrow.

"You know I cannot ward against a dark creation's link with its master," Camoe said, setting his spoon on the table. "However, I have solid reason to believe this one has no link or he somehow severed it while traveling with us."

Caven regarded his brother with a sharp eye. "Indeed? Is such a thing possible? I've never heard of the like in all my years of study. If that is truly the case, what shall keep others from doing it?"

Camoe shrugged. "The only thing I can say for certain, Burl saved our lives as we escaped the Dark Citadel. Other defections from Dark Users remain to be seen."

Caven sat straighter. "You gave it a *name?*"

Camoe shook his head. "Not I. Jade did. Burl follows her."

"You did not bring it here for the brothers or the Browns to study?" Caven asked, the surprise evident in his tone.

"Burl has a name," Jade said.

Neither man acknowledged her comment.

"No, we have come here seeking aid in locating Jade's sister," Camoe replied. "I hoped you could convince some of your connections within the Browns to gather information as to her whereabouts."

Caven spread his arms wide. "I am but a simple monk, the brown robes do not listen to me,"

Camoe frowned. "Do not attempt to placate me, my *froman'atu.* You are the prominence. The Browns still do your bidding if it serves them, and I have some small coin."

Caven slumped in his chair, oblivious to his unfinished meal. "You had better tell me everything."

Jade leaned back in her chair, her hunger sated for the time being. Now, if she could coax a hot bath out of someone, she would be happy to let the brothers hash out what was to come next.

FIRST LIGHT

The solid silver door Atoi opened for her was what Crystalyn expected to find guarding the chambers of a ranking member of the Circle. Beyond the threshold, an ornately furnished greeting room highlighted the way deeper inside. A man stood near the room's center, both hands clasped in front of his silken robes of stark white. His lengthy hair and long beard matched the color of his robes, though his tanned complexion and smooth skin suggested he was not much beyond middle-seasoned.

The white-robed man gestured toward a row of plush chairs lining a set of three silver-gilded small tables. "Please, select a seat." The man's baritone voice was pleasant to hear.

Crystalyn motioned to Atoi to sit beside her.

Once seated, the man startled her by clapping his hands together. Crystalyn stiffened. He flashed a quick smile. "I apologize for my abruptness. I have signaled for the chamber servant. Refreshments should be most welcome after your journey. Would you prefer mulled wine or a revitalizer draught?"

Crystalyn looked to Atoi. "What do you want?" Staring at their host, her young companion didn't reply, but a strange look of anger mixed with fear flickered across her pale face. "Water, or whatever you have in abundance, will be fine," Crystalyn said when it was obvious no answer would come from her young guide.

A matronly woman wearing a plain dress strode into the room, her gray hair fixed in a bun.

"Bring a decanter of both wine and draught. Crumb bread, too, if it's ready," Crystalyn's host said brusquely.

The woman's face tightened, but she gave a small obeisance and left the room.

"Now that refreshments are forthcoming, let me introduce myself if you do not already know," the middle-aged man said, raising a bushy white eyebrow.

"I don't," Crystalyn said. Even though his expression remained neutral after her admission, his lively blue eyes were alert. "I've traveled a great distance."

"I see. It is of no moment. However, I do know your name, Crystalyn Creek. And, I have followed some of your journey here." Crystalyn was somewhat surprised but let it pass. "I am Durandas, First Light of the Circle of Light, a title I have held for many, many years."

Crystalyn stared with surprise. He wasn't just a high-ranking member of the Circle of Light; he was *the* highest. What could he want with her?

His eyes boring into hers, Durandas let his words penetrate before moving on. "You are likely wondering why I called for a private meeting with you after the Circle refused one, though our definition of *private* differs greatly, I am afraid," he said, flicking a quick glance at Atoi.

"Atoi is her own person and will not leave my side."

"Then I may speak frankly before this child?"

"I know Atoi's a host to an ancient entity. She's much more than a child. You may speak your mind."

Durandas' eyes flickered at her declaration. "Very well, I would ask you keep matters mundane until we've been served, however. Unlike you, I do not believe I can wholly trust many who call me master or colleague."

Crystalyn had no idea what he considered mundane, but she did have matters to discuss, pressing matters. "Is the Circle of Light really too busy to meet with me?"

Shifting in his seat enough to keep an eye on the door the servant had used, he chose his words with care. "The Circle of Light is…divided. There is some dissension between us that I—*we*—would not care to reveal to the outside world. Ahhh, here we are," he said with a smile as the servant woman strode into the room carrying a tray. Plopping the tray on the center table, the older woman reached for a red crystal decanter. Durandas waved her away, pouring the red liquid into cups personally. The servant woman backed away from the table, strolling from the room much slower than when she arrived.

Crystalyn opened her mouth. She had so much to ask.

Durandas' lively eyes swung toward her. "One moment," he said. Raising his glass, he sipped slowly. Finally, he took a long swallow, setting the glass down with a sharp clink. "A ward is installed on each entrance. Should anyone come close, I will know. We shall be able to speak as we will for a time."

Crystalyn wondered how he'd set the wards; the procedure hadn't been visible to her eye. Perhaps she could achieve the same task with a symbol, but she had too many other questions. "Your politics will have to wait. I only journeyed here at the Lore Mother's suggestion. How much do you know about me?"

Durandas smiled. "In part, the Lore Mother is the answer to both your questions. You already know she is capable of a contacting."

"So she's been in contact with you. How often did this happen?" Crystalyn asked, irritated at herself. How could she be so unobservant?

"Do not let it concern you too much," Durandas said quickly, leaning forward. "Three times the Lore Mother performed a contacting with only Lore Rayna to assist."

Of course, Crystalyn thought. *It took them both to reach Jade. If they'd reached Jade at all; the viewing had ended almost before it began.* Now she wondered if they'd actually attempted a contacting. Had the Lore Mother staged the whole thing to get her here? Had the naturists duped her into a perilous journey? She wouldn't put it past any of them; the three of them kept as many secrets as the administration's political faction. "How does the Lore Mother fit in here? She never mentioned a close tie, only that the Circle of Light was my best chance at finding my sister."

Durandas sat back on the cushion, his eyes widening slightly. He paused for a few moments, regarding her. "The Lore Mother is my Interrupter; occasionally I have a need to use her...services remotely. The Lore Mother's power is without peer in her field, which is why she is Second Light of the Circle."

Crystalyn was astounded. "Are you saying the Lore Mother can supply you the Flow through a contacting?"

Durandas beamed. "That is one way of saying it, a good way. Accomplished by our most talented Interrupters only to a certain extent, it is quite dangerous and not risked often. At least, with most Light Users, it is not. The Lore Mother has always been somewhat arrogant with her ability. Even so, together we make a strong team. We were a powerful duo against the Dark Users during our younger seasons." His tanned face grew serious. "Alas, age has caught up to her, even though she was the same age as your young companion eternally appears to be when we were first adapted to each other." He gave a brief nod toward Atoi.

"Wait! Did I hear right? Did you just say you were a child when you first started using?" Crystalyn asked. Trying to put together a timeline, her confusion grew.

"By sweet Onan, no," Durandas replied, chuckling. "I have limited memories of childhood, which is likely a good thing since I was a vagabond, but that is for another time. Suffice to say, back when the Lore Mother went by her true name, her predecessor still lived. I was not much younger than I am at present. I assumed the Lore Mother had explained at least one of the glaring differences between an Interrupter and a User. Of course, now that I think about it, she is not one to dwell on being out of time—"

Crystalyn interrupted, beginning to get annoyed. "What are you going on about?"

Atoi spoke for the first time since entering the room, her voice hollow. "He means that an Interrupter's frail life is shortened, while a User's weak life is extended. By the nature of how the Flow conducts through the Interrupter, minute quantities of the Interrupter's vitality siphons into the User. Some races are able to resist it longer than others, but eventually all Interrupters' lifespans are shortened."

Surprised at Atoi's candor, Crystalyn glanced at her companion. Atoi wasn't staring at her or their host but at the wall across the room where a full-length tapestry hung to the floor. The brooding but picturesque scene was elaborate with colors that would be at home on a painting.

Standing, Crystalyn went to it. An enormous gate made from dark gray stone speckled with light gray flecks glinted like granite, spanning a great distance between two walls of a canyon. Pinned to the cliff face above with black iron, three massive doors overlooked the gate and the blighted meadow below.

Suddenly, weaves of varying color threaded swiftly throughout the tapestry, drawing additions to the scene with chilling detail. White-robed Users flanked three rows of silver-armored soldiers gleaming in the bright sun. The white-robed figures hurled golden comets at a dark-armored army now pouring out of a purple gate so dark it appeared black.

The doors wove open upon the cliff face. With a splash of dark colors, black-robed and red-robed Dark Users appeared upon the great thresholds in the midst of hurling black cones and red missiles.

Alone, between the two armies, a youth with a sword at his side stood holding a staff topped with a crystal that glowed with an azure hue. Something about the youth seemed vaguely familiar, but she couldn't think what it could be. A spot beside the youth blurred with color.

Crystalyn choked on a breath. A figure now stood between the two armies. Auburn-haired, the figure was taller than most that battled around her; she wore the same Kell leather as the boy. The young woman had two symbols hovering near her raised, outstretched arms. One white symbol faced the Dark User horde pouring from the gate, while the other, a black symbol, faced the Light Users. Her blue eyes lifelike and stony, the girl looked toward neither army, staring toward the youth instead. The symbols she held were beautiful but unfamiliar to her, though she should know them. The woman's smooth face was her own.

"Remarkable," Durandas said from beside her.

Crystalyn jumped. "What is this, Durandas? Why didn't you show me this from the beginning?"

"I would have bypassed all pleasantries for you to view this, since you seem to be involved in it," Durandas said, still gazing at the tapestry, "but this was not here when you arrived. I am privileged with a first look."

Crystalyn touched the tapestry; it felt soft and warm to her fingers, but an underlying current thrummed through it. "It's real enough to the touch, what's supposed to be here?"

"A plaque bearing my family tabard was the only thing adorning this wall. Truly remarkable, I would say," Durandas said.

"What does it mean? How did it—?"

The tapestry faded from the wall, replaced by a plaque with crossed swords behind a great tree supporting a large lizard. The lizard reminded Crystalyn of the glowing, green ones prominent in the desert regions of Lower Realm.

"Blast them!" Durandas swore. "I should have expected this. I am afraid my wards are not sufficient. We shall have to meet again under better circumstances."

"Wait!" Crystalyn said. "What was that? What's going on?"

"Someone has stolen the Surbon Codex. Such an occurrence is the only thing that would allow the tapestry to reveal so much. I am one of the two people who would know this. I suspect whoever has it had access to the Dark Oracle or it would never have been located. They must have worked with the Crypt Druids too, though I wasn't aware their using had advanced so far," Durandas said, shaking his now white-hooded head. "We shall continue our conversation when privacy can be assured. For now, I must meet with the Circle."

"Wait!" Crystalyn repeated. "What was that tapestry? Is it the Surbon Codex? Why was I involved in it? What's a Dark Oracle?"

"This is not the place for your questions, young one, though I understand your need for answers. I must move with haste. Can you see yourself out? I shall send for you when the time is ours." Without another word, Durandas hurried through the door.

Crystalyn shot a glance at Atoi and then stormed through the doorway after the First Light. Durandas was nearly to an intersection in the great hall. "You're going to the Circle? Why can't I go with you?" she called after him.

Rounding a corner, he vanished without a reply.

Atoi kept the door propped open with a tiny foot. "Should we go through his quarters? We might discover something useful."

Crystalyn considered, glancing both ways along the hallway. No one had entered from either direction. She made up her mind. "No, let's go back to the room. I want to check on Broth and see if Hastel's back. Checking on the horses shouldn't have taken very long."

In truth, as much as she needed answers, Crystalyn didn't want to stumble across one of Durandas' wards. It could be fatal for all she knew about them, and the last thing she wanted was to alienate the Circle of Light. If they wouldn't aid in her search for Jade, she at least didn't need them as enemies.

Nevertheless, the bloody Circle politics had added a frustrating delay to her growing sense of running out of time. What was so hard about hearing her request? It sounded like Durandas already knew what she was going to ask. Had he already talked to the Circle about it? Was she the reason for the dissension among them? Crystalyn ground her teeth; she had no answers to her questions, and they were multiplying at an alarming rate.

CIRCLE OF LIGHT

The assembly hall for the Circle of Light seemed more an arena than a hall. Leaning back as far as she dared, Crystalyn stared at the unadorned white marble pillars lining both sides of a wide walkway, rising up and up in stoic splendor. Each pillar rose higher than the one before, balancing the great dome overhead. A marvel of ingenuity, the top of each pillar matched the dome's curvature with precision; she couldn't tell where the pillar ended and the dome began. Her mind reeled at the enormity of the task of raising the dome and the pillars to support it.

At her feet, a beautiful golden rug carpeted the floor, providing some cushion. Required to remove their footwear before entering the hall, she flapped along the rug in the low support sandals the steward provided upon request. Now she was glad she had since the hall ran as long as two of Ruena's warehouses placed end to end.

"The Circle of Light awaits your esteemed presence," the gray-haired steward intoned beside her.

Dressed in a white uniform with a golden sun emblazoned on his chest, the steward was the first person she'd seen not wearing robes since her arrival four days ago. The man had come for her just as she was about to throw another early-morning tirade at the two white-robed guards stationed outside her chambers for her supposed protection. With Broth and Atoi near, and Hastel coming and going, she'd felt safe enough, but her protests were ignored. That was, until the pompous steward had showed up at her chambers.

The steward spoke in a slow monotone, as if everything he had to say was of the highest importance. "I shall remain behind. The wondrous Circle of Light, highest of all, awaits. Do not delay."

Crystalyn nodded for her two companions to follow. The annoying steward hadn't been happy she'd brought them along. He'd scowled and intoned a feeble protest as they left the room, which she ignored. Her companions were coming; their support helped keep her stable. Letting her volatile anger best her before the bloody Circle of Light wouldn't do; she was already annoyed to be in a place that didn't allow animals inside its pristine walls. The warden wasn't a beast; he was a dear companion and hailed from a particularly noble race that protected the borders of the White Lands, many times without help from others. Perhaps the Circle knew it; they'd not voiced a word about him, good or bad. No one had.

Her annoyance at having to wait, not to mention leaving Ferral at the gate by the *bloody Circle of Light's ordinance*, might be coloring her assumptions, but suppose her anger was justified? Either way she was prepared, having taken her dwindling supply of retina meds for the day. Though compressed, the med cylinder would eventually run out. That day was still days away, but she needed to be home before it happened.

The pillars' majestic march stalled at a circular pit where they doubled in circumference before rolling around each side to continue lining the hallways joining from three other directions. Crystalyn made for the large crater in the floor.

The circular pit was as large as everything else sheltered under the great dome was. Stone benches lined the bottom, and four stairways climbed down to a smooth glass-like floor big enough to race hovercraft around it. A multitude of people in colored robes sat in the first two rows at the bottom. Without having to ask where to go, Crystalyn began the climb down, her mouth dry. She'd never been any good in front of a crowd.

Reaching the bottom required several minutes, while most of the hooded heads followed their progress. Crystalyn did her best to ignore them, concentrating on the twelve robes seated behind ornate white marble tables widely spaced in a circular formation around the flooring. Crystalyn wondered why they sat so far from each other. The dissension between them must be worse than they wanted the common folk to believe.

Stepping onto the polished surface, Crystalyn strode to the center where a round white marble dais resided. She nearly lost her footing when she glanced down. The Flow's hoary storm raged with all its turbulent glory below her feet. Lest she be mesmerized, Crystalyn wrenched her eyes from it, her stomach feeling weak like the first twisting plummet on a zip cycle. Whenever she'd flown, she'd found it was better to focus on the destination and not look down. *Don't look down.* Nevertheless, the Flow was there. How could she not reach out to it?

She stepped onto the dais, going to the pedestal. Raised chest high as if blown from the Flow itself, the pedestal formed a clear toadstool, flashing with the brilliance of the Flow. A hollow, clear tube, attached like a wheel around the top, writhed with the Flow.

Not knowing what to do next, she looked around. Durandas sat stiffly at a long table, only a moderate horse field away, his white hair and beard providing the only recognition beacon she needed. He made grabbing motions for her to place her hands on the tube, which she did.

An appalling force wrenched her arms, pulling her away from the tube, only to reverse, flinging her at the pedestal with enough force to ram her knees into it painfully.

Durandas was suddenly within easy speaking distance, his expression pained. "I must apologize," he said. "You have never been instructed here. Most Light Users have been through rigorous trials to adapt themselves to the Flow. They know well what to expect when touching the Light Podium. Again, I must ask for your forgiveness. It is too easy for us to forget that we sometimes have…unusual guests. The Light Podium is unique with many powerful uses. For now, think of it as a way to personalize your plea. The podium will travel to whoever wishes the floor, so to speak. Do you understand?"

Crystalyn refused to gasp. Standing straight sent a jolt of pain rocketing from her hip to her thigh. Clamping her jaw closed, she gripped the tube in silence. When the pain reduced to a dull throb, she took a moment to glare at the Circle's First Light. "I think I comprehend how it moves. My plea hasn't changed. All I'm asking for is a contacting to locate my sister's whereabouts so that I can go to her. Or, give me a valid reason why you can't do it. If payment is required, name your price so we can get the negotiation over and get on with it."

Without warning, the Light Podium wrenched her in front of a middle-aged, white-robed man with shining gold hair similar to the User who had accosted her party at the Dome of Light's main entrance.

The entire moving platform thing was getting annoying. Now she was half a warehouse away from the First Light. Loping along the glass floor toward where she'd been a moment before, Broth switched direction, heading where she was now. Atoi stood watching near the center where they'd all begun. *Please go to Atoi. Keep her away from the center in case this thing returns there.*

Without slowing, Broth reversed direction. *I do not like this situation, my Do'brieni; it is far faster.*

I will be fine. Let's get through this.

"Fourth Light has the podium," Durandas' voice intoned, booming throughout the dome.

The golden-haired man regarded her in silence for a long moment. "State your plea," he finally said, his tone annoyed.

Crystalyn started. "Oh! I've been told the Circle of Light could help me locate my sister."

The golden-haired man frowned. "So it was spoken when the First had the podium. State your plea," he repeated.

"What bloody plea?" Crystalyn's annoyance with the entire blasted Circle was rising. "Are you going to perform the contacting or not?"

Another wrench deposited Crystalyn before a dark-haired woman in yellow robes, whom she'd never met.

"Ninth Light has the podium." Durandas' voice echoed throughout the dome.

The woman's blue eyes regarded Crystalyn shortly. "A

contacting has been attempted before, has it not?"

"Yes, but—" Crystalyn began.

"What resulted from this contacting?"

"Resulted? I don't understand. It wasn't successful, if that's what you asked."

"I asked for results. Was contact made?" The woman's voice boomed through the dome like Durandas' had.

"Oh, yes, we did. With who, I cannot say, it was too short," Crystalyn said. Her voice boomed, too. The acoustics of the dome were amazing…or enhanced with magic.

The woman leaned forward slightly. "Was a member of your party injured?"

Before Crystalyn could reply, the pedestal put her before another woman, a woman she *had* met.

"Third Light has the podium." Durandas' voice boomed.

"Did you use your special…abilities to heal a party member from the backlash of an improperly severed connection?" Kara Laurel asked. Garbed in white robes, her hood pulled flush with her beautiful, aristocratic face, the woman she'd met in the aftermath of the Carnage Field battle looked as regal as ever.

The question didn't help her plea, but she had no choice but to answer. "I suppose I did."

Another bone-jarring wrench left her gelled and quivering beside her two companions. Thankfully, neither made any move to join her on the dais. It was all she could do to maintain her grip on the tube.

"The Circle of Light has the Light Podium," several voices boomed in unison. "Show this healing to the Circle," the voices commanded.

Not hesitating, Crystalyn set the symbol she'd used on Lore Rayna hovering in front of her on the dais, wary enough to keep her double grip firm on the tube.

Some voices gasped, and several cried out in surprise.

A wrench brought her before Durandas.

"First Light has the podium," Kara Laurel's voice intoned.

Durandas' voice was low with excitement. "It is beautiful! Such an intricate pattern, yet I cannot fathom how it is used. I can detect no trace of the Flow anywhere in its constitution. Yet you have performed an advanced healing with it, as great as any Enhanced User could!"

"Enhanced?" Crystalyn asked.

"A User enhanced. A powerful User augmented by another User and a strong Interrupter. Together they enhance the magic of the User. Yet, you seem to do it as a matter of course, without the Flow. You must show me how this was accomplished."

"I do—"

Loud shouts broke out behind Durandas. A projectile shattered against his chair near his shoulder, peppering Crystalyn with sharp stings. Durandas' hand flew to his shoulder, where a red stain blossomed. A transparent sphere of white sprang up around him. A second projectile ricocheted from it, spinning to the glass floor beside the dais. A barbed steel arrow clattered to the floor.

Curses joined the shouts, growing louder still and then quieting. The crowd behind Durandas scattered, making room for a writhing mass of white robes. The white-robed group parted, shoving something large forward to face the First Light.

Wrapped from chest to knees with white luminescent cords, Lore Rayna snarled, pulling on the glowing ropes like a wild animal caught in a snare. Lore Rayna's fury doubled upon seeing Durandas so close, her limbs shifting from tree bark to flesh every other second as she bit and pulled at the bonds binding her. Flung from their feet, two of the white-robed figures thudded into her, but the rest pulled tighter on the cords attached at the end of their arms, where hands should've been. Lore Rayna tumbled to the glass with a crash, squirming and gnashing at her bonds.

Crystalyn was stunned. Lore Rayna was here in Surbo, and she'd tried to kill Durandas. What was going on?

Leaving the Light Podium, she got a closer look at the big woman's bonds while staying out of range of Lore Rayna's thrashing body. The Flow circulated inside her bonds grew denser as Lore Rayna fought, the ropes constricting tighter. If Lore Rayna didn't stop resisting soon, the bindings would cinch tighter and tighter, enough to do serious damage or cause a fatality. Crystalyn had to help her friend, somehow.

"I am a great fool!" Durandas exclaimed. He said it with a suddenness that made Crystalyn's heart pause for a moment. "I should have caught the signs from the Lore Mother's descriptions. Now that the vile thing has activated, she is beyond saving."

"What's been activated?" Crystalyn asked, alarmed.

Durandas regarded her, his blue eyes sorrowful. "A mind worm, I am truly sorry, Crystalyn. I know she was a companion of yours. There are many of us that love her, too; she was headstrong but valiant."

Crystalyn frowned. "What do you mean, she *was?* You talk like she's no longer alive."

"You do not understand. A mind worm has infected your friend, likely during a contacting. The worm will rip through her brain, eating away all that is good about her, molding her into its own evil image. None here has the skill to remove it, nor do I know of anyone else in the White Lands who can. It is too powerful, too fast. I should have caught the signs when the Lore Mother mentioned her erratic behavior."

Crystalyn hated worms; their mindless wiggling was enough to make her cringe. Worse, Durandas sounded like he'd already given up on Lore Rayna before they'd assessed the situation fully. "How do we get rid of it?"

"You truly do not understand, we might have had a chance had we caught it early enough, but it has triggered and will consume her. There is no cure. I am sorry, Crystalyn. She only has minutes before she fades."

But she does have minutes, Crystalyn thought. In an instant, her lovely white-gold symbol was sinking into her large friend with her awareness attached to it. Concentrating on Lore Rayna's neural pathways, Crystalyn exulted in the power thrumming through the pattern.

She found the worm almost immediately, in her large friend's frontal lobe. She should've expected that, since the cerebrum controlled motor functions and reasoning, among others. The darkness invading Lore Rayna's mind doubled in size, resembling a millipede. Thousands of writhing tendrils supported a lengthy oval shape that elongated as it moved. The millipede marched along the cerebellum pathway, changing gray matter black by attaching a tendril to a nerve ending in the cortex. Soon it would reach the back region, which controlled respiration, heart rate, and spinal functions.

Crystalyn couldn't allow that. Halting the foul thing's growth then may destroy the big woman with it, once it tapped Lore Rayna's spine.

Elongating the symbol to match the oval body, Crystalyn enfolded the worm within her healing pattern.

The dark body flattened. Tendrils snaked from under it, attacking the symbol with an inhuman frenzy. The white pattern in her symbol steamed, costing the worm a tendril as it blackened her white, touch by touch, tendril by tendril. Her white pattern reduced to dwindling fragments in seconds.

Crystalyn would've been worried she'd conjured the wrong symbol, except the gold pattern was holding strong. Noticeably diminished, the tendrils worked on destroying the few ragged dots remaining of her white pattern. The tendrils froze as the last of the white vanished, a large tendril swinging toward her.

Crystalyn stretched the gold symbol around her awareness the second before the first tendrils broke apart on it: the worm was coming after the source of the symbol, after *her*.

The attack went on for many seconds, or milliseconds; it was hard to tell though it seemed like hours. Tendrils bombarded her golden cage. Unable or unwilling to quit, the worm destroyed a large part of itself flinging its feelers against her cage—even pulling back and attacking with the tendrils it had attached to Lore Rayna's nerve endings. Drifting to the bottom of the neural path, the last tendril faded away, and the worm reverted to the size it had been earlier, her gold pattern tightening around it.

Now she was in a quandary. There wasn't anything left of the white pattern to disinfect the worm, though she had it netted with the gold. She couldn't trap it much longer; her body needed her awareness to function, to keep circulation flowing. Nor could she leave the worm in its present state. It would soon regenerate, continuing with its evil inside her friend's mind. What could she do?

There was one thing she could try: taking the foul thing out with her. Lore Rayna's nasal cavities made a plausible exit nearby. Gathering her will, Crystalyn dropped through Lore Rayna's mucus walls, pushing the worm before her. Gaining momentum, she released her attachment to the symbol when she judged they'd broken free.

Her awareness restored, Crystalyn's mind reeled as all her bodily functions requested attention at once. Dizziness assailed her as her mind tried to sort out her motor and neural functions faster than she was capable of assimilating. Not fighting the sensation, she let her brain handle the job until the dizziness cleared. A burst of energy rippled through her.

Kara Laurel knelt beside her. The woman's usual iron haughtiness was nowhere to be seen; concern mixed with awe shone in her eyes. "Are you well?"

She was so weak it was hard to speak. "Don't let it get away," she managed to say.

Kara Laurel's quick smile was reassuring. "Durandas has it magically sealed in a white crystal. It is fascinating; no one has actually seen a mind worm before. We have a team of healers seeing to your friend. The preliminary word is, there is some possible scarring, but she should recover. How far remains to be seen."

"No!" Crystalyn shouted, her voice coming out barely above a whisper. "You must destroy it!"

"I do not understand much of what you're trying to say, but you must stop fighting sleep," Kara Laurel said. "You have drained yourself dangerously. I have replenished what I can, but you must rest to recover."

"But the worm is still active!"

"Durandas will take care of it," Kara Laurel said.

Sure, he will. He's taken care of all of us so far, Crystalyn thought just before unconsciousness claimed her.

THE POINT

Somehow managing to look foppish in his plain monkish robes, the little man droned on about ceremony etiquette and then inventory consumption for the entire past week. Jade swallowed her irritation and kept silent. The Order of the Great Mother's ruling council of monks had insisted they come to the meeting to ask their questions. So far, no one at the long table facing them had acknowledged the two of them beyond a speculative glance. Camoe appeared unconcerned, slouched over on the bench beside her, but she heard his sharp intake of breath when the little man seemed to have finished and then began anew.

Caven's blue eyes regarded them a short while later. Holding up a hand, he silenced the little man midsentence as he opened his mouth to begin another monologue. "The Council of the Great Mother's Brethren will partake of a short recess at present."

Surprised, the yellow-toothed monk snapped his jaw closed, a glower of disapproval flickering across his bushy brows. Executing a stiff bow, he spun on a heel and left the room. Jade almost applauded.

Caven locked eyes with Camoe and then glanced to the antechamber beyond the main entrance.

"Come," Camoe said, springing to his feet. "We shall go while given the chance."

Jade stayed on his heels; getting away from the stuffy room sounded wonderful to her. Camoe halted at the far end of the long foyer, waiting for the Brown Recluse's prominence to catch up. They did not have to wait long.

Caven strode through the council chamber doorway, making his way to them in a surprisingly short amount of time for a man his size.

Several monks milled about, though no one ventured near.

Jade was happy to keep it that way. So far, the monks had been a tiresome lot, asking the same old questions about the Dark Citadel's layout, where she found Burl, and why he followed her. No one seemed to want to answer any of her questions. Caven looked carefully around to ensure no one had wandered too close. "Accept my apologies for the wait. Brother Kern means well, but he can go on about simple mundane tasks while wording his ferreting reports so that only I may know what is happening beyond the monastery walls besides these infernal ceremonies. The man has a flair for tediousness to repel anyone accidentally catching on."

Camoe's eyes widened but then his face slackened, as if he battled a bad case of boredom. "Kern is your intelligence gatherer?" Camoe pursed his mouth to whistle and then caught himself. His face smoothed to studied indifference.

Jade understood Camoe's amazement. A small man, Kern hadn't seemed capable of anything beyond taking exhaustive inventories or recounting each step of every ceremony performed in recent memory. "I don't understand," Jade said, "why do you worry about what is happening outside your monastery?"

Both men looked at her. "Brown Recluse is not the haven it has been in the past." Caven took a quick glance around, and then his blue eyes returned to her, his portly face serious. "The monastery still seems safe enough, tucked away up here on Brown Recluse Mountain, but the town of Brown Recluse has tripled in population over the last decade. In the beginning, the town housed mostly pious, hardworking farmers and tradesmen. Sadly, most have abandoned their homes or rebuilt along the outskirts, which holds its own dangers.

Jade hadn't realized the town had such harsh problems. Everything had seemed so orderly when they had passed through, except for the animosity toward Burl. Perhaps there was a reason for it. "Why? What could be so bad that they would leave their homes behind?"

Caven's face grew solemn. "There is a Dark lord setting up a base of power somewhere close. As of yet, we do not know where, only that it must be near. In many of the outlying provinces young men and women are missing during the night, the same here. The town and most of the surrounding countryside have grown a healthy hatred for all Users, with no regard to what power the User wields. They may have solid justification. I have witnessed much vileness in the name of the Light for the pursuit of power in my lifetime. Corruption wears many guises. Some magic should remain untouched."

Jade was aghast. The Light was supposed to help them, the Light was good, dad had always taught her and her sister so.

Caven turned to Camoe. "So far there is no word of anyone matching her sister's description, and you could probably answer most every question the Order asked. Perhaps I should get one of the brethren to guide Jade around the monastery and recount its history. What do you say?"

Camoe looked at her, his blue-gray eyes unreadable. "Would you want to listen to a tiresome monk or tour the monastery guided by an equally tiresome monk droning history at you?"

"Hey," Caven said, "I resent that."

Jade smiled briefly. "I would like to see some of the culture here."

"Excellent," Caven said. "Allow me to set someone to the task." Striding off, he vanished beyond the entrance to the foyer.

"He shall not be long," Camoe said. Jade turned to find his earnest blue eyes fixed on her. "Promise me you shall be watchful of your surroundings. Caven will have a trusted acolyte accompany you, but even here it is not as safe as it once was."

"I will," Jade said, quickly. She wasn't too concerned. So far, the whole place had been the embodiment of delay. Besides, listening to Kern's prattling the rest of the afternoon would make her want to throw the man at a patch of swamp sunflowers.

"I am not too troubled. You have the ability to recognize danger, perhaps even gather a sense of some intent. The essence of a druidic soul lies within you. Alas, I will have to endure Caven's Kern for a while yet. Pray it is not too long or I may have to fall on my sword."

Camoe looked so morose Jade curbed her smile. "Don't even think about it. I need you around when I get back."

Camoe smiled then, but it was brief.

True to his prediction, Caven returned a moment later, bringing a younger, red-haired monk with him. "This is Dirk," Caven said. The monk gave a short bow. Jade attempted a slight curtsy in return. "He's been at the monastery for the largest portion of his young life. This last season he accepted the appointment as personal assistant, after my old one grew ill and went to meet the Great Mother. You'll like him, though he has a tendency to talk too much about history, which makes him a good guide for your purposes. Is this acceptable?"

The monk, Dirk, watched her, his boyish face—barely older than hers—was stony, but his lean frame seemed tense. "Yes, so long as he answers my questions as best he can."

Dirk smiled, his rigid stance relaxing a little. "Then it is decided. Is my lady ready?"

A bell tinkled. Caven nodded farewell and headed back the way they'd come, albeit reluctantly.

Camoe grimaced. "It sounds like they're ready in the council chamber," he said. "Have a care, Dirk. Treat her well; she is a lady in every sense of the word. Treat her well," he repeated. "Or deal with me."

"I will show her the same respect as I would my sister," Dirk said.

Camoe glanced at him sharply his eyes gray, and then strode after Caven. "See that you do," hung in the air long after he caught up to his brother.

Abruptly, Jade was alone with the young monk. The tenseness she'd sensed in his manner had vanished with his easy smile. The smile suited his narrow, clean-shaven face and confident stance. Bowing slightly, he made a wide, sweeping motion with his arm, indicating their departure path, the same open door he'd entered with his Prominence. "Shall we begin, my lady?"

Passing through the main hall, Dirk held the main entrance door wide. Jade strode out into the golden brightness of the morning sun. The monastery square was abuzz with activity. Several monks strolled nearby, deep in conversation. Many hurried past on some errand known only to them.

At the front of a temple, scaled down and built to resemble the great cathedral they'd dined inside of the first night, some half-dozen monks knelt on mats, their heads bowed. Through the paned windows and open double doors, a miniature winged statue of the woman resided, carved with the same breathtaking detail as the original. Bright, potted flowers lined stone shelves on three sides.

A shadow shorter than hers came to a standstill in front of her. "Exquisite, is it not?" Dirk's soft baritone voice came from beside her.

"Who is the winged woman inside?"

"Do you not recognize the revered Mother Mary? Come, I will take you to the most beautiful representation of the Mother to be found anywhere on our great world."

"If you mean the one in the cathedral, don't bother. I've already been there."

"Then how can you not know the revered Mother? I'm afraid I do not understand."

"Let's just say we are from two different backgrounds and leave it at that. I'd like to see the monastery from the *outside*. I've been inside too long."

Dirk hesitated, a quick smile flashing across his lips. "As you wish, my lady; we shall tour the monastery's battlements, though I fear beyond this square, there is only one other sight worthy of your captivating, lovely eyes."

Jade flushed at the compliment. Not certain how to respond, she chose to ignore it; after all, they'd just met. "Sounds good enough to me, lead the way."

"No, please, walk beside me. Our path lies at the end of the square behind the temple."

Dirk set an unhurried pace around the shrine, folding his hands in front of his brown, monkish robes. The robes weren't bulky on his lean frame as they were on every other monk she'd seen.

Behind the shrine, the wall ended on two sides, leaving a wide space open to the rest of the mountaintop's leveled grounds. They went through, moving toward some of the tall structures with the statues paired at the entrances. Jade thought of something to fill the silence. "Tell me about the statues in front of the buildings. Do they have a history?"

Dirk's ebony eyes regarded her sharply. Then he smiled. "At first, I believed my lady jested, but your interest appears genuine. There are indeed chronicles relating to them as with all the structures. He pointed to a large, rectangular stone and wood building off to their left. A gigantic pair of winged statues gazed upon the cobblestone walk with expressions of unnerving ferocity. "The sleeping quarters are designated by the gargoyle. The masons of old believed the creatures would frighten away nightmares, being as fearsome as the frights themselves. Birds bring food to their young. He gestured toward a squat but high-peaked structure on their right. "Those statues over there are meant to designate a place to acquire sustenance in the refectory sculleries. The dragon marks the armory, farther along the walk, which is where combat training and the making of fine chain mail are taught."

"You all wear chain mail under the robes?"

"By the great kingdom of Light, we do not! Only the elder monks do, aiding in battle when the Light or the revered Mother are threatened."

"What about the monk statues at the tallest cathedral? Are they Dark lords?"

"Dark lords? Nay, lady, they were but simple prominences known for their wise leadership, though the necessities of war forced them both into becoming master strategists and commanders in the wars against the Dark Users."

"Wouldn't that make them battle lords? After all, they directed battles."

Dirk's narrow eyes rounded. "By the Great Light—may He shine for eternity—no! They were but pious monks flung into the War of Countless Sorrows when our fledgling monastery came under fire from the horde of Dark Users. It was their downfall. Over ten seasons they assaulted our fortress. Finally, the rest of the White Lands regrouped and forced the dark ones to retreat. It was the monks' worst and greatest seasons in history."

Jade almost smiled at his enthusiasm. Dirk was proving to be affable and knowledgeable, not to mention handsome in a plain, monkish way, an odd combination. Much different from the usual string of suitors she'd had back home. To be fair, he wasn't a suitor—at least, not yet—nor were there any monks on her world. The sect leaders probably had the closest bearing to them.

The hours flew by as her escort guided her through three large buildings with high cathedral ceilings, stained tile, and picturesque scenes, each as exquisite as the one before it. In the late afternoon, they stopped at the kitchens for a quick bite. Dirk led her to a small, two-person table placed off to one side. Dropping the tray of goods on the table, he plopped into a chair and grabbed a goblet of water. After taking a long, noisy gulp, he set his drink on the table and smiled. "Forgive me, my lady. I've regaled the day away. Has my supreme knowledge of all things pious and historical kept you captivated beyond hope of redemption?

Jade laughed, longer than his comment merited, but it felt good to laugh again. It seemed so long ago. She bit into a pastry. The sweet tartness of strawberries tingled on her tongue, awakening a fierce yearning for the carefree days on the farm with Crystalyn. Would she ever see her again? She finished the pastry and drank half her water before answering Dirk's question, though he probably never expected one. His flirting was transparent. "You've certainly mentioned a lot of the monastery's rich history. Tell me a little about the world beyond this place. I know you came here at a young age, do you remember much of it before coming here?"

Dirk's mouth tightened. He picked up a pastry and then set it down untouched. "There's not a lot to mention. Brother Alexander found me begging at the Brown Recluse markets below our esteemed monastery when I was seven or eight—no one knows the exact season that I drew first breath. He convinced me to climb up the mountain and plea for the rite of passage and become an acolyte. The rest you know. His most excellent Prominence Caven likely spoke of it."

Jade flashed a brief smile. "I'm glad you climbed the mountain and that you're still here. I really needed a day like this. You've very knowledgeable and fun to be around, thank you so much."

Dirk stood. Smiling, he executed a small bow. "It has been my pleasure, my lady. However, the day is not over yet. I have a final wonder to show you."

Jade nodded, her excitement rising as she stood.

Dirk strode outside.

Jade rushed to follow. This time, he seemed to be in a hurry as he swung sharply left, his path taking him beyond any fabricated structure. He moved toward the highest cliff where no border wall loomed.

Climbing a gentle upward slope, Dirk halted a few steps beyond where it leveled off. Jade followed slowly, her view expanding outward with each step forward. Distant mountains loomed vague behind a forest of monstrous falun trees far below. A great river cut through it, widening into a dark lake and then emptying into the swamplands she'd crossed in the east. Below her, cultivated land spread to the trees.

Awed, Jade stopped beside her guide. "Are those farmlands down there?"

His reply was slow to come. "Yes, yes...I suppose they are."

"Can we visit them sometime? I have a special fondness for farms. I grew up on one."

Dirk started, catching her eye. "Really? Good, good, you can see them better from over there. We call it the Point. It is highest spot in Brown Recluse. The view is unique."

Jade looked to where he gestured. The cliff's edge tapered to a sharp point above the farmlands. The Point was farther away from where they stood than she'd first thought. "Are you certain it's safe? It looks kind of fragile."

"Yes, go on. The Peek has been here hundreds of seasons, millions. Go look."

Jade took a step forward. The longer she looked at the point, the more transparent it seemed. *Transparent?* The whole edge of the mountain peak out to the point seemed transparent now, and open sky gaped below. As she looked, the area dimmed again, and a new cliff edge faded into view, much too close.

Jade focused on her guide, opening herself to her view of his aura. It was dark, and stayed that way as she slowed the rotation. A hooded man stood behind a faceless warrior in the first image. In the second, a flowery meadow shifted to sand and back to the meadow. The third frightened her. A foreboding, unidentifiable dark shape leaked blood into a growing pool about the bottom from many places. Jade lost her grip on the rotation. The aura spun.

"Go to the Point, take a peek. Look now," Dirk suddenly said.

Jade started. "I've seen enough. I want to go back inside now."

Dirk's small but strong hands slammed into her shoulders, pushing her backward. "You have to view the Point," he mumbled, loud enough to hear.

Frightened, Jade dug in her heels, pushing back against him. "Why are you doing this? What have I done?"

"I'm sorry, Jade. Your being here will ruin everything, *He* has spoken."

"Who's 'he'? Please don't do this! I thought you liked me!"

"I do, Jade. I am truly sorry." Dirk spoke in a monotone as he pushed her backward with a strength belying his size.

"Then don't do it! Please, stop pushing!"

Only the scraping of her heels on rock answered her plea. Dirk's silence was as chilling as the maniacal determination embedded in the darkness of his eyes, the set of his jaw, and the rigid, jerky movements of his body. He pushed her forward mechanically. Loose rocks under her feet clattered behind her and then silenced with a frightening abruptness. The long drop was close, too close.

Staring at his slack face, Jade dug her heels in deeper. She slowed, and so did the dark vortex raging around him, one of the scenes continuing.

With one brutish hand gripping Dirk's head, the warrior forced him to his knees, a sword gripped in his free hand. The hooded man's biceps bulged under gold bands as he unstopped a vial. Leaning forward, two hourglass eyes peered redly from the shadows of his cowl. The warrior pulled Dirk's head back and then jabbed his sword into the acolyte's right foot. Dirk opened his mouth in a wide, soundless scream. The hooded man reached out with the vial. The image spun away.

Jade stomped on Dirk's right foot with her own.

Grimacing, he let go and hopped backward.

Jade scrambled past, running madly, but he knocked her to the ground before she got very far. Rolling her on her back, he grabbed her legs and pulled, dragging her toward the edge. Glancing desperately about, she saw only smooth stone, nothing for a handhold. "Who was the hooded man, Dirk? What did he do to you?" she asked in desperation.

Dirk stopped, inches from the edge. He frowned. "How could you know? I have never told anyone."

Jade sat up. "What was in the vial he made you drink? What did it do to you?"

Dropping her legs, Dirk sobbed. "I cannot tell you, not anyone, not ever." He straightened. A sad smile crossed his lips as a look of utter hopelessness dulled his eyes. Turning slowly, he stepped over the edge and vanished, the sound of the uprising wind slackening briefly.

Only inches away, Jade scrambled from the edge, her heel catching on a rock. She fell back on her hands and bottom. The icy wind from the immense open space below blew her hair back, a chilling reminder of the great summit she sat upon alone.

Shock and sadness warring within her, Jade crawled away.

FIVE SETS OF EYES

Crystalyn bolted upright, her heart thumping against her sternum. The worm had returned. A bloodied Lore Rayna savagely killed a white-robed man. Dark red blood gushed from five holes in his stomach where she impaled the man on five digits of her wooden, elongated hand. Her other hand gored another. The poor men died without the strength to scream, though their mouths gaped wide with agony, and their eyes bulged with shock and terror.

Crystalyn's eyelids sprang open. The vision faded.

Leven's wary face faded from sight, replaced by Kara Laurel's clinical one. "How do you feel?"

"Weak, my head throbs. No surprise there."

Kara Laurel flashed a brief smile. "I believe I know why. I did not see a link from your symbol back to you as it sank into the Valen, Lore Rayna. You did not *ground* yourself. It takes a conscious effort on a User's part to do it, something requiring training beforehand. It is a process we never discussed in our last…encounter. From what little I know of your…using—I imagine that is what you are doing—you will need to attach a constant link to your magic, somehow. Some part of the symbol's pattern, perhaps. Then, as long as you are in contact with the ground or touching something that is, you shall have a proper ground. It should work with you as it does with every other User. All magic requires stabilization for some semblance of control. Some magic should remain untouched. As humans, even the other races, cannot access too much power at once, our bodies cannot take it. The Flow is too powerful. We shall begin training as soon as you are well enough for it. Can you sit up?"

"I'd rather not try, right now. Can't we just talk for a while?"

Kara Laurel nodded, squatting beside her. "There is no rush. What matters is your health. After the…incident with the worm, you fell into a comatose state, your breathing stilled. Leven has supplied you with as much energy as his adept ability was able to, scarcely enough to keep you inhaling oxygen. It was a narrow escape, and he's much stronger at it than I am. He believes you may well be beyond his ability should it happen in the future."

A sudden chill swept through her. Whether from the lack of her apparent oxygen, or from Kara Laurel's matter-of-fact statement, she wasn't sure. She'd never considered her use of symbols would ever put her in harm's way, let alone in death's way. She needed to learn more about this grounding of her symbols when she'd healed. "Tell me more of the worm. How would Lore Rayna get the infection?"

"Somewhere during your travels, Lore Rayna must have attempted a contacting through a dark veil. Though rare, it has happened when someone attempts a contacting into the Dark Lands where creatures like dominion wraiths—an old and particularly vile evil—lie in wait. The Dark Users have learned how to attach a neural spell, a mind worm, to the wraith without affecting its evil purpose. Whenever a contacting brushes against a wraith, the worm slips into the link and follows it back to the source. This particular worm was magically instructed from the outset to command its host to kill Durandas, a feat only accomplished by their most powerful."

"Did they want Durandas the man or the First Light on the Circle of Light?" Crystalyn mused.

"That, I cannot answer for certain, though I suspect they were after Durandas the man. He is quite powerful and so has numerous enemies. Instructing the worm to differentiate between a person and a political position would be quite involved."

Crystalyn gave a weak nod. It made sense, somewhat.

Someone had covered her to the neck in a soft blanket and shoved a firm pillow under her neck, yet the hard flooring added to the chill through her backside.

A small glance around informed her she was still in the assembly hall at the base of Durandas' table. The vast room was devoid of all but a few robed people gathered into small groups. Other than a frowning Leven hovering behind Kara Laurel, the others in white robes kept their distance. Her friends stood grouped nearby, but she didn't see her large friend, the worm carrier. "Lore Rayna! Did your healers save her?" Crystalyn asked, suddenly worried she'd failed after all.

Kara Laurel smiled, longer this time. "Remarkably, she seems near full recovery in just a few short bells."

Crystalyn found it hard to believe. "I've been out for hours?" It didn't feel like hours, only *an* hour. Her body still needed some rest.

"Yes, nine bells, to be precise. We did not deem it wise to move you, not with your breathing so frail. Lore Rayna's asked to see you, so have your three companions. I shall not permit it until you are able to sit on your own."

Crystalyn sat up, the blanket falling to her lap. The expected nausea, coated with dizziness, washed through her in tidal waves. Eventually, the waves of affliction, as she thought of it, lessened to a level she could live with, as before. She hoped that living life with her mind affliction episodes had raised her tolerances for such attacks.

Kara Laurel continued to regard her with a critical eye, her face impassive. "Bring them here. All of them," Crystalyn said. She was proud that her voice remained steady, though unusually weak.

Raising a fine dark eyebrow, Kara Laurel uttered her own set of commands to the white-robed group with Leven in their midst. "Bring food and drink to speed her recovery, see that her companions are summoned."

Leven inclined his head and strode away. "Why does he follow your orders?"

A hint of surprise flashed through Kara Laurel's green eyes, but her face remained smooth. "Not only is Leven a healer and my Interrupter, he is indentured to me for training for a position on the Circle. Perhaps someday he will be bestowed a seat, should someone abdicate or be involuntarily abdicated. I do believe he has the capability."

"So the appointment to the Circle of Light is for life?"

"Yes it is. However, we've had a few renunciations in our history, though one or two have been forced."

"By forced, you mean, asked to leave or face worse punishment, I assume," Crystalyn said.

Sadness flickered briefly in Kara Laurel's green eyes. "Yes, except the worse punishment is execution within the golden pyre."

The approach of her friends making their way around the stone benches spared Crystalyn the necessity of replying. Execution was a barbarous custom, though some very evil people had sometimes left limited alternatives for those passing judgment on her world. Crystalyn's eyes went first to Lore Rayna, who looked well, though her big companion kept her golden-haired head lowered as though abashed.

Broth sprang over a bench and sprawled at her side, slipping his head under her palm, contentment flowing through their link. Crystalyn stroked his fur gratefully, feeling better already.

Atoi was close behind. "You're pale, like me," she said without preamble.

"Thank you, Atoi," Crystalyn said with a smile. "Your concern is touching."

Atoi gazed at her unblinking.

Hastel laughed, taking a seat on a nearby bench. "That's our Atoi. I don't know what I'd…uh…we'd do without her bluntness to keep us humble. How do you feel?" he asked quickly, his one good eye glancing away.

"I've been asked that already," Crystalyn said, nodding toward Kara Laurel. "I'll survive is the answer. Have you checked on the horses recently?" she asked, eager to change the subject. There were only so many ways to politely tell someone you would rather be unconscious than face the pain the day promised to bring. Besides, Kara Laurel was listening to every word; she wouldn't hesitate to send them away if she thought they were detrimental to her recovery.

Hastel smiled briefly. "Every day, like you asked. They're energetic but doing well for the most part. Oh, there's one other thing you should know. The stable master has refused to accept payment."

Crystalyn's eyebrow rose. "Why would he do that?"

"Not sure, he would only say we'd been placed with the Circle." He dabbed at the weeping scar with a cloth.

"You know, there may be one here who could heal that," Kara Laurel interjected.

Atoi spoke, her voice taking on a faint echo quality. "Many of your best have tried; some high on your Circle. All have failed."

"Yes," Hastel agreed, sighing. "I thank them for the effort, but this scar wasn't made with conventional steel. I don't think it *can* heal. Someday I may even divulge how I got it, but not now."

Kara Laurel looked pointedly at Crystalyn. "I wasn't speaking of any of my people."

Five sets of eyes regarded Crystalyn, even Broth. "*Stop it, Do'brieni! I don't know why she thinks I can.*" Broth lowered his head to her lap, bemusement flowing through to her.

Hastel's one eye opened wide; he looked as if struck by an errant arrow.

Atoi stared at her, a thoughtful look on her usually impassive face.

Lore Rayna's head rose to face her, a broad smile on her lips.

Crystalyn regarded her companions, amazed. "What's wrong with all of you? What makes you think I can heal it when so many others have failed?"

Lore Rayna straightened to her full height, her smile firm. "You've healed me, twice, when no else could. I am indebted to you, and I will be older than the Lore Mother before it is repaid. Command me as you will, my lady, as long as it doesn't interfere with my studies."

Crystalyn almost expected a salute from the gigantic woman. Vibrant and green, Lore Rayna's dress shifted with each breath she drew, forming a cover over her lush body only where needed, but it was lively. A sure sign the big woman was in good health since the dress seemed to mimic her physiology. What about those fragile aspects of Lore Rayna's Valen mind? Had the worm destroyed some tiny, but integral, part of her friend?

She'd have to keep a sharp eye out for signs of brain trauma or differences in speech behavior. Hopefully, the Valen had recovered completely from the effects of the worm. Time and patience would be the key. "It doesn't mean I will be able to help Hastel like I helped you, but I'll certainly try," Crystalyn said quietly. She still felt wholly drained, as if she never would have enough energy to do what she promised. "But you all must know by now, I failed in healing *my* spiderbee wound."

"Your Valen friend has already taken care of that," Kara Laurel said.

Crystalyn's hand flew to her stomach. The puncture wounds were gone, not so much as a scar left behind. "How is this possible?"

Kara Laurel stood. "Lore Rayna is a rare Valen who can use the Flow to manipulate her affinity with flora, specifically trees. As for attending to Hastel, it will have to wait until I have had a chance to train you on *grounding* yourself after your recovery." Folding her arms to her stomach, she looked around Crystalyn's little circle of companions. "For now, she needs time to heal the old way. Do I make myself understood?" She glanced at each one of the companions in turn. Every head nodded, even Broth's. Kara Laurel's imperious gaze fell on Lore Rayna last. "Can you carry her back to her quarters?"

Lore Rayna scooped her up, lifting her with both arms with ease. Her strength was no surprise to Crystalyn, not after inhabiting the big woman's body back at Four Bridges. Lore Rayna could no doubt carry her for days.

Watching her footing, Lore Rayna climbed from the pit while Crystalyn's three companions followed close. Strolling side-by-side, Kara Laurel and Leven trailed the group deep in conversation. Crystalyn strained to overhear, but the distance was too great, so she focused her thoughts on her living transport while gazing ahead. "Do you recall how you arrived in Surbo? When last we parted, the three of you had left for your homeland."

Lore Rayna spoke softly for her ears alone. "I remember the journey but no reasoning or motive for it. I was allowed to see as a prisoner would, caged beside a mute wagon driver, viewing the path forward clearly but helpless to change course. Part of my mind screamed *this is wrong* the entire nightmarish time, no matter where the driver went, what *it* did. I still recall every tiny, horrific detail." A shudder wracked her large frame, vibrating through Crystalyn from the woman's chest and arms. Crystalyn gave Lore Rayna's neck a weak squeeze, the best she could.

Lore Rayna went on, her voice a dull monotone. "On the first night of our return to Vibrant Vale, the mind worm waited until everyone but the watch was asleep. Slaying a guard who I knew well, I slipped away from my beloved city and trudged without rest through the dense forest of the Vale to Surbo. I made many attempts to regain control. The worm batted me aside as if I was an annoying blood fly; it paused thrice during the journey to drink water and partake of sustenance. I arrived at Surbo on the third day. You know the rest."

Crystalyn could imagine the big woman's horror at having to watch her hands kill someone. She shuddered, fervently hoping a similar situation never happened to her. "Have you been in contact with the Lore Mother and Cudgel yet?" she asked in order to change the subject.

"Yes. A contacting occurred while you slept. Durandas initiated it. Once things are stable at the Vale, they are to meet us here."

"Durandas can contact?" Crystalyn asked. Her voice sounded sharper than she intended.

"No, but being on the Circle, he always has a Master Contactor at his disposal. Surely he has informed you of this."

"You would think so, wouldn't you? Has he mentioned attempting to contact my sister, yet?

"No. No one has mentioned it. I would have expected this to have occurred as well, by now," the big woman said.

Crystalyn stayed silent, quietly fuming. Why hadn't Durandas mentioned from the start that he could have ordered a contacting? She knew the answer. He'd been afraid of the very thing that had happened to Lore Rayna. Now that he'd seen her heal, that reason carried less weight, though Crystalyn wasn't sure she could do it again, but he wasn't aware of that. The golden symbol had held, but who could say for how long? Her white one had crumbled in seconds, but no one knew that, nor would anyone as long as she kept it to herself. So why had the Circle flatly refused to help?

LORD CHARN

The aging tavern woman thumped two mugs onto the table. She glared at Crystalyn as if holding her personally responsible for having to wear the drab, too-tight clothing and work in such a dingy place. Seizing the coins Atoi had set standing on edge, she gave her a final glare and strode away.

The woman's reaction was typical, happening whenever Crystalyn found herself around women her age or older, usually when she wore new purchases. Youth and fashionable clothing triggered the female rivalry gland for some reason. Perhaps at middle season it would happen to her, too, though she preferred not to think about it now, as the day had been too grand. They'd squandered some of Atoi's wealth spending much of the day finding suitable clothing, which always seemed to be among the most expensive the merchants offered.

Atoi had paid for everything without protest, without a single scowl, but she rarely smiled either. Crystalyn hadn't asked how the little girl always seemed to have the coin available, extracting it from a thin leather belt worn under her clothes. Did she really need to know? After all, the lacy blue dress—donned right after its purchase—did go well with her eyes. Not to mention, she would now blend in better with the locals: even the Kell leather she'd gotten from Hastel had stood out.

With the assortment of outfits they'd bought, they'd had to purchase large bags. Interestingly, silver seemed to have greater value than gold; she'd gleaned that much from their travels.

She was tired but pleasantly so. The shopping experience had been therapeutic. After a week of recovering from removing the mind worm and then another week demonstrating her symbols, she'd needed to get away before she throttled the entire bloody Circle of Light, starting with the First Light.

Durandas had contacted the Lore Mother about her student's recovery, but he had refused to risk another worm encounter looking for Jade, not without the Lore Mother's help, he'd finally admitted. She'd at least gotten him to commit to performing one when the old woman arrived, but only after she'd threatened to stop demonstrating her symbols for the Circle. Fervently, she prayed Durandas would stick to the bargain. She didn't want to put anyone in danger again, but she had to locate Jade. All of her companions from the journey to Surbo she counted as friends, the Lore Mother included.

Kara Laurel's rigorous training designed to keep her from frying precious oxygen in her blood whenever she used her symbol had gobbled up much of the past week. The training had made the demonstrations for the Circle easier, though she felt like some weird, newly discovered technology on display.

Now here they were at some seedy inn, waiting on Hastel. The Creeping Vine Inn, he'd called it. "Did the note say why Hastel wanted to meet here? Why not back at the Dome of Light, in our room?"

Atoi's green eyes shone briefly. "I didn't know a man would offer an explanation, particularly when it's a drinking establishment."

Crystalyn smiled. Atoi's humor was old for her age, and funny. She had to keep reminding herself how ancient her young companion really was, especially now that she seemed to have gotten over her fear of being in Surbo, at least for the moment.

"To be truthful, it looks like he has started on the drinking part as scrawled as the note is. Do you want to see it? He wants us to meet him here after the fifth midday bell, which it is," Atoi said, lifting her mug for a swallow.

Raising her own mug, Crystalyn tasted a semi-sweet red liquid with a faint acrid taste. She took a longer draught before setting it down. "I'll accept your word on that. How long do you want to wait? Myself, I want to sort through all these wonderful clothes."

Atoi shrugged her petite shoulders, taking another swallow.

"What about your clothes? Don't you want to go through them, even though they look nearly identical to what you've been wearing lately?" Crystalyn looked at the black pants and matching shirt Atoi wore. They fit the young girl snugly and felt strong and supple when she'd handled the ones Atoi purchased. "What material is that anyway? I've been meaning to ask."

Atoi glanced down at herself. "It's a blend between black wolf and Kell, expensive but worth it. I like the way it feels on my skin. It's rare, so only the bigger cities carry it. The wolf material is hard to come by and kept secret, but I have ways to acquire it."

"Tell me of the Kell, do I know what they are?"

Atoi regarded her over the rim of her mug. For once, the little girl seemed to be quite lucid. Atoi's ancient entity residing in her was a keg of knowledge Crystalyn wanted to tap during those moments of lucidity. Most times, though, she didn't know if she was talking to the shade or the child. "You may not," one of the Atois was saying. "It's a furry river creature found only in one place on Astura—though they are fairly abundant there—the Black Wolf Valley."

"Well, that's convenient for you, isn't it? Both materials for your silky, shadow clothing gained from bloodshed in one place, does it matter to you that it's made from living creatures?"

Atoi blinked.

Crystalyn regretted her irrational outburst almost as soon as she'd said it, even though she probably couldn't have stopped it. Her mind spat what it would from her mouth sometimes. Nevertheless, a moody, defensive companion was the last thing she needed right now. "Don't answer that. We'll save it for later. When Hastel gets here, help me pressure him into going before the Circle with me. He seems to know how to get things done. Perhaps he'll have better luck with them. They've kept me waiting for days with their petty politics. I'm not asking for them to hand over the world, just a little help."

"Your scarred companion won't be successful," a female voice said.

Face smooth, a dark-haired woman from the Circle of Light—who so far had argued the most against helping them—sat down. Crystalyn couldn't recall her name, if she ever had known it. "Most of the Circle now believes as I. A contacting would be extremely risky to those making the attempt, for the sake of finding someone who may or may not be found," the woman went on, her light blue eyes boring into Crystalyn's. A hooded red shawl draped across her thin shoulders stood out over a skirted yellow tunic. Much different attire than the yellow robe she'd worn at the assembly hall.

"You haven't been invited to share our table," Atoi said, her voice low but distinct.

The woman ignored the comment, gazing at Crystalyn as if expecting something.

Crystalyn tried to recall which position the woman held on the Circle. Ninth? "Did you stop by to gloat or tell me I'm wasting my time? I'm not giving up on finding my sister, even if I have to camp outside the Circle of Light's bloody assembly chamber."

The woman leaned forward slightly, lowering her voice. "A contacting isn't the only way to find someone on Astura. I have... other ways at my disposal, should you be interested."

Atoi banged her mug on the table and then leaned forward. "Don't trust her, Crystalyn. I don't like her or any of those like her. Their assistance always comes at a steep price."

Her smooth face unperturbed, the woman's blue eyes stared placidly at Crystalyn, showing no indication she'd heard Atoi. She looked prepared to wait patiently through the night for a response, though a flicker of haughtiness marred her composure now and then. Tiny streaks of red pulsed along the blue of her corneas, an indication of her addiction to the Flow and a mark of her strength as a User, according to Kara Laurel. "Why would you help me?"

"I, too, have a sister."

Good answer, she thought. Perhaps the woman could help; she was on the Circle, and the Circle of Light was supposed to be working for the good of the White Lands. It should be safe to work with her, yet one never knew. What did the woman hope to gain by helping her?

Atoi made eye contact with Crystalyn. "How do we know she has a sister?"

Crystalyn looked to the woman. "Good question. Can you offer proof?"

Her smooth façade crumbled with a frown. "You don't have to accept my word; my *proof* is far from here in another…city." The woman arose. "Do as you will. I simply offered aid, nothing else."

Crystalyn rose to her feet. "Wait! What's your name?"

Pulling the red hood over her head, the woman paused, her face shadowed, but her pale blue eyes shone brightly before fading. "You may know me as Khiminay."

"Okay, Khiminay, how do I find my sister? What other methods are there besides a contacting?"

"Follow me. I will answer your questions, perhaps all of them," Khiminay said softly, walking away.

"Wait!" Crystalyn called.

Khiminay's pace never slackened; soon she pushed through the tavern's front doors, letting them swing closed behind her. Crystalyn scrambled to gather her bags. "Hurry, Atoi. I don't want to lose sight of her."

Atoi slipped her purchases over a shoulder. "I don't know what the big hurry is," she said, though she remained close.

Crystalyn spotted the red hood as soon as she stepped onto the market street. Winding her way to the crowd's center, she found Khiminay's eyes upon her, staring from the hood's shadow. She was comfortable nestled inside the throng about her. No one jostled her, several even stumbling over each other to keep their distance. The red hood provided plenty of advance notice, practically shoving the throngs aside. Apparently, everyone in the city knew the woman or the woman's place on the Circle from the sight of the hood, perhaps both.

"Come, I have an offer to help find Jade I don't dare refuse," Crystalyn sent to her link mate.

Broth loped up beside her from the side street where he'd

waited. Merchants had been aghast when he accompanied them inside their store as they shuffled through clothes. The tavern may not have minded, but Crystalyn hadn't argued when he suggested keeping vigilance in the alley.

As with Khiminay, the crowd scattered out of his way. *"Exercise caution, Do'brieni. Do not let your desire cloud your judgment. This side of Surbo is relatively lawless."*

Khiminay eyed Broth but said nothing. "One of my…outlying residences is not far from the bazaar. Please follow me and stay close." Without another word, Khiminay started down the street, striding through the crowd as if she were out for an after-dinner stroll.

Crystalyn didn't have to work hard to stay close, at least not until Khiminay swerved into a side street heading east toward the lower-class part of Surbo. The mob thinned noticeably, allowing their guide to set a faster pace.

Crystalyn refused to run on most occasions; she'd never been a runner. After a few blocks of her fastest walk, she began to wonder if she ought to run. By the time she strode through a gate leading out of the city, Khiminay had widened the gap by a hundred yards.

She finally broke into a sprint, charging past the gate and its two guards in time to spot the red hood ducking into an unobtrusive tent among an ocean of canvas. Crystalyn slowed. Roped hitching posts dotted the open space in front of many tents, some with horses tied to them, grazing passively on frugal grass below. A slight breeze brought the foul scent of waste and manure. Wrinkling her nose, Crystalyn kept her gaze fixed on Khiminay's tent while trying to watch where she stepped.

"This place has the repugnant smell of unwashed humans and equestrians." Broth observed, echoing her sentiments and making her smile. *"Wardens do not inhabit such a place, nor would we wish to spend any length of time away from our beloved forests."* Crystalyn draped her arm over his shoulder, sending feelings of fondness and sympathy into the link. She understood how hard it was to be away from family and loved ones, to be traveling through unfamiliar places,

uncertain if she'd ever see home again. Tears stung her eyes, but she forced them away.

Once she stood outside the tent, she glanced at Atoi, whose tiny, white face was impassive. Not even the smell could get to her. Thankfully, the guards had remained where they were. "What is this place?"

"Surbo's illustrious temporary city," Atoi said, gazing into the distance as if she could see an end to the tents. Perhaps she could. Who knew what the Dark Child could do? "It was built at the beginning of the Hundred Season War as a refugee camp for the destroyed towns of Gray Dust and Grit Eye City but has been long since adopted by the Great Plains nomads and those wishing to remain anonymous from the rest of Astura. The city has persisted as landscape clutter, blocking Surbo's easternmost gates for twice that of the war. It's one of Astura's seedier places, particularly after nightfall. The best part is the mighty Circle of Light has not been successful in getting them to move, though they have managed to enforce the restriction of permanent shelter construction. Bringing wood and rock across the flatlands is difficult; the distance is too great due to the Circle of Light controlling the nearby quarries. The nomads who roam the Great Plains on their horses are most comfortable in their tents anyway, preferring to pull out anytime they choose."

"It's been a tent city for a hundred seasons?"

"Yes, humans hold onto an infatuation with temporary cities."

Crystalyn whistled softly wondering at Atoi's choice of words. Or was it Atoi speaking? Likely not, since she'd spoken of humans as a different species. "What's this place called?"

"Welcome to Rancid City. It is one of my most profitable haunts," Atoi said. Then she blinked. "I am surprised someone like Khiminay would own a place here. Didn't we see her on the Circle?"

Crystalyn frowned. "Yes, ninth position, I believe. Why would someone on the Circle have a tent? Surely someone associated with the power and prestige of the Circle of Light would own something permanent, such as a palace, or two."

Atoi glanced around. "Methinks Hastel should be used to discover more about this Khiminay before we agree to a business arrangement."

"Yes, that would be the wise thing to do since it's likely some sort of a trap. She did push us to follow, but I'll be ready. I can't let the chance go by, however slim, she may lead me to Jade." Crystalyn nudged Atoi forward. "Come, let's see how she can help or betray us before the sun goes down. I want to be back in our room long before then."

Slipping past the tent's flap, she stepped inside, pausing to let her eyes adjust to the dimmer light.

Two guards stationed inside the tent's foyer pulled long swords from their scabbards.

Crystalyn's net symbol took shape in her mind.

"Hold!" Khiminay shouted from farther inside. "Let them pass."

Crystalyn eyed the guards. She let her pattern dissolve from her thoughts only when their swords were stowed away. "I hope this isn't a prelude for how you treat guests you invite to your quarters, though why you'd have a place here is beyond me," she said, staring at the woman. It hadn't taken long to spring the trap—not much time at all.

Ignoring her comment, the Circle woman turned to speak quietly with a tall, muscular man wearing a massive suit of black plate armor. A horned, full-faced greater helm protected the man's head. Three men wearing chain mail and open-faced helms stood behind the man and Khiminay, next to the rear tent wall.

Crystalyn grew irritated. She strode to Khiminay, shouldering past soldiers—a man and a woman in black plate. The conversation between the dark-haired Circle woman and the dark-armored man cut off abruptly when they both turned to regard her, measuring her progress as she threaded a path through a field of silk cushions and plush rugs.

Khiminay had removed her shawl's hood. Her fine eyebrows and ice-blue eyes regarded Crystalyn boldly, ignoring the brute beside her. "I hope there's a good reason we chased across half of Astura to come here. Can you help me or not? What do you want in exchange?"

"There is *reason*, I assure you," the dark-armored man said. His pleasant, concise voice drifted down from within the horned helm—a long way down. He towered over her by a full span in height. *Great! A possible kin to Lore Rayna,* Crystalyn thought. "Whether the reason is *good*, I leave to your judgment." He turned to Khiminay. "You may leave us."

Curtsying deeply, Khiminay brushed past Atoi and Broth, leaving the tent without saying a word of farewell. Crystalyn wanted to protest against her going but kept silent. The dark-armored man was intimidating, and the massive hammer fastened to his side added to the feeling. Its double-headed black metal pulsed with a faint, dark purple hue. Crystalyn wrested her eyes from it. The brutal thing was hypnotic.

The big man laid a gauntleted palm on Big Brutal. "Let us advance to the point—or should I say, to the blunt end—of why we are gathered here. You are right to believe I want something from you, I do."

Crystalyn frowned. She knew it.

Atoi laughed without mirth. "No surprise there."

The horned head swiveled in Atoi's direction briefly. "If it is permissible to continue," he said, "I *shall* find your lost one. Once found, I will discuss payment. You will not know disappointment as soon as an agreement is reached."

Crystalyn admired his confidence. Perhaps she was finally at the right place after all. "Who are you?"

"I am Lord Charn. It is a title I've retained for the last one hundred and fifty-four seasons."

Atoi gasped.

"Garrrrr!" Broth's growl barreled through her mind. *"Do'brieni, this User has been the cause of much of my race's destruction. I do not doubt that he has knowledge of where those missing from the White Clan are. Please, stalk with care, but help discover if they live. I beseech you!"*

"What do you want from me, Lord Charn?" Crystalyn asked,

keeping her voice at a neutral tone. She was determined to hold her composure, even around apparent nobility, especially around nobility. It wouldn't do to have one of them believing they could order her around.

"I shall speak my intentions one final time. Discussion of payment will occur after you learn the location of your missing…sibling?"

"Yes, my sister," Crystalyn said. She glanced at Atoi, gauging her reaction to the man. Her face was her usual pale impassive mask, though there was a flicker of curiosity in her eyes.

Lord Charn continued. "I shall require your sibling's name when we begin. First, we have to travel to a scrying device, a journey made in an instant once we have an agreement. Have we reached one?"

Crystalyn kept her eyes on Atoi, raising a questioning eyebrow, and then her legs grew weak. The green in the girl's eyes revealed nothing, except…something shadowy moved in the background, the Dark Child, perhaps. Was it trying to tell her something?

Deliberately, Atoi turned away from her.

Crystalyn reined in her flaring anger. She couldn't grab the little imp by the shoulder and spin her around, as she wanted. It wouldn't do for them to argue in front of nobility. "Surely you would expect me to be obligated to you in some way. I don't like having a debt with anyone."

Lord Charn hesitated. When he finally spoke, his voice was low but distinct. "I do not wish to make you uncomfortable. Tell me then, what sacrifice are you unwilling to make for a reunification with your sister?"

His words gave her pause. "I won't agree to anything if it goes against any belief I may have or has a remote chance of hurting anyone, animals included. I'll find my sister on my own if that is the direction I must go," Crystalyn finally said. "And my friends come with me, or no deal."

"What do you think, my link mate? It may be my best chance to find my sister."

"I shall not expect you to do something you're not comfortable with. You may simply refuse this offer, and we shall part on even terms," Lord Charn said. "Your friends may go as well, though they may not have the same liberties as you." His great helm swiveled toward Broth.

"This is a grievous mistake, Do'brieni. No good will come of working with this man." Anxiety reverberated through her mind. Whether it was Broth's or hers, she couldn't decide.

"I thought you wanted to find those missing ones of yours. We have an opportunity here," Crystalyn sent, trying to exude confidence.

Broth was silent, though flashes of disquiet filtered through; his hourglass eyes had changed to deep red, echoing his inner turmoil as his wolf head moved constantly keeping everyone in view.

Crystalyn turned to Lord Charn. "When do we start?"

Lord Charn slapped his mail gauntlets together, his demeanor brusque. Two of the open-faced helmed guards brought a pair of objects forward from the tent's rear. "Excellent. We begin by going to the Dark Oracle." Quickly booting cushions to the side, the guards set two violet crystal obelisks a door-width apart.

Crystalyn swallowed her gasp.

"So you know their purpose," Lord Charn said more as a statement than a question, his expression still unknown behind the helm.

Crystalyn nodded mutely. Dark purple in color, the obelisks spanned the same height as the sapphire crystal ones that had brought her here. A nagging doubt had crept in that she would never see their like again. "Where will the obelisks take us?" she asked, regaining a measure of composure.

Lord Charn's mailed palm rested casually on Big Brute again. "To the Dark Oracle, where you shall ask to be shown your sibling."

"Will they return us here?"

"Alas, no, the journey back shall be accomplished by mundane methods. Attuned to a specific location, the obelisks are one way only. Please, step through with haste. The gates require a large amount of

Flow to hold open," he said, sweeping a muscular arm toward the curtain of stormy darkness swirling between the obelisks.

"Stay beside me, my Do'brieni." Broth leapt next to her, brushing her shoulder with a gentle and precise control belying his size.

Trying to shake the feeling she was going the wrong way no matter which way she turned, Crystalyn shifted her bags, grabbed Atoi's hand, and stepped into another gateway.

DARK ORACLE

The obelisks deposited them inside an antechamber to a much larger room. A large, open space beyond the smaller room beckoned to Crystalyn. She passed through a wide, iron-banded wooden door, side by side with her warden, pulling Atoi with her.

Ahead, three gilded chair backs inlaid with glistening tiled designs presided over a great room, and massive statues lined cavernous walls. Rounding the leftmost and smallest chair, Crystalyn paused to gaze around the immensity of it. Five curved steps, carved from brilliant amethyst, sloped gently down into a wide walkway.

The statues faced inward as though to watch a gathered crowd. Their backs to the wall, the statues depicted dark-armored men and women holding weapons, blunt and sharp, standing next to menacing red-robed and black-robed Users, each spanning the great distance from floor to ceiling. Carved in eerie, lifelike detail, they expressed various stages of war.

Crystalyn could believe the fury expressed on one Dark User's face or the raised axe of a soldier was for her benefit for having the audacity to enter the great throne room. For a throne room it was, she realized. Whirling to confirm her suspicions, she found Lord Charn sitting at ease in the high-backed seat built between the two smaller ones. *Not a seat, a throne,* Crystalyn corrected herself. A chill crept down her spine. She hadn't even sensed his arrival. His massive armor had made no sound.

Broth's soundless wails roared in her mind, making her head reel. Agitation mingled with self-recrimination flowed at her in strong surges. *"This is the stronghold of the enemy. Desiring to find my clan members, I have put us in grave peril, Do'brieni!"*

"Calm down! He seems to want to help us. We will find out if your people are here." Crystalyn added a comforting sense of a friend inviting someone over for a relaxing visit.

"You do not understand. This is one of their great Dark lords, possibly the greatest. I let my desire cloud my judgment. Your protector is not something I deserve as a designation."

"Stop, Do'brieni! Stop, now. We'll find Jade, see what this lord wants in exchange for his help, and then leave. Everything will be fine." Though he chose not to respond, Broth's agitation seeped through, but she couldn't change her decision, not now. Enemy's lair or not, she had to follow it through. It may be her only hope for finding Jade.

Lord Charn waved an arm expansively. "Impressive, is it not?" His pleasant, masculine tone resonated with pride. "Though, I would daresay your warden companion may not agree. I would believe it safe to say he is the first of his kind to enter here. Most of his…race spends their entire lives attacking my forces along our borders. He may not be well received," he added, his voice letting slip a trace of venom.

Crystalyn grew resigned. It hadn't taken long for things to turn ugly. Squeezing Atoi's hand, she went over her acidic symbol in her mind. Lord Charn's grand armor shouldn't be able to protect against it completely. The man should have mentioned an issue back in the tent, but then, she would've refused his offer of aid.

Lord Charn raised a gauntleted hand. "Please be at ease. I will not let any harm come to you or your companions while you are under my care. I simply wanted you to be forewarned."

Crystalyn let the symbol's image fade from her mind, for now. She had to believe him; there was no choice now, not unless she wanted to fight her way out. She wasn't prepared to battle blindly in an unfamiliar enemy stronghold.

Taking her silence as an end to the subject, Lord Charn turned to look out upon the room. "I selected an hour when the nobles are not allowed to stand around listening as most daylight bells permit. We are late into the evening. Do you appreciate the hall of thrones?"

Her fingers frozen, Crystalyn released Atoi's hand, shifting her bundles from her palm to her elbow. Tingling slightly, her hands warmed as she rubbed them against each other. "'Spectacular doesn't begin to do it justice." She wondered if she should address him as "Your Majesty" or something. "Are you the king here?"

Lord Charn gave a small laugh. "There are no kings here; only Dark lords and their generals; one great Dark lord and a few desiring to become the great Dark lord. For that, they would have to destroy me in single combat. Most are content to keep their ambitions well hidden. Some few, however, have believed themselves worthy enough to attempt, those all ended recruited to the Dark Regiment. In the end, we all are subject to the Great Master's will," he said, rising to his daunting seven-span height. "Come; let us make haste to the Oracle. I am certain you are anxious to locate your lost sibling."

Crystalyn wondered what he meant about a "Great Master." The "Dark Regiment" she could guess already. She rushed to follow him down the stairs. His long stride kept her scrambling to remain a step or two behind. Broth stayed close. She didn't have to look into his hourglass eyes to see the wariness there; she felt it in the tenseness of his shoulders whenever he brushed against her. Atoi trotted along behind, her gait easy.

Two great golden doors loomed into view after they'd gone some way along the grand hall of thrones. The doors opened slowly as they neared, assisted by ornate uniformed guards, each toting a spear. Lord Charn passed through without pause. Four guards with spears and swords stood on a landing beyond the doors, two on each side. Their guide climbed down a set of three dark amethyst steps to a great, pillared hallway.

Sensing perhaps her shorter strides, Lord Charn slowed, allowing her a quick view of the pillars as they strode past. Engraved with men, women, and animals of every sort—some creatures she recognized and some she didn't—each pillar was cluttered with scenes of people and creatures enacting some activity.

Crystalyn slowed a little to gaze over Broth's shoulders at the pillars on his side. They too had carvings all the way around to the top, two stories high. Crystalyn idly wondered if the carvings might tell a story if one had the time to circle the pillar from bottom to top.

The carved pillars ended at an intersection heading forward and to the right, where polished stone replaced the engraved scenes. Lord Charn selected the hallway leading right. Crystalyn trailed behind, glancing back to gauge Atoi's progress. The little girl seemed contented, though her too-white expressionless face made it difficult for her to read.

Beyond the short hall another intersection appeared, this one taken up by something large, round, and surrounded by Dark Users, mostly in black robes but interspersed with a few reds.

Lord Charn strode purposely to the closest section of the object, halting behind the shoulder-to-shoulder ring of people. He spoke, his voice amplified unnaturally. "Use of the Oracle is mine, disperse!" The last echoes of his command boomed throughout the hall as the robes scattered.

In seconds, the intersection was devoid of any breathing souls except them. Crystalyn was impressed with the respect their escort commanded, but then, he *was* a Dark lord with his own throne room. She doubted he'd claimed his position by asking nicely.

Atoi stopped close beside her on her left. "Keep your back to me while we are at the Oracle, Atoi. I can't watch behind me once focused. You too, Broth," Crystalyn said in as low a tone as she could muster and still be heard.

The warden's sienna head tilted to one side, approval glinting in his now golden feline eyes, presumably, for expressing her wariness. He worried about her becoming too complacent.

Atoi looked around the wide hallways. "You shall have warning, should the need arise."

Crystalyn continued across the hall. The lighting was dim, but Lord Charn stood out, his formidable dark shape standing in front of an oblong shadowy area rising to his waist. Joining the big man there, she found the Oracle was nothing less than a half wall of pitted lava rock encrusted with black moss and filled a few inches below the top with brackish water. The water swirled slowly counterclockwise, stirred from some unknown force.

Crystalyn leaned close. Tiny white-capped waves rose to within a hand's reach before plopping softly down to meld with the base of the next rising wave.

Lord Charn's clipped words intruded upon her. "Do not touch the water. The Oracle has an effect on living souls, most adverse."

Crystalyn snatched her hand back, disconcerted. Why had she been reaching for it?

Lord Charn placed his gauntleted hands on the rim. "Are you aware how to activate the Dark Oracle?"

"No."

"Use the Flow to roll the Oracle's water while you visualize your interactions with your sibling. Call your contact by name as you maintain your focus on the eye. I can add strength to the call if you permit me to know your sister's name."

Feeling like she should know, Crystalyn had to ask. "Are you calling the center—where the water is churning around—the eye of the Oracle? Jade, her name is Jade."

"Yes, of course, the center is the eye." Lord Charn's pleasant tone had a hint of impatience. "Is Jade her full name? I...*we* need to use her complete given name."

"Oh! Jade Creek, her full name is Jade Creek."

Straightening from where he'd been leaning on the Oracle's rim, Lord Charn's right hand flexed open and then closed once, his fist hanging not far from the monstrous hammer. She couldn't get the ugly thing out of her mind. "So, she is a true sibling to you?" he asked quietly.

"We have the same father and mother, if that's what you're asking."

Lord Charn's stance relaxed. "That is good. It will make the contacting less taxing.

"I cannot believe we are present before the fabled Dark Oracle, Do'brieni," Broth interjected into her mind. *"For long my clan has believed it a legend."*

"Have a care; we don't know what your legend is capable of yet."

"Agreed, my Do'brieni."

Atoi spoke. "Someone comes."

Lord Charn's horned helm tilted forward slightly as he looked at the girl. "One of my most promising generals is here by prearrangement to assist us. He will add strength and shall direct your sibling to the closest gateway we have attuned to the citadel."

A voice she recognized drawled from the edge of the light, sending a warm thrill racing through her. "I live to serve, My Lord." Slipping from the shadows in the hall, Darwin Darkwind suddenly stood opposite her at the Oracle. He looked different in a black robe with the hood pulled back, but he still had the same clean-cut, handsome look.

She wasn't certain how she felt about the robe. The black robes had fought her on the way to Surbo. Or had they? Thinking back, they were attacking Kara Laurel and Leven; they had only started attacking the companions after Atoi had intervened. Malkor hadn't really attacked her at the ruins either until she goaded him; he'd wanted Atoi. Had she been too quick to use her symbols? Was she addicted to using her symbols and the power contained within them?

Gazing at Darwin, she couldn't help but return his warm smile.

Lord Charn scraped a heavy boot on the floor, shifting to include Darwin and Crystalyn in his field of view. "Let us begin. Increase the whirlpool."

Crystalyn had no idea how she was supposed to get the water swirling faster when all she had was her symbols. Perhaps she could modify the knockback symbol to suit her needs. Forming the symbol in front of her, she altered it slightly by unraveling the bottom edge enough to keep a string, which she attached to her wrist. Her feet on the cavern floor completed the grounding.

Lord Charn's roar boomed throughout the cavern. "What folly is *this*?"

Crystalyn's concentration wavered, and so did her symbol.

Darwin spoke up. "Please, Great Lord, let her continue. I believe it is how she uses."

"Very well, proceed," Lord Charn said. "Darwin, you and I will discuss at length your reasons for not informing me of this…unorthodox way of using."

Darwin lowered his big brown eyes.

Crystalyn's concentration wavered, again. The symbol paused, hovering over the center. Darwin's eyes would have to wait. Immersing her symbol halfway into the dark water, she released a portion of its energy.

The Oracle's roiling picked up substantially, the lazy waves becoming smaller. The splashing grew into a roar.

"Yes, you're getting it!" Darwin said, his voice full of glee.

Lord Charn spat commands. "Faster! Go faster!"

Crystalyn's excitement grew as she dribbled energy into the agitated water, whipping the Oracle into motion like a vat of plasicrete stirred by machinery. The top waves flattened, picking up speed. The Oracle spun faster with a growing roar, bringing back the awe-inspiring memories of Misty Gorge before the spiderbees carried her off.

His voice hugely amplified, Lord Charn shouted, "Feed it! Feed power to it!"

"Keep going, Do'brieni!"

Crystalyn released most of the symbol's remaining energy, churning the dark water faster and adding a raging fury to the frothing turbulence around the eye. If Lord Charn wanted power, he'd get power. Spinning at an incredible rate, the dark water rose to the Oracle's lip.

A funnel opened downward in the center, curving smaller the deeper it went, swirling into a vertical cornucopia. Oddly, the roar of the water spiraled down within it, traveling downward. As it flowed into the bottom, the cavernous hallway went from a thunderous boom one moment to eerie quiet the next, the last vestiges of the din silenced with the suddenness of death.

"You have succeeded! Call out to your sibling by her name, her full name! Visualize her image in your mind," Lord Charn shouted. As the words left his helm, his voice fell oddly downward, echoing around the cornucopia until it too ended abruptly.

Though Lord Charn's words had sucked down into the Oracle, Crystalyn heard enough to comprehend. "Jade Creek! Can you hear me? I've been searching for you! Jade, are you there?" Her voice leapt from her lips and vanished into the maelstrom.

"Good! Keep speaking! Lord Charn and I will amplify your words. Maintain her image in your mind—" Darwin's voice floated past her hearing before fading down the tube.

"Jade! Jade Creek! Can you hear me?" A memory from seasons ago drifted into her thoughts, when she'd called out for her sister many times during a camping trip at the farm. She recalled the wide circle they'd hiked from camp searching for Jade. Crystalyn had been so frightened then, not knowing what had befallen Jade. Finally, she'd found her little sister asleep in their tent. "Jade Creek, where are you, my beautiful little sister?"

A tiny sound erupted with an unexpected volume from the cornucopia.

"Oh, Crystalyn, is it finally you?" Jade's voice resonated oddly, as if forced from a great pit.

Crystalyn's eyes welled with tears. The sweet, familiar voice she'd longed to hear echoed throughout the hall. "Yes, Jade, it *is* me! Where are you? I've been searching so hard."

Jade's voice drifted out of the pit below. "I am in the town of Brown Recluse, waiting for Camoe to decide where we go next. I knew you'd be worried. I've been looking for you, too."

Crystalyn spoke without glancing away from the maelstrom, not caring which of the two standing at the Dark Oracle answered. "Do you have a gateway there, in this Brown Recluse?"

"I have a pair of obelisks at the outskirts of town," Lord Charn said. "Command her to go to the Staunch the Flow Inn, ask for the owner, Craight, two days hence. Let him know the great lord requires a debt paid. He will provide the path here."

The spinning, brackish water was mesmerizing, but Crystalyn kept her focus. "Did you hear that?"

Jade hesitated. "Yes, but, Crystalyn?"

Crystalyn wanted to comfort her sister, to reach through the eye of the churning cornucopia somehow and give her a hug. "What is it?"

"Make haste!" Darwin shouted. "The contacting is closing!"

"Where am I going?" Jade asked.

Crystalyn felt the vortex slow perceptibly. She blurted a reply. "To the citadel, but we can talk about it when you get here. Go to the Staunch the Flow Inn in two days."

Jade's gasp resonated out of the maelstrom. "You don't mean the Dark Citadel, do you? Crystalyn you're—" Jade's voice broke off.

The maelstrom slowed quickly, returning to its normal rate after a few rotations. The funnel filled quickly from the bottom up, replaced by the slow, churning blackness.

"No!" Crystalyn reached for her symbol, but it was gone. "Should I get it going again?" she asked, though she felt woozy. Gathering energy from around her instead of from her by grounding herself had helped, but it still had its limits. The magnitude of energy required set those limits, and the Dark Oracle must require a huge amount.

Lord Charn confirmed her suspicion. "No, it has drained us. We cannot risk another attempt this soon."

Crystalyn was disappointed but jubilant: she'd heard Jade's voice for the first time in weeks, and they *were* on the same world. They'd be together soon. Together, they were stronger.

"I don't understand." Darwin's voice was heavy with fatigue. "Why couldn't we see her sister? I put far more into it than any other contacting."

"There was supposed to be an image?" Crystalyn asked. Oh,

how she would've liked to see Jade.

His voice soft but distinct, Lord Charn leaned on the Oracle's short wall. "Always, at the bottom of the maelstrom, there is an image of the contact, but some kind of light blurred it this time. I couldn't bring it through, though I attempted many times, strange—" He stared into the Dark Oracle's murky depths and was silent. After a while, his horned helm swung toward Crystalyn. "Your sibling should have seen your image in her mind as well, but it is of no consequence now. Provide Darwin with a description. He will deliver it to the gatekeeper."

Crystalyn recalled the awful day in the Big Ugly, when she'd opened the Sapphire Gate. "Jade is two inches taller than I am, over six feet, reddish-brown hair with dark emerald eyes. She was wearing blue jeans and a black tee when I saw her last, that's the best I can do. Thank you for helping us, Lord Charn." Crystalyn hesitated. She already owed the dark-armored man so much for this, not to mention his promise to bring her here so they could be together. The last thing she wanted was to alienate him, but she had to know the cost. "What is it you want in return?"

"Nothing too demanding, I assure you, my wishes are simple," Lord Charn said. Then, he too, hesitated for nearly a full rotation of the Oracle's slow-churning water. Inhaling a small breath, he continued. "Now that you know I am going to follow through with reuniting you with your Jade, I shall enlighten you. I want you, your sibling, and anyone else you desire and can vouch for, to join me in the battle against the lies and corruption we've lived with too long on this world. Khiminay has informed me you've been subject to some of it from the Circle already." He paused, letting her absorb his words for a long heartbeat. "We'll talk later on the deceit practiced daily coming from the White Lands. At present, please, exploit what we have to offer as my guest. Your decision can wait until you've been given information and after your reunion with your sibling."

There it was. At least he'd been up front about wanting something. Crystalyn didn't know what to say. His desire went beyond a simple favor for a favor. He wanted a long-term commitment. She wasn't certain how she felt about it, but at least, she didn't have to provide an answer right away, not before Jade arrived. *Now that I've found Jade, what to do about getting home?* Crystalyn asked herself, gazing at Darwin Darkwind. Was it really such a big hurry?

Dad would be worried, for certain, but a few extra days shouldn't cause him any additional anguish than he experienced now. Besides, once Jade was with her, they still had to find the way back. Lord Charn wouldn't be eager to help with that one, no matter what her answer to his offer. He had nothing to gain by them going home.

Her host's pleasant voice broke into her thoughts. "Other matters require my attention. Darkwind will show you and your companions to your quarters. He will instruct the servants to attend to your every whim, however small. Make use of them as you will."

Crystalyn inclined her head. *"Stay close, Broth, please."*

"I will, my Do'brieni. Please, do not dwell here long. Danger awaits us here."

"Oh? How is it you know this?"

"I have heard...tales, dark tales."

"Then we will have to decide for ourselves if there is any merit to these tales, but I will take extra care."

Gripping Atoi's icy hand in her own, Crystalyn began an intercept route to the robed boy's side. Darwin's tanned face looked striking under the dark hood; it suited him. *Of course, it probably wouldn't matter what he wore even had he worn nothing.* Her face heated at the thought.

Darwin started along the great hallway as Crystalyn joined him at the Oracle's end. She wondered what it meant for him to wear the black robe and not the red, as Malkor had. Did the color mean a certain rank? If so, which was higher in rank? Perhaps Atoi would know. Strangely, everyone seemed to know her, for no one paid attention to her wherever they traveled, which was disturbing in itself. How much was the Dark Child and its host withholding from her?

"One other thing," Lord Charn's deep and pleasant voice called out when they approached a nearby intersection. Crystalyn paused, looking back over her shoulder. "I will send for you tonight. Please accept my invitation to dine at my table."

Crystalyn nodded, deeper this time.

Lord Charn inclined his head in return.

Resuming their walk, Crystalyn stayed by Darkwind's side gathering details of her surroundings, committing them to memory. She wanted to be able to find her way back on her own.

The intersection opened at another grand hallway supported by massive pillars stoically holding the purple granite roof high. Provided from clear crystals, the lighting hung from rigid wires from somewhere up above. She started to ask about the crystals, but something else caught her eye, something that made her breath catch in her throat. Standing nearly as tall and majestic as the grand hall, a pair of topaz crystal obelisks stood as two magnificent beacons heralding the hallway's beginning. Spectacular by their sheer size alone, the obelisks were the largest she'd yet to stumble across.

A smile pulled at her lips. The situation had just ascended from awful to decent. Perhaps it was a way to send two lost girls home. They *could* be home in a few short days after Jade arrived, regaling Dad with all that had happened. Crystalyn yearned to see him, to be in her room with Jade. Home was where they belonged.

DARK MAN

Yet another brown robe—Browns, as most monks called the Users in Brown Recluse—stood outside Jade's doorway in the monastery. For days, the monks had pleaded for a chance to study a live dark creation—though he'd never been, nor ever would be alive—after she'd made the mistake of taking him outside after Dirk had attacked her. Now she was paying daily for wanting the protection.

Neither she nor Camoe was naïve enough to believe the Browns intended harmless studies only. They'd caught quite a few using the Flow on their mute friend. Some seemed designed to help Burl, like bombarding his pinched arm with a healing spell—that had failed utterly. Their healing magic had no effect on dark creations.

Other experiments were destructive. One User hit him with ice through a window, trapping him inside a block. Camoe forced the haughty woman to release him, but she never expressed any remorse. No one had. To them, Burl was the perfect lab rat for their experiments with the Flow.

Jade was tired of their transparent subterfuges; they had such single path minds. Not one seemed to understand that Burl was more than some User's creation. "Why are you still speaking to the Brown, Cam? Send him on his way. I need to talk to you."

Jade raised her voice just enough to be heard from where she sat in the little alcove, trying to read. Saddened and angered by the betrayal of his acolyte, Caven had shown them to the securer room the same evening. She'd found the nook with the stuffed bookshelves immediately. She read to ward off boredom, keep her mind off Dirk's actions, and simply for the pleasure of it, something one could do alone.

Most of the time, Camoe was busy meeting with every monk in the monastery. Caven had sat in on many of the meetings, usually held in the room adjacent to the kitchen. At first Jade had felt left out, but the wondrous leather-bound books had stifled the feeling. Astura's history was rich with evil tyrants wielding dark powers and ancient wars lasting hundreds of years. The Dark Citadel was the farthest anyone had beaten back Virun.

Camoe's reply drifted from the entrance doorway. "Perhaps we should give this one a few minutes. He claims to know how to end the experimentation attempts on our resident dark creation. His words, not mine."

Jade looked up from the book titled *The Dark Empire* with more than a little reluctance. The chapter had detailed the violent shifts in power throughout User history in graphic detail. She'd discovered a reference to a codex called the Surbon Codex. The author—a renowned scholar and Light User—hinted at an adverse User erupting on the world causing untold destruction, eventually bringing an end to a war at great cost.

Jade had some concerns. The codex failed to mention what war and which side it ended with; apparently, it could shift either way. Right after, it mentioned an anomaly moving through the world at the same time, which may, or may not, affect the outcome of the chosen side. It was almost as if the book remained vague on purpose.

Folding the book over her hand to mark her place, Jade went to deal with the intrusion. Peering over Camoe's shoulder, she gazed at the man standing with his arms folded into the wide sleeves of his tan robes. The material was lighter in color than the monk's dark brown tunics or even the brown silken robes they so piously donned for daily rituals.

Unlike the Browns who had made such a nuisance of themselves, this one had left his hood hanging at his emaciated shoulders, exposing curly blond hair. The lack of a hood called attention to his gaunt face and dark, haunted eyes that had…seen things. "What do you want?" Jade demanded, in no mood for pleasantries.

A pained look crossed the man's face. "May I enter? This open hallway provides an opportunity for an easy ambush. I don't wish to have my backside shaved by a fledgling User."

Jade wanted to trust him but only at arm's length. "You have one minute to convince me you can help. If not, you leave."

Camoe flicked a glance at her but said nothing.

Peering over Camoe's shoulder, the man inclined his head. "Fair enough," he said.

Camoe swung the door wider but stayed blocking the threshold. "Step back first."

The man complied.

Glancing both ways down the hall, Camoe finally stepped aside and motioned the man inside, closing the door on his heels.

"That's far enough," Camoe said. "We have never met, so I cannot vouch for you."

"Let me correct that oversight. I am Vancid, at your service." Not looking around, he stared at her. "Now let's move onto why I'm here. Simply put, I wish to help you."

Jade waited for him to continue with his explanation. When he didn't, she asked, "You don't know us, yet you offer aid. Tell me, what 'services' can you provide?"

"Ah-ha! Very astute questions, very astute, I say!" Vancid exclaimed, rubbing his hands together. Dropping them to his side, he stood still.

Something's not right, Jade thought. For the first time since Dirk had tried to kill her, Jade switched her view to his aura.

Vancid's spinning aura was cloudy and brackish, like much of the swamp water she'd waded through before Brown Recluse. Jade forced it slower. A blackness roiled behind the aura's grayness, gaining power with each rotation, poised to break...*through!* "Camoe!" Jade cried, "He's not what he seems!"

Vancid's face darkened, and his eyes bulged to grotesque

spheres. The tan robe he wore bled into a dull black color, elongating to twice its size. A man-shaped darkness detached from Vancid, stepping out from him as one might discard soiled clothes. Vancid's deflated form slid to the floor.

Jade screamed.

Camoe's sword passed through the shadowy torso, lopping their wooden garment stand in half.

Jade's mind lurched, slowing the scene around her. A single mahogany wood chip floated in the air, lazily striking the shadowy head then rebounding slowly away. Her mind shifted back; the chip fell away at a normal rate, but not her rising fear.

The light in the room *bent* around the murky shadow as it advanced toward her.

Jade backed away, filled with dread. The sense of the dark man floated through her awareness. A single touch meant death: its evil would replace her bone marrow with shadow as it absorbed the rest of her internal matrix over time, feeding on organs and nerves until she became a dark one, a slave to a dark mind. No, more than a mind, an over mind. The same evil she'd sensed in the dominion wraith, and again at the wall, as it chased them into the swamp.

Camoe's sword flashed, once, twice, diagonally from shoulder to pelvis, slashing a crisscrossing pattern across the dark torso from behind, parting it like pitch-black smoke.

The sword's pattern merged with the dark man, leaving no trace behind. The black shape slid toward her.

The small of her back rammed against a table, halting her backward momentum. The dark arms began to raise, to reach out.

The memory of the wood chip intruded into her mind. "Camoe!" she cried, leaning back. "Go for the head!"

The druid's sword rent the shape's head from ear to ear.

The dark man froze for less than a beat of her thumping heart as its head reformed. It reached out again.

Instinctively, Jade brought the book up in front of her like a shield. The shadowy hand touched the book and recoiled. Jade scrambled over the table, confused. The dark shape glided cautiously around the table, moving relentlessly toward her.

Slipping around the table to keep it between her and the dark man, Jade thought furiously, *The book stopped it, yet Camoe's sword to the head didn't, why?* A fraction later, it occurred to her. *Paper! The book was paper! Paper was a product made from wood. Why didn't it like wood?*

The black shape glided around the end of the table, coming for her.

Dropping the book on the table, she shoved the table with all her might.

The heavy table pinned the shadow to the wall, slicing through. Half of the dark man fell onto the table and fragmented into smoky filaments that soon dispersed.

Afraid of what she might see, Jade squatted, searching under the table. Nothing but normal shadows lay underneath. At least she hoped they were.

Straightening, she leaned on the table, touching its smooth texture with reverence. The wooden object had saved her life. The attack was odd, but devious, in an evil sort of way. What warrior would use wood as a weapon?

Camoe exhaled an explosive breath. "By the true power of the One, what was that thing?"

Suddenly Jade was tired, too tired to stand for long. Taking no chances, she sat on the table cross-legged, setting the book on her lap. "You're asking *me?* Why was it after me? Why does everything and everyone seem to be after me?"

Camoe looked taken aback. He sheathed his sword with a soft clang. "I don't know, but you are right, the darkest evil..."

Camoe's voice faded away as a new voice rang in her mind. One she'd desperately wanted to hear for many, many days.

"Jade Creek, where are you, my beautiful little sister?" Crystalyn's voice called out in her mind sounding clear yet so far away.

"Oh, Crystalyn, is it finally you?"

"Yes, Jade, it is me! Where are you? I've been searching so hard."

"I am in the town of Brown Recluse, waiting for Camoe to decide where we go next. I knew you'd be worried. I've been looking for you, too."

"Do you have a gateway there, in this Brown Recluse?" Crystalyn asked someone else.

Jade was confused. Then a pleasant masculine voice echoed through her mind. *"I have a pair of obelisks at the outskirts of town,"* the voice said. *Command her to go to the Staunch the Flow Inn, ask for the owner, Craight, two days hence. Let him know the great lord requires a debt paid. He will provide the path here."*

"Did you hear that?"

"Yes, but, Crystalyn?"

"What is it?"

"Make haste! The contacting is closing!" a new male voice said, sounding younger than the other one.

"Where am I going?" Jade asked.

"To the citadel, but we can talk about it when you get here. Go to the Staunch the Flow Inn in two days," Crystalyn said, her voice urgent.

"You don't mean the Dark Citadel, do you? Crystalyn, you're in great danger!" Jade shouted into the recesses of her mind. Silence met her call. *"Crystalyn, are you there?"* No answer, her sister was gone. *No!* Crystalyn couldn't have meant the Dark Citadel, could she? An involuntary shudder racked her bones. What would she do if Crystalyn were at the same horrid, evil place she'd fought so hard to escape? Would she go back after expending so much effort escaping from there?

She had no choice. She would do whatever it took to reunite with her sister, for them to go home, though she might be creating anxiety over nothing. There must be other citadels on the planet. Crystalyn could be in a different place, one without the evil.

Camoe eyed her, his eyebrows slightly elevated.

"I'm sorry, what have you been saying?" she asked.

"Other than asking what's wrong with you? I said I wouldn't have thought anyone else would know or care about your being here on Astura."

"My sister does now. Crystalyn contacted me."

Camoe's aging face darkened. "What? When?"

"It just happened."

"Oh! Then she is still alive. Try to recall everything she mentioned."

"She wants me to go to the Staunch the Flow Inn to make contact with its owner, a man named Craight."

"No, not there, I forbid it. The owner hates Users to no end, all *Users*, no matter how small their ability." The druid looked at her pointedly. "His patrons detest Users as much as he does. When I'm recognized, most everyone in there will attack me. They would not kill me, or there would be recriminations, but that does not mean they would not beat me to near death. It is too dangerous, even up here with the monks. Have you forgotten about that acolyte, Dirk, so soon? Down in the town of Brown Recluse, murder from dueling or assassinations is an everyday occurrence."

Jade moved to the pantry and peered inside. "I'm guessing the owner of the inn has a gateway that will take me to her. If he hates Users, if *they* hate Users, what will they think of a User's creation?" Burl's unblinking yellow-orange eyes regarded her.

Camoe didn't reply immediately. "It is irrelevant. I told you I forbid you from going. You and I should not ever be caught near a place such as that," he finally said, his voice firm.

"Oh, Camoe," Jade replied, her voice catching in her throat. "You know I have to. It's what we traveled here to do, find my sister. Now she's found *me*. I have to go."

Camoe gazed at her, a frown creasing his forehead. His jaw worked, but no sound escaped his throat.

Jade's resolve weakened. There had had to be some other way, but nothing came to mind.

Camoe turned away. "I suppose there is no stopping you, but you shall not go alone."

Jade was frightened but determined. "I won't be alone. I have to figure out a way for Burl to accompany me. He can't stay here, and you cannot go. You can't defend him forever. I won't put that responsibility on your shoulders. He has to go with me. I owe him too much, and I won't let you risk the inn to help me, either. I will be safer without you." She hated herself for saying it, but it was true.

"Of course, Burl has to go with you. I could not stop him if I wanted to, which I don't. He has proven to be a good protector. As for me, a seasoned druid with abilities would give you away immediately. Craight knows me too well to risk a disguise, but I can insist Caven accompany you."

Jade's eyebrow rose. How much use could his portly brother be? She'd never seen him touch a weapon. "You're going to send Caven?"

Camoe relaxed slightly, picking up the book from the table. "He is more versatile than you may think. Consider it settled then. I would speak of this, *The Dark Empire,* before you depart. I spoke with Caven on the matter yesterday; a copy of it is rarer than you know, even in Virun. He wanted to see it immediately, but I have delayed to give you the opportunity to peruse it with your particular insight. As far as we know, there are only two in existence; both were in the Dark Lands after the White Lands' copy vanished from Surbo. The codices have gained interest of late, due to their uncanny accuracy. Monks have spent their lives trying to glean meaning from the cryptic tomes, the Virun Codex especially. Though deemed too dangerous to study alone, I believe some of our monks with the most arrogance still peruse it in secret, believing they alone can resist its evil. Apparently, someone, or something, wants you to read it. Have you come across anything referring to the Surbon or Virun codices in the book?"

Jade gaped at her friend and protector. "Yes I have seen it mentioned. That's what I wanted to discuss before that...*thing* jumped out of Vancid's skin, if that was his real name."

"I believe it may have been. I've seen him around the taverns here before my time at the Dark Citadel. He has been reporting to Caven since he was good at gathering intelligence, which is why I thought it well to hear what he had to say. But, come to think of it, he has been asking about the codices in exchange for information regarding lower Brown Recluse."

Jade felt a chill begin to form in her stomach. "But that would mean—"

"Yes, at some point in the last one or two days, the dark man, or whatever it was, consumed him."

Jade's stomach switched from chilled to nauseous. "Do you think it was after me all along?"

"Again, I do not believe it so. It is possible, I suppose, that the Dark Users at the Dark Citadel know about you. But that would mean Burl told them. I do not think it, though. Had they known about us, they could have sent armies to hunt us, or worse, long before we had escaped the citadel. Someone else, perhaps a sole Dark User, went to a great deal of trouble to get a particularly vile evil close to you. Perhaps when they could not kill you through poor Dirk, they grew desperate and expended a valuable espionage commodity to get to you. Caven chose Vancid to replace Dirk solely for the man's skill as an instructor; he was to train a new acolyte for Caven. Vancid was a member of the Order of Brethren, serving the Great Mother. He had a lowly position but was a member, nonetheless."

Burl's yellow-orange eyes continued to regard her unblinking from the darkness of the pantry. She'd commanded him to stay in the cramped room days ago, but there was no hint of resentment in his eyes, only enduring patience. Like Camoe, she didn't believe he'd been in contact with his creator; whoever sought her had taken advantage of her proximity. A single hidden enemy could be worse than an angry mob, as her dad might say. For now, all they could do was stay alert. Staying alive and healthy was an even bigger priority now that Crystalyn had found her. But she couldn't escape the fact that something else had found her, too.

HIGH-ANXIETY EVENING

A soft metallic sound clinked against stone. Fine porcelain clattered together softly. Crystalyn woke from a dream of wandering in thick woods with Jade calling her name from somewhere near. She'd dashed toward the sound of her sister's voice, tearing through thorny branches that ripped at her clothes. Plunging through a wall of greenery, she had broken out into a clearing. The calls grew distant, and Jade's voice faded.

Even though the urgency the dream instilled in her had not gone away, Crystalyn shunted the feeling to the back of her mind. It was a dream, nothing else. Jade would be beside her soon, she reminded herself, yet it didn't quite quell her uneasiness. *A manic episode must be coming on*, she thought, glancing around for her pack. How had she fallen asleep so easily in a place she'd never been and only heard bad things about? The Dark Oracle must have sapped a lot of her energy.

The woman who had made the sounds that awoke her had left a tray on the bedside table and was now rifling through the room's wardrobe. At last, she fetched Crystalyn a blue gown. "It's good you have awakened. The great lord does not like to be kept waiting." Seasoned past her middle years, the woman clutched the dress as a prized possession she hated to loan.

Crystalyn sat up, only now recalling Lord Charn's dinner invitation. She had no desire to go, but she couldn't think of a way out of it. Until Jade arrived, compliance with the great lord's wishes was critical.

Broth's comforting presence stemmed from the next room. Atoi lounged beside him. Crystalyn hoped there would be time to spend with them after dressing.

Slipping from bed, she stripped down to her undergarments. So exhausted when Darkwind had taken his leave, she'd only removed her boots. The woman's face was stony with disapproval as she slid the dress over Crystalyn's shoulders, buttoning it in place almost before it had come to rest. "Tell me what to call you, please," Crystalyn asked, feeling the first stirrings of irritation. The woman's brusque manners had begun to grate on her patience. She had low tolerance for such things. Patience for a person's idiosyncrasies was for normal people.

Smoothing an errant lace on the dress, the light-haired woman hesitated, her blue eyes cold. "I am Deonna, head mistress for the citadel," she said. Grabbing an ornate metal comb from the bedside tray, the woman pointed toward a plush chair placed in front of a gilded vanity. "As a rule, I have staff to take care of our guests; my duties are to the citadel and the great lord. You must be important indeed: the great lord himself requested I assist you with your evening attire."

Crystalyn crossed the room to sit in the chair, which didn't feel as soft as it looked. Facing the beautiful, gilded mirror, she gazed at her haggard reflection in silence as the woman prattled on about the many great lords she'd personally served. Her irritation showed with the deepening of her blue eyes, so dark as to be almost black, but the woman, Deonna, wouldn't know.

A symbol with interlocked squares transposed in place of her auburn hair for a moment. She recalled it from the aggression section in the black-lettered book, and it had a silencing feel to it. Perhaps she could use it to quiet the woman. Another flash of irritation raced through her, this time with herself. Deonna probably wasn't as bloody snobby as she seemed. Was she becoming too dependent on her symbols? The thin, smooth face looking out at her from the mirror had no answers.

"Do'brieni? Are you well? I sense unrest." Crystalyn was grateful for the surge of friendship that flowed into her mind, soothing her irritation. The warden's presence was good for her. She hoped he

got as much out of it as she did. *"I am better now, my Do'brieni. You bring out the best in me. I don't know how I'd do this without you. I can't wait for you to meet my sister Jade. I do hope you two get along. I can't imagine why you wouldn't, but it's been weeks since I've seen her."* There it was. The true source of her irritation, not Deonna at all, though she'd added to it. Jade might have changed. Had this harsh, violent world taken her loving nature?

It didn't matter. They would work through it. Jade was *alive*. Somehow, her sister had survived, and that was all she wanted. *"Are you and Atoi coming to dinner with me, Do'brieni?"*

"No, we have dined while you slept. There is no place for a warden at a lord's table. Please remain alert; though I perceive you have to take any path offered to find your sibling, this is the dominion of the greatest evil known. We are in the lair of the great lord. We cannot remain long."

Broth had been disappointed with her quick decision to come to the Dark Citadel. She felt it strongly. He did not hide it, nor did he focus on it. Wariness flitted in the link, something he hoped to instill in her, as it wove around his devotion and support. Crystalyn added warmth and love, mixed with a deep affection to the mix. *"Try not to worry over much, my Broth. I will be careful enough for both of us. We'll get through this, I promise."*

"You do have such beautiful hair, though we should do something about the color," Deonna was saying. "The bright red within it is almost overcome by the drab brown."

Deonna yanked the metal comb downward, tugging through the tangles. Crystalyn sat up straighter, bracing herself against the long strokes. It didn't help much. "It's my natural color," she said through clenched teeth.

"Natural?" The woman raised a thick golden eyebrow. Plotting her path in advance, Deonna pulled the steel comb as gently as she could. It still felt like the stout woman was pounding through the snarls with a hammer. "Why haven't you highlighted it? A tone enhancement would do wonders. I could order one of the red robes to cast it for you.

Or perhaps you could do it yourself should you be a User of even small ability." Deonna raised her other eyebrow to match the first.

So there it was. The woman was as transparent as an old holo image. "If you want to know something about me, simply ask. I may even be inclined to answer," Crystalyn said, keeping her face smooth. Having her reflection in the mirror to look at made it easier. Blunt to the point of sarcastic, she'd never been good at holding things inside.

Deonna looked away for a moment. When she turned back, she kept her eyes downcast, ostensibly concentrating on Crystalyn's tangles. The tugging lessened. "I am here to look after the great lord's well-being. Becoming familiar with dining guests is a small, but important, part of my duties," she said quietly. Raising her head, she gazed into Crystalyn's eyes, and yanked the comb downward.

Pinpricks of pain tore through Crystalyn's skull, snapping her head back. Gazing once again into the mirror, she met Deonna's smug stare with a stony one of her own. "Do that again, and you will be dismissed from my service." Her voice never cracked once, though her head throbbed with the grating pressure of a pulse engine out of discordance.

Deonna's blue eyes widened. "I am truly sorry, my lady. Please, forgive me. I don't know what I was thinking. I will report myself to the great lord. He will no doubt have me flogged for which I am most deserving," the matronly woman said, her face aghast.

Crystalyn felt some remorse. "For now, there will be no talk of reporting or flogging. See that it doesn't happen again and I'll overlook it, this once. Let's just concentrate on the task at hand, shall we?"

"My lady is too kind," Deonna replied in a small voice, lowering her eyes. A flash of haughtiness flitted briefly across Deonna's smooth face. With difficulty, Crystalyn kept a sigh bottled inside. Perhaps Broth was right about this place.

Tonight was going to be a high-anxiety evening if the preparations were any indication. Where had she dropped her pack? It was high time for her meds.

EMPTY GRAYNESS

Lowering her head slightly, Jade was grateful for the robe's deep hood. The tavern of the Staunch the Flow Inn was booming with patrons loud with drink for such an early evening hour. Caven had expected as much, and he'd planned their entrance when most would be socializing with known acquaintances early on. Later, after the imbibing was in full fruition, the hardy ones, heavy with drink, would circulate around the tavern intruding upon conversations. Some would inevitably accost latecomers demanding to know things best kept private.

Jade still harbored doubts Camoe's portly brother was the right one to get her and Burl where they needed to go, but so far no one had questioned them, and the robes he provided blended with the crowd. Apparently the monks of Brown Recluse proper liked their drink; no one gazed overly long at Caven's two acolytes standing at ease at the end of the bar while he ordered another round.

Burl, nonetheless, was a cause for concern. He remained in the exact position she'd put him in upon their arrival: his back to the wall behind her, head tilted toward the floor, and hood pulled forward to hide his telltale eyes. Jade worried about his lack of motion. If Caven delayed too long broaching the subject of speaking with the tavern owner, someone may notice one of his acolytes failed to draw breath.

"Another round, monk?" the nondescript man behind the bar inquired as he swiped the counter in front of Caven with a stained rag. Of average height and build, the man's only outstanding feature was his scraggly black goatee.

"Certainly," Caven said, sliding his tankard closer to the man with his fingertip. "Keep them coming. Set one up for Craight as well. Oh, and let him know I'd like a word in private at his leisure," he added, almost as an afterthought.

Reaching for the tankard, the bartender hesitated, frowning. "Is he expecting you, *monk?* What is it he would want with *your* kind?"

Caven sneered. "If I told you, it wouldn't be *private*, now would it?"

Jade cringed inside. If there was going to be trouble, it would be now.

"Replenish my ale, get one for Craight, and deliver my message as I asked," Caven said, his voice a low growl. Leaning forward, he gazed hard into the man's eyes as he slid his hand toward the man, palm down. "This should cover it, with the remainder staying with you for your…gracious effort," he added, inching the coin forward with his fingertips.

The man's eyes narrowed and his frown deepened. For a long moment, he stared at Caven. Finally, he dropped his eyes to the table. The coin vanished with a flash of gold. Pouring the tankard to the brim from a dented pitcher he produced from somewhere behind the bar, he sloshed it in front of Caven. Filling another tankard less full, the nondescript man regarded the three of them briefly before vanishing through a door into the back.

Caven leaned back on his stool, taking a small sip, looking around surreptitiously.

Jade followed his example, glancing around quickly, not letting her eyes linger in one place too long. Staunch the Flow Inn and Tavern—as the sign posted out front read—worked a thriving business. Townspeople lined the bar sitting on plain-backed, high stools or standing and leaning on it with their elbows and arms. The wood chairs and tables taking up most of the remaining space on both sides of a narrow aisle sustained a fair amount of patrons involved in conversation.

A pitcher similar to the barkeep's occupied the center space on every table but two; those supported three castle-like miniature structures, which several people stood around tossing implements similar to dice. Jade would've liked a closer look at them, but glances her direction had already grown frequent from different places throughout the room. One in particular seemed to have taken an interest in her; a scowling, broad-faced man in silver-black armor sitting at the bar's end glared boldly in her direction. Certain that he'd now made eye contact with her, the scowl deepened, bordering on rage.

"Don't trade looks with him, Jade," Caven said in an undertone barely loud enough for her to hear. "It will only encourage his kind to start something."

Jade locked eyes with Caven. "Why does he hate me so much? I've never done anything to him, have I?"

Raising the tankard, he downed a decent swig of light amber ale. "They hate anyone they suspect is a User," Caven said, his tone somber.

"But, I'm not a User!"

Caven glanced around, a yawn breaking up his slack face. His blue eyes slid past her without lingering. "Are you sure about that? When you look at me, what is it you see? I mean, really *look* at me," he said quietly. "But keep your head down."

Jade slowed the tempest rotating around the portly monk. Three images of a younger and older Caven abounded within the rotation but not for long. An indistinguishable shape, slightly lighter than the gray vortex spinning around Caven, floated behind the images, consuming them one by one until it alone remained. Drifting inside the vortex for another full rotation, the shape slowly blended with the now empty grayness surrounding Caven.

Shocked, Jade let the vortex go. Then, with some trepidation, she tried again, concentrating on Caven with all her will. The monk's aura obediently slowed, but there was nothing to view, only the impenetrable gray.

Jade dropped the viewing feeling as if she'd brushed against frost cold enough to burn. She was cold inside. What did it all mean?

One minute the viewing was there and the next it was gone, which brought to mind an urgent question. What swallowed them?

The coldness inside deepened. Not for the first time, she wished Camoe had come along so she could ask him. He would have an answer. Even if he were uncertain, he'd have some sort of practical opinion on the matter.

Jade sighed. Wishing was irrelevant most of the time, so it was now. Camoe would've been in immediate danger had he accompanied them here. She wouldn't want him to get hurt or worse, simply because she wanted his advice.

Caven was regarding her, a question shining in his blue eyes. Jade didn't know what to say. She'd never had an image slip away before, not in such a manner. What could she tell him? That he had no images now?

Thankfully, the barkeep appeared from the back motioning for them to follow, sparing her the need to reveal the viewing. The stool creaked loudly in protest as Caven lifted his bulk from it. Swaying slightly, he scooped up his tankard, drained it, and then waddled after the barkeep.

Towing Burl by the hand, Jade followed, trying to shake the feeling things didn't bode well for them.

CAUSE OF STRIFE

The fetching, dark-haired Darwin arrived to escort Crystalyn not long after Deonna left. The prim, older woman had obviously informed Darwin that the common girl was ready. However the woman might infuriate her, she was admirably efficient.

"I hope you had a refreshing nap, and I trust the head mistress wasn't too insensitive with waking you," Darwin said, one fine eyebrow raised. It was almost as if he'd heard her thoughts. Without waiting for a reply, he stepped into the hall, pausing and offering his arm. Crystalyn slid her arm in his delighted with the strength inherent in his muscles. "She can be brusque, but she likes her duties here and does them…well enough. You are so beautiful in your blue dress," he added, changing the subject smoothly.

"Oh! Thank you for saying so," Crystalyn said lamely. He looked so glamorous in his black chain mail. "Where is your black robe?"

Darwin laughed easily, a divine sound in her ears. It was the first time she'd heard him laugh with delight, but she hoped not the last. "I wear many outfits, for I have many duties, my lady. After our meal, I must inspect the state of my regiments. It is a duty I neglect at times, though Lord Charn forever reminds me of it. All soldiers invited to the great lord's table are required to follow his example. You will see much armor tonight."

Crystalyn wondered how many functions Darwin served within the Dark Citadel. "Why don't you like it? Is it simply because it is a duty?"

Darwin's brown eyes swept over her, sending an involuntary

thrill through her. She had to be on her guard here: she *was* in the lair of the enemy after all according to…some she'd met on this world, such as her *Do'brieni*. "I see you do not have a military background, which endears you to me. I detest anything designed to make a man efficient at destroying another man. Life should never be taken for granted."

Crystalyn let his assumption pass without comment. Having her dad as head of security had forced many hours of tactical studies upon her and her sister. "I'm afraid I don't understand," she said, frowning. "Why wouldn't you want your men to fight well and live? Aren't you a captain or something? Isn't it your duty to train them?"

Darwin flashed a brief smile. "I am a general with many captains under me. I simply meant I would like to end this war without having to destroy half the lives of the people and creatures living on Astura."

"Then why don't you throw down your weapons and walk away? Wars are messy things, anyway. No one really wins," Crystalyn said as they entered an unfamiliar intersection. Guided by his gentle pressure on her arm, she turned down a narrower but opulent passage. Bright banners hung on the walls above stone shelving displaying silver wrought figurines and dining ware. Black, white, and red tiled flooring brightened the polished gray stone. A warm feeling raced through her as their hips brushed together.

Darwin laughed, gazing at her with his dark eyes. "That's what I always say, but we've been so oppressed here in Virun so long, no one knows much beyond soldiering."

Crystalyn halted, pulling her escort to a standstill by his elbow. "You call yourselves oppressed, but the White Lands claim to be on the defensive against the Dark Citadel's aggression."

Darwin's merry features vanished. His smooth face took on a serious cast. "I have heard they promote fear and distrust of the Dark Citadel. Some in the White Lands no doubt believe it," he said, his brown eyes earnest. "I can't say I blame them. There have been some…tyrants, in our history, and in the White Lands' as well. We used to be one people, living together in harmony when this world was young and devoid of some of the darker dangers, before some Users learned how to become so powerful."

"Yes, I've heard that you were all a family in the past; it's one of the things both sides agree upon. It sounds like you're having trouble accepting it though," Crystalyn said, following his strong but tender guidance. Plush carpets and gilded rugs lined the hallway, growing quite intricate the farther they strolled. Crystalyn would have liked to spend some leisure time perusing them—they certainly deserved an extended look—but it was hard to keep her eyes away from Darwin too long. *What's come over me?* She was starting to act like Jade, mooning over every handsome boy who happened by.

"I do not accept it," Darwin said with his quiet baritone. They strode up to a bronzed door guarded by guards in dark armor, holding the now-familiar spears and swords. "Our world need not be in constant strife."

The faceless guards nodded at her host as they passed. Their helms depicted the heads of spiderbees with chilling, alien detail. Crystalyn shuddered, moving past a half step ahead of her guide. Recalling her near-death experience with the hive, she wasn't about to linger.

The room beyond the doorway curtailed a great stone and glass table that gave up space in the big room only when necessary to the mob of well-dressed people standing behind plush chairs. Servants moved quietly in the background of the table's startlingly clear glass.

Lord Charn stood tall, dark, and powerful, standing at ease at the table's gleaming onyx head. A large head the table had, too; Crystalyn took in the sinuous body, the illusionary delicacy of the fine membrane wings, and four powerful legs of a magnificent black dragon holding up the glass. Lord Charn gestured for her to take the seat next to him.

Darwin pulled the chair out for her, sliding it forward to stop at the most comfortable spot for her reach, before claiming the seat on her right side. Lord Charn settled in next to her. "You may all be seated," he said, his voice carrying the table's great length with alacrity and volume, yet he didn't seem loud to her.

The men and women wearing the elegant clothes sat nearly in unison. No one sat to the left of Lord Charn for there was no chair, only a glaring vacant space. Servants appeared as soon as the last person was seated, watched over by Deonna's appraising gaze from where she'd stationed herself at the far end of the table.

In a surprisingly short amount of time, the glass top abounded with steaming bowls, heaping serving plates, and crystal decanters. Conversation dulled to a background drone as everyone served their table neighbors from the wide variety grouped together upon similar trays along the dragon's back. The better-dressed servants at the dragon's head brought forth colored crystal decanters, entire cooked birds, ornate brim-filled salad bowls, breads, cheeses, grapes, and sliced melons.

The serving trays spread from Darkwind all the way to the former empty space by Lord Charn. A manservant trimmed with lace and sporting chin-length sideburns, the color of snow, stood there, waiting with arms clasped behind his back. After a time, Lord Charn nodded. The servant sprang into action; reaching on both sides of Lord Charn's chin, he released a catch, and a portion of the dark helmet dropped into his hand.

Any hope Crystalyn harbored of getting a glimpse of her host's features vanished as the manservant began to hand feed Great Lord Charn as if he were a mere child. Crystalyn gaped. Realizing she was being impolite, her face heated, so she glanced at her closest table companions, looking away from Darwin. The last thing she wanted was for him to inquire after her flushed face: her embarrassment would escalate into utter shame.

"Have you caught something vile?" a beautiful, dark-haired woman sitting across the table from her asked. Her lacy black dress peeked out from the loosely tied silky red robe, revealing a plunging neckline underneath. "There are many diseases floating around I wouldn't care to share."

Two men wearing red armor on the woman's left abruptly broke off their conversation to look at Crystalyn. Older than her by half, one sported a thin scar across his right cheek. The other kept a plain, clean-shaven face. They regarded her with thin lips and icy eyes.

Crystalyn's skin grew hotter.

"Have a care how you speak to our guest, Correlda," Darwin said. Our great lord may decide you have overstepped your station in life."

Correlda's dark eyes smoldered. "Do not think you are ready to test me. Not too long ago I was still your Flow master. You cherished my teachings then. Or did you? Perhaps you only ever treasured my other…ministrations."

Darkwind's countenance darkened. Locking eyes with the woman twice his seasons, he spoke softly. "Have a care, Correlda. I may accept your offer to meet at the Dark Dais, if that is what you intended when you opened your scathing mouth. Though I fear it would be your last challenge."

Correlda's face blanched slightly, but her dark eyes never lost their smolder. "The day shall come. At this moment, you may tell me who you've selected to take my place beside the great lord at his table." Her eyes fixed on Crystalyn.

Halting the servant's feeding with a raised, gauntleted hand, Lord Charn's horned helm swung toward Correlda. "My guest is not your concern, nor that of your cronies," he added, his head moving toward her male companions. As he did, Crystalyn caught a glimpse of smooth sienna skin. "If you still believe you must know everything you're not privy to, meet *me* at the Dark Dais this night. I shall expect you to bring along your two lackeys and rid myself of their disease, at the same moment."

His masculine tone still carried, though it was higher without the mouthpiece. Conversation had quieted in an instant. All heads had swung their direction, even the full helmed red- and-black-armored lords and generals at the dragon table's tail end. No food sat in front of them.

Correlda gaped at him for three long beats of Crystalyn's heart. Finally, she lowered her eyes to the table. "Please punish me as you will, My Lord. I do not wish to be the cause of strife in your greatest of domains, the Dark Citadel," she mumbled.

"Do not test my patience! Speak to be heard!" Lord Charn said, his throaty voice ringing throughout the room.

Correlda straightened as if backhanded. "Yes, My Lord! I do not wish to be the cause of strife in your greatest of domains!" she shouted into the silence at the table. Her face was flushed with anger or perhaps her own embarrassment.

Lord Charn waved a dismissive, gauntleted hand. "Very well, you may leave us. Return for sustenance in the morning; no morsel shall pass your lips before then."

Her face livid, Correlda slowly stood, glaring at Crystalyn, a moment before it would've been too obvious an infraction. Then the red-robed woman stalked from the room, trailed by the two men. Almost immediately, the table buzzed with conversation as if there had been no interruption. Crystalyn ladled something soupy into her bowl, and began to eat, carefully keeping her gaze on the now empty chair across from her. For the first time, she wondered if she'd made a mistake by coming here.

LOST ONE

Pulling Burl along by his good hand, Jade kept close to Caven as the barkeep showed them to a small chamber behind the main bar, made up of two rooms. After ushering them into the first and largest room, the bald man with the dirty goatee left without a word, a scowl still affixed to his lined face. The room was crowded, so Jade crept next to Caven. Four men sat in pairs on each side of a burly, black-vested man seated in an armchair, his large feet propped up upon a rickety table. Empty, dented pitchers littered the room.

"What are you bothering me with this time, Caven?" the burly man asked without preamble, his blocky face set. "Now that you're heavy with drink again, are you going to persuade me to let your brother back inside my tavern? His worthless User carcass isn't welcome here."

A brown scraggly-bearded man with lean, solid muscles sitting to his right chuckled venomously. "Perhaps we should let him inside your establishment, Craight. I could use the entertainment of converting him to a worthless User cadaver."

Several of the men laughed.

Craight smiled as he thumped his booted feet to the floor, standing with a speed belying his too-beefy stature. "I wonder if you have the same User blood flowing in you. Speak. What is so important to warrant pulling my man away from selling my ale? Or perhaps, you've brought me a…volunteer barmaid." He glanced at Jade, his tone ominous.

Jade lowered her head quickly, looking through the hood of her robe at Camoe's brother. The big monk swayed back and forth worse than a decayed tree losing its last roothold next to a lively stream. Jade's irritation flared. *Why did he pick now of all times to down so much ale?*

Caven looked around for something to lean on. Seeing nothing in the immediate vicinity, he settled for pulling a chair to him and leaning on the back. "My associates are not your concern. But if you must know, I was asked to escort these two by someone high enough up the chain of command for me to have no choice but to accept the request," he sniffed, his voice slurring noticeably. The chair creaked loudly in protest when he swayed forward, catching himself at the last minute.

One of the men, an older man with a gray beard, sneered. "You chose to accept it so you could drink a pitcher for free—or two or three. For a man as wide as you are, you should be able to drain a cask, yet look at you; your monkish brain is a sodden mess!"

A chorus of laughter followed.

"Silence!" Craight roared. The room stilled, except for Caven's labored breaths.

Craight glared at each of his men in turn and then at Caven. "Who requested your assistance, and what does it have to do with me?"

"I had thought to speak with you in private. It is a matter of some urgency," Caven replied evenly. "Yet I have this nagging feeling you will ignore my request."

Jade shot a quick glance at her escort. Caven's slur hadn't manifested with his last words.

Craight paused, his face smoothing. He gazed at Caven as if he'd shed his skin and changed into a flicker or something. Then his stony expression resumed as he glanced sidelong at his men. Something unreadable flashed briefly in Craight's blue eyes as he straightened, his hand resting on the pommel of his sword. "I would hear what a drunken monk thinks is urgent enough to interrupt my men's leisure."

"As you would have it," Caven said, his voice as heavy as his body. "I was asked to inform you the great lord requires a debt repaid."

Several men gasped.

Craight's sword swept from its sheath.

Exploding with blurring speed, Caven smashed the sturdy wooden chair solidly into the face of the sneering man sitting at the table. The man's smirk vanished with splintering wood and a sickening thud.

Craight's sword jabbed through the throat of the man nearest him, his backswing chopping the hapless man next to him partway through his torso.

From somewhere in his robes, a long knife appeared in Caven's hand, his free hand hurling the table to the side. The long knife stabbed deep into the chest of the fourth man as he attempted to scuttle from his chair.

Jade was stunned. In the blink of an eye, four men's lives had been snuffed out with brutal efficiency.

Using his foot to pry his sword from the corpse, Craight spun on Caven, his face livid. "You've cost me four good men, monk! Your master better be grateful."

Calmly wiping the long knife on his victim's black tunic, Caven straightened and faced his accuser, a frown creasing his forehead. "Lord Charn is far from my master. I serve the Mother. From the message, one would assume you followed the great lord."

Craight stuffed his sword in the sheath at his side. "Hardly, I accepted his coin to build this place, not knowing the blasted citadel was behind the funding until it was too late. I had begun to believe they'd forgotten about the debt, until last night." He glanced at the door. "Perhaps we should continue our conversation in my private room." He motioned toward the door at the rear. "First, let me get someone started on cleaning up this mess."

Cracking the door leading to the bar open, he spoke too softly for Jade to hear and then strode to the room's rear door, carefully avoiding the pooling blood. Slipping a small chain from his neck over his head, he produced a key and turned the great lock on the door with a sharp, well-oiled click. Pushing it open, he stepped inside, indicating Jade should follow. She did, bringing Burl by the hand.

Caven filed in after, joining her in front of a rough-cut wooden desk, smoothed on the top surface only. Craight closed the door, locking it from the inside, moved to the desk, and sat on the edge, eyeing the three companions long enough that Jade began to feel uncomfortable. "Well? Is someone going to tell me why four of my men died?" Craight asked, his blue eyes blank.

Jade started. "But you killed two of them!"

Craight's oval eyes flicked to her before resting on Caven. "Is she a User? You brought one *here?* Am I now forced into helping a blasted User?"

"Nay, she is no User. Just someone lost, trying to find her way," Caven said. All trace of drink had vanished from his voice.

Craight looked relieved. "That is well. I always pay a debt, but I'm not certain I could've convinced myself to do it this time." He stood long enough to move to the chair behind the desk. He sat down heavily, using one hand to mask a quiet cough.

When he raised a shaky hand to point to a pair of objects covered with unadorned rugs, she tried to read his aura, to get a sense of the man. She slowed the images around him, marveling anew at her strange talent. A black hole floated next to a circular shining eclipse of light. A red substance, resembling the blood congealing in the next room, pooled on dusty ground made up the second. In the final image, a stooped, old man dressed in rags looked away into the distance. The vortex tugged strong at her mind. She winced and let it go back to rotating around him.

Craight pointed toward two objects covered with blankets. "Those arrived early this morning with a cryptic note: 'Your services will be required for a lost one. Do not hesitate.' That's all, two simple sentences with a hidden meaning I now know. My men's lives lost, for a lost one."

Jade gawked at the stocky man.

Craight raised a brown eyebrow, his eyes on her. "What? Do not feel too bad for my fallen men, lost one. Hired as they were as bouncers and guards, but in truth, they were nothing but thugs. Nay, your compassion is better suited directed at me. Now I have to search for the right mindset for replacement lackeys—not too intelligent or too ambitious. It takes months of conditioning getting them to perform precisely as I require. Now, if you please, do what you have come here to do. I have much work ahead of me," he said with a nod toward the rugs.

Caven swept the rugs away with a flourish. A pair of crystal obelisks, russet in color, brought a gasp to both Jade's and Caven's throats.

"Yes, that was my first reaction this morning, too. Impressive, are they not? Can you imagine my surprise when a duke's fortune showed up here, yet they are not mine? I don't suppose any of you are capable of activating them. Not even your silent friend?" Craight glared hard at Burl.

Caven dropped the rugs in a pile. Spreading the obelisks a few feet apart, he stepped back, his hands going to his rotund waist. "No, we can't activate them. I don't need to reiterate how that's going to be a problem."

"Who is going?" Craight asked.

"My two associates," Caven said.

Craight sighed. "I suppose I will have to bring someone in. You all are being no end of trouble. However, you, monk, will have to leave."

Caven turned to Craight, frowning. "I do not see the need for my withdrawal."

Craight leaned back in his chair, his arms going behind his head. "Nevertheless, it is but one of two conditions for receiving my help. Your acolytes must also be blindfolded."

Caven glanced at Jade. "He cannot be trusted, but I don't see a choice."

Jade nodded. She had to get to Crystalyn.

Caven sighed. "Very well, I will be at the bar, and I expect you to show me the active gateway once they've passed through."

Craight dropped his big arms to his lap and stood. "If that is what you wish."

Caven strode to the door. He glanced one final time over his shoulder; a small smile pursed his lips, and there was a glint to his blue eyes. He stepped through and the door clicked closed.

Jade was surprised how sad she was to see him go; he'd been a good friend in his own way. She wondered why he seemed satisfied with something. Turning toward Craight again, Jade found him next to her, holding two dark rags. "Tie this tight over your friend's eyes. I will check, so make certain it is," he said, handing her a rag. Jade did so, taking Burl by the hand when she finished. The room darkened as the second one stole her vision. Rough yet firm hands guided her by the shoulders to stand at a particular spot. "When I tell you, step forward," Craight said from behind her.

A few moments of darkness went by before he said, "Step forward."

As Jade did so, she realized Craight's hands had been firm on her shoulders. There was no evidence he ever shook at all, like Caven's vanishing drunkenness. Was everyone on this whole world full of subterfuge? More importantly, why did they have to use it?

REUNION

Crystalyn fiddled with the buttons on her dress, dark emerald today. Deonna had woken her promptly at the late afternoon hour she'd requested after another pleasant, yet exhausting, morning touring the citadel with Darwin. It was far bigger than she had expected, and Darwin had assured her she still had more than half of it to see. He wanted to show her soon. She wasn't looking forward to all the walking, but she did want to spend those days with him.

So far, he'd been the model of a man, apologizing several times for that horrid evening at dinner while explaining the citadel's rich history at length. She missed his company as soon as he left each day.

Today, he'd delayed those duties to be at her side for the big reunion, as he put it. She was grateful, but her anxieties remained. A lot had happened since Jade touched the gateway she activated in Ruena's office. "What am I going to do if Jade is still mad at me for stranding her here on Astura? Suppose she hates the sight of me now."

Darwin gave her hand a gentle squeeze. "Your sister may still harbor grievances at first, but she has to be yearning to see you, who wouldn't be?"

Crystalyn couldn't bring herself to smile at his thoughtful attempt to cheer her up, but she appreciated every word. "Your world has to have changed her though, it's changed me. All these battles have an effect, good or bad. What do I do if it's bad? I'm not sure I could take it if her loving, good-natured self is gone."

Darwin let go of her hand and put his strong arm at her waist, pulling her close. "Whatever her nature, you will guide her to where she should be."

Crystalyn did smile at Darwin then, but she had reservations. Jade had always listened to her, doing what she'd asked with minimal complaint. Crystalyn had needed that as she took on the role of guiding her sibling after their mom's disappearance as shaky and error ridden as it may have been. Would Jade still want guidance from her? Did she still need it?

Crystalyn caressed the black crystal candle tucked away inside the dress pocket on her hip. The candle helped soothe her anxiety, a memento of home and an augment to her symbols in an emergency. She was still uncertain if coming to the Dark Citadel was the right decision; she feared putting Jade in unnecessary danger. The One knew she'd done a horrible job so far of keeping her safe. The shock of suddenly finding oneself thrown into Astura had to be affecting Jade hard, which was why she'd left Atoi and Broth behind. There would be time for introductions after Jade had adjusted to the citadel's martial atmosphere.

Lord Charn appeared to loom next to her, his normal somber self—as much as she could tell with his ever-present helm—yet, she thought she could sense a kind of…eagerness about him. Most likely, she was picking up her own innate signals. Darwin dropped his arm and stepped back. Crystalyn let him. She wanted to see her little sister so much her chest ached, and she owed Lord Charn a large debt of gratitude for clearing the area around the gate for a mostly private reunion.

"Behold! The topaz gate activates!" Lord Charn said, boyish excitement leaking into his voice. "I shall leave you to your reunion for a time." He strode inside the gate's southern guard quarters.

Near the top of the gate, two dark horizontal lines shot forth to meet in the center, twisting into a swirl. As wide and deep as a many-storied river, the now-familiar dark swirling curtain dropped to the floor. Crystalyn held onto a breath. A blindfolded, brown-robed figure appeared at the curtain's stormy base, leading a second brown robe by the hand. Crystalyn looked beyond them to the dark gate, her anxiety rising. Where was she?

The figure pulled the brown hood down and untied a dark cloth covering her eyes, revealing long, black hair and wide, emerald eyes. Grabbing the brown robe's hand again, the figure raced toward her.

Then everything was right for a few sweet moments as Jade gripped her in a tight hug. As Crystalyn stroked her sister's long hair, tears misted her vision. "Oh, Jade! I'm so sorry."

Jade hugged her with a fierce embrace, tears falling onto her shoulder. "I'm here, I'm here!"

Crystalyn bawled with joy. For many moments, she let her emotions roll out of her. Cries of relief mixed with soft, joy-filled laughter. They held each other until the tears subsided on both sides. Finally, Crystalyn stepped away, holding Jade at arm's length, looking into her striking emerald eyes. "Oh, Jade, I'm so sorry I lost you. It won't happen again, I'm not letting you leave my side!"

"It wasn't your fault! I didn't listen. I should've stayed away from the Sapphire Gate," Jade said in a rush, smiling through her tears.

"I have so much to tell you," Crystalyn said, her excitement mounting. Now she finally had someone she could share *anything* with; Jade would never judge her. She couldn't wait to introduce her to Darwin. She turned toward him, but he was gone.

Lord Charn walked around the four guards stationed outside the guardroom, striding toward them. "I am quite certain you both have much to discuss for your reunion, but I would ask you return to your room so the gate's function can return to normal. Do you wish your sibling in the same room?"

"Oh yes," Crystalyn said immediately.

Jade's smile vanished as Lord Charn spoke. She gazed up at the dark-armored man with frightened eyes.

Crystalyn smiled up at the big man. "Oh, Jade! This is our host, Lord Charn. Without his help, you wouldn't be here."

Lord Charn looked beyond Jade, toward the hooded figure standing by the topaz obelisk. "I was not aware there would be two of you," he said, his voice frosty. The second person who'd arrived with her sister stood motionless, the brown hood pulled far forward.

Jade started. "Oh, right! He's my servant. He doesn't speak," Jade said too quickly.

Crystalyn took Jade by the hand, pulling her gently along the hall. "Come, Lord Charn has a point; we should be going to our chambers. You must be tired and hungry. We can talk while you eat."

"Yes, yes, I am," Jade agreed.

As they strode past Lord Charn, Jade's eyes followed him. Crystalyn would have to assure Jade when they were alone the imposing man meant them no harm. Yet she did wonder why he hadn't pressed her to join with him again since the night at the Oracle, but she was glad he hadn't. So far, she hadn't dwelled on it too much.

"Would you mind if we returned to our rooms alone? We have a lot to catch up on," Crystalyn asked. "I know the way."

Lord Charn's reply was immediate. "The evening is your own. I have duties to attend to at present, but we shall meet again in the midmorning. My personal guards shall escort you. Please ask them for directions should you get turned around." He nodded toward the group of guards who had trailed them since he'd collected her from her room.

Crystalyn found it odd. For all Lord Charn's supposed prowess in battle, he never went anywhere without several guards with him. Did they follow him into the toilet? How did he go with all that armor on? She almost laughed, but she recognized her thoughts for the nervous relief they were for finally getting Jade back. "Thank you, My Lord. We will look forward to it."

Glancing now and then over her shoulder as they left the cavernous hall, Crystalyn looked back at Lord Charn. He watched until they drew out of sight.

Before they'd gone very far, Crystalyn realized Jade was pulling *her* by the hand, moving them ahead of the guards by several paces. She looked around and frowned as they moved toward her chambers. It was almost as if Jade knew where they were going.

FULL CIRCLE

Jade struggled to believe she was right back where her horrific ordeal had begun. Would the nightmare never end? Worse, Crystalyn had ended up here, too, but under better circumstances, it appeared. Appearances were deceiving more often than most realized. As glad as she was to walk next to her sister, no real happiness would come until they escaped.

They had a way out, providing they could get to the bathing ponds. Certainly, at some point, they'd have to bathe. Camoe had already provided her with a small light he called a glimmer shard, assuring her it would last a week or beyond once uncovered. With it tucked in her bag alongside the white candle, she felt better about the whole plan.

Worst-case scenario, Burl could lead them to where Camoe would be waiting at Fetid Fume Swamp's edge. She hated to think about making the journey, let alone crossing the swamplands again. But what choice did they have? Even with Caven's years of studying the Dark Citadel's fortifications, he couldn't foresee a way in or out without great loss.

After she'd convinced the druid she had to come back to rescue her sister, the three of them had sat up for most of a night and on through the next day discussing alternate escape routes to no avail. All others would have worse hazards than the one they'd thought of first, the same way they'd escaped last time. It wasn't going to be easy, for the citadel had to have stationed better-equipped guards at the waste tunnels by now. With Crystalyn's help, perhaps they would survive.

Jade tried not to think about it too much. It all seemed hopeless, especially now that she was here in the frightening place again. She lowered her voice to a whisper as soon as they were out of earshot of the guards that trailed them. "I'd hoped I wouldn't find you here, but it's not hopeless. I know a way to escape this awful place. With luck, we'll be gone by nightfall."

Crystalyn slowed, though her sister kept her grip on her hand. She too, kept her voice soft. "What do you mean? I found you with a contacting at the Dark Oracle. Remember? I wanted you here. We might be able to find our way home now. It's our best chance."

Jade frowned, though she never slowed, tugging Crystalyn along. "I don't understand. How can this horrible, evil place help us return home?"

"It may be scary at times, but I don't believe its evil," Crystalyn said, looking away. "Life here is just different than we're used to. We'll discuss it in our chambers. I can't wait to show them to you, they're grander than a room. Imagine! Our very own chambers and they come with servants." Crystalyn picked up the pace.

Jade clamped her mouth closed. The soft chink of metal-shod boots scraping against granite testified to the fact the two guards had drawn closer. Jade gave a silent *tsk*. Camoe would've given them a disapproving stare had he been here. Of course, if he had come with her, he might've attacked the guards on sight. Certainly, he would've sprung at Lord Charn after what happened to his daughter. The druid had a hatred for all Dark Users, but Lord Charn topped the list as the one who had given the order to fire the arrow that took his daughter's life.

Crystalyn took the lead, taking them toward the great golden doors Jade recognized from weeks ago. Those days had passed in a frightening blur. They strode past the iron door glaring ominously at her—the one leading to Lord Charn's armory she'd peered so fearfully out from weeks ago. She'd come full circle, back to the place of terror where the harrowing nightmare escape had begun. Her nearly healed lower lip she'd chewed ragged could attest to that. She was a fool for coming back, but her sister was here, in great danger.

Moving past the golden doors, Crystalyn selected a smaller passage veering off to the left. Stealing a quick glance over her shoulder at the one she led, Jade made sure Burl's disguise was intact. Hood draped partway to his drawn-on nose, her raggedy companion kept his face shadowed with his dangling arm in a sling under the robe as she'd shown him this morning. So far, the ruse had held. Having such dim light in the places they'd passed through helped; she couldn't chance his being recognized and reclaimed by his creator.

A short hike later, Crystalyn pulled her through an ornate door opened by one of the two guards standing watch outside of it. Jade got a glimpse of their escorts returning the way they'd come as the door closed.

"Well? Isn't it lovely?" Crystalyn asked, her smile beautiful. Jade hated to destroy her mood, but they needed to talk. She got the feeling Crystalyn was trying to distract her.

Jade tackled one of the most critical issues first. "How are you doing with your meds?"

Getting comfortable on a benched alcove overlooking a sunken dining area, Crystalyn replied, "I haven't been taking as many as I should, so there's a half month's supply." Her big sister didn't seem to be too concerned with not taking them, which surprised Jade. Crystalyn had always stuck to her schedule when it came to controlling her anger.

Jade sprawled gratefully opposite her sister on the bench. It'd been a long, frightening day. "Why haven't you?"

Crystalyn sighed, long and deep. "I've been too busy doing things…like nearly dying. Stabbed with a poison dagger, impaled twice, attacked by brigands, and sauntering into the middle of a battle has caused some hardship, but I muddled through. Honestly, I don't know why they seem to like me here; I've killed enough of them that I wouldn't like me."

Jade gasped. Not her big sister too, how could Crystalyn already speak so casually of killing like nearly everyone else she'd met here? Something dark flickered within Crystalyn's blue eyes when she'd spoken about the violence. Or had it? Whatever Jade thought she'd seen was gone. "That's my point; this is a violent, deadly place. I've been in the Dark Citadel before—the Sapphire Gate brought me *here*—and I don't like it at all. We are in grave danger and need to leave," Jade said in a rush, afraid Crystalyn would interrupt.

Crystalyn looked at her with wide eyes, her mouth open, as if she'd suddenly shed her skin and become something alien.

Jade sighed, as long and deep as Crystalyn had. "Perhaps I should start from the beginning. I have a lot to tell you, and it sounds like you should apprise me of some things. I'll go first," Jade said, feeling immensely tired. Already it was shaping up to be a short night.

*****

Crystalyn gaped at Jade. Her sister had been through more than she realized. Though Jade hadn't been hurt too bad physically, in many aspects her journey had been as grueling as hers had, perhaps worse.

The fault lay with Crystalyn; had she not opened the *Tiered Tome of Symbols,* none of it would've happened. Now, she'd have to tell Jade her plan to open the book. Well, both tier one and tier three books of symbols actually, on a regular basis. Darwin was supporting her practicing of some of the cryptic symbols in the two books, even suggesting it. One of the symbols catalogued under travel might get them home with the right obelisks.

Jade's journey had been frightening, but it left a question careening around inside her head. "This Camoe you spoke of and his companion, did he ever say why he and his daughter were running in the first place? What did they do to merit being attacked?"

Jade looked troubled. "I don't think he mentioned why, only that they were both druids. I gathered they were on some sort of infiltration mission, which I assumed meant this place."

"But you don't know for certain. Even if it was this place, perhaps they shouldn't have been here. Espionage always comes with a high amount of danger. I'd venture a guess the White Lands, assuredly the Circle of Light, would take similar measures with an enemy agent.”

“When did you get to be so cold, so…clinical about life and death? She was his *daughter!*”

“I know, and I’m truly sorry. There had to be a reason they were running. We just don’t know the whole story—” Crystalyn felt badly. Jade was right, the young woman was the man’s daughter. It would make anyone bitter. Yet Crystalyn wasn’t certain how far this druid could be trusted. She’d never met him. If he was anything like those on the Circle, she didn’t care to. A large part was due to the Circle not helping with a contacting and Khiminay’s dubious help, they’d all ended up here. Perhaps it was for the best. They might discover a way home.

“I’m not one to care if I don’t know it all. I trust him. If not for him and Burl, I wouldn’t be alive right now.”

“Okay. If you trust him, then I will too. By keeping you safe, he’s put me in his debt. And I promise to be suspicious of the things happening here,” Crystalyn said. She glanced at the immobile form by the door, suppressing a shudder. No breath rose and fell under the robe. She gathered her resolve. “Let’s have a look at Burl.”

A look of relief shone in Jade’s green eyes. She smiled. “Burl, come over here.” Obediently, the brown robe crossed the room to stand by Jade.

“This is my sister, Crystalyn. You may pull your hood down when she’s the only one in the room with me,” Jade said with a commanding voice. Crystalyn was surprised: she didn’t even know Jade had one. They *did* have some catching up to do.

Jade’s companion reached up with one hand, dropping the hood to the back of his neck, and then pulled a dark rag over his head and away from his eyes.

In all her time wandering through this world, Crystalyn had never seen anything like him, not even here at the citadel, where Jade said she’d discovered him, at least not alive. His skin resembled those odd-skinned ones lying about Carnage Field. Vibrant yellow-orange eyes gazed at her above a scrawled nose and mouth. Staring transfixed at those eyes and the intelligence lurking behind them, Crystalyn's worry of how Jade would react to Atoi, and especially Broth, lessened.

If Jade could befriend a…non-breathing creation, she shouldn't have any problem with her friends. Perhaps it was time for everyone to meet. Crystalyn sent a silent request to Broth to bring Atoi. Broth agreed to the request with enthusiasm mixed with trepidation. He was right to be worried. How would Jade react to the linking?

Crystalyn was about to find out.

SHADOWY PASSAGE

Something about the red robe moving across the hall drew Jade's eye. It wasn't that the wearer hobbled with such an obvious limp, though the gait had first caught her attention. No, it was something else, something about the person's...actions. Glancing both ways along the great hall, the red-robed figure shambled from one pillar to the next, poking the hooded head around each one before continuing on to the next. The furtive procedure repeated for several pillars, until the robe vanished behind the one across from her.

Jade glanced at Atoi, who sat next to her on a stone bench. The young girl seemed to have not noticed the robe's movements. Or, she had no particular interest in them, which was probably the case. Jade really had no idea what did interest the strange little girl, but she was an amicable companion, only speaking when Jade asked her something. Jade preferred it that way.

She waited, focusing beyond the pillar, expecting the strange behavior to continue down the great hall. Yet, only servants made use of the wide hallway, hurrying on their errands. Jade was disappointed. The weird mannerisms had provided a welcome distraction to her aching hamstrings.

The poor guards had followed her and Broth and Atoi for hours around the massive Dark Citadel while they wandered up and down stairwells, down into dank dungeons and dark side halls, performing another methodical but fruitless search.

They still hadn't found another way out after days of daily searches. Nor had they found any of Broth's clan anywhere, even though Crystalyn said he'd insisted they'd vanished somewhere inside.

They had come across several more creations like Burl doing menial tasks. None would acknowledge her presence in the slightest. She hadn't pressed them much for fear of alerting their creator.

Today had been especially grueling, for they had climbed to the top of a dark tower. From there, she'd seen the citadel from a different perspective. The curvature of the gate was quite pronounced and the canyon a bit steeper and narrower than she'd first seen with Camoe. A cave halfway up the right side captured her interest for some time, but she couldn't see a way up or down to it. At the road below the last curve, the cave wouldn't be visible from the bottom; a landing-like ledge had sealed that. While the view from the tower had been breathtaking, no exit presented itself, though she left wondering about the cave. It still nagged. If it led to the citadel, they'd not yet found the entrance.

The red robe hadn't exited from behind the pillar. Jade stood. "Come on, you two. There's something I want to check before heading back to my sister's chambers."

As he raised his sleek body to all four powerful legs, Broth's haunches glistened from the small stream of ground water next to the bench he'd lain in to cool off. Though he couldn't speak to her as he did to Crystalyn, the big canine-like creature with his beautiful, hourglass eyes seemed to understand her well enough.

Having Broth's presence near her had made the days here bearable, as Atoi had, unlike her sister. Crystalyn had been no help plotting their escape. Her time spent with the young general, Darwin Darkwind, was all she talked about, and Jade had begun to wonder if the handsome Dark User had cast a spell on her.

Crossing the width of the great hall didn't hurt as badly as she'd expected. Her overtaxed leg muscles loosened after the first hundred paces or so, and the burning faded to a dull ache. Prepared to stride on by when she got close to the furtive red robe, she rounded the pillar at a fair pace and then slowed. No one was in sight. How strange. She wouldn't have missed the robe's departure, not with such a noticeable limp. "Atoi, will you and Broth loiter around the backside of the next pillar down?" Jade asked. "Pretend you're gazing at something near the ceiling, and make sure the guards see you doing it."

Atoi complied without comment, and Broth followed without hesitation. Once they were in place, Jade moved on to the cavern wall where a half-dozen woven tapestries hung on the rough-cut stone, which she found odd. Why hang them in a dark section of the great hall? Wall hangings as intricate as these deserved the appreciation of people seeing them.

Another oddity caught her eye. A beautiful tapestry depicting a rich banquet hall filled with carousers draped closer to the floor than the others did. It rustled softly, but she couldn't feel any wind. She pulled the tapestry aside. A shadowy passage, as tall and as wide as a door, ran deep into the wall. Did she dare follow it? It was now or never: her companions wouldn't fool the two guards who'd drawn the duty long. They'd been diligent, though they had to be tired from packing around all that armor.

Jade climbed into the tunnel, letting the tapestry fall in place behind her. It was darker than the hall, but a dim light ahead indicated the passage wasn't long. A few quick strides brought her to a slit of brightness slicing through the darkness from ceiling to floor. She crept close, peeking through a crack in the wooden wall. Storage shelves filled with mugs and pitchers lined a small room.

A set of open double doors opposite her allowed a peek into a larger room beyond where a black table strewn with maps and miniature figurines stood. The red robe's back was toward her, presumably, speaking to someone unseen at the table. Inching away from the light, Jade crept the way she'd come.

Slipping past the tapestry, she rejoined her companions, motioning for them to follow. The guards fell in behind when they strode past. As she made her way back to their chambers, Jade mulled over what she'd seen. The passage could be a way out, or—if nothing else—a way to shake the guards when the escape route was found, though she'd have to convince Crystalyn it was time to go. It wasn't going to be easy.

EVERYDAY OCCURRENCE

Crystalyn let Darwin drone on with his in-depth theories on how Users, Dark and Light alike, manipulated the Flow. She'd heard his ideas a few times in the past few days. He'd outlined a theory he'd nurtured, he claimed, where she could tap into the Flow using one of her symbols as the recipient. The symbol he'd grown excited about when he pointed it out in her second book of symbols was under the heading absorptions.

From there, it had been a tricky matter of combining it with an aggression symbol, but they'd managed after a few volatile results where she'd had to heal them both, more than once. Darwin's excitement was contagious every time she'd made a breakthrough. Most notably, when she'd combined her absorption symbol with multiple aggressions and manufactured a larger black-and-white one. They'd been working on that one alone for the better part of a week.

He was quite knowledgeable in most aspects of the Flow, but as far as they'd been able to discover, her symbols used something besides the Flow. What that something was, they'd not been able to determine. Crystalyn didn't mind too much, as long as they spent time together, and she was getting better.

In theory, he was studying her symbol magic and training her in using them safely. But they hadn't been able to substantiate if she interrupted the Flow to create her symbols. Darwin had insisted that must be the case. Though she'd demonstrated in front of many Dark lords and Users alike—whomever Darwin wanted—no one in the Dark Citadel had proven it so. Everyone simply assumed the Flow was integral to her magic.

Crystalyn wasn't so certain. She had tried to access the Flow on Glacier Mountain against the Lore Mother's instructions, and it hadn't gone well. Yet they found she had the same limitation as Users when it came to barriers. She could only install a physical *or* magical barrier; her symbols dissolved every time she had tried to combine the two.

Thankfully, Darwin had moved on to assisting her with deciphering the meanings of most of the symbols in her two books. He even brought it to her attention that at least one other volume must exist, since tier two was missing. Something she hadn't thought about for any length of time.

Crystalyn sighed with wistfulness. She'd love to get her greedy hands on one or two added volumes for her collection, but most likely they were on another world. Ruena probably had them stashed away somewhere.

Most days she spent accompanying Darwin as he handled the routine military tasks involved in the upkeep of a large and militarized dwelling. For a while, Atoi or Broth, or even Jade, had insisted on coming along, but they'd quickly become bored, preferring to roam on their own.

Jade seemed to have given up asking her to leave, which was a relief; she was learning so much that leaving now would be foolish. Jade's motive for exploring the citadel was clear: she looked for an obscure way out, which was fine with Crystalyn. It gave them all something to do. The three of them got along well with Jade becoming the group's unspoken leader from the outset. Even Atoi stayed close by her, though she spoke as little as usual.

Crystalyn felt twinges of something missing now that Atoi didn't tag along after her, though her constant link with Broth filled some of the void. They had found limitations with it. There were dark places in some dark corners of the citadel, and the link severed with no warning at all. Most times Jade's little group went around such places—Broth refused to go through those areas—but it still sent a shock through them both whenever it happened.

In a way, Crystalyn envied them their freedom to roam around the citadel at will. Well, nearly at will. Some places the little group found guarded and barred to them. Lord Charn's ever-present guards had claimed it unsafe to venture there. The day Jade had complained about the off-limit areas, Crystalyn made her promise to adhere to the decrees without question. Jade agreed, though reluctantly. One of the places cordoned was the route she'd left from the first time, the gated waste tunnels.

There was little point trying to leave, and Jade must know that. Though they had the run of the place, it was never without an escort, even when they bathed. Her face still heated when she thought of the first time. The male guards had laughed when she and Jade had refused to remove all their clothes at the nobles' bathing pool. They'd found it hysterical that two women quick-scrubbed in their undergarments. Now, after Darwin had spoken with Lord Charn about it, female guards handled the duty whenever they bathed. They had even gotten into the helpful habit of using their bodies to shield them from the bulk of lordly male eyes lounging at the opposite side.

"Am I rambling again, dear one?" Darwin asked.

Crystalyn started and then smiled sheepishly. "I suppose you are, but it's one of the things I like about you." She shivered a little. The breeze blowing up from the bottom of the monstrous wall still carried the slight nip of winter. The golden sunrays piercing the barren land beyond the wall throughout their inspection made up for the wind, a bit.

The bright sunlight brought the promise of midday warmth, though she doubted they'd be outdoors much longer, which was unfortunate. She wanted to soak up enough warmth to last through the night, for the citadel always seemed to have a chill about it. But Darkwind had delayed longer than his normal allotted time for inspecting the ramparts and the soldiers garrisoned along the wall's great expanse. Perhaps he enjoyed the time outdoors as much as she did.

"It's the *only* thing you like about me, you mean," Darwin said, a smile tugging at his lips. "I am so crushed. And here, I thought I had many other qualities besides my supreme expertise in all things known and unknown, all that is, all that was, and all that shall ever be, forever."

Crystalyn laughed. Echoing loud across the battlements, it sounded strange to her ears when it returned. With difficulty, she clamped her mouth closed, but her smile remained. Darwin had a way of wrenching laughter from the depths inside her where she'd kept it safely locked away. If he kept at it, she'd develop horrid lines around her eyes at an early age.

Darwin's smile faded, his features growing earnest. "It's all right, you know. You can be happy. All that's required is that you trust me. Together we can accomplish anything, for there is little that can block our desires. You know this, don't you?"

"I'm…beginning to," Crystalyn said, hesitant. She wasn't sure why she all of a sudden felt such reluctance. Was he offering her something?

"Not the reply I was hoping for, but I will accept it as an assurance you will want to speak again on the subject soon."

"Broach the subject whenever you wish," Crystalyn said, relieved.

"Do you promise?"

Crystalyn smiled. "You have my word."

"Then seal it with a kiss," he said, his brown eyes shiny, a sheepish smile tugging at his lips.

Glancing around, Crystalyn pulled him behind the gatehouse and stepped into his arms. Long and lingering, the kiss stirred something deep inside, awakening her to every nuance of her body and stealing her breath. Finally, she stepped back, feeling heady. She could go on for hours locked in his strong, firm arms. If only they could. She leaned toward him, and he leaned toward her. The second kiss held passion, more urgent than the first, and Crystalyn's blood heated, coaxed alive by his fervent lips, her body responding to the firm caresses. As his loving hands moved closer to her sensitive places, she found she wanted him there and…she pulled away. Someone might come upon them. It wouldn't do for the general's men to see them as love-struck adolescents, though her breath came in gasps and her body still tingled from his touch.

Darwin sighed deeply. "Before I give you back to your sibling and companions, I think we should get a final practice session completed for this day."

"Okay, my magic absorb again?"

"Precisely, I feel like we are close to a breakthrough."

Crystalyn agreed, though it did seem to work well as protection against magic attacks. It wouldn't work for anything physical. Providing he was right, tying his magic or someone accessing the Flow to hers would provide both barriers at the same time. "Well, here goes," she said. Bringing out her cross-patterned absorption symbol, she combined it with the airy one under the heading multi-aggression in the black-lettered book. The same one she'd almost used on Lore Rayna when she'd drawn her bow in the meadow.

"Good, now mold it over and around you like a dome," Darwin said.

Crystalyn did so, marveling how easy she accomplished it now.

"Mind you, keep it away from the ground, as I've mentioned."

Crystalyn lifted the beautiful, smoky symbol with its intricate white crosses several inches above the stone of the wall. Darwin had to remind her nearly every time. It was an opposite method from *grounding* herself as Kara Laurel taught. She found it hard to shed the habit.

"This time I shall throw a tiny burst of dark flame at you. Are you ready?"

"Yes."

Darwin's right hand vanished behind a glow of black. As before, whenever someone accessed the Flow, the stone below bled clear, the captivating river of white frothing below. At least for her it was white; Darwin had described it as black when she'd asked. A black fire shot from his hand and struck her shield. This time, not only did the crosses on the symbol—a radiant white resembling the river at her feet—pool at the top center, the intricate pattern along its full length glowed and then faded. "Did you see that?"

Darwin smiled. "Yes. We *are* getting close. I think soon, you will be able to use the excess Flow in your barrier to your advantage. That is enough for now. I have an unpleasant duty ahead of me and must attend to it. I would like you to go with me, but I have kept you from your family and companions long enough."

Crystalyn was intrigued. "They will wait."

"I suppose so. They appear to be content, even the Dark Child," Darwin said softly, taking her arm. "Except for the quiet, brown-hooded one, I cannot ascertain his demeanor. Or is *he* a *she?*"

"I imagine *he* would be correct. I've never actually spoken to him, since he's mute." They began the long climb down the wide stairway leading to the courtyard behind the wall, the same set that seemed never-ending just days ago. Now she barely noticed them. How long could Jade keep Burl's identity undisclosed? Was it even a secret? Crystalyn had a nagging feeling that Lord Charn knew. After Jade's first day at the citadel, Lord Charn hadn't mentioned her sister's companion, not once.

Nor did he ever mention Atoi; no one but Darwin had. They all ignored her as if she weren't there. Crystalyn found the whole thing odd. If it were the other way around, she'd be trying to coax information from them. "What is it you have to do? Is it something I can help you with?"

Darwin's countenance darkened. "If only you could, but alas, it will not be permitted."

They descended the stairs in silence. Crystalyn felt his tension through the solid set of his arm and the rigid way he moved. She preferred the relaxed, easygoing Darwin, but she couldn't think of a single thing to say.

Striding under a stone arch, they passed into the courtyard. Armored soldiers and black-robed and red-robed—even some brown-robed—Users lined the perimeter. The milling crowd parted for them, opening a path to a small, raised area cut from black marble flecked with gray.

Darwin strode straight to it, not once halting to chat with a known soldier or a familiar robed User, as was his usual behavior. Crystalyn wondered at the solemnity of the occasion. Halted at the platform's edge by a gentle pressure on her elbow, she glanced at him. He watched her expectantly. "What do you have to do here?" she asked.

"A challenger for my position has come forward," Darwin said, his dark eyes unreadable.

Crystalyn frowned. "How often does this go on? Are you going to be all right?"

Darwin's smile was roguish. "It does not happen often; I've retained this position for some years now. We shall soon see how I fare." His smile faded as he glanced at the dais.

Crystalyn followed his gaze. A heavily armored man—nearly as big as Lord Charn, though smaller than Cudgel—strode the perimeter. Slung over one shoulder, a long-hafted, double-headed axe gleamed with the dark onyx brilliance she'd come to expect from the citadel. The man rested a large hand on the handle as if the axe's sole purpose was a resting place for it. She disliked it immediately. The long haft bespoke a design to incapacitate from a distance, possibly from horseback. Yet the brute packed it around like a favorite sword. Surely, such a weapon would render a disqualification in a challenge.

The bulky man climbed on the black stone, two of his cronies supporting him from falling backward, from the weight of his armor, with a rough push forward.

His chain mail armor no hindrance, Darwin vaulted onto the dais, his sword still sheathed at his side. "Are you quite certain this is what you want, Gard?" he asked, coaxing a tight-fitting gauntlet over his right hand.

Gard's lip curled. "Your reign is about to come to an abrupt end. You're too young for it, anyway. It's time to let those older and wiser run the kingdom." Perfectly balanced, the axe stayed horizontal as the man let go to adjust his armor around his large waist.

"I have no reign, only duties," Darwin said softly, yet his voice carried. Several voices from the ring of men surrounding the dais murmured appreciation at his declaration.

Gard scowled. "Bah! Enough talk! Let's get to it." Gripping the axe, he set it gently down on the dark stone, leaning on the haft with both hands. He nodded toward Crystalyn. "I shall have my evening wine and meal waiting for me in your chambers, with your lady friend there."

Several raucous voices laughed at the comment.

Crystalyn's face heated.

Darwin stiffened slightly but otherwise showed no reaction to the taunt. "Raise the barrier," he commanded, glancing to the sides and ends of the dark stone dais. For the first time, Crystalyn noticed four black robes stood by themselves on four sides of the circle, forming a square around it. One palm downward, the other gesturing upward slowly, the Dark Users began lifting a clear, smoky box upward around the circular stone as if they were pulling it from the ground. Perhaps they were, and the barrier roiled with the frothy turbulence of the Flow.

Before the black robes had raised it higher than a sword's length, Gard charged.

Glancing over his shoulder at the barrier's progress, Darwin appeared to not notice.

"Darwin!" Crystalyn screamed.

Darwin spun toward her, his back now facing his opponent. Another scream welled in her throat but died there. Darwin's eyes smoldered with excitement and something else…something dark.

Axe blurring, Gard swung for Darwin's unprotected head.

Crystalyn blinked. A barely perceptible transparency outlined Darwin. He'd installed a personal barrier, but she couldn't tell if he had used the one to protect against Flow-enhanced attacks or a physical repel shield.

Brilliant sparks exploded beneath the half-moon axe blade, leaving behind a trail of molten white sparks as Gard's favored weapon bounced harmlessly to the side of Darwin's head, answering her unspoken question. Gard cursed, launching a series of ineffectual two-handed blows.

Forced into the rising box barrier, Darwin pushed away from it, turning to face his attacker. The weapon barrier he'd been teaching Crystalyn how to use reflected the morning sun at odd angles. The personal shield absorbed the brunt of the two-handed blows, though she recalled enough well-aimed blows to the same spot could compromise it.

As she feared, jagged cracks soon spider-webbed in two spots on Darwin's head and back, though they didn't seem to hinder his movements. Darwin's long sword appeared in his hand in time to parry a succession of blows. *It's horrible how the barrier leaves the weapon hand unprotected,* Crystalyn thought, though she knew the reason why. The weapon had to be beyond the barrier in order to use it. Even a glancing blow from the brutal axe would maim for life. She couldn't watch, yet it was impossible to look away.

Beginning as an overhead chop, Gard's axe swept into a side cut, and then reversed midway to hack at Darwin's sword-bearing arm. Twisting his wrist, Darwin tilted his sword tip downward slightly. The long sword took the brunt of the blow with a loud clang, forcing the axe to slide to the tip.

Gard danced away to avoid Darwin's counter stab, his breath coming in gasps. Oddly, the big man removed his left hand from the axe, putting his arm behind his back. Even with one hand, the axe blurred as he parried with surprising speed.

Darwin advanced, jabbing his sword tip at Gard's armored throat. His sword, too, met resistance inches from the weakest point of the plate armor at the big man's neck. Fine sparks of molten white bloomed with every blow landed. Darwin was landing blow after blow, snaking through Gard's slower parries; if not for the bigger man's barrier, he would have sustained heavy damage. Jagged cracks branched out from Gard's neck, racing upward along an unseen sphere to vanish behind the top of his head. Vision impaired, Gard panicked, swinging his brutal axe back and forth with all his considerable might, forcing Darwin back a step and then two. Darwin's shield faded and then brightened as his connection to the Flow lapsed. Grinning maliciously, Gard batted Darwin's sword to the side and then lunged, throwing his bulk at the smaller man.

No! Crystalyn screamed into the recesses of her mind.

"Do'brieni?" Broth's anguished query joined with her scream.

His movements quick and fluid, Darwin shifted to the side, chopping at the wrist that gripped the onyx axe.

The axe clanged against the cobblestone, loud and surreal in the sudden silence. Gard's right wrist hung limp at a weird angle under his gauntlet. He left his useless palm pointing to the ground, bringing his other arm from behind his back. "You'll not win this easily!" Gard bellowed. Dark flames shot forth, enveloping Darwin in a black inferno at close range.

Nooooo!

"I am coming, Do'brieni!"

Darwin stepped out of the debris of the onslaught, his left arm raised. A ball of black flame rocketed from Darwin's hand, burning through Gard's barrier and exploding inside, turning the inside of the barrier an oily black. The blackened barrier toppled to the ground. The only part recognizable—Gard's free hand—convulsed once and went still.

Crystalyn was stunned. Just like that, it was over. The challenge met. Darwin was alive. *"It's okay now, Broth. I am well."*

Relief flowed through the link in waves. *"I still have some distance yet to reach you."*

"No, please return to Jade. She needs watching over."

"Provided you are certain of your own safety, I will do as you wish."

"I'm certain. Take care of her for me, please!"

"I will, my Do'brieni."

Irrationally, Crystalyn felt anger toward the corpse for putting Darwin in harm's way, for attempting to kill him. But a closer look at the pile revealed Gard's personal barrier had dissipated after the ball of black flame struck—as it should have since Gard still had his weapon shield installed. Darwin must have switched his when his barrier dimmed. Interesting to her, it hadn't been instantaneous; the switch was noticeable to someone keeping a close watch. Grotesquely, Gard had burst inside the unnatural container. Nauseated, Crystalyn turned away from the steaming lump to find Lord Charn beside her, his horned helm tilted in her direction. She was surprised. He'd maintained his distance after her reunion with Jade.

"Your Darwin is a true champion of the Dark Dais, but you know this now. To lose is to die. Can you still hold him in high regard knowing he is subject to any who wish to challenge? Have you prepared for the eventuality that even the mighty Darkwind will fall?" he asked, his pleasant voice soft.

"I am not certain I know what you are referring to when you say 'my Darwin,' My Lord," Crystalyn said. "I can assure you no mention of future plans has been the topic of our discussions."

Lord Charn laughed with some mirth. "Well answered, Crystalyn. Tell me, what do you think of our little succession custom here?"

"I'll have to go with the obvious: It's barbaric."

Lord Charn chuckled, but then his voice took on a serious tone. "Indeed it is. I am not surprised you view it as such. Come, walk with me, Darwin has monopolized your company from the start."

Crystalyn matched the Dark lord's pace as he made his way around the milling crowd, most attempting to get out of the way when they noticed him. Lord Charn strode as if he cared nothing for what happened around him. The box barrier was gone and the four black robes already dispersed. Raised to protect bystanders from errant energy flung from either party, the box raising had ended before full installation from the corpse's premature attack, which likely made it easier to take down.

Darwin smiled as they strolled past him, but he continued speaking with a group of armored men she'd never met. Crystalyn smiled back hesitantly, avoiding looking overly long at the lump dragged away behind him. This citadel, *this world,* was proving to be violent. With a casualness she found disconcerting, a man's life ended. It shouldn't have bothered her, the man had attempted to slay someone she cared about, but it did. Perhaps it was time to seek a way home. Now, if she could just get her Darwin to go with her.

ANOMALY

Where Lord Charn had led them, Crystalyn thought of as the citadel's left wing. It was one of those off-limit places to them, so she was surprised for a fourth time today. The first had been the challenge Darwin had her attend, with the second immediately after when Lord Charn had taken her away. The third and most puzzling was when he stopped by their chambers and collected Jade. He'd kept his silence afterward, saying only he had something he wanted them to see.

Crystalyn looked at Jade. Her younger sister's green eyes were round with wonder, looking much like her own, she suspected. Was he going to ask her to make a choice about living here at the citadel with him?

Crystalyn had considered it. She'd been leaning toward staying until witnessing the challenge today. Did she really want to subject Jade to this bloody environment? How could she leave Darwin now that it was going so well? How could she leave Dad with his weak heart and stay here?

Yet she and Jade would want for little here. If she were to marry someone like Darwin, for instance, she'd acquire duties running a noble house while he oversaw a garrison. Would it really be so bad?

She'd mulled over the same set of questions for so many days, but she was no closer to resolving them than she had been at the start. Now would be a good time for her meds, but she hadn't thought to grab them when they'd collected Jade.

Rounding a corner of the east wing hall, Lord Charn halted at a stone railing installed between the great black pillars, chest high. Leaning on the rail, Crystalyn gaped at different levels of the citadel carved from the mountain and open on one side to a great chasm dropping away into darkness.

Each level had thin but sturdy iron railing pinned to the stone like the one on their side of the chasm, the one she leaned upon now. The iron rails kept the rows of iron beds from slipping off the edge of each level as red and brown robes moved busily throughout the rooms. The smell of blood drifted heavy in the air.

Crystalyn glanced at their host, raising an eyebrow.

"I did not think to trouble you with our trials, but you should be aware of the ugliness war brings. Those of us left here in the Dark Citadel—those that think as I do—wish for this to end. I have desired this one thing for hundreds of years. What you see there, across the Gap of Thundering Darkness is the infirmary. Sadly, over the past one hundred years, it has expanded to consume an entire wing, where one or two floors sufficed in the past. I cannot stomach such suffering and wish it finished. I am but a gust of breath away from convincing some of those that lead in the White Lands into treaty negotiations bound with the Flow. At the very least, scaling the battles' frequency back—I have considered proposing one season of war, two without. Yet I no longer believe I can, or should, accomplish this alone..." he said, trailing off as if speaking to himself.

Crystalyn shot a glance at Jade. Jade spread her hands wide. Her sister had no idea what he wanted either. Crystalyn thought about asking him, but opted to be patient instead. After all, they were here by his choosing.

After a while, Lord Charn stirred. "Indulge me for a tiny bit of history. Do either of you know anything regarding the codices?"

Jade spoke first. "I have read a limited amount of the Surbon Codex and perused a paragraph or two of the Virun Codex. It is the same case with the AM Edicts."

Lord Charn's helm swung toward her. "You surprise me. Your knowledge is advanced for one not long on this world."

"I've heard mention of the Surbon Codex with a passing mention of the Virun Codex, but nothing about the AM Edicts," Crystalyn said, recalling the strange appearance of the tapestry in Durandas' quarters.

Lord Charn's helm shifted to include Crystalyn in his field of vision. The dark-armored man's attention was always intimidating. Crystalyn felt Jade's hand in her own and gave it a gentle squeeze. The immediate answering squeeze made her feel bolder. Dad always said together they were stronger; together they would prevail. Now she had an inkling of what he meant, and she missed him. "As I should've mentioned, you *both* continue to surprise me with your knowledge. I am uncertain how much you've gleaned, so I will ask for indulgence should I touch on subjects already familiar to you. The AM Edicts— the Aftermath Edicts, as they are known to the scholarly—were written after a great war, when this planet was younger, back when it was known as planet Earth—"

"Wait! Astura went by a different name?" Crystalyn asked. "Why would you change an entire planet's name?"

Lord Charn hesitated for a long moment. A deep sigh vented from his helm. He continued. "Our planet was made nearly uninhabitable after the war. Only a single island named Astura in ancient times remained with a river flowing through it. Even the island and the river were not wholly unaffected by the war, but they provided habitation. Humans discovered the Flow there then, or it was always there and the knowledge required to access it only occurred with humanities last hope for survival. No one can say. After the Flow enabled the fledgling Users to clean the air we now breathe, most left the island. Separating into two factions based on their affinity with the Flow, either dark or light, they worked to make the planet habitable. Each side believed they had the better vision to accomplish it. War broke out again. Seeing their work destroyed, they penned the Aftermath Edicts. The edicts permit warfare without destroying our habitation beyond irreparable harm. They have held for the most part throughout our long history. Any ruler not abiding by it faces annihilation by the rest."

Lord Charn paused, letting his words penetrate. Crystalyn appreciated the respite as she grappled with the enormity of it all.

"The Surbon and the Virun Codices appeared in written form much later. Each is infuriatingly vague. No one I am aware of knows for certain when, or even where, they originated from," Lord Charn continued. "Legend has it that scholars woke up one morning to discover the codices added to every major archive overnight."

Lord Charn spoke softly, his pleasant baritone accentuating the eeriness of his story. He spoke with a distinction any king's administration professor would kill to mimic, drawing her into the narrative and carrying her along with his tonal inflections. The history of his words made her thirst for knowledge, as it always had. How old was Astura? How long had the two sides been at war? What could possibly be worth warring over?

"The two codices are vastly different from each other from many aspects, but there are some points they both agree upon without deviation. Each corroborates that a single symbolic User will decide the fate upon which this world hinges and that the outcome *may* have influence from an anomaly. Until you arrived, Crystalyn, no one knew precisely what a symbolic User was, though there were many hypotheses. Knowing this makes it easier to ask what I must of you, but even so, I am reluctant."

Well, here it comes, Crystalyn thought.

"As I mentioned when convincing you to come with me, I wish for you to join me, both of you. Help me put an end to this ugly war, to stop the persecution instigated by the White Lands. You must know by now that we are not the monsters they claim we are," Lord Charn said, his words made all the stronger by the moans and uncontrolled weeping echoing from above and below. Crystalyn's heart wrenched. She wanted to go to them. Her healing would be of great use.

"What about flickers? How can you deny those...*things* are not monstrous?" Jade asked, her voice cracking at the end. Jade's description of the creatures was still muddled in Crystalyn's mind. She had trouble picturing them, though they sounded horrible.

Lord Charn waited a beat to answer. "I will admit there are some...*beings* born in the darkness of this place. Most have succumbed to the control of man. Some we have learned to coexist with, some of the powerful darker ones we have learned to avoid altogether."

Jade tensed. "But, don't you people turn the flickers loose at night to consume the souls of prisoners captured in this war, to swell their ranks, to…to…*feed* them?" The horror of her words made her voice soft. Crystalyn gave her hand another squeeze.

"How would you know of these things?" Lord Charn asked, his voice much louder than before. Taking a deep breath, he went on. "It does not matter. What you speak of is true, or at least it used to be. Recently, I've convinced the Obsidian Table to forego this practice. The flickers have been contained elsewhere for a time."

Crystalyn wasn't sure she liked the sound of that. "What does that mean?"

"They shall not be used unless the war slips too far from our favor. I must apologize. It was the best concession I could get from the Obsidian Table."

"What is the Obsidian Table? I thought you ruled supreme here," Crystalyn asked. It was odd. Darwin had never mentioned it.

"It is a mix of our war generals and the most powerful Users who govern the citadel. Originally established to oversee the progress of the war, it has devolved into a deadly game of politics. Your Darwin sits high within it, providing me with information while working to keep the Table focused on what is truly important. Unfortunately, many on the Obsidian Table now control over half the regiments, which has given them the idea to become a ruling class of their own. I have not allowed it, though I cannot hold them at bay much longer. One of the first things the Reformed did, as they call themselves, was to install the flickers 'for protection.' It has taken me nearly two seasons to wrest the concession from them to contain them elsewhere. Yet I did not bring you here to talk about the trials of the past, or the politics within my citadel. I am here to ask for assistance from both of you, as you have likely conjectured."

Jade spoke. "There's something I don't understand. How could I help you? I can see you wanting Crystalyn, but I can't do anything. I don't even know how to use a sword, nor do I want to."

"It is not for what you can do, Jade," Lord Charn said, his deep voice soft. "It is for what you are, and for what you may yet be. I have studied the scrolls for many seasons—longer than you have lived—yet I only now have come to a stunning conclusion since the two of you arrived on Astura: I believe *you* are the anomaly mentioned in the cryptic codices."

Crystalyn exchanged a look with her sister, questions arising in her mind. How could Jade be an anomaly? What did that even *mean?* And, what did Lord Charn want with said anomaly? She was beginning to feel lightheaded, either from the smell of the infirmary or from the huge revelations Lord Charn had dropped on them. "Thank you, Lord Charn, for being so candid, though you've only added questions to those already clamoring in my mind," she said, gazing up at the one responsible for bringing her sister to her and wondering anew about his motives. What did the person under all that massive armor really look like? Could he be trusted? *Stop it!* Crystalyn admonished herself. After all the things Lord Charn had done for them, she should trust him.

But she didn't, not yet.

"I am aware my words have given you both a lot to think about," Lord Charn said. "Please give my offer careful consideration. There is no haste at this time; there are a few days still. The Dark Citadel and I can be of great use to you: your every want shall happen with alacrity, more so if we put an end to this ugly war. Together we can, I am certain. For now you two have much to discuss; can you find your way to your chambers unescorted?"

Crystalyn held back a frown. She still had a thousand questions. "Finding our chambers won't be a problem," she said, suddenly realizing what he had offered. No guards would be trailing behind.

"That is well. I have pressing matters to attend to now. I dismissed my own guards at the courtyard. You will have none on the way back, yet you should be safe enough. I know your power. Join me for dinner two days hence, both of you, when you have arrived at a decision. Good day to you both." Turning his back to them, he strode away.

"Good day to you, My Lord," they replied in unison. Whether he heard them or not, Crystalyn couldn't really say. "Come on, this place is giving me a nauseous headache. As he said, we have some things to discuss. There's greater security when we walk," Crystalyn said, though it sounded false in her ears. Who knew what kind of magical listening devices were active in a citadel of Dark Users?

*****

Putting the sounds of suffering and dying behind her, Crystalyn strode in the opposite direction Lord Charn had taken. They passed through two narrow hallways before Jade let go of her hand. Crystalyn was reluctant to disengage. The warmth of Jade's hand was a great comfort. Dad was right. They were stronger together.

Crystalyn had anxiety. Should they stay or should they continue with the search for a way home? She didn't have the faintest idea where to go next looking for a sapphire gateway similar to the one she'd unintentionally activated to bring them here. She wasn't even certain she could activate a set a second time. Lord Charn's offer was sound. Everything they could possibly want handed to them, *and* she'd get to see Darwin Darkwind on a regular basis.

The downside was that she'd have to assist with ending the war somehow. Of course, she wanted to see the war end, but how was she supposed to do that, exactly? Dark, enigmatic, Lord Charn had failed to mention how. Did he want her to kill for him? Could she bring herself to do it? She'd have to answer that provocative question before making any kind of decision.

There was danger here, some very strong danger, she believed Jade about that. Lord Charn hadn't wanted to admit it, though she found it hard to blame him. Obviously, he didn't want to frighten them off. His offer seemed heartfelt and his reasoning compelling. Who wouldn't want to end a hundred-season war?

She was homesick. Many days had passed. Dad had to be beside himself with worry, and the credit debts piling up there probably required a thrust cycle to reach the top by now. Perhaps they could go back and get him and plan for a return. They could carry a gate through with them if a second set was located. The debts wouldn't mean much if the three of them went to another world.

"I want to go home," Jade said, breaking the stillness abruptly.

Crystalyn hesitated, but not for long, making up her mind. "I think I do too, Jade. But I don't know how I'm going to accomplish it."

Jade's relief was evident by her wide smile. "I was hoping you'd say that. The truth is, I've been hoping for a while. Follow me. I may be able to help with this." Jade's eyes shone as her stride lengthened into a fast walk, then a trot. Crystalyn was quick to match her pace. A couple of brown robes conversing in the middle of the east wing hall halted their conversation to gawk as they passed by. Crystalyn ignored them. Jade never slowed.

Keeping up with her younger sister was difficult yet exhilarating. They leapt down short staircases, flung themselves around corners to careen off walls, and sprinted at top speed down long hallways. It was as if they were children again, racing around the big house to the consternation of their parents.

Crystalyn reveled in the familiarity of it. Gathering a second wind, she pumped her legs, sprinting down yet another stretch of narrow hallway, closing the distance Jade had put between them.

Whipping out into the great hallway, she was only a dozen or so steps behind as they raced past a servant carrying a tray. Crystalyn caught a flash of Deonna's usual scowl, and then they were past, zipping at full speed from pillar to pillar. As they flashed by, a stitch began to develop in her side, and her heart beat wildly.

Suddenly, Jade slowed, winding down to a semi-trot. Gulping for air, Crystalyn matched her pace.

"Over there," Jade gasped, glancing up and down the hallway and then nodding toward a dimly lit portion. Changing direction, she darted into the shadows.

Crystalyn found her sister catching her breath while leaning against a wall haphazardly covered with half a dozen frayed rugs. Not caring if she dirtied her dress, Crystalyn sat beside her, putting her back to the wall.

Jade slid down beside her.

Crystalyn enjoyed the run immensely but was honest enough to admit that she was out of shape. They weren't in their early teens running around the farm. The world was carefree then, right up until the Hartwig kid arrived to join his prominent scientist father. Crystalyn missed those worry-free times every day. At least, she'd been able to find Jade on this world.

Now all she had to do was get them back home.

Glancing around the shadowy area, her breathing slowed. "How did you find this place, Jade? It's so peaceful here. With the bend in the hall so close, I'll bet most who pass by don't even know this little area exists. I know Darwin and I have passed this way many times, and I never noticed it."

"To be honest, I didn't really think about how secluded this is. That's not the reason I brought you here." Jade spoke softly, her tone crisp but neutral. Something bothered her.

"What is it?"

"I know you…care for Darwin. He seems attentive enough, he's always checking on our needs. He's the only one in this whole place who has shown any kind of respect for Broth. Though with Atoi, he ignores her as if she doesn't exist, just as everyone else does. Don't you find that odd? And Darwin has never asked about Burl, even though I have noticed his gaze lingering on him now and then. Again, just like everyone else here, Deonna included. You'd think she, at least, would ask about them. She's pestered us enough about our past."

Crystalyn stared at her sister but the shadows hid her face from scrutiny. Jade had obviously been thinking about this for some time, going over some of the same things she herself had, and coming to the same conclusions. But she doubted Jade was finished. "There's something else on your mind besides Deonna, however right you are. The woman is a pompous busybody. What is it?"

Jade sighed. "The whole time we've been here, you've spent it with Darwin—"

"That's not true. I've eaten nearly every dinner with you, with our companions."

"Let me finish. I've gotten to know your friends well. Though Atoi doesn't say it and Broth can't, they miss you a lot. No one is at all certain what your intentions with Darwin are, which includes me. What are you doing, Crystalyn? Do you plan to marry him? If so, what happens to us, to my friends? I don't even know if Camoe and Caven are still out there waiting for us at the beginning of Fetid Fume Swamp. We agreed on two weeks only and not to try a contacting, it is too dangerous here, which I'm glad they considered after hearing about your Valen friend. We're way beyond that allotted meeting. They have likely moved on to the escape vent of the Brooding Mountain just outside the citadel."

Crystalyn swallowed a harsh retort. Hadn't she just been thinking about what she was going to do about Darwin? What *was* she going to do? She couldn't stay here, nor could she leave Darwin behind, she couldn't! Yet Jade was right, it was something that needed to be discussed soon. "We've never talked about marriage, Jade. I don't know if he wishes it, but you are right to question. It is something I may bring up soon. I don't think we can stay here. I wouldn't without you anyway."

"I know you wouldn't. It's just that I miss Dad and Camoe. I don't like it here, but I didn't like Brown Recluse much either. I suppose I should show you what I found," Jade said morosely, shuffling to her feet. Her tone had lost its previous excitement.

"This wasn't it?" Crystalyn asked, climbing to her feet with reluctance. It was good to relax with her sister for a change, something she hadn't been able to do for ages, it seemed. She wasn't about to complain, though. The time spent with Darwin *had* been worthwhile.

"We're going to have to be quiet. I'm not sure what we'll find this time."

Before Crystalyn could ask what she meant, Jade's shadowy form pulled the center rug to the side, holding it open for her. "You go first, Crystalyn. It's not far, and I'll be right behind you," Jade explained, her voice hushed. Feeling suddenly wary, Crystalyn stepped from deep shadows into darkness.

MIX THE FLOW

The passage seemed darker this time around. Jade groped until she found Crystalyn's hand. Several minutes of shuffling forward revealed the reason. The lights at the end had dimmed. Jade slowed to nearly an infant's crawl as she crept up to the slits of dim light. Permitting her eyes a moment to adjust, she looked into the storage room.

Crystalyn shifted carefully into position beside her. The room beyond was darker than before but otherwise unchanged. Of the two amber crystals in the room, the one closest to the shelving shone with its normal brilliance; the other next to the inside doorway had some dark cloth hung over it.

A movement by the door caught her eye: a figure squatted there.

Jade raised a finger to her lips. Crystalyn nodded slowly. How had the shadowy figure not heard them arrive? She thought it a stroke of blind luck, but was it? What would they do if the figure advanced toward them? Now that she thought of it, she realized it was a real probability. The figure had to vacate through some exit, likely where they stood. Jade prepared to run if that happened, keeping her grip on Crystalyn's hand firm.

For what seemed like ages, they stood gazing through the cracks, afraid to fidget lest someone heard. Every compulsory breath Jade drew roared like the engine of a thrust cycle in her ears. Finally, the figure shifted, standing abruptly and reaching for the covered light. The light bloomed, forcing her to squeeze her eyes closed. *We have to run!* Jade wrenched her eyes open. The figure vanished through the doorway beyond, a flash of red silk fading from her vision. She released a silent sigh of relief.

A small catch halfway up the wooden shelves glistened, smelling of fresh oil. Thumbing the latch, the shelf swung inward on quiet hinges. For a long moment, they both stood there, gazing into the room. Nothing moved. No one appeared at the inner door. Releasing her sister's hand, Jade bent over and entered the room in a crouch, staying close to the wall as she worked her way to the door the figure had vanished through. A glance behind showed Crystalyn followed, shadowing her movements. Comforted she wasn't alone, Jade halted inside the doorway and peered out, shying back from the bright light of a large, well-lit room. Crystalyn crept to the opposite side of the door, staying in the shadows.

The flash of red she'd seen stood nearby. The dark red robe of a hooded, medium-sized man stood in front of someone who leaned on a glossy, black table, circular in design. That person, whoever it may be, wore gauntlets of black armor.

Crystalyn shifted position, her foot scraping against stone. Jade froze. Thankfully, neither person in the room glanced toward them. Instead, they focused on the arrival of a third person. A broad-shouldered man, wearing a deep cowl over his head and shoulders that left his beefy arms bare, strolled across the lengthy room. Two gold bands encircled his massive biceps.

Beyond him, a man with a shaven head, taller than the black-hooded man, halted in a sentry posture near a doorway at the room's far end. The man seemed vaguely familiar to her, but he was too far away and the lighting too poor for her to see clearly.

The mouth of the man wearing the dark hood was moving, yet Jade couldn't hear anything. Surprised, she strained harder. All three should've been well within hearing range. Still hearing nothing, Jade focused on reading his aura instead. Oddly, jagged lines, a paler shade of ruby, stretched along the doorway vertically. Jade pushed through, concentrating on the hooded man's aura. Sound exploded from the room. "There had better be good reason for me to return so soon after our last meeting," the hooded one was saying. His voice was silky and masculine but held a promise of steel. "A course of action has been chosen by the Obsidian Table. You heard it. What do you wish of me? My time is much too valuable to spend it all at your citadel."

"You know well I would not have asked for your return without careful consideration, but the need for a private conversation has arisen," Darwin Darkwind said, coming into view as the red robe moved closer to his side.

Jade shot a quick glance at her sister. Crystalyn's blue eyes had widened, mirroring Jade's surprise. *Should we be eavesdropping on him?* Jade wondered. Darwin catching them would ruin things for her big sister. He was the type of man who wouldn't forgive. She wanted to sneak away while they still could, but her legs refused to move.

"First, I have finally located a pair of sapphire obelisks. The cost for them was beyond what I could garner here without arousing suspicion, so I had to resort to other…much baser ways to obtain them," Darwin said with a grimace.

"They are here? Is that wise?" the man with the hood asked.

"They are safe in my chambers until the exchange can be arranged. There is a second bit of knowledge I must impart, which you will find far less satisfactory. My…associate has arrived from the Vibrant Vale. The situation has become dire there. Unfortunately, the Valen naturists are proving to be more resilient than we believed." Darwin moved to the table's head. Halting behind two high-backed chairs, he flicked a gesture at them. "Will you be seated?"

"I have no time to lounge. Have your man give me a full summary. Tell him to keep it brief but thorough," the hooded man commanded.

Darwin looked to the red robe. "You heard him, Malkor. Speak to him as you would me. Hold nothing back."

A squeak from Crystalyn went unnoticed. Jade shot her a glare anyway, but she was staring into the room, her mouth hanging open.

"I will endeavor to hold to the relevant details, as you wish," Malkor said. His voice screeched, nearly as high as an aerial predator if such a thing could speak. Or like someone afflicted with enormous pain. *On this world, who knows what's possible?* Jade thought, as an image of Broth came to mind. "Our attempt at stealth has failed. A fledgling earthen naturist detected your Flow worms draining the Flow from underneath their precious Vale. I know not how. The Vibrant Vale has switched from attacking our creations in full force to holding them at bay, while they concentrate on the infestation. I believe it's only a matter of time before they discover the simplicity of shielding the queens from the source of power. Our one advantage now is they have to remove every single worm unless the weakness of the queen is discovered."

The hooded man raised a palm, and Malkor bit off whatever he was opening his mouth to say. "I shall develop a way to bypass the queen's limitation, but that is another matter. Do not speak of it aloud again. How the enemy discovered the ploy concerns me. They should not have sensed any alteration to the Flow until it was far too late…unless someone alerted them to it." The man's black cowl swung toward Darwin. "How well do you trust this information?"

Darwin started. "Malkor is loyal. The information is sound."

"Then I suggest you search for a Vale agent hidden among your commanders. Bring all of them to me for questioning, including yourself, and this one," the man in the dark hood said, stretching a muscled arm toward Malkor. "I have potions which will weed out the traitor soon enough. As for the battle, if it's as bad as you say, I shall remove the worms rather than risk their capture. You are to scale back your attack. Bring your men here until I remedy the limitation."

"As you wish, Great One," Darwin said, executing a small bow.

The man in the hood regarded Darwin for several seconds. "Have you made progress with the prophesied vessel? We can still salvage your ineptness…providing you have had success."

Darwin and Malkor exchanged a look from the corner of their eyes. "I am ready to broach the subject. It is a delicate matter for her, yet I am confident I can persuade her to join with us."

"You no longer believe you can convince her to trade one life for many?" the man in the hood inquired, his silky voice predatory.

"No, that path of persuasion will chase her away, I am now certain. She questions fanaticism in any form, a worthy trait for one so young," Darwin said.

"Proceed with caution, Darwin Darkwind. You sound like you have developed an attachment. Do not forget who installed you in your position and whose potions ensure you stay there." The dark-hooded man's soft voice held the promise of violence.

"Your threats are premature," Darwin growled. "Due to the failures at the front lines, I must move ahead faster than I'd planned. But, as I said, I am confident she will supply aid at the appropriate time in the areas with the most pressure."

"Supply aid? Do you not realize the end result? With the potion enhancements I gave you to slip in her food and drink, her power has grown exponentially. The vessel now has the potential to destroy half the White Lands, certainly the Circle of Light if you place her where I ordered. She may destroy a larger area, if she's in contact with one of the great artifacts I've been searching after. How are you going to get her to commit to genocide of that magnitude, knowing she will not survive it?" The hooded man's voice held a passionate fervor Jade had heard only at the farm before.

"I won't have to convince her," Darwin said, his voice both sad and smug at the same time, giving it an odd student quality. "She will believe she's merely there to intercede in a small part of the battle. Once she attempts to interrupt the Flow and mingles it with her own symbols, she won't be able to sever the resulting influx. She will detonate. The explosion will lay waste *to half our world,* not just half the White Lands. Though I have not viewed it personally, I now believe she holds one of the greater artifacts, which she acquired somewhere on her own. She has the potential for so much power, so much destruction, it is almost inconceivable! Great One, their capital city of Surbo, with all its arrogance, will become a barren pit for centuries. The destruction may very well reach as far as the Vibrant Vale, making our efforts there all for naught."

A strangled noise rose from Crystalyn.

Suddenly terribly afraid, Jade wrenched her attention away from the conversation in the room and looked at her sister. Crystalyn was on her feet, and a diamond-shaped, black-and-white symbol hovered before her.

"Leave this to *me, Crystalyn,*" a new voice boomed.

Lord Charn stalked past Jade and Crystalyn, his brutish hammer in his hand. Dark flames raced around its huge double head, making no sound and giving off no heat.

Crystalyn kept her symbol out but stayed silent, unmoving. She seemed to be on the verge of another violent breakdown, ready to lash out in anger. Jade had seen her sister's symbols during training sessions, but they seemed so surreal to her. Up close, they dried her mouth; Jade forced down the stark taste of fear.

Darwin's betrayal had revealed just how much power her sister wielded. He'd been teaching her to mix the Flow with her symbols for the sole purpose of creating a weapon of almost unimaginable destruction. A weapon detonated from within the woman he professed to love. Jade grappled with the callousness of the whole design, biting back her disgust. Her sister needed her now.

Lord Charn advanced cautiously into the room, his backbone rigid. "Your betrayal, while disheartening, is not wholly unexpected, Darkwind. I have watched you beat down many challengers, proud as any vain lord and instructor could be, so foolishly unaware that you had been enhanced with Flow saturation potions. I should have expected those. Any intelligent instructor should realize his best student would eventually repay his teaching with an attack for supremacy. I had never expected you to be such a worm as to betray your entire race, however."

The red robe, Malkor, had spun at the sound of Lord Charn's voice. Jade caught a glance at his face as he shuffled behind Darwin. A hawk nose and brown goatee marked his most prominent features. His dull brown eyes seemed afraid and angry.

The ring of steel echoed faintly through the room as Darwin unsheathed his sword, gleaming in his steady grip. "So you heard everything. Quite foolish of Malkor to not include his usual eavesdropping entrance when setting his privacy wards."

Malkor made a choking sound. "I am certain I set the entire room—"

"It makes little difference now. Yet you should be aware, Lord Charn, I have no desire to challenge you. You have my utmost respect as my master and our great lord," Darwin went on with a deep sadness in his brown eyes. He kept his sword raised.

"Is this what you call respect? Attacking the Vale without a direct command from me while working with this one and using his foul potions?" Lord Charn said, implicating the hooded man with a thrust of his hammer.

The man in the dark hood hopped backward, throwing his arms out. "I am only here to provide a service. Don't take your aggressions out on me."

Darwin's gaze swung upon the hooded man. "You are not going to stand beside me?"

"It is your internal affair, Darkwind, not mine." Spinning on his heel, the dark-hooded man stomped away. The big man by the door fell in behind him.

Jade watched him go; she tried hard to shake the feeling she should know who he was.

VICIOUS LOOP

Crystalyn's mind reeled. Practicality, independence, and many of the stronger emotions vied for supremacy all at once. Disbelief, rage, hatred, remorse, coldness, relief, embarrassment, pity, and great sorrow all swept through her in torrents. It was almost as if someone had deliberately terminated her wiring to the wrong circuit and then waited for her to flick the switch on. In a way, someone had, her Darwin. *He's not mine, not now.*

Her emotions raged, threatening to succumb to the emotional loop all over again. She quelled it. The time for feeling sorry about life's unfairness, the time of crying, the time of despair at its blackest, would come later. Right now, she would keep Jade from harm. At least the man in the black hood had gone. There was something animalistic and predatory about him. And he'd been one more foe in the room, someone she knew nothing about.

Symbols from the *Tiered Tome of Symbols* scrolled through her mind. Selecting a black, airy one from the directional chapter and a white, loamy one under the cascading heading, she combined them. A diamond shape, black on one side and white on the other, formed in her mind. The pattern inside, drawn with glowing lines, formed intricate crystals. The overall feel of it was one of glass. Crystalyn set it to hover before her, but she wasn't certain she could use it against Darwin. She had harbored thoughts of marrying the man, after all.

Darwin spread his arms wide. "Why are you so furious, Great Lord? I would expect your satisfaction to run deep knowing the troublesome druids had taken such a hard hit."

Lord Charn advanced one shuffle forward at a time. "I am trying to end the war which ruins our world, not destroy half of it. An attack upon the Flow goes against the Aftermath Edicts of protecting our resources, but you would not care, for you would destroy a world. It matters naught. I have deduced your twisted scheme. You never meant to challenge me, not soon. You could not take the risk of an accidental death from *my* hand. Then, you wouldn't have had to, for you meant for me to die beside your ultimate weapon when your plan came to fruition. You know well, I would be at the front line, commanding my troops in a battle that size. I struggle to comprehend. How could you destroy your own men? Men trained by you? Or did your plan include withdrawing your men on some pretense long before? A coward such as you would be elsewhere when the weapon you created detonated. I despise you. Enough talk. There *will* be a challenge this day, by my decree. You *will* fight me to the death. Your Flow master lackey *will* interfere at his own peril."

Crystalyn shifted from hurt to stunned, struggling to think beyond the moment. "Do not worry about Malkor, Lord Charn. He won't be interfering with anyone here, isn't that right?" Crystalyn glared at the man who had attempted to kidnap Atoi and kill her at the ruins. Broth had nearly died. She couldn't forgive that.

"I am coming, Do'brieni!"

Flicking his tongue across his lips, Malkor gazed wildly around the room. "I may not be of much use to you right now, Master. Kill the great one and we will triumph over these two together." His narrow, shifty eyes paused on Jade and settled on Crystalyn.

Looking at her, Darwin opened his mouth and then clamped it shut. Raising his long sword with a flourish, he gave a mock salute and slipped around the rounded black table to meet Lord Charn in the largest opening in the room. *Why, Darwin, my love, why did you do it? Was it your plan to use me from the start?* He looked so brave, so confident, as he sauntered to a fight to the death against a man who towered over him. Perhaps he had cause to be confident. Crystalyn *had* seen him cook the hapless axe man, Gard. What would she do if the Great Lord Charn lost? Could she fight the love of her life?

Presenting as small a target as possible, the two armored men pirouetted into a side stance, holding hammer and sword out with arms bent. They began a slow circle around each other searching for flaws in their opponent's defenses. Darkwind struck first. Switching direction mid-step, he lunged at Lord Charn, jabbing for the softer underarm of the arm holding the hammer.

The dull ringing sound of iron against steel echoed as Lord Charn bludgeoned the sword to the side with a twist of his arm, stepping into the blow and following the sword's edge toward the hilt. Jumping back a step, Darwin disengaged before the brutal hammer could smash his hand or wrist. Lord Charn followed. The fight began in earnest with the two trading jabs and hammer swings.

Crystalyn glanced at Malkor. His beady brown eyes glared at her from behind the faint glow of a barrier. She wondered why he hadn't used the magic protection barrier the first time they met; the outcome may have been different. He had been concentrating on opening a gateway to haul Atoi through; perhaps he couldn't handle both at the same time.

Malkor slunk closer to the fighting in the makeshift arena, giving her a better view of the lanky man. Stark hatred shone in his eyes, as she had expected, along with…something else. Giving the battle a cursory glance, Malkor's eyes darted to the side, gazing at something she couldn't make out behind one of the square roof supports.

Then he shifted his gaze to include her once again with hate-filled eyes. Suddenly she understood. Malkor was humiliated and ashamed. He'd never rest until he'd exacted vengeance. No one near her was safe while he was around. Crystalyn moved to stand beside her sister, keeping the red robe locked in her sight. "Keep your eyes on Malkor, Jade. He's up to something," she whispered.

"I will."

A cry of pain drew Crystalyn's attention to the struggling men. Darwin's left arm—his non-sword arm—hung shattered and useless at his side; a jagged piece of bone protruded from his injured elbow. Blood gushed from it. "Did you think the same ploy you used on Gard would work on me?" Lord Charn said with disdain, backing Darwin into a corner. "I periodically test every barrier against my weapon during a battle for precisely that reason as I watch for the subtle dimming of the shield. You've grown too accustomed to switching to it. Now it's only a matter of time. Your life's essence is fleeing your traitorous body, Darkwind. You are dying. I could simply step back and wait, but I shall not. I am going to smash your treacherous bones into tiny bits. Though you've managed to reinstall your weapon barrier, you are weak. It should not take long to break through."

With a roar, Lord Charn flailed on Darwin's shadowy barrier, amethyst sparks flying with each blow. Fractures appeared after only a few blows. Crystalyn's breath caught in her lungs, forgotten for a heartbeat. Could she watch Darwin die? He *had* hatched an evil plan designed to destroy half a continent with her as the centerpiece. He'd even provided the training; she could see that now. It was all one big, deadly sham conceived by the man she loved.

His betrayal was made all the worse by the fact she couldn't trust the training now. It made her ache deep inside thinking about it. She'd pushed so hard, never dreaming how versatile her symbols could be.

Except, there was one they hadn't perfected yet—the symbol she'd modified without him. Crystalyn used it now. Dismissing the black acid rain symbol, she brought out the barrier wall symbol, reforming it around her and Jade for protection against magical attacks. It should suffice for now, since she did not intend to get close enough to any weapons to require a physical barrier.

"Your physical barrier is weakening like your battered body," Lord Charn said almost amenably, landing another blow. "I wouldn't have expected it to last this long with your blood loss, though you have always been one of my strongest. Perhaps I will bestow the honor of a quick death upon you after all." Standing tall above his opponent, Lord Charn tapped the hammer's flaming head against his free palm. Could she *really* watch him die? Grotesquely distorted under the crumbling barrier, the man she loved was no longer recognizable. Only his legs remained clear. *Darwin!* She couldn't watch him die.

Taking Jade's hand, Crystalyn raised her shield a little, as she headed for the fallen man, an idea taking shape. If she could get close enough, she could switch to a physical barrier and drape it over Darwin long enough to calm Lord Charn. Then she could heal Darwin.

She froze, not making it far.

Black webbing passed through Lord Charn's barrier and wrapped around him, pinning his arms and the hammer to his waist.

Malkor had his hand raised past his shoulder. A flaming javelin appeared in it. He threw. Flying with uncanny accuracy, the javelin sank into Lord Charn's chest inches above the luminous webbing.

The webbing tightened, yanking the great lord backward off his feet. He crashed to the floor with a resounding *clang*. Lord Charn's barrier winked out, the javelin and webbing dissolving with it. Features hidden in the shadows of a heavy cowl, a black-robed figure, aglow with a barrier, stood beyond the fallen man. Without pause, the figure flung a volley of dark cones across the room. Crystalyn watched them come, her mind reeling. Things were happening too fast.

"Crystalyn!" Jade screamed.

Malkor's red laser-like missiles, aimed at Jade, struck her symbol even as the black cones sought her out. The Flow ripped into her symbol, sending bolts of excruciating power flowing through her body. Too late, she realized Darwin had perfected her symbol. But not in the way she'd expected. He'd made it for use on the battlefield. A raging torrent of raw power coursed through her neural pathways, too much, too fast, as each magical blow landed. Some of the Flow escaped through her eyes, blinding her with a white-hot haze of pain, which reabsorbed into her barrier and then into her mind. Vaguely, she sensed power building up inside the vicious loop under her symbol.

Her vision burned away into a crackling inferno of white light. Still the Flow poured in, the pressure rising until she ceased to comprehend anything but the white-hot agony in her skull.

She screamed.

ABSORPTION

Frightened, Jade gripped Crystalyn's hand. Flowing down from the symbol above, a bar of glowing white flowed into the top of Crystalyn's head and blazed from her eye sockets emanating no heat. Her open mouth dispelled the substance, disconcertingly quiet where it vanished into the symbol's patterned wall before them. Crystalyn's agonized scream had broken off as soon as the light exited her mouth, which in itself was a bad sign. Her sister was in trouble, bad trouble. Jade didn't know what she could do, but she had to do something. The power loop Crystalyn had somehow created was destroying her; Jade felt the pressure building. Perhaps she could sever the loop's link to her sister.

Raising her free hand, she slipped her palm into the bar of white light where it met Crystalyn's head.

Her perspective changed in an instant, filling her with awe. Now she could see a frothy white waterfall crackling with an immense energy along the bar of white going in and out of Crystalyn and into the symbol creating the dome. The energy flowed along the intricate, glowing pattern that loomed overhead and around them, as if some powerful entity had drawn a divine symbol in the night sky from horizon to horizon. It was beautiful and frightening.

Jade could tell it was dangerous for her to interact too close, so she kept her awareness a breath away as she followed the torrent from Crystalyn out to the brilliant pattern. Once near, she realized the streams of energy flowing through Crystalyn's symbol pooled at the top center. The problem was obvious: the energy followed the only path set for it. Though the pattern traced a long and intricate route, in the end it flowed back into itself—through her sister's head from the pool above, out from her eyes and mouth, and then back into the symbol.

Not able to interact with so much of the energy, Jade couldn't see any way to reroute it, but Crystalyn might if given a chance. Jade drew some of the hoary white energy in through her hand, sensing it racing through her, moving down, seeking its mother source. Putting her lips to Crystalyn's ear, she yelled as loud as her voice would allow, "Set the symbol on the floor! Do it now!"

Crystalyn lurched as if struck in the head. The symbol touched the floor. The waterfall of power flowed back into the symbol and from there into the floor. Jade suddenly groped empty air.

Crystalyn's piercing wail vibrated her eardrums. The wail stopped abruptly when her older sister clamped her jaws closed. Crystalyn gazed at her, her blue eyes round. "How did you know? The symbol was a trap, designed to trigger with first contact with the Flow—even a magical attack—the mastermind behind it counted on it. The Flow was bloating me with too much power. A few seconds and…" A shudder racked her tall frame.

Jade pointed at Malkor and the black-robed figure. "Shouldn't we be worried about those two throwing their power at your symbol? Their onslaught hadn't slowed an iota."

"I suppose we should end this, their attack is affecting my barrier, but I can hold them off for a while now, thanks to you," Crystalyn said, her voice full of wonder. "Let's see if we can push this thing onward without it unraveling or leaving the ground. Stay with me, little sister." Crystalyn took a step forward. Jade moved with her. The symbol maintained a precise distance from them, moving a step forward as they did. Crystalyn smiled. "Looks like we're in luck, now let's see what we can do with it."

Like the arc of a rainbow one could never quite catch, the symbol's outer rim moved along with them as they strode toward the fallen form of Lord Charn. "I don't know if this will work…" Crystalyn said, trailing off quietly.

Jade realized what her sister meant at the last moment. Coming upon the fallen man, the symbol molded around him, shrinking in for his neck and then rising to pass over his comatose face. Before Jade had time to marvel, Crystalyn squatted to feel under the chain mail covering Lord Charn's neck with her free hand while maintaining her grip on Jade's hand with the other. Jade was grateful. She didn't want her sister to let go; the contact was comforting, particularly after what had just happened with the power loop trap. Together, they were stronger.

"Is he alive?" Jade asked after a short time.

"Yes, though his pulse is weak. I could possibly heal him if the damage isn't too great, but I'm not sure I dare," Crystalyn said, her tone somber.

"You wouldn't be able to keep the protective symbol if you did, right?" Jade asked, fearing the answer.

Crystalyn looked at her sharply, as if she hadn't considered it. "I'm not certain. I have to…attach…part of me to the healing symbol and access the damage from there. I don't know if I could split my…awareness in two places. It takes gobs out of me to heal and nearly as much to run the absorption symbol."

"Can you transfer the absorption symbol's focus to me and sort of…*tie* it off there. I'm sure all it needs is a path to you. I won't let go of your hand. I think we have to try for his sake."

Again, Crystalyn gazed at her hard. "I would have to release the absorption symbol to launch an attack. It would be risky; the timing would have to be perfect. But you seem to be aware of some of this. Shifting the symbol's focus to you should work as long as we are in contact, though it will likely drain you, so we wouldn't have much time." Crystalyn hesitated. "Though, I'm not sure I want to try."

"Why? Is it too dangerous?"

"It's not entirely that. We're in danger *now*, severe danger. My symbol is weakening me the longer I hold it. What's worse, I won't be able to heal either one of us if we should get hurt or anyone else for a few days after." Her eyes flicked to where Darwin lay. Jade understood her hesitation at last. *How could she still be worried about him?*

"Make your choice," Jade heard herself say.

Crystalyn regarded her and then chuckled without mirth. "You're right, I don't have a choice. If I can heal him, I have to try. Don't let go of me, no matter what happens," Crystalyn said, her voice a plea.

At once, Jade felt an all-encompassing…*awareness* of the symbol pulse within her hand that gripped Crystalyn's hand. It exploded up her arm, along her neck, and into her mind. The feeling wasn't sharp or painful but insistent, like a toddler demanding attention every time she acknowledged it.

Below, a river of power flowed, as infinite as an ocean current. Awed, and a little intimidated, yet helpless to stop herself, Jade reached out with her own delicate awareness, stretching it toward the river in small increments, reaching ever so slowly.

The moment her awareness touched it, power filled her. Instinctively, she severed the connection. Once again, she was awed, almost to the point of stupor. Many heartbeats thumped by as she reveled in the feeling of newfound energy. All her fatigue had vanished. She felt so alive and so full of energy, enough to climb to the top of the black tower again had she wanted.

Except…it was becoming difficult to contain it. The power raging inside her demanded an outlet. Her mind and body was heating at a frightening rate. The power needed a…release. What could she do?

The answer arrived almost as soon as the question occurred. She could disperse it. Funneling energy into the symbol was a simple matter of sending a small quantity through the symbol's link. The tugging at her mind quickly dissipated, replaced by a feeling of completeness. All well and good, but there was so much left; she'd barely tapped into what she had inside, so she fed a large stream through her palm into Crystalyn.

The effect was profound. Crystalyn's slumped shoulders straightened, a grin bloomed on her lips, and a warm glow flushed her young face. A golden symbol appeared over Lord Charn's comatose form, vanishing on contact. Time passed, how much she couldn't say, and then Lord Charn suddenly sat up, swiveling his horned helm to look at them both. "I cannot say how, but you've mended a death wound. You have my gratitude," Lord Charn said, his voice a fragile parody of its former self.

Crystalyn regarded her but spoke to the armored one. "I'm not certain what my sister and I have done, but we can sort that out later. We need your help. Can you stand?"

Lord Charn rose to his impressive seven spans. "I can move," he said, sounding surprised. "What is it you would ask of me?"

"I cannot lower my symbol to fire at both those attacking us. Can you take out one of them?"

Lord Charn's head spun, his helm assessing the situation. "I see. I did not realize the battle still raged. I shall remove the coward who attacks from behind," he said, his voice soft but firm. Hefting his hammer, his outline glowed briefly as he raised his personal barrier inside Crystalyn's symbol of protection and then strode toward the black-cloaked figure. A sharp tug on Jade's mind mirrored his stepping through.

Crystalyn locked eyes with her. "Are you ready? We're going after Malkor."

Not trusting herself to speak, Jade nodded. She wondered what they could possibly do when they got there without removing the symbol's sheltering pattern. Doing that would leave them as vulnerable as Broth without claws or teeth.

A FLASH OF RED

Malkor shuffled backward toward Darwin, hurling a series of attacks at Crystalyn. Hardened, multicolored crystals shattered against her symbol, jagged lightning bolts struck from above, and shadowy insect-like creatures swarmed to bite. Crystalyn felt them as mere pinprick annoyances, not the excruciating drain they'd been before she tied her symbol to Jade.

A flow of energy surged from their clasped hands. Healing a wound as dire as Lord Charn's should have left her a sleeping babe for a day, but not now. With Jade strengthening her, she was determined to stop Malkor while she could. How she was going to accomplish it for the moment was beyond her.

The absorption symbol required her as the power source even though she'd tied it to Jade, which meant she had to be diligent with its upkeep or watch it dissolve without a link back to her. Jade, bless her sister's heart, had relieved a lot of the pressure by providing that extra boost from somewhere, but it was up to Crystalyn to use the symbol. Every hit was taking a toll. Even now, she could feel the black candle heating inside her dress pocket.

At the rate Malkor was firing, she hoped he would soon drain himself. Crystalyn switched direction. The evil man could squander his power on the symbol while she tended to Darwin's wounds. She must hurry; even with Jade's help, each hit required her to use energy to sustain it.

The onslaught ended with an abruptness that made her pause. Standing above Darwin, Malkor turned his back to her. How odd. Was he that confident in his abilities? Had he guessed her predicament? Did he know she'd have to release her sheltering symbol to switch to an aggression symbol? Or, was he waiting for her to make the switch so he could lob an attack? She wouldn't put any of it past a man like Malkor. Her best course of action for the moment was to keep it in place.

Spinning on his heel, Malkor turned and hurled a dozen black cones one after the other. As the last few struck, he scooped Darwin into his arms, as though the bleeding man had a child's weight, and jumped behind a pillar.

Dropping the absorption symbol, Crystalyn brought out her trusty knockback symbol; she couldn't take the chance Malkor's actions would aggravate Darwin's wounds. Symbol readied, she waited for Malkor to appear on the pillar's far side. There was no way she'd let him leave with Darwin, *her Darwin!*

Tense heartbeats passed. Then a slow-dawning realization struck her, spiking her frayed anxiety. Malkor wasn't going to reappear.

Dropping Jade's hand, Crystalyn dashed around the pillar where she'd seen the two men last, finding what she'd feared. Two topaz obelisks stood a narrow doorway apart. "Great!" Crystalyn shouted at the empty air between the obelisks. Spinning, she released her symbol at the black-robed figure.

Scurrying away from Lord Charn's whirling hammer with a long dagger in hand, the figure noticed her symbol only when it flew through the smoky barrier. At the same instant, Lord Charn's hammer connected with the figure's shoulder. Batted across the room, the black robe thudded into the wall, fell to the floor, and lay still. The dark cowl fell to one side. Correlda's waxen face lay exposed to the light of the room. Drops of dark blood dribbled from one corner of her red, full lips.

Slipping his hammer through the ring on his hip, Lord Charn went to the fallen woman. Removing a gauntlet, he dropped to one knee, checking her pulse. He stood, pulling on the gauntlet. "This is…disturbing yet not wholly unexpected. Correlda had always shown affection for young Darkwind, yet I foolishly believed she had moved on to someone else or some other addiction."

Crystalyn felt ill. Had the two of them been together secretly?

No wonder the woman had treated her with such animosity.

Lord Charn's dark helm turned to regard her. "It is unknown if the traitor ever returned the affection."

"Will she live?" Jade asked. Heat rose in Crystalyn's face. She should have asked the question before Jade had. She was the healer in the family.

The helm swung toward Jade. "She may if I send for a healer soon. I have not yet made the decision to do so."

"I might be able to do it with Jade's help," Crystalyn said. It was a big *might*, though. She was feeling the consequences of so much symbol use.

"I'm not sure I could do it again, but I will try," Jade said.

Lord Charn's helmed head swiveled between both of them. "I do not believe I comprehend your meaning."

The sound of voices coming from the room's entrance drew their eyes. Broth leapt inside, followed by Jade's strange dark creation. Burl had discarded the hooded robe.

Four guards charged into the room, glaring at Broth and Burl. Atoi strolled into the room and leaned on the wall. Folding her arms, she gazed at them impassively as if she'd been there all along. "Leave them be!" Lord Charn bellowed. "One of you shall fetch some healers, make haste!"

The guards straightened as the anger upon their faces shifted to embarrassment. They sheathed their swords, standing straighter still. Without a word of discussion, one broke away, slipping from the room with a fleeting flash of his golden, elite armor.

"The rest of you will guard Correlda. If she lives, bind her and take her to holding. She shall be judged for treason by the Obsidian Table." The guards' faces grew blank as Lord Charn went on. "General Darkwind and Flow Master Malkor are hereby given the blood mark. As enemies of Virun, they will be hunted down and executed upon sight," Lord Charn decreed. The guards' eyes widened, but they did as ordered, taking up position around the woman. Lord Charn's helm fixed on Burl and then swung toward Jade.

"Do you know where they went?" Crystalyn asked, as she moved to the topaz obelisks wondering if she could activate them. Even if she could, she had no way of knowing where Malkor had taken Darwin. Jade stayed close by her.

Lord Charn moved beside her, his voice low. "I am aware of the general area; the color of the crystal denotes the region but not the precise location."

"So you *know* where they went?" Crystalyn pressed, getting excited. She might be able to help Darwin after all.

"The topaz crystals would likely be attuned to somewhere in the Blistering Sands, a large and arid region southwest of here. I will set up a contacting to one of my…field contacts." Lord Charn nodded slowly toward a guard, who immediately trotted to the entrance door and spoke a few words to someone beyond the doorway. "Even with every troop garrisoned there searching, spotting them will not be simple. The region is nearly the size of a continent."

Crystalyn's excitement fell. How would she find him there?

Jade pointed at the topaz obelisks. "Wait! A Sapphire Gate brought us here; couldn't Crystalyn make these take us home?"

Lord Charn hesitated, his helm moving to include all in the room. He lowered his voice. "Alas, no one is certain how the gates are constructed or how to tune them. The knowledge has been lost when the ancient people who built them vanished. It is one of the tests I had wished to conduct with you. It may be possible one of your symbols could change a gateway's attunement with controlled experimentation. The advantages of such an accomplishment would be of tremendous value. It would require extensive research and development, something I am eager to assist with simply for the scientific knowledge alone."

Crystalyn gaped. Now he wanted to talk of experimenting. A woman was dying. Darwin had vanished and might be…no, she wouldn't let herself think it.

Lord Charn's helm looked toward the door. The guard still hadn't returned. He continued. "At present, a positive return to your home world would require a pair of sapphire obelisks, but they are rare. I have the entire Dark Citadel scouring Astura for a set, but no one has reported success."

Crystalyn exchanged a look with Jade. "Not everyone has been truthful with you, it seems. We overheard Darwin and Malkor mention one."

"Are you certain? Did they speak of a location?"

Crystalyn answered readily; the conversation burned into her mind. "We're certain. Darwin had recently come into possession of them. He mentioned his rooms." Trotting past Atoi, the golden-armored guard returned to resume his position by Correlda and the other guards not far away. The woman stirred. Opening her eyes, she stared up at Crystalyn with a furrowed brow. "Sureen? Why are you here?" Closing her eyes, she slipped back into unconsciousness.

Crystalyn was startled. "What did she just say?"

Lord Charn was already moving. "Send a messenger to me as soon as the healers have finished here. We shall be in the traitor's former chambers." He strode past the guard.

"As you wish, My Lord," the guard replied to Lord Charn's receding back.

Crystalyn grabbed an obelisk. "Bring the other one," she said, slipping past Jade.

Running past two guards stationed outside the doorway, Crystalyn caught up to Lord Charn in the great hall. Even with the weight of his armor, Lord Charn moved too fast for questions, his anger fueled by Darwin's betrayal.

Crystalyn couldn't bring herself to believe he would have gone through with the dark-hooded man's plan. Had he felt nothing for her? The man in the hood had seemed to think he did. Her disappointment ran deep, deadening her emotions as her affliction did to the point of not caring about his fate, but she didn't want him to die. She had to find him somehow and keep him alive. She could change him; *she could.*

Lord Charn stalked to the end of the hall, choosing a sharp branch to the right in silence. Crystalyn and her companions struggled to stay close, particularly her and Jade since they carried the obelisks. But not Broth; the warden loped beside them with ease.

"Stay close to Lord Charn, my Do'brieni. We can't lose him now."

Broth leapt ahead. *"Be at ease. I shall follow."*

The pristine pillars of the command quarters sprang into view. Darwin's chambers were the first ones in the opulent section. Crystalyn's chambers were farther along the grand hallway. Two of Darwin's personal guards barred the way to his room, standing alert with their two long pikes crossed.

"Stand aside," Lord Charn commanded, halting out of range of the barbed weapons.

Crystalyn used the reprieve to catch her breath but kept her eye on the guards.

Jade wheezed nearby.

Broth growled low in his throat.

Squeezing in between Crystalyn and Jade, Burl positioned his odd burlap body protectively beside her little sister, his charcoal face providing no clue as to why he did. Raising his one good arm, he held up her pack and Jade's bag.

Setting the obelisk in the crook of an arm, Crystalyn took her pack, working it onto her shoulders. Jade retrieved her bag. Atoi stood with her back to a pillar, her small hand resting near the slit in her dress.

"Our most sincere apologies, My Lord, but Great General Darkwind's command was explicit," one of the guards was saying.

"His orders were no one but himself or Malkor shall pass, but surely he didn't mean to exclude the great lord," the other guard hurried to add.

"Your *great* general is likely drawing his last breath. You will join him if you don't stand aside," Lord Charn said, his voice low and deadly.

The guards exchanged a look. Then, as one, they moved to one side, setting the pikes' dull ends on the floor, barbs safely pointed to the ceiling.

Lord Charn swept past, halting at the door. "Locked and warded," he mumbled aloud. "An inferior ward, however. The *great* general was a fool not to set it himself," he sneered, raising a hand toward the door. A flash of red left Crystalyn's vision spotty. There was an audible click as the door swung inward. Lord Charn stalked inside. Crystalyn followed with her sister and companions in tow.

SAPPHIRE GATE

Setting the topaz obelisk down, Jade took a step closer to Lord Charn. Stamping his metal-shod boot with impatience, the huge, black-helmed man seemed preoccupied with gazing around Darwin's airy bedchamber. While his attention focused elsewhere, she wanted to attempt a reading. The one time she tried before hadn't gone so well. His rotation had refused to slow enough for a proper viewing.

For the second time, she fought his stormy aura slower, bearing her will down upon it. As before, it barely slowed. This time, she drew heavily from the power contained within the white candle—or from whatever source that the candle drew from when she touched it. Perhaps it was a catalyst for the Flow; the energy gleaned from it felt much the same as when she'd circulated it to Crystalyn.

Whatever the case, she blessed Burl's dark heart for bringing her bag and Crystalyn's pack along. Rotating slower and slower, she strained to make out images in the turmoil of Lord Charn's aura. The arrowhead amulet grew warm under her shirt, and the whirlwind revolving around him slowed little by little.

A black dragon barreled out of the darkness. Gigantic maw open wide, it spewed forth darkness more absolute than the rotation's abyss from where it came.

Startled, Jade loosened her grip. The aura twisted into a raging cyclone, whipping the dragon's image away with it. Her mouth dried. The dragon's red eyes had *glared at her. It knew she was here! Somehow, the bloody dragon knew!*

Lord Charn spun, his horned helm leaning down toward her. He straightened. "What do have around your neck? How did you come by the arrowhead artifact?" he asked and then continued without waiting for an answer. "With it, you may be able to discern if the obelisks are near."

Camoe had been right all along. Lord Charn's armory was where she'd first found herself on this world. The amulet must be his, but she wasn't going to offer it back.

Crystalyn glanced at Lord Charn. "Jade can? How is it used?"

"Your sibling has to bend her will to the artifact, attune it to detecting that which is hidden."

Jade frowned. "How am I supposed to do that?"

"That artifact will extend any innate ability for…observing that which is hidden from use of the Flow. Keep it in contact with your flesh—as you seem to know—while you peruse the room. Search for anything that seems to…want to appear as something other than it should be."

"Could you be any more cryptic?" Jade asked with a frown. "Never mind, don't answer. I'm going to look around, but don't expect too much." She turned away, feeling uncomfortable inside Darwin's bedroom. The man had two full suits of his black armor in the room. Several more had lined the outer room. How many did one man need?

The bedroom looked similar to many of the other plush, someone-of-high-station living quarters she'd been in since coming to the citadel, complete with a four-poster bed, massive wardrobe, cushioned alcove, and luxurious grooming table. All looked ordinary, at least for a room this rich.

Except…her eyes returned to the two suits of armor. They looked much the same as the others they'd passed on the way but darker on one side, as if they stood in shadow there. Acting on instinct, Jade walked to the closest one. Pulling off the helm, she reached inside and pulled out an oblong object. The suit vanished, the helm dissolving in her hand. A moment later, a second azure obelisk stood beside the first.

"Oh! Well done!" Crystalyn cried.

Lord Charn moved close. "Yes, you do not disappoint."

The sapphire obelisks were indistinguishable in size and style from the pair that had brought her to the Dark Citadel and begun her grueling journey. Jade still found it hard to comprehend. After all those terrifying months, they stood on the brink of going home. So why did she feel sad? Camoe and Burl…how could she leave them?

Jade clasped the butterfly amulet hanging from her neck, the medallion still warm to the touch from its recent use, *her* recent using. That's what she grappled with: *she* could use artifacts, and *she* could unlock their hidden use. Perhaps she wasn't so helpless after all. Though she suspected she could only unlock certain artifacts that fit her ability. How had Lord Charn known?

"By the One God, they are beautiful," Crystalyn said, smiling. "I was half-convinced we'd not see the blue ones again, great job."

"Yes, yes, yes, *excellent* work," Lord Charn said, a trace of glee in his tone.

Jade began to feel a little uncomfortable with the praises but only a little.

Atoi spoke, her voice a monotone. "One is curious, Great Lord. How did you know the sister would be able to use the medallion? You could have demanded to use it yourself."

The dark helm swung toward the little girl. Jade looked to her, as did everyone else in the room, including Broth. Atoi spoke so seldom, the question seemed odd, though it was close to what Jade had been asking herself. "In truth, I considered it. But the medallion grows stronger with association—she's worn it for some time, I believe. Even so, the User would also need the ability to read the object's reveal. I have reason to believe it is so with her, which has strengthened my suspicion that she is the anomaly mentioned in the scrolls."

"Crystalyn has to be the one to open…the Sapphire Gate, right?" Jade asked, wanting to change the subject. She didn't feel like an anomaly; it wasn't a flattering description.

The horned helm settled on her. Not for the first time, Jade wondered what he looked like without it. "Yes, that is so. I will repeat an earlier question. How would you know this?"

"Like you, I didn't, but it stands to reason. Crystalyn brought us here. She should be able to take us back to our home world, back to our world of Terra," Jade said, eyeing her sister. Crystalyn gazed back the way they'd come. She seemed so sad, so forlorn, though one hand rested on Broth's great shoulder.

Going to her, Jade held her hand in her own and pressed her lips close to her sister's ears. "Are you ready, Crystalyn? Darkwind was bad from the start. Try not to let it hold you back, he made his choice. Someday it will haunt him, if he still lives. Let's go home. Please? I miss Dad."

Crystalyn stirred, a look of resolve shining in her blue eyes though the sadness never lessened. Cupping her hands together, a symbol, identical to the interlocking lines and complex curves on the gateway, floated away from her sister and locked between the two obelisks. Rotating, the symbols spun into a maelstrom. The black veil dropped in place from the top down, twisting into a swirl almost before the symbol had fully faded like the one in her ISP's office, seemingly so long ago. Crystalyn was becoming adept with her symbols.

Jade found her gaze on Atoi. Was the little girl going with them?

Looking oddly out of place on her too-white face, a wide smile crossed Atoi's face.

It was the first time Jade had seen her smile. It didn't suit her. The smile didn't look malicious, but it didn't emanate any warmth either; it seemed forced and…alien.

Jade focused on the tiny girl's image. Her aura spun much faster than any other aura she'd yet viewed. Jade concentrated on slowing the blurring whirlwind, still flush from the victory of finding the sapphire obelisks and seeing through Darwin's illusion—seeing its reveal, as Lord Charn called it.

The cyclone slowed minutely, but a wave of vertigo rushed into her mind. She counteracted by dribbling the vertigo into the dark cloud, making her feel better. The cloud slowed a little. Atoi glanced at her, the smile gone. Without a word, she dashed through the gateway.

Crystalyn cursed. "Blast it, Atoi! I wasn't quite ready to leave yet, but now we have no choice. Jade take the topaz obelisks through, you and Burl are next, then Broth. I'll come last. Will you do us the courtesy of making certain no one follows, Lord Charn? The gateway should close as soon as I go through, but it's possible someone could reactivate it. I don't want any surprises."

Lord Charn looked at Crystalyn. "You are correct. The gateway will close, but I shall not be here to view it, I shall accompany you. A new world to study is something I cannot ignore. I have always harbored a science inclination before becoming a battle lord, though I will wait to go through right before you and stand guard here as long as possible. Your safety is fragile here now that Darwin's cowardice has surfaced."

Now he wants to follow a scientific path, unbelievable! For many reasons, "scientist" didn't fit Jade's mental image of the dark-armored man. Though Lord Charn's aura didn't show anything specifically threatening toward them, it was still full of something dark. The bloody, red-eyed dragon had shown her that.

Though he had given them exceptional hospitality, he'd claimed he wanted a resolution to the war, and he'd fought for them against Darkwind, nearly losing his life. For that last reason alone, she should trust him. "Don't expect too much, Lord Charn. Our Terra is not the world it once was. Are you certain you want this?" Jade asked.

Lord Charn stood tall. "You misunderstand how much I *do* desire this. I go with you or no one else shall step beyond the Sapphire Gate."

Jade looked to Crystalyn. "Well, I suppose that answers my question. Can't Broth do the guarding?

"I guess they both can, before following each other through. Now go. I don't know how long the gate will stay active."

Jade didn't argue. Excitement settled inside. They were finally going home. She'd wanted to get away from this horrible world from the start. Now they could go back to being a family again, her, Crystalyn, and Dad. The family would be different now, but at least they'd still be a family. She'd miss Camoe, but Crystalyn was also leaving friends behind. If her sister's heart could do it, then so could she.

The dark curtain awaited them, impatient and ominous. With a last glance at her big sister, Jade handed Burl the obelisks, grabbed his hand, and stepped through, feeling confused. Crystalyn's image had changed. Inside her slow-moving cyclone, a double-headed hammer now rotated.

BOUND

Garn followed the Alchemist at a respectful distance, not too close to intrude, but not so far back he'd waste precious moments reaching the man in case of attack. The Alchemist never mentioned how far behind he should be, though he did give him a look of modest approval at the beginning. Garn didn't care for the hooded man's approval, but he accepted it. He needed the proximity to him if the man was assailed, no *when*, he was beset. The Alchemist had many enemies. No one was going to slay his captor, not before him.

The Alchemist strolled with purpose away from the massive obelisks they'd used yesterday to enter the great underground hall. Garn had nearly missed a step when they'd appeared at the towering obelisk's threshold. The two brown crystal obelisks they'd stepped through had been about the same size as the blue ones that had brought him here.

He would've liked to examine those closely, but the hooded man's command had been as specific as Codar's had been the first day after his captivity in Corteezsha's room. Keep up or die. He chose to keep up, at least until he killed the hooded man or found his missing daughters, whichever happened first. So far, no one at the keep had heard of his daughters' whereabouts, but he hadn't given up. They had to be somewhere on this world.

The Alchemist's pace wasn't taxing, nor was it slow, unlike when they'd left the meeting with the man in dark chain mail and the red-robed one, when the huge man in his dark plate armor had shown up. Garn took it then that the meeting hadn't gone well: the Alchemist had left in a rush.

As he noticed the day before, anyone they passed in the great hall reacted much the same toward the Alchemist as the townspeople had when he'd followed Codar in Grit Eye City. Armored or robed alike, it didn't seem to matter. All avoided eye contact to the point of crossing to the other side of the wide hall or turning to look the opposite direction.

Garn preferred it that way; it made his job easier. Ambushing a man without looking in his direction was hard to accomplish. Therefore, when three red-robed men glanced surreptitiously their way as they strolled along a wide intersection, Garn's instincts took over.

*****

Holding Broth back by a slight pressure on his shoulder, Crystalyn motioned for Lord Charn to precede them through the Sapphire Gate. Casting a last look around, the tall, dark-armored man vanished through.

Crystalyn breathed easier. Lord Charn was used to giving commands and having them followed without question. Well, he'd have to get used to following her commands now if he was going to live in harmony on her world of Terra. He'd have to rely on his scientist side, if he truly had such an inclination. Perhaps she'd get him researching the glaring commonalities between their two worlds. Astura's ancient name was Earth; Terra was another name for Earth. Coincidence? There was no way she believed that.

His giving up supreme power on Astura in order to live a menial life on another world was a little hard to concede. Yet, she could understand how taxing it would be to constantly fend off the younger, up-and-coming great lord wannabes attempting assassination after assassination, challenge after challenge.

Eventually one of them would get in a lucky blow by moving a tad bit faster as he slowed with age. If Lord Charn was truthful, he'd lived half as long as Atoi, if not longer. The Dark lord hadn't said it, but Crystalyn suspected there now was a potential threat strong enough to displace him from his black throne, or at least, there might've been as Darkwind honed his battle techniques. Lord Charn had to know it was just a matter of time before someone else came along.

No challenge would come from Darwin now, not after what he'd done. He'd wanted to use her as a weapon and not just any old weapon; a weapon he'd helped create when he'd cunningly put her in harm's way several times on the journey, forcing her to build power. At the back of her mind, she'd known it as soon as she'd seen his connection to Malkor.

By convincing the brigands to attack as she climbed Glacier Mountain, possibly even staging the battle blocking their way forward, and sending Malkor to kidnap Atoi, he'd begun the process of creating a weapon of great destruction to destroy half the known world. It was an ambitious undertaking. One he'd nearly pulled off, probably would have, had it not been for Jade finding the hidden entrance to the secret passage. Though he claimed to have a total disregard for the vessel— for her, the man in the hood had seen otherwise.

Crystalyn struggled to understand.

Her dark and handsome Darwin Darkwind had betrayed her right when they were getting along well, so well she'd made the choice of convincing him to leave Astura and go back home with her. If he hadn't done what he did, he'd likely be here with her instead of Lord Charn. *Oh, Darwin, why did you throw it all away?*

Crystalyn quelled her budding tears. She needed a good cry but not now.

What was she going to do with Lord Charn on her crumbling, technological world? He couldn't saunter around, seven feet tall and wearing a pile of black armor. For that matter, how would she explain Jade's raggedy man? Not to mention how she would explain a four-hundred-season-old child and a larger-than-average canine with color-changing hourglass eyes. Animals were rare enough as it was. How would they all fit in?

Crystalyn had no idea, but they'd all been friends to her or to Jade, helping them when it mattered most.

Broth's thoughts flowed beside hers. *"My excitement to see the home world of my Do'brieni is high."*

"We are bound together now, Broth, whatever world. Nevertheless, I must warn you, Terra is a dying world. Overuse of technology has polluted it and turned the once-vibrant mountains into a barren, artificial wasteland."

Nudging Broth forward, Crystalyn stepped through the sapphire gateway alongside her most intimate friend. She couldn't help but feel Broth's apprehension that stemmed from her last declaration of thought.

DARK FLAMES

Jade curtailed her excitement at finally setting foot back on her home world. Not everyone had come through the gateway yet, and there was more information she wanted to gather. Putting the topaz gate beside the conference table, she motioned for Burl to do likewise and then slipped the white crystal candle from her beaten wayfarer bag. It was too dangerous not to know.

The hammer in Crystalyn's image concerned her. Lord Charn *insisted* he accompany them. The hammer had to mean something, but she'd failed twice to get more than a few shadowy images from the dark lord—besides the red-eyed dragon—no matter how hard she concentrated. It was time for the heavy hardware, the white candle, and her newfound knowledge of how the amulet worked. She'd begun to suspect that at least one of them was a great artifact the hooded man had mentioned. Perhaps she could force a reading. Now she needed a subject.

She didn't have to wait long.

Lord Charn materialized next. Showing no interest in the technology in the room—odd for one wishing to play scientist studying a new world—the plate-armored man turned to face the wall where they'd arrived.

Holding the white candle in one hand and palming the arrowhead amulet in the other, Jade concentrated on slowing the shadowy storm spinning around the man. It took enormous effort, but finally the images whirled slower, the shadows drifted drifting lazily, as they came into focus. Was the dragon still in there?

The horned helm of Lord Charn swung in her direction. "Desist what you're doing," he said, his voice as hard as the great hammer hanging from his side. "It has been no small task to keep you at bay."

Startled, Jade lost her hold. The image twisted into the dark raging cyclone she normally viewed. So, he'd been resisting her all along. Perhaps she should've known. Was it why some people were harder to read than others were? It made sense. Some she'd read must've resisted her, likely not even aware they were doing it. Even then, she'd been able to force a reading from most everyone. This attempt had some little success too. The shadows around Lord Charn had slowed enough she'd glimpsed two of them. The dragon, in flight this time, came before a great hammer trailing it.

The dragon she couldn't fathom. She might never find out what it represented for the man; it wasn't as if Lord Charn begged to volunteer information. Perhaps she could wheedle it out of him later now that he was on her world and away from his fortress.

Broth popped into the room with Crystalyn not far behind. Crystalyn glanced around. Running her thumb along the arrowhead's edge out of habit, Jade slowed her sister's rotating aura. The hammer rolled around to the front, displacing a symbol with a pattern she'd yet to see, only to be displaced by an azure crystal so covered in blood it was hard to recognize it. Jade shivered. With the concentration broken, the aura whirled.

Jade frowned. She'd wanted to stop the hammer and focus on it. Now, she'd have to start from the beginning. Perhaps she'd seen enough to tell if it was identical to Lord Charn's hammer.

As Jade looked at the big man, the awful war hammer was in motion, swinging toward Broth. A brilliant purple flash engulfed the warden. Taken unaware, Broth smashed into Crystalyn, propelled by the unnatural force of the dark-flamed hammer.

Jade wanted to scream, but her lungs refused to draw breath.

Crystalyn smashed into a shelf, splintering it to pieces. She fell to the floor, gasping for air, with Broth on top of her.

Broth didn't stay down long. Snarling, he sprang through the air, latching onto Lord Charn's weapon arm. Faster than Jade thought possible, the dark-armored man spun Broth in a circle. The force of the spin ripped the warden's grip from his jaws, flinging him into a smoky glass wall. The wall shattered. Broth crashed into the warehouse and lay still.

Ignoring the angry red gashes streaking down his arm, Lord Charn advanced on Crystalyn, raising the cruel double-headed hammer high. The dark flames arced back and forth on the hammer's head, glowing with the intensity of a silent lightning strike.

Jade found her voice and screamed.

HER BLOOD RAN COLD

Crystalyn was delighted when the Big Ugly sprang into view. She hadn't been quite certain the Sapphire Gate would open to the same place they'd left—though Lord Charn had seemed confident it would. The Dark Citadel's great lord stood tall and forbidding, his back to the wall beside Broth, as if he were cautious about stepping too far from the gateway. Atoi gazed in wonder at the images flickering on the desk.

Crystalyn sought her sister. Jade and her doll man, Burl, lounged by the conference table ahead, watching for her arrival. Jade had grown cautious from their trials on another world. Rubbing the arrowhead with one hand while holding the white candle, Jade stared at her, but not into her eyes, and then moved on to look at Broth. Was she using her ability?

Jade's eyes widened with shock.

Something heavy crashed into Crystalyn, ripping her legs from under her, smashing her against something that crumpled under her. White-hot pain ripped through one of her legs as the weight fell across her chest, stealing her breath. The world began to blacken. *No!* She hadn't fought this far to lose it all now. She pushed with all her might against it. Incredibly, the weight sprang away. She gulped for breath, watching as Broth latched onto Lord Charn's arm. Lord Charn spun in a tight circle, hurling Broth through one of the walls of tempered glass.

"Arrup!" The lone yelp rang through Crystalyn's mind as Broth crashed into the warehouse and lay still.

"Broth! Broth!" Stark silence rang loud through the link. She couldn't feel his presence, the link hollow and empty.

"Nooooo!" With the last of her scream dying in her ears, Crystalyn looked up at Lord Charn standing above her, the glowing hammer raised high. Jade screamed. Inching backward, Crystalyn met the glass wall. She reached for a symbol, knowing it was too late.

Absorbing the light around it, the double-headed hammer fell, trailing a shadow of blackness.

With a sharp *ping*, the hammer froze. Atoi's dagger stood between it and her skull, inches away. Gazing upward, her face as passionless as ever, the tiny girl stood to one side, the hand gripping the dagger outstretched.

Lord Charn bellowed. "What is this? You *dare* to interfere, Dark One?"

A voice resounded from Atoi, hollow and distant. "Your selfishness *will not* ambush the vessel; to triumph, you must defeat the prophecy on equal terms..." the ringing voice said, dropping away. The dagger withdrew.

Atoi's distraction was enough. Grounding the symbol to her, Crystalyn released it.

The hammer continued its downward arc.

Crystalyn threw out her translucent black symbol with its intricate weave-like pattern and wrapped it around her head and torso. The hammer bounced harmlessly away, inches from her skull.

"Blast you!" Lord Charn cursed, swinging the hammer in rage. He pounded on her absorption symbol as if trapped inside a cave. Quickly, she wrapped the symbol around the rest of her.

The pounding drained her somewhat, as she reinforced her symbol, but otherwise didn't hurt her. Even better, it gave her time to prepare another symbol during the rampage. Crystalyn sat up. Blow after blow pounded on her symbol, *not* with abandon as she'd first thought but with expert skill. The dark flame hammer's great head landed on or near the same spot near the top of her head.

Jagged cracks, purple in color, had begun to spread across it. Alarmed, she cast away the net symbol and shored up her shield with another protection symbol. The cracks vanished. She pushed her way to her feet, wincing from a stab of pain in her leg.

Breathing harder, Lord Charn lowered the hammer. "I may not be able to reach you yet, but there is someone else here mentioned in the codex." Whirling, he threw the dark hammer. Leaving a trail of purple darkness in the air, the hammer flew at her wide-eyed sister's heart. Shocked, Crystalyn couldn't even shout a warning.

A shape appeared in front of Jade only to vanish behind the far end of the conference table along with her sister as the hammer collided with a loud thud.

"Jade! NO!"

Lord Charn laughed. "The scrolls mean nothing now."

Anger pulsed, clouding Crystalyn's vision red as it soaked into her coherence. Lord Charn would pay! The red haze blew away as coherence reestablished in her mind. Her anger dissipated leaving behind an empty place devoid of emotion. The pain in her leg dulled beyond notice. She knew what to do. Holding nothing back, *grounding* be damned, she released the knockback symbol.

Accelerating faster than the eye could follow, the symbol's concentric circles struck the great lord full in the chest. Lord Charn smashed through the wall of glass and soared into the warehouse, landing heavily on his back where he lay still.

Five beats of her dull heart passed. Perhaps she'd finished him.

Lord Charn jumped to his feet, vanishing deeper inside the warehouse.

Crystalyn's anger pulsed back, swamping her vision with the red haze. How could she have been so stupid? Her angry heart thumped, and cold clarity settled in. Crystalyn clung to the coldness, following the shattered trail toward the path of gloom. She would destroy Lord Charn, no matter the cost to herself.

As she stepped through the broken panes, a dark cone streaked toward her. Leaning to one side, Crystalyn felt the cone zoom over her shoulder, shattering some of the tempered glass, peppering her with sharp shards. Blood blossomed on her bare arms, and a warm wetness on her cheek trickled into a corner of her mouth. The taste of blood brought the red haze back.

She'd tasted her own blood before, during an act of aggression against her. The Hartwig kid had been the one then, hitting her repeatedly after she'd refused to lie down with him. Ramming her med cylinder into his eye had been instinctive then. She'd lashed out in a rage.

She hadn't meant for him to die.

This time was different. Lord Charn had killed Jade and her one true friend, Broth. He would pay.

Crystalyn released a symbol, the one she'd not wanted to use again. Whirling faster than a hover engine, the splinter symbol threw its wicked spikes throughout the room, punching through crates. Wood, metal, it made little difference. They ripped into it all. A walk-in transport container's steel bent outward emitting a loud, metallic groan, as it shredded into large, pointed strips. Lord Charn hid behind it; a shadowy glow surrounded him. Destroying a good portion of the room, her symbol wound down and then broke into wisps of smoke that dissipated quickly.

The glow around Lord Charn winked out.

Crystalyn brought out her wall symbol, barely in time. A string of Lord Charn's dark cones mixed with fireballs smashed into it, forcing her back a step. Pushing her wall outward, Crystalyn moved forward one difficult step at a time, remembering to *ground* it to the floor. The great lord's onslaught lasted several drawn-out moments, stopping abruptly as the last few missiles bounced off her barrier and exploded into containers.

Lord Charn moved from behind the ruptured transport, dragging a leg behind him, a wide strip of shrapnel protruding from his shin. *Your bloody armor did you no good there, murderer,* Crystalyn thought.

Lord Charn hopped over to a rectangular container and flung the splintered lid to one side. Inside, polished silver lances gleamed. One of the few containers in the area she'd dot mapped long ago.

Her blood ran cold. The symbol she had out was set to repel

magical attacks. The lances wouldn't have anything magical infused in them. Anything mundane could penetrate her symbol wall.

Crystalyn halted her advance.

Snatching a lance from the crate, Lord Charn cocked his arm and threw. Wobbly, the lance missed its mark by a wide margin. Taking his time, Lord Charn reached for another.

Crystalyn was at an impasse: she couldn't dissolve her wall to launch a symbol or Lord Charn would attack with the Flow, nor could she stand by and wait for his aim to improve either. She had to finish him off somehow, but even wounded, he was as strong as she was. Perhaps stronger, given he had armor and a container full of weapons at his disposal.

She was at a loss what to do.

YELLOW-ORANGE EYES, DARK HEART

Jade ceased trying to push Burl off her. Fireballs and some other black bolts shattered the glass panes above her. High and low, glass exploded on the side of the office Crystalyn had strode through. One of the largest panes nearby crashed to the floor, shattering into sharp cubes.

She crawled out from under Burl as soon as the fallout stilled. Rolling over, he used the table to help pull himself to his feet. Jade did likewise. Her breath caught in her throat. The double-headed hammer had left a large rectangular hole in his chest. A black tarry substance oozed out in great quantities.

Crystalyn needed her.

So did Burl.

Expending precious time, she ripped off a strip of her dress to the thigh. Wrapping it around the raggedy man, she tied it off in a knot at the back. The oozing slowed substantially. Booming and crashing sounded. She'd given him all the time she dared. Jade stepped over the massive hammer, the purplish flames now quiescent, leaving it where it lay as she peered through the broken glass.

Atoi was nowhere in sight, but Crystalyn stood close by. Glowing like a displaced entity from an astral dimension, her sister towered behind a symbol, facing a hunched Lord Charn, his leg mangled grotesquely under his protective shield.

Jade dashed to her sister's side, gripping her hand.

Crystalyn stiffened and then smiled, tears flowing down her cheeks unchecked.

Jade was suddenly afraid. Crystalyn bled profusely from gashes on her arms and neck, soaking her to her breasts. Deep cuts reddened her cheeks to her chin, the wounds begging for immediate attention.

"So your sibling survives. It is but small consequence, for it provides another recipient for my spears," Lord Charn said with a sneer, the effect lessened by his hoarse voice. He hefted the spear in his hand easily and then lowered it slightly. "What is this? You brought the dark creation in here. I had thought my hammer destroyed you both," he rasped. Then he laughed.

Jade looked behind. Burl marched inexorably toward her; gripped in his good left hand, Lord Charn's wicked hammer gleamed dully. "No! Drop it, Burl!" Jade screamed.

Extending his left arm, Lord Charn made a closed-fist gesture at Burl.

Burl froze in mid-step. Jade was suddenly afraid for him; he looked so helpless. "Did you think to control a creation made in the citadel? I am a lord of the citadel, and now master of the creation." Lord Charn's voice boomed louder and stronger. "Creation, bring the hammer to me!"

Burl shuddered as if struck with an axe. Resuming his march, he altered direction, moving toward the dark-armored arm extended toward him.

"Burl, no!" Jade screamed.

There was no sign Burl heard. High-stepping past her, her loyal companion's eyes never left his new master.

"Halt!" Lord Charn commanded. Maniacal laughter escaped from under the dark helm. "I have a better use for you, my creation. Destroy them both with the hammer!" Lord Charn said, raising a lance and his left hand, palm down.

Pivoting on one heel, Burl spun. Advancing toward her and Crystalyn, Burl lifted the hammer high, the double head shining with an ominous, dark gleam.

The rush of energy through their clasped hands was all the warning Jade had. "Crystalyn, NO!"

The black-and-white pattern protecting them traced quickly to gold as it snaked outward to a triangular point and then swirled into a twisting, golden cyclone of sharpened, gold fragments, which spun into her companion. Countless blades sliced through Burl, his tattered form dropping to the floor. The hammer thumped dully against the plasicrete flooring to lay still.

"NO!" Letting go her sister's hand, Jade ran to her friend, falling to her knees next to the largest recognizable lump. Burl's yellow-orange eyes regarded her brightly for a moment and then faded.

*****

Releasing the golden cyclone symbol on Jade's companion had the adverse effect of dissolving her protection symbol, which Lord Charn may have intended when he sent the creation after them.

Crystalyn was ready; whichever way the lance flew, she would dive the other way, installing the magic barrier as she did. True to form, Lord Charn cocked his arm back, but his angle was wrong. The lance aimed at…*Jade!* Crystalyn prepared a shield symbol and sent it to hover in front of Jade. Too late, she realized she'd used the spell absorption, not the physical.

Lord Charn stiffened as the lance left his hand, and his barrier dimmed as he released a burst of black cones.

Time slowed. Crystalyn watched in horror as the lance, gleaming with a deadly brilliance, sailed toward Jade's unsuspecting back. Time sped to normal. "JADE!" Crystalyn screamed in desperation.

Jade's vision locked on her, an accusing look in her green eyes.

The lance sailed over Jade's shoulder with a petrifying inch to spare. The cones exploded upon Crystalyn's symbol bursting it apart with the last hit. Losing momentum, the lance dropped, *clinking* along the floor.

Lord Charn collapsed in a heap.

Exercising the same dispassionate demeanor as when Crystalyn had first encountered her, Atoi reached down and pulled her dagger from the hole in Lord Charn's armored shin. Glancing around, she looked for something to wipe it clean. Finding nothing but plate armor and plasicrete containers, the white-faced girl strode toward the Big Ugly.

Dazed, Crystalyn staggered past Jade, squeezing her shoulder gently, hoping to ease her sobbing, as she walked by. Her sister would need time to grieve. Jade had grown close to her…magically animated companion.

Kneeling beside Lord Charn, Crystalyn found him alive, though his breaths had grown shallow. Feeling for the release under the chin, Crystalyn slipped a hook from its catch and slipped the helm from his head.

Then she sat back stunned.

Her Indenture Service Provider, Ruena Day, stared up at her.

"How can this be?" Crystalyn managed to say.

"I see your confusion, though you've always been a bright student…much like your mother. Perhaps I followed a false promise," Ruena said. Though her voice was weak, it sounded as it always had, like her and not Lord Charn.

Crystalyn frowned. "What do you know about my mother?"

Ruena coughed. Pink, foamy blood oozed from one corner of her mouth. "Your father met me here, looking for you. Did you know that? I activated the obelisks, pushed him through, and then I traveled to my…citadel later," Ruena rasped, the corners of her mouth rising slightly. Another cough, deep in her chest this time, pushed dark red blood from her upturned mouth.

Crystalyn cradled the dark-haired woman's head in her hands. "Where did you send him? Please, tell me!"

As Ruena Day convulsed up and away from Crystalyn, her throaty voice rang strong and clear throughout the warehouse. "I am not dying!" she shouted and then fell back in Crystalyn's arms. Her dark heart stilled.

RAGTAG GROUP

We make a ragtag group but a rich one, Crystalyn thought. Broth *clinked* and *chinked* like an olden-times prospector's mule carrying the mother lode of diamonds, which she supposed he was in relation to the bags strapped to his long, sleek back. Better yet, the mother lode of jewels, nearly every kind of precious gem, lay inside the bags. She was glad he was so resilient; he'd responded to her healing, though it had been another narrow heal. The hammer had crushed many of his internal organs, but he was still drawing ragged breaths when she'd gotten to him.

Jade carried the two sapphire obelisks they'd discovered in the warehouse slung over one shoulder along with the confounding surprise of Lord Charn's great hammer—rather, Ruena Day's brutal weapon of choice. The hammer hung from a silver ring on Jade's waist. When she'd picked the hammer up from where Burl had dropped it, the purple flame vanished. In its place, a brilliant white shone from head to haft. Jade claimed the hammer was light, no heavier than a metal goblet. Crystalyn still found it hard to believe, since she struggled to lift the white hammer beyond her own waist. Jade's bag bulged with exquisite, finely wrought jewelry.

Crystalyn looked at the youngest-oldest member of her little family. Atoi carried a bagful of artifacts, strapped to each side of her tiny hips, which nearly reached the ground. The little girl claimed they would come in useful at some point. Crystalyn hadn't argued about the booty, though she did require the little girl to bring the topaz obelisks. The artifacts Atoi had gathered would, by themselves, set them all up handsomely in a fair-size kingdom, yet the gateway was beyond their value considerably.

Crystalyn's own pack weighed heavy on her back. She'd packed two other symbol books; perhaps she could discover how Ruena had come by them, where they had originated. Crystal candles, amulets, and rings, carefully stowed so as not to bang against one another, stuffed the rest of her space inside. One never knew, perhaps the amulets and rings would enhance their abilities the way the candles and Jade's arrow amulet did. She couldn't wait to experiment with them.

Ahead, the early evening lights of the Muddy Wagon Inn grew into view. With any luck, Hastel would have made his way back to his tavern by now, and they could enlist his help. It would be nice to see the crusty one-eyed man again, she admitted to herself, along with those in the Vibrant Vale.

They would visit Brown Recluse after that, at Jade's insistence.

Crystalyn had agreed without too many reservations. The more friends they could gather, the better chance they had of finding their father. Jade's druid and monk friends would help immensely there. And, word of their mother? Crystalyn still wasn't certain what Ruena had meant when she mentioned her. It might not be too farfetched to believe that their mother had found her way here. After all, hadn't the rest of her biological family traveled to another world?

Shifting the heavy pack straps back onto her shoulders from where they'd slipped, Crystalyn pushed open the back door to the Muddy Wagon Inn and strode inside.

THE SPEAR

Garn dove past the Alchemist, executing a forward roll that brought him to his feet behind the closest red robe. Pinning the man's arms behind him with one hand, he pushed him forward as a shield, unsheathing his long sword as he went. Both the remaining red robes dropped any pretense of looking away. Palm down, they formed fists of angry fire and flung them at the Alchemist. Flinging the first red robe in front of the black-hooded man, Garn's whirling blades cut down both men before they could release a second bolt.

The Alchemist calmly stepped around the burning corpse, barely slowing. Garn hurriedly wiped his blade on the less messy of the two red robes. Sprinting, he fell into his former position behind the man. His captor moved with a purpose, choosing the left fork of the great hall's intersection. Garn kept pace with minimal effort, in tune with his new body. Technically, the same old body but magically enhanced with potent chemical attributes courtesy of the Alchemist's experiments. He was in better shape than he could've dreamed of being in during his twenty-fifth season.

The hallway led past a large group of Users surrounding a dark stone basin of some sort. Thankfully, the Alchemist went past without stopping. Security in such a large crowd would've been difficult, if not impossible, particularly if every User present fired one of their fireballs or some other magical attack.

Once past the stone basin, the Alchemist stayed with the left passage at the next intersection. Though ornate, this hallway wasn't as high or as wide as the great hall, and less people strolled about. Garn relaxed slightly, glancing around. The few persons milling about wore colored robes of silk or some other supple material. Most wore black, red, or brown, though an occasional gold robe was interspersed in the mix. Red, brown, or gold, all bowed before any black robe in this quarter. Garn wondered what the difference was between this section and the great hall. Perhaps the number of black robes in the hall meant one would spend his entire day prostrating and never get anywhere.

Ahead, two massive doors loomed so dark they seemed to swallow light and exude darkness back into the eyes of the beholder. They stood closed and foreboding. Garn found them disconcerting to look at for long.

The Alchemist slowed almost imperceptibly. The two black robes positioned in front of the double doors scrambled to push them inward before he had to pause outright. They opened without a sound. Garn followed his master inside, not liking the looks of the room's interior. Rectangular in shape and lined with silver statuettes, the room had intricate paintings hung on the walls like signs leading to a massive fire pit ringed by ornate chairs and sectional, curved stone tables. Every set of ringed tables had Users seated around them. Hung from the high ceiling, half a dozen ornate chandeliers provided light from countless glimmer shards. Two stone stairways, one to each side, climbed above the paintings and thick walls to become walkways running halfway along the room's length. Several darkened archways leading deeper within presented security concerns.

At least in the room two days ago, he'd had a view of nearly all of it beyond the huge, rounded obsidian table, though he'd disliked not being able to see where the hulking one in the black armor had entered. Garn had almost been to the point of breaking the command to stand guard at the door, though the Alchemist would've most likely attacked him for it. But it had turned out to be a non-issue. The Alchemist had wisely vacated the room when the man with the horned helm had shown up.

The Alchemist made for the largest, and most occupied, table in the room where several black robes sat, conversing in heated tones. All conversation grew quiet in the vast room as the Alchemist claimed the topmost, most ornate seat. Keeping his face stone smooth to cover his surprise, Garn settled into a standing position behind the hooded man, very much aware how exposed they both were. How could he keep them both alive if things got out of hand with this many people in the room?

Garn counted eleven black robes, hoods pulled deep over their heads, seated around the main table. The Alchemist made twelve, though he didn't wear a robe. His dark hood trimmed below the shoulders left his prominent gold-banded biceps bare for all to view, but it also singled his charge out, making him an unmistakable target. Garn wanted to grind his teeth in frustration; the one time he'd brought it up, the man had tersely informed him to do his job and never speak of it again. The hooded man was too arrogant for his own good, daring to conduct a meeting with hundreds of Users in the room.

Every hooded head faced the hooded man in silence.

A dozen heartbeats passed before the Alchemist spoke. "I ask your indulgence for this…unexpected hearing," the Alchemist said. His soft silky voice somehow carried to the farthest table in the room. No one in the crowded space asked him to speak up. "I think you will all agree it has much merit once the details are known. Events have unfolded faster than my portents revealed, faster than the oracle could have seen, and faster than the scrolls or the tapestry foretold, yet the symbolic one and the anomaly have…" He paused, the hood looking to those around the table. "Where is the Spear?"

At first, no one in the vast room full of robes spoke. Then the black robe to the Alchemist's right stirred. "The Spear's location is unknown. My…associates and my creations are scouring the citadel. One progress report I've received is…disconcerting. Heavy wards prevent access to the Spear's quarters, still. Betrayal is looking more likely."

"Surely the warding isn't so strong *you* cannot dispel it," the Alchemist said.

"All of my strongest were called to this unexpected hearing," the black robe said, her pleasant, feminine voice slightly on edge.

"Your highest concern should be the Spear's wards. Yet, I detect discontent in your tone, possibly even a challenge. Have you decided to challenge this day?"

"I have not," the black robe replied immediately.

"Perhaps there is some wisdom residing somewhere inside you, Kara Laurel," the Alchemist said. "I shall see if that holds true. This hearing is postponed until I have a report on the Spear within the hour."

Several hundred black robes stood and filed from the room in an orderly fashion. Some were women, Garn noted from the quick flashes of smooth faces or the way they moved. Most revealed a masculine gait as they filed out. In seconds, the room was clear except for the two of them. The Alchemist remained sitting, facing the long room as if he expected an answer to his most pressing concerns to come gusting in at any moment. Perhaps it would.

Gazing up at the darkened alcoves one by one, Garn pondered. He had no idea what the hooded man had just allowed him to overhear, but it sounded as if the promised cataclysmic events had been set in motion for this world. Like it or not, he was part of it, and so were his daughters. For now they were—until he found them and brought them safely home.

The End

R.V. Johnson lives in the beautiful mountains of Utah with his wife, Savidtri. His inspirational father lives with them. R.V. enjoys hiking, camping, and outdoor activities. Having time to spend with family is important to him.

He strives to be the gem the dragon hoards.

Other books by R.V. Johnson: *Beyond The Dark Gate*, Book 2 of the thrilling *The Flow of Power epic fantasy series* and *Beyond Terra*, An engrossing novella set in the same two worlds.

FREE DOWNLOAD

Sign up for the author's new release list and receive a free copy of the stunning new novella: *Beyond Terra* in *The Flow of Power*. Get it here: http://www.authorrvjohnson.com